UNDER THE LIGHT OF FIREFLIES

A NOVEL BY LEE SANDERS

Copyright © Lee Sanders, 2024

All rights reserved.

No part of this book may be
used or reproduced in any manner
whatsoever without written consent
from the publisher, except for
brief quotations for reviews.

For further information, write info@catalystpress.org

In North America, this book is distributed by
Consortium Book Sales & Distribution, a division of Ingram.
Phone: 612/746-2600
cbsdinfo@ingramcontent.com
www.cbsd.com

In South Africa, Namibia, and Botswana,
this book is distributed by Protea Distribution.
For information, email
orders@proteadistribution.co.za

Library of Congress Control Number: 2024942210

9781963511062 ISBN E-book
9781963511017 ISBN Paperback

Cover Art by Gary A. Dorsey

For the Father

CHAPTER ONE

The summer I was twelve years old, I watched a teenage boy die.

May 30th, 1981 was the last day of school my sixth-grade class would ever attend at Kennedy Elementary. In those days, junior high began in the seventh-grade, so the next year we'd be moving up, which made this last day a small but epic step in our quest to become teenagers. At the podium in front of the class, a girl was delivering a final report about our recent school year for our teacher, Mrs. Dent, who collected these reports at the end of each year as a memento. Mrs. Dent had asked the class to choose a student to write it, so we took a vote and naturally picked Jill.

Jill Newcastle was one of the smartest kids in school and close to perfect in everything she did. She made first chair in clarinet, won the spelling bee, and even got the title in the horseshoe contest, which was somewhat annoying. I'd never won anything. I was good with my grades and played lots of sports, but any big achievement always fell beyond my reach.

Jill, though, was good. She was also decent. And whatever she did, she did without some cheap motive. I'd had a secret crush on her since the first day of school.

On my desk sat a small yearbook, being more of a paper booklet, which contained our class pictures. I was supposed to sign it with some statement or farewell, preferably witty, then pass it back to its owner. This particular book was Jill's, and I was spiraling into a small panic. I'd worked on what I would write in it for days but had left my notes at home. I previously mentioned it to my older brother, Jack, who was in high school, and asked him for his thoughts. He'd told me to write that the whole blonde thing was really working for her and she was a dead ringer in the horseshoes. I felt that was too crass.

"That's how you've got to work these things," he said. "She's just some snot-nosed, honor-roll chick you've known since you were six."

"Since I was eight, Jack. She moved here from Knoxville the week after Thanksgiving of my third-grade year."

"What do you mean...you're in love with her?"

"No. Why would you say that?"

"Look, just write something simple," he sagely advised. "The last thing you want to do is sound weird and screw it up."

To no one's surprise, Jill's report turned out great. It was funny, subtle, and even made us feel strangely sentimental. When she finished, Mrs. Dent was then presented the report along with a yearbook that Jill had gotten everyone to sign. We gave a round of applause to which our teacher smiled humbly and said thank you. The students congratulated Jill on a job well done while she coyly sauntered down the aisle as if ignorant to all the fuss. Like all things for her, it was an easy success. And there I was with her yearbook in hand and nothing to write. So, of course, I rushed it.

Jill, Super job today. I hope you don't stay in Tennessee all summer because I need you to teach me how to speak and spell. Haha. Let's get together sometime and throw them shoes! —*Noah*

Horrified at what I'd written, I quickly slipped the yearbook back onto her desk with mine on top, hoping she wouldn't read the disaster I'd penned and instead write me something deeply alluring. Then ten minutes later, the impossible happened. The final countdown began. 3...2...1...

The last bell rang and pandemonium broke out school wide. An unwavering scream filled the air as kids dashed out of their classrooms and down the halls, gleefully throwing papers and books into the air. Every face had a smile. Every step had a bounce. Even the nerds delighted in the mayhem. Near the exit, I found my two best friends, Dusty and Sam, and together we burst through the door without a single book in our hands.

"You know what, Rosie," Dusty said to me. "Today is a righteous day."

Rosie was the nickname that Dusty had conferred upon me for reasons concerning my first name, but more importantly for its feminine ring. Dusty was a tall and athletic kid with shaggy hair and brown resolute eyes. Outgoing, precocious, and interested in all things from famous battles to outer space, there wasn't a subject he couldn't find a question for. He was also quite the card.

"What do you say we blow off the school bus and head over to the mini-golf course for a round?" I asked.

UNDER THE LIGHT OF FIREFLIES

"I'm a little short today," Dusty said.

"I can cover you."

"Is there anything better than free?"

"How are you getting back?" asked Sam.

"Sammie, baby," Dusty said and put his arm around him. "Have you ever heard of a little thing called walking?"

"But it's over a mile home."

"Well, we better not go home then."

Sam's shoulders slumped and his face went long. Sam was a skinny careful kid raised by skinny careful parents who smoked cigarettes by the pound. They were also notoriously protective. If Sam didn't arrive at his scheduled bus stop on time, his folks would instantly jump into their cars and canvass the streets like wolves.

"Come on," I told him. "I've got enough money for all of us."

"No, I can't."

"Then I'll still see you later tonight for our big venture, right?"

"I guess so," he replied and sluffed up the steps onto the bus.

"There goes a broken man," said Dusty.

The mini-golf course sat on a main road near our school, but it wasn't the refuge I'd envisioned. When we arrived, some boys I loathed were standing at the counter. They were a grade above us, and many years we attended the same school together. They were also bullies, cheats, and notably popular. Torturing kids was their favorite game. Many was the innocent child who got dogpiled or had his books tossed simply for turning the wrong corner. They lived in a different neighborhood than

4

we did and had a treehouse-club they called the "Wandering Stars." They even stitched special patches onto their backpacks and jackets. Dusty, Sam, and I also had our own treehouse club which we'd dubbed the "SLP Loafers." If any competition existed between the clubs, however, the Stars certainly weren't aware of it.

"Well, if it isn't the galoot Dusty and his little sidekick, Noah," said their leader Fenton. Fenton was a tough, thick, curly-headed kid who possessed skills in most everything whether it be football, skateboards, or yo-yos. He never liked me, although I couldn't remember doing anything to the guy.

"You want to play a round against us?" he asked.

"Noah's a loser," said another kid named Tyler. "He'll only slow us down."

The son of a rich attorney, Tyler was a pretty boy with a beautiful sweeping coiffure whose parents arrayed him in fancy shirts with logos. He was the squirrelly kind who always got away with things like cutting in the lunch line or skipping school.

"How much money do you got?" asked the last one, Billy.

"Two dollars," I lied.

"Good. I bet you that other dollar that I can kick your butt."

"I have to buy Dusty's round too."

"You didn't say you were on a date."

Billy was tall and rangy and known in school as a master thief and vandal. His coal black eyes emitted strange waves which girls found captivating but made me wary. He'd never spoken more than one sentence at a time to me.

"Don't kiss and tell," Tyler sneered as they walked away.

After they left, I stepped to the side and let the folks behind us move in front, then I pulled Dusty over.

"Maybe we should leave," I said.

"That's not a very strong move."

"I really hate those guys."

"Just avoid them," he said.

"We could go to a movie instead."

"But we're already here. Forget about it, man."

"For your information, I'm the one who's paying."

"Which is exactly why I think we should stay."

Over the fear of sounding like Sam, I dropped the argument and bought us two rounds on the opposite course from the others. We grabbed our putters and balls then went outside.

"What do you think of Kimberly Crowder?" Dusty asked as we walked to the first hole.

"Why are you always asking me about Kimberly? I thought you liked Sandra."

"A man should have options."

"Kimberly's good-looking but she's too stuck up."

"Have you ever called her?"

"Only once," I said.

"What'd you talk about?"

"School and baseball and stuff."

"I'm sure she found that fascinating."

"Then what did you talk about?"

"*High Risk.*"

High Risk was a gaudy R-rated flick that we'd snuck into a month before and loved every minute of it, mainly because it was filled with car chase scenes, guns, and nudity. R-rated movies were strictly forbidden by our parents, so it was an excellent subject to discuss with a girl, and one that I would file away for future reference. The fact was that many times Dusty and I competed for the same girls. He was better at it than me. For one, he wasn't awkward. He also happened to be tall, handsome, and funny, which helped. I could score a joke here or there, but I found girls to be more of an elusive breed.

"What do you think about Sandra's neighbor?" I furtively asked as we started to play.

"You mean Jill?"

"Yeah."

"I think if I wanted to cheat on a test, I'd sit next to her."

"I wouldn't put her on the spot."

"She's more like a sister. I prefer fast women."

Satisfied with his response, I dropped the subject. I hadn't told him yet that I liked Jill because I feared that once I did, he'd see her in a new way, the same way that I saw her. I didn't want him to see her at all. It was the only secret I ever kept from him.

Next, some racket broke out from the other course. It was Fenton and his crew. They were playing on a hole where the ball was rolled up a ramp that curved upside down onto a topside green. Facing such a task, there existed only one way for those guys to execute it, and that was to swing as hard as possible.

Fenton had cracked the ball and sent it flying, but it missed the ramp and struck a post on the next hole, ricocheted, then shattered a bottle sitting on the ground. A cry of glee erupted from the boys, which sent the manager hustling outside.

"Every time you kids come here you make some kind of

UNDER THE LIGHT OF FIREFLIES

trouble!" he fumed as he marched over. "Which one of you did it?"

Silence ensued as the entire place stopped to listen. Acting like it was more of a nuisance than a situation, the boys rolled their eyes and sighed.

"It was an accident," Fenton said at last.

"Bottles don't break themselves!"

"What do you want from me? I had to swing extra hard to get the ball up the ramp."

"Balls go up that ramp all day long and things don't get broken."

"Fine then. You got me."

The manager hesitated, surprised by the candor, then replied, "Fine indeed. You'll be the one who cleans it up too. Once you're finished, you have to leave."

The manager strode off to get the sweeper, and as soon as he'd disappeared inside the maintenance room, Fenton shouted, "Let's go!" They all broke for the fence, hopped over the rail, then sped away on their bicycles. Right afterward, the manager emerged with a broom and dustpan in hand. Searching and finding them gone, he dropped everything and ran to the exit.

"You little punks!" he yelled with a raised fist. "That's the last time you disrespect this place! Don't you ever come back here again!"

Riding away untouched, Tyler looked back from his deluxe bicycle and smiled victoriously. They cut into traffic, forcing a line of cars to slow down, and then were away. After they'd gone, the manager dropped his fist and gripped the rail a long moment. He picked up the broom and went to sweep up the glass as everyone stood and watched.

"I wish they'd get busted just once," I said.

"Don't hold your breath."

Dusty won our match by a hole, but I didn't pay him the quarter we'd bet. We never paid our bets. I bought us sodas and gum instead. We left and were walking along the road blowing bubbles when I heard the quick beep of a horn. Turning, I saw a small green car drive past. It was Lisa, my big brother's girlfriend, along with another girl.

They pulled into a grocery store where we ran over to meet them. Riding with the windows down, the girls donned sunglasses, spaghetti strap tops, and cutoff shorts. Their wide smiles shone with lip gloss as the smell of suntan lotion drifted from the car. They were the picture of the American teenage summer.

"Hey there," Lisa said out the window. "What are you two hoodlums doing?"

"Hi Lisa," I replied as I checked out the other girl. "We skipped the bus today."

"I can see that. Would you like a ride?"

"Absolutely!"

We jumped into the backseat where Dusty immediately hung his lanky arms over the front and started in with the questions.

"What kind of engine does this thing have?" he asked.

"I have no idea."

"Are these leather seats?"

"Vinyl."

"What are you listening to?"

"Fleetwood Mac."

"Is that what girls like best, Fleetwood Mac?"

"We like all kinds," she replied with a strange look.

"But in a date-like situation, what do you prefer?"

"Who are you?" asked the other girl, twisting sideways.

"I'm Dusty Schaeffer. Who are you?"

"Desaray Parker."

"That's a very fetching name you have, Desaray."

"Don't play with me. You're not that cool."

We already knew who she was. We lived in a Texas town called Texarkana which had a twin city in Arkansas, and teenagers were our soap opera. Desaray was a big star. With a gorgeous face, black mane, and piercing eyes, she was an exotic creature who'd moved from the Arkansas side to Texas just that year, instantly assuming the mantle of every boy's fantasy. Being asked for a ride with her was like stumbling upon a golden idol.

"Noah," Lisa asked, "what do you have planned for the summer?"

"Playing on the Little League all-star team, I hope. Later on, we'll head to my grandmother's cabin for a few weeks."

"Is Jack going to the cabin too?"

"I don't know. He's got Legion Baseball and lifeguarding. Do they let people off work for baseball?"

"Jack pretty much does whatever he wants," she said with a side look at Desaray.

I found that comment to be very true. Lisa understood. She'd been his girlfriend for a year, and they were practically inseparable. Whenever she came over, she always made sure to say a few nice words to me. Sometimes we'd sit next to each other on the couch, and I could smell her soft perfume. I wondered what it would be like to have a girl like that in your life, something soft to wait for you in this hard world.

We rolled up to my house where Dusty and I said thanks and crawled out. My brother Jack and his best friend Keith were in the garage with the door up. Jack was working on a model airplane like my dad had taught him. Since before I was born, my dad built model airplanes. Not the plastic kind either. These were made of wood with real engines and they flew. Every so often, Dad gave the old one away and started another. My brother hadn't perfected the craft yet, although he was trying.

"What's up, kids?" Jack said as we walked up.

"How's the plane going?" I asked.

"It's getting there."

I looked over my shoulder and noticed Lisa's car still idling on the street.

"Are you going to talk to Lisa?" I asked.

"I'm in the middle of setting these pieces. Go tell her that I'll call later."

"But she's your girlfriend."

"Go now," he said and motioned backward with his thumb.

I paused at first, testing him as always, then trotted to Lisa's car and told her. Feigning a smile, she sighed deeply and drove away.

"What'd she say?" Jack asked when I got back.

"Okay."

"How'd she look when she said it?"

"She looked bummed."

"Who's she with?"

"Desaray Parker."

Jack and Keith looked at each other.

"Are you sure it was Desaray?" he asked.

"Positive."

"Hey, Jack," Dusty said. "What kind of gas does that engine run on?"

"It's 3-in-1 fuel."

"But is it gas or diesel?"

"Methanol and nitro."

"And it doesn't explode?"

"Are you for real?" Keith asked with a hard look.

"Let's go inside," I said and pulled Dusty away before we both got tossed to the turf.

"I need to go home," he replied. "I have to use the bathroom."

"You can use mine."

"I need my privacy."

"Whatever, man."

If anything, Dusty was original. He'd walk straight up to a cop and ask him what caliber of pistol he carried, but then he was too shy to use his buddy's bathroom. Inside, my mother was cooking in the kitchen. I opened the refrigerator, grabbed some juice, and sat at the table.

"How did the last day of school go?" Mother asked.

"Good."

"Did that extra money come in handy?"

"Sure did. Thanks."

She tossed a dish into the oven, then cleaned off the counter and washed her hands. Mother cooked dinner almost every night. If she wasn't cooking, she was reading a book or playing with my little sister, Sally. Mother's hair was starting to gray, and small crow's feet had formed at the corners of her eyes. Although she wasn't old, I worried she was becoming that way.

"Is there something wrong with Jack and Lisa?" I asked.

"Not that I'm aware of. Why?"

"They were acting funny."

"They're teenagers, son," she said and whisked off her apron. "It's their job to act funny. I'm going onto the back porch. Sally is at Charlotte's playing, so I'm doing nothing. Would you like to join me?"

"No, thanks. I think I'll just go upstairs."

"Is everything all right?"

I nodded.

"Okay, darling," she said and kissed my head.

I climbed our stairs and stopped to peek inside Sally's room. It appeared spotless as usual even though she was only five years old. Sally was pure. She loved dresses and shoes and putting bows in her hair. Everything that was hers had to be perfect, though she would share any of it with anyone. Mother's friend had once visited with her two-year old daughter, and Sally played tea-time and dress-up with the girl, even giving her a small stuffed giraffe that the child had taken a shine to. I always kept an eye on Sally. I even liked how clean she kept her room.

By contrast, my room was normally a semi-wreck. On my walls hung posters of planets, dare-devils, and baseball players. A few participation trophies lay scattered on a shelf. Above my desk sat an aquarium that I actually took decent care of. At least the fish were alive.

13

My room was clean that day because apparently Mother had come for the laundry. Along the way, I guessed that she decided to make my bed too. I laid down and tossed a baseball to myself. At some point I dozed off because when I opened my eyes, the shadows had changed and I could smell chicken casserole. In the other room, I heard my sister's innocent voice singing a nursery rhyme, one that she sang daily.

"Daddy finger, Daddy finger, where are you?
Here I am, here I am, how do you do?"

Then I started to cry. Later, Mother appeared in the doorway and told me it was time to eat.

"I'll be down in a minute," I said and rolled the other way.

"What's wrong?" she asked and sat on the edge of my bed.

"Nothing. School's out, so that's good."

"Yes. You have a whole summer to do as you please."

I sat there feeling my pillow, breathing slowly.

"It's going to be okay, Noah," she said and stroked my hair.

"I know. We've talked about it."

"We can talk more."

We sat there a few moments in the still of the room. Mother waited.

"I don't understand how it happened," I said, turning to her. "He was so smart and so strong."

"Accidents happen. Even to strong people."

"Will we ever know why?"

"Sometimes, we just have to accept things as they are."

"I miss him so much."

"I know how you feel, son," she said. "He was an amazing husband as well."

CHAPTER TWO

"Come in, Houston. Come in, Houston. This is Apollo. The eagle has landed."

It was later that evening when Dusty's official communication crackled through my walkie talkie as I relaxed on my bed. Although Dusty lived behind me a few houses down, we were still in transmission range because his dad, who was an electronics buff, had given us a real set of walkie talkies.

"Apollo," I responded, "state your position and status."

"Approaching re-entry. Arrival time is t-minus fifteen minutes."

"So, then the Eagle *hasn't* landed."

"Correction, control. The eagle is due for touchdown shortly."

"Roger that."

I hung up and checked my backpack for the night's supplies. Flashlight, pocketknife, lighter, yo-yo, and other assorted necessities. I always kept our needs in stock, although I didn't

UNDER THE LIGHT OF FIREFLIES

have any bottle rockets or firecrackers yet.

Downstairs, Mother and Sally were sitting on the couch together watching TV.

"Dusty should be here in a bit," I said.

"Will Sam make it too?" Mother asked.

"He said he would. I haven't heard from him since this afternoon, though, so it's hard to say."

"Okay, darling. There's sandwich stuff in the fridge and leftovers if you all get hungry."

"Where's Jack?"

"He's in the garage with a couple of his friends for now."

"I'll go say hi."

"Be careful not to bother them."

Jack didn't mind me hanging out for small stretches. He knew I liked being around him and his teenage friends. I just needed to avoid saying anything dumb or getting pulled into some crazy stunt. Mines lurked everywhere in the land of teenagers. The strategy was to ease in, establish coolness, then slide out unscathed.

"Noah, what are you doing out here?" Jack demanded.

"Waiting for Dusty to show."

"Dusty Schaeffer? That kid's a pest."

"He won't come in here. He'll go straight to the treehouse."

Jack slung a dart with all his might. Then another. And another. His two friends, Keith and Travis, were seated outside the garage being quiet.

"What's wrong?" I asked Jack.

"What do you mean?"

"You're throwing darts like you're mad about something."

16

LEE SANDERS

"Don't sweat how I'm throwing darts."

"I'm just asking."

Then Keith blandly spoke. "Barry didn't make the Legion Baseball team this summer."

"Barry Vaughn?" I said. "But he's like the best outfielder in high school. How'd that happen?"

"There's this new coach. Atkinson. He put his own son on the team over Barry."

"Is that legal?"

"Coach Atkinson told the committee Barry has a summer job that won't allow him to play."

"Working for Ark-La-Tex Lumber," Jack said with a bitter laugh. "Who let Iggy play baseball last year without any problems."

"This is crap," said Travis. "That Atkinson kid is only a sophomore."

"He's terrible. That's the main thing."

"I pray they don't let him pitch."

My mother opened the door and called me. "Noah," she said. "Sam is here."

"Well, surprise, surprise. The local kid does good."

"His father is here too. He wants to speak to you both."

"Oh boy," I said. Then to my brother and the other guys, "Sorry about Barry. Raw deal."

When I walked into the den, I found Sam and his dad both standing there, each looking nervous in their own special way. Sam wrung his hands like he was squeezing a lemon, and his dad predictably had a cigarette dangling from his lips while his shifty eyes scanned the room for an ashtray.

17

UNDER THE LIGHT OF FIREFLIES

"There you are," Mr. Wooderson said with propped cheer when I walked up. After a formal greeting and a vigorous handshake, he gave Mother a respectful nod, appeared to gather his thoughts, then got straight to the matter at hand.

"Noah," he began, "I want to speak to you about the sleepover you're hosting here this evening. But before I start, I'd first like to acknowledge what a fine young man you are. You don't ride your bike over people's lawns, or let the air out of neighbor's tires, or steal things from their garages. In addition, you have a most polite demeanor towards adults."

He smoked his cigarette and darted his eyes for that missing ash tray.

"What I'm here to say," he continued, "is that it's the first night of summer, and it could be very enticing to engage in some form of mischief. So, with your mother's approval, I'm officially instructing you boys not to leave the premises, for as soon as you do, the temptation starts. Sure, it's easy to look around and see other kids toilet papering houses, or egging cars, or vandalizing mailboxes—which is a federal offense by the way—and think: gee, it might be fun to to push Mr. Wooderson's lawn mower down the park hill into traffic. But let me tell you right now, whenever they catch the punks that did that, they will replace my mower and spend the day in Juvie. Understand?"

"Yes sir," I replied.

"Furthermore, I believe that if you kids would apply this same standard each and every time you're together, then one and all can enjoy a summer unfettered by..."

He noticed that his cigarette ash had grown exceptionally

18

long, forcing him to pause his lecture just when he was getting hot. What he didn't know was that my mother—aware of his propensity to smoke as well as sermonize—had shrewdly hidden the ashtrays. Mr. Wooderson's search came up fruitless, as expected, and he turned to Mother with a blush.

"I'm sorry, Lauren," he said. "But I can't seem to locate an ashtray."

"That's all right, Gerald," Mother told him. "I think the boys understand perfectly well what you're getting at. Right boys?"

"Yes ma'am," we responded.

"Great. Then you two can go find a snack."

Mr. Wooderson acted confounded by Mother's casual disregard for his address, but when she opened the front door for him, he had no choice but to go outside and ash.

"See you later, Mr. Wooderson," I said, yanking Sam towards the kitchen.

"I'll be just down the street, son," Mr. Wooderson called back. "Only a phone call away. Avoid temptation!"

"Goodbye, Dad."

Once in the kitchen, we felt safe and sighed in relief.

"The first thing we do," I said into Sam's happy face, "is blow up the Nelsons' mailbox."

"What?" Sam responded with a tragic smile.

"Just kidding, amigo. But tonight, we ride."

After getting a few sodas and snacks, I fetched my backpack, and we headed outside to my treehouse. When we climbed up, we found Dusty already inside with candles lit everywhere as if this was some kind of ritual. He had a towel draped over his head like a monk while he kneeled behind a small table.

"Hear ye, hear ye," he solemnly spoke. "The brotherhood of the SLP Loafers will now come to order. Come inside and submit your tokens to the commandant."

"Hopefully the 'commandant' likes potato chips for tokens," I said.

"Does the brother have any grape soda?"

"Cola."

"The commandant prefers..."

"Knock it off, man."

"Fine," he said and tossed off the towel.

After giving him the snack, we emptied my backpack to inspect the goods, then Sam and I played with the yo-yo and whittled sticks. From his own pack, Dusty produced a cutout magazine article and sat against the wall somewhat theatrically to read it. I was almost afraid to ask.

"Go ahead," I said. "Tell me what you're reading."

"It's a sports piece," Dusty replied. "It's about the rise in Major League salaries."

"Gee. That sounds exciting."

"It's very informative."

"Baseball players don't make nearly enough money."

"They can barely eat."

"So why is the article a cutout?"

"My dad's brother, Uncle Ned, gets *Playboys*," he explained. "He takes out the sports features so I can read them."

"You couldn't score the whole magazine?"

"My mother would flip if she knew I even had this part. To her, anything inside a *Playboy* is certifiably lewd."

"Maybe you've been busted looking at one before."

"Maybe you were with me."

"That was a special day," I said.

"Not as much for you."

"My folks weren't quite as proud as your dad was."

"That's because I didn't pin it on Uncle Ned."

"You know the code. So, who did you pin it on?"

"The exchange student down the street," he replied.

"Hanz? But I thought he only loved chocolate."

"It was easy," Dusty said. "He'd already flown back overseas."

"Never to learn of his illustrious status as the pervie foreign guy."

"My advice is to always blame the German kid. Then people will say, 'Oh, he's from *Europe*. It's a culture thing.' That's a permanent free pass for me and you."

"You've seen a naked lady magazine?" Sam asked.

"Of course," I replied. "Haven't you?"

"Not me! My folks would kill me."

"If you want to spy some leg," Dusty told him, "then you've gotta be willing to risk it all."

"I don't think I could take the shame if they caught me."

"You're the sensitive type. Perhaps a career in bird watching is in your future."

"Shut up."

The alarm went off at 9:00. Time for action. After convincing Sam to come with us for about the tenth time, we climbed down the tree and crept to the side yard for our bikes, peeking at the kitchen window as we went. My mother didn't mind if I rode at night as long as it wasn't too late, but after the speech

Sam's dad gave, it was best to slip away undetected.

Walking to the street, I saw our garage door was shut and that my brother had left. With the coast clear, we jumped on and pedaled silently away. A full moon hung in the sky and its light shone clear and bright, making it a perfect night for an excursion. At the bottom of the hill where my lane ended, an overgrown field hunkered between my neighborhood and the park. This sat beyond Sam's threshold for riding a bike. In fact, this sat beyond Sam's threshold for everything.

"My dad's gonna kill me," he said.

"He'll never find out," I replied.

"But everyone at Sandra's will talk."

"Is your dad plugged into this town's social network? No. All he does is smoke cigarettes in that dark den and watch *Hawaii Five-O*."

Sam's head bowed from the mortal sin he was about to commit. He then followed us onto the trail through the field to the park road. We crossed over and went underneath a group of pine trees casting shadows from lights at the Little League field. The late game was almost done. Groups of people mulled about the grounds, and we heard the fielders' dull chatter as they goaded a batter to swing. Sam demanded we take a wide berth around the baseball diamond to avoid being seen. Dusty and I didn't make a big deal of it and followed him towards the park's lake.

We had a big park for a mid-sized town, aptly named Spring Lake Park because there was a spring and a lake, except the lake was actually a large pond. A springhouse fed the pond through a heavy pipe that gushed crystal water over a concrete burn into a grassy creek. On the west side where a pavilion stood, hidden trails weaved beneath towering pines which had grown so thick that they blocked out the light. At the creek, a bridge crossed over to a playground sitting in front of the water. Beyond that opened the park's entrance. A row of sleepy homes lined the lane, and in the first house lived Jill.

When we got to the edge, we coasted along the pond's shore and rode up the creek. It wasn't a long creek, maybe sixty yards to the springhouse. Rich grass grew along its banks, filled with crickets and croaking frogs. We crossed the stone bridge to the playground with swing sets, monkey bars, slides, and a spinner. A small distance north of the playground stood a small hill cut in half by a brick wall. We biked up and sat with our feet dangling over the bricks, looking towards the row of homes.

"Do you think they're still up?" Sam asked.

"You mean Jill's house?" I replied.

"No. I was asking if you think Sandra's parents are awake."

"Oh. I guess I heard you wrong."

"Why would I ask about Jill?"

"I was wondering the same thing."

Sandra lived next door to Jill, and their houses sat on the east side where the park began. Each side of the entrance was flanked by a stone lookout built like a little castle, both about fifteen feet high with a ladder inside and a window at the top. The house nearest to the entrance was Jill's. Sandra's house, though, was where our attention was focused. That's where the pajama party was going down. Pajama parties were the holy grail for pranks. It was our intent to crash it, and to crash it well. After several minutes of intense observation, we saw a set

UNDER THE LIGHT OF FIREFLIES

of girls' shadows float past the windows.

"Bingo," Dusty said. "Let the freakout commence."

"How are we going to work this?" I asked.

"I have two schools of thought on the subject. First, we could sneak up to the house, lightly tap on the glass, and scare the girls when they open the drapes. Or second, we simply wait for shadows to appear and then beat the windows like savages."

"You mean a bull rush? That sounds too crude. I like the bait and hook better."

"It is a strong move. However, there's no guarantee when they hear the tap that they'll go for it. They might get scared and run away."

"Which blows the gag."

"That's why the bull rush is so smart. There's almost zero chance of failure."

"Fascinating."

"I'm scared," Sam announced.

"What?" I said. "What've you got to be scared about?"

"Sandra's dad. I see his car."

"I already told you," Dusty said. "He's out of town on a fishing trip."

"Then why is his car still there?"

"You ever heard of catching a ride?"

"What I've heard is that once during Hell Week, he pulled his gun on a teenager."

"That was the boyfriend of Sandra's big sister. And her dad was only cleaning his gun on the coffee table."

"So, then it's true," Sam said. "Her dad's a gun freak. This could be very dangerous, guys. There's a good chance that we

24

could get shot, or go to jail, or maybe even both. My dad would say this is an impossible risk."

"Sammie baby, stop," Dusty said and squeezed his shoulder. "This conversation humiliates us both."

"You don't need me. Why don't y'all go ahead. I'll stay here and watch your backs."

"Listen to me," I said to Sam. "You've been avoiding the danger factor your whole life, and if there's one thing chicks dig, it's danger. You have to take off your diapers someday."

"Today is that day," Dusty said.

Sam seemed as distressed as I ever saw a guy, searching in despair for a counter argument, but peer pressure is a demanding mistress. He held his hands prayer-like like to his mouth and muttered something indiscernible. After several moments of arguing with his absent father, he dropped his hands in defeat, and whispered okay. Dusty and I looked at each other intently.

"Go time," I said.

"It's on like *Donkey Kong*." Dusty nodded.

Then we put our hands together, Sam included, and on the count of three we chanted, "Loafers ride!"

Across the lawn near our destination, we hid our bikes behind a tree and hurried onto a gravel lane leading to the houses. As we got closer, we tip-toed to a bush to have a look around. Yet again, we saw a group of shadows drift by the windows. When they were gone, we quietly scooted behind the house then crept beneath the sill.

"So which plan did we decide on?" Sam whispered.

"Bait and hook," I said.

"Bull rush, bull rush," Dusty countered.

UNDER THE LIGHT OF FIREFLIES

"Shhh," said Sam as shapes reappeared.

Apparently, some girls had heard something and were now standing near the windows to take a listen. I gestured for the guys to be quiet, and we waited. The girls stood a small distance away but wouldn't come closer. After another moment, I gave the fellows the thumbs up, then raised my hand and gently tapped the glass. Instead of opening the drapes, though, the shadows quickly scurried away in a burst of chatter. I thought I'd blown it for sure and began to ponder the other strategy. But a minute later another figure appeared in the window. The fellows and I waited with bated breath as the shadow drew closer and closer to listen. After several motionless seconds, two hands reached carefully out, touched the curtains, then moments later ripped them open.

"Now!" I cried, and we shot to our feet and screamed at the top of our lungs, "*BOOO!!!!!*"

The next thing we saw was the horrified face of a grown woman followed by a bloodcurdling shriek that nearly shattered the glass. Dumbfounded, all we could do was shriek back, turn, and run for our lives. And run we did. In fact, we ran so hard that Sam forgot to look up and crashed blindly into a row of trash cans. He rolled backwards over the top where he lolled about in a state of bewilderment. Dusty and I had to stop to help him, and that's when we came to our senses.

"That was Mrs. Prince," I said. "We're busted."

"You are correct," Dusty agreed.

"She saw our faces. My mother would be super mad if we kept running and didn't stop to clean up this mess."

"Yeah, my dad wouldn't be too proud this time. He'd beat

me like a mule."

"Are you crazy?" Sam cried as he staggered to his feet. "You can't be thinking of staying. We've got to get out of here. We've got to run!"

"Sam, hold on," I said. "Mrs. Prince could turn out to be cool."

But it was too late. Sam had already taken off in a blur of elbows and shoe soles. He even abandoned his bike. Dusty and I watched him zigzag wildly into the night, wondering how far he'd get before realizing he was completely alone. As Dusty and I picked up the trash cans, the light to Sandra's driveway flicked on and the back door swung open.

"What in the hell is going on out here?!!" a woman's raspy voice hollered. "Who is that?"

Mrs. Prince staggered outside wearing a short night gown and slippers while holding a crystal whiskey glass. She hopped down the back steps and waltzed through the carport with a smoldering sex appeal, if that was possible for a forty-year-old woman.

"I said who is that?" she demanded.

This was the moment of truth. Dusty and I bowed our heads and regretfully stepped forward.

"It's Noah Ellis," I said sadly.

"Sam Wooderson right here," Dusty added.

With those words, we plunged into an instant war to stave off howls of laughter.

"Noah Ellis," Mrs. Prince said as she walked up. "What in the world? And Sam. I didn't know your folks let you out after lunch."

UNDER THE LIGHT OF FIREFLIES

"They needed more air for smoking."

We both sucked in sharp breaths and let out involuntary snorts.

"Say what?" Mrs. Prince said. "You seem awfully tall from what I remember. Come here and let me see you."

Dusty shuffled over. Mrs. Prince had known us for years, and as soon as Dusty got to her, she lifted his chin.

"Well, Dusty Schaeffer! I should have known."

"Sorry, Mrs. Prince," he said, busting out a string of obnoxious giggles.

"Have you lost your mind?"

"No ma'am. We were passing by and saw that your trash cans had been knocked over, so naturally we stopped to pick them up."

"Oh, cut the crap," she huffed. "You came here to raid a pajama party, didn't you?"

"Pajama party? What's a pajama party?"

"I'll tell you one thing. You almost gave me a heart attack."

"We're sorry," I said.

"Don't sweat it, Ellis," she replied and gulped her drink. "Who's your friend?"

We looked behind us, and towards the playground we saw Sam's head timidly peeking around a tree like a rabbit.

"I can't believe he's still here," Dusty said.

"He's scared of the dark," I replied.

"So *that's* Sam," said Mrs. Prince. "Well, guess what now? I own all three of you."

The back door opened again whereafter a passel of girls' faces appeared one atop the other like a totem pole.

28

"Yoo hoo!" Mrs. Prince called. "Ladies! Your clumsy knights are here to win your honor."

The girls giggled, then came out and tiptoed to the edge of the carport under a streetlamp. They were all barefoot with their pajamas on, but still acting very prim. I was there for one person alone. A blonde with a ponytail and freckles. And then I saw her. Jill. Instantly, my heart leapt in my chest and my throat swelled shut. My hands clung together, worriedly wringing Sam's invisible lemon. After that, a sagging, depressed feeling arose because it was painfully obvious that I wouldn't be able to speak.

"What is this, a bar mitzvah?" Mrs. Prince asked. "You all can talk to each other."

"I have that effect on women," said Dusty.

"Oh shut up," a sassy girl named Eloise told him. "You're the only person here in love with you."

"That's fairly aggressive. But you've always been a little touchy."

"Just remember that it was me who knocked you out in the kickball tournament."

"Yeah, well, that was a year ago and you're a grade older."

"We still beat the pants off you."

This was partly true, which burned Dusty deeply. His class had been the fifth-grade champs in kickball the year before, but they lost the school title to the sixth-grade champs. Eloise, who was on the sixth-grade team, had beaned Dusty with the ball for the final out. Afterward, he was inconsolable. If there was one way to get to Dusty, it was sports. And more specifically, sports losses.

"Winning by two runs doesn't mean you beat the pants off anybody," he said. "And if you want to play again, then name the time and place and I'll be there."

"Better watch out," I whispered, "you don't want to over-impress them."

"Talk about your Casanovas," Mrs. Prince said before ambling to the house with ice tinkling in her glass. "You've got five minutes, ladies."

We all stood there for a moment, wondering what to say. Sandra's cousin Michelle whispered something in Sandra's ear.

"What are you talking about?" Dusty asked.

"Don't worry about it," Michelle replied.

"Seriously. Don't keep a secret."

"I was just saying how you almost killed my aunt."

"Well, we didn't know it was her at the window."

"Then you ran over the trash cans and woke up our whole neighborhood."

"That wasn't my fault."

"You guys are dorks."

I looked over, and incredibly Sam had reappeared.

"Thanks for sticking around, pal," I said. "That was very heroic of you."

"Did you give Mrs. Prince my name?"

"No. Just your phone number."

"Why'd you do that??"

"I worry about you, Sam."

The girls were now rustling around and chatting. Dusty slyly eased into the middle of the pack and started to judge their attire under a chorus of giggles. Sam and I walked over too and tried to mingle, instead hanging around the outside looking in. Then I heard someone say my name.

"Noah Ellis. I'm surprised at you."

It was Jill's voice.

"Hello there!" I said and spun around, perhaps too quickly. "Hey, it's cool. We weren't trying to hurt anybody."

"Hurt anybody? Give me a break. Mrs. Prince loved it."

"Really? She's pretty neat. No, wait. I mean cool."

"Yes. In a premier sort of way."

Her words lingered there, as if imploring me to engage, but I was stiff as a board. Jill, by contrast, rested an elbow in her hand and looked as casual as the stars.

"Are you doing anything fun this summer?" I asked her at last.

"Nothing special. Just modeling camp."

"Modeling camp. What's that?"

"It's a camp for supermodels. I'll be gone most of the summer."

"That's a long time. What happens at this camp?"

"They teach things like the art of hairspray. Hairspray is very important, you know."

"Extremely," I said, unsure how to proceed. "Anything else?"

"How to be skinny. And to smoke. All models love to smoke."

"Hmm. Maybe you could learn to smoke yourself skinny. Sam's parents could teach you how."

"Ha ha!" she laughed.

Score. With that I felt the sudden urge to exit while I was

UNDER THE LIGHT OF FIREFLIES

ahead, but then again, I was in love.

"So, Mr. Ellis," Jill said with a smirk, "I've been meaning to talk to you. Are you missing something?"

"Like what?"

"Something sentimental."

I had no clue what she was talking about and drew a blank. It must've shown on my face because Jill chuckled again.

"You have no idea," she said.

"I can't think of a thing."

"Then you should drop by sometime," she said in a discreet voice. "Maybe I'll show you what it is."

With those words, my heart almost exploded, and my mind went radioactive. Was it possible she was flirting with me? Or was she just being witty? Should I try and flirt back? What if I made a wrong move and screwed everything up? As my mind raced inside this unsolvable dilemma, the back door flew open and saved me.

"Ladies!" Mrs. Prince hollered. "Time to get your hineys back inside."

"Aww, come on, Mrs. Prince," Dusty pleaded. "We were just getting to know each other. Won't you join us?"

"Don't push your luck, honey," she said and came onto the carport. "Now let's go, girls."

All the girls scooted off. When they'd filed through the door and were back inside, Sam ran over and said, "Mrs. Prince. If you ever run into my parents somewhere, could you please not mention anything about tonight? Please, ma'am?"

"Your parents? Why, I don't believe I know them."

"We're the Woodersons. My dad's name is Gerald. We live

32

over on Palm Drive."

"I know who they are, son," she sighed. "Your secret is safe with me. Now you all clean up these cans before you get in trouble. You wouldn't want Mr. Prince to come out firing."

She walked off as we all looked at each other in disbelief. Then the back door slammed shut and the lights snapped off.

"Wow," Dusty said. "Mrs. Prince is fine."

"Can a woman be fine after having three kids?" I asked.

"This one can. Did you not see that red négligée she had on? Reeeoww."

"That's mostly inappropriate."

"I stand by my statement."

"So we're going home now, right?" Sam asked.

"Sammie," Dusty said. "You crash one set of garbage cans and now you want to quit?"

"We have a lot more damage to do," I said.

A look of consternation overcame Sam's face that was heartbreaking. I relented.

"Tell you what, why don't we take a slow ride back through the park," I offered. "Then we'll go to my house, make some popcorn, and watch a movie."

"That'd be great!" Sam cried. "But hold on. Are you kidding with me?"

"Not this time, buddy."

"You did good, Sam," Dusty said and slapped his back. "You made those trash cans look like tackling dummies."

After cleaning up the mess, we grabbed our bikes and pedaled lazily through the playground without a care in the world. Across the park, the baseball game had ended. There wasn't another soul to be found. The full moon now hung at its zenith, casting a glow so luminous that the pond's lily pads seemed to hover like holograms. As we arrived at the stone bridge, we happened upon a family of ducks crossing our way and we stopped to watch. Ducklings were cute, even to boys. When they'd almost made it over, I took an innocent step forward but stopped. Without warning, the mother duck emitted a sharp hiss and drew her wings protectively over her ducklings. I never once thought I could be intimidated by a duck, but there it was. Without debate, we left the bridge and traveled up the creek and around the springhouse. High above us the pines rustled and swayed rhythmically as the warm breeze brushed our faces. This night was our first night of freedom, and it intoxicated us. There were so many more to come. Bathed in the blue light, we took the long way home, reveled in our conquest, and pondered the endless possibilities of summer.

CHAPTER THREE

Coach Darrell was a wiry man who wore a mustache, gold rimmed glasses, and a baseball hat bent straight down the middle like a rooftop. He reached for a bag of charcoal, ripped it open, then dumped it all into the grill. After stacking the briquettes into a neat pile, he poured on half a quart of lighter fluid, lit an entire book of matches, then tossed them in where a wonderful burst of flames shot up.

"Whoa," I said. "That's quite a flame."

"I refuse to be the guy whose fire went out at a barbecue," Coach said then crunched his beer can and tossed it in the trash.

Coach Darrell was an assistant for my Little League team, the Franklin Cardinals, and that afternoon was our annual trophy ceremony at the pavilion in the park. That was also the day where we would learn who made the all-stars. Our head coach, Coach Pritchett, had not shown up yet. Both of my coaches were fireman, but Coach Pritchett was a station chief, and I wondered if his duties would keep him away.

UNDER THE LIGHT OF FIREFLIES

"Can I get one of those?" asked one of the parents, Mr. Thompson, gesturing at the cooler.

"Only if you like 'em cold."

Rifling through the ice chest, Mr. Thompson found a beer, cracked it open, then slurped the foam off with his purplish lips. Coach followed suit and got himself another.

"Where's Pritchett?" Mr. Thompson asked.

"Oh, I got some bad news. Bethel Methodist is on fire."

"Like hell! You kidding me?"

"I'm telling the truth, I'm sorry to say."

"When did it start?"

"Over an hour ago," he said and pointed his beer can eastward.

On the horizon, a black plume of smoke rose in contempt of the bluebird sky. Some parents overheard, and the word quickly spread around the tables so that everyone turned to watch. Mr. Thompson scratched his neck and sized up Coach Darrell a second.

"Ain't you supposed to be over there?" Mr. Thompson asked.

"I was over there," Coach replied with his eyes narrowing.

"That fire's still a burnin'!"

"For your information, it's in Arkansas and I'm not even on duty. They already got every dang fireman in the city running around like it's the second coming!"

"Settle down, settle down," Mr. Thompson said, producing a pack of cigarettes and offering one. Coach thought it over a second then accepted and lit up. The other parents were still listening.

36

"Somebody had to hand out the trophies," Coach said aloud. "Otherwise, I'd have stayed. Not that it would've done one bit of good."

"How's that?"

"That church is toast," he replied, blowing smoke from his nostrils. "The whole thing's engulfed in flames. Some woman went into hysterics about the antique windows of all things."

"Excuse me," a mother asked with a worried face. "Is everybody okay? I have a sister who goes to that church."

"Oh yeah," Coach answered with a quick nod. "The Sunday service ended hours ago. Everyone's safe."

"Thank the good Lord for that."

After cooking the hot dogs and burgers, the trophy presentation commenced. It wasn't much of an affair. We'd earned second place in our division, but the plaques didn't mention it. All that was stenciled was the year and our names. Though the younger kids seemed excited to receive one, I already owned a stack of worthless trophies. All I cared about was who made the all-stars. I was twelve and this was my third and final chance. I'd played a good season, and many people figured I was a shoe-in. After giving the last trophy, Coach searched his clothes and pulled a folded paper from his shirt pocket.

"Here's Coach Pritchett's list for who made the all-stars," he said as I nervously clenched my fists. "Donovan Johnson. Leroy Hailey. Brian Pritchett. Congratulations, boys."

He then wadded up the paper and threw it unceremoniously on the table. That was it. I didn't make the all-stars. Everybody went back to talking, but I could only sit there stunned. Mother laid her hand on my back and rubbed it, but I didn't respond.

37

My body was cold from rejection. I'd been third on the team in batting average as well as RBIs. I didn't make an error all season. *How could this happen?* I wondered. But I understood perfectly well how it happened. I glanced around for Brian Pritchett—the coach's fortunate son who was a whole two years younger than me—but he hadn't shown either. How convenient. Some of the other parents noticed me and averted their eyes.

"Noah," Sally asked. "Do you want some ice cream?"

"No," I replied.

"I can get it for you."

"I just want to be alone, please."

"Okay," she said and scooted away.

A Black lady with bouffant hair and horn-rimmed glasses walked up. She was the mother of our best player, Donovan. Mrs. Johnson was one of the nicest and happiest people I ever knew, and we were always pleased to see each other.

"Is this Sally Ellis we got sitting right here?" she asked with her head cocked playfully. "I was hoping that you'd be here today, you pretty little thing. Aren't you just a blessing?"

Sally giggled as Mrs. Johnson showered compliments on her.

"And Noah," she said with her hands on her hips, "you did so good this year. I always say that if that ball gets anywhere near centerfield, you gonna catch it. And catch it you did."

"Thanks, Mrs. Johnson," I said with a forced grin. "Donovan got MVP and made the all-stars. He deserves it."

She looked into my face and could see everything at once.

"Don't you go hanging your head, Noah Ellis," she said. "You deserved it too, and your day is gonna come. You just keep doing it right."

38

Then Donovan came trucking over and barged right into the middle. "Momma, can I have another ice cream?" he asked.

Donovan was a big, strong kid with a tall afro and attentive eyes. Nobody ever messed with him because he didn't take any lip, but he wasn't a bully either. He could hit the baseball a mile. We'd been friends and teammates since pee-wee.

"Donovan, did you say hello to everybody?" Mrs. Johnson asked.

"I said hi to Noah back there," he said and motioned at the buffet.

Mrs. Johnson stood and waited.

"Hold on," he said and rubbed his face. "Mrs. Ellis, hello. Hi ya, Sally. That's a pretty dress you got on."

He took off his hat and shook their hands, dropped his chin to his chest, then returned to his mother with those beseeching eyes.

"Yes, you can have another ice cream," Mrs. Johnson said. "Just don't overdo it."

"Thanks, Momma. Noah, you want one?"

"Sure," I replied and got up.

My mother watched me with a cocked eyebrow and nodded at Sally.

"Sally," I asked. "Can I get you a bowl?"

"That's okay," she replied and placed her chin on the table. "I'm not hungry."

We hurried to the buffet and pulled the dripping carton from the ice bucket. Without an adult around, Donovan carved several large slabs into a bowl and then gave me some. After a few bites, we looked out across the pond. There at the

UNDER THE LIGHT OF FIREFLIES

playground, aimlessly patrolling on his massive bicycle, rode Connor Strait. He was a former eighth-grader who'd moved to town earlier that year.

"Do you know that dude?" Donovan asked, pointing his spoon that way.

"I know who he is," I said. "I try to avoid him."

"He's kind of a weirdo, though, ain't he?"

"He's a thug."

"His dad's crazy, I heard."

"How so?"

"He's some kind of hillbilly who stayed up in the mountains too long," he said, then peeked around and snuck another scoop. "He has a shop near our house. Pop says that he don't bother us, so we don't bother him."

A pudgy teammate of ours named Joey was standing next to us, listening. Joey, who also attended the same church as me, was holding a small figurine of Darth Vader. To say Joey was a *Star Wars* fanatic would have been a large understatement. The second movie was released a year before and Joey had seen it about ten times.

"Do y'all remember this past spring break when someone broke into the junior high and sprayed it with fire extinguishers?" Joey asked.

"And then those books went missing," Donovan said. "The teachers' editions."

Joey checked behind us then drew in closer to Donovan and me.

"What I heard was that they found one of the teachers' books in Connor's locker. There was a big meeting at the front

40

office with the principal, the superintendent, and Connor's dad. Even a cop showed up. They were going to expel Connor permanently, but his dad made a big scene. I heard it got out of hand."

"How out of hand?" I asked.

"His dad's a big man, and he supposedly got mad and went after the principal."

"Did he hit him?"

"No, but the cop had to hold him back. Instead of getting expelled, though, Connor got sent to Lincoln Street for the rest of the year. I haven't heard much since then."

"Dang," Donovan said. "That's messed up."

We watched Connor drifting towards the far side of the park while Joey handled his figurine. Finally, I couldn't stand it any longer.

"What is it with you and all the *Star Wars* stuff?" I asked.

"What do you mean?"

"How many times have you seen it?"

"That would be hard to say."

"Please. You know exactly how many times you've seen it."

"Are you counting both episodes?" he asked.

"Probably I shouldn't have asked."

"I like it because it's about life."

"It's science fiction, Joey," I said. "Spaceships aren't real."

"You don't get it."

"I guess I don't," I said and picked up the wadded all-star list to double-check the names. "So. Would you have done it?"

"Done what?"

"You know," I said, indicating the figurine in his hand. "If

UNDER THE LIGHT OF FIREFLIES

you were Luke, would you have partnered up with your little dad there to rule the universe."

"It wasn't the universe," he snorted. "It was a galaxy. Nobody could rule the whole entire universe, unless of course you can answer the question..."

"You're disturbing me."

"So you want to know if I would've turned to the dark side with my dad?"

"Well?" I asked.

"Yes. I would have."

"You serious?" said Donovan. "That Darth dude is evil. Like, for real evil."

"It's the only way to save the galaxy," Joey replied.

"By making everybody slaves?" I asked.

"It wouldn't be like that."

"Sure, it wouldn't."

"How else can you win?" he declared. "The dark side controls everything."

"It doesn't matter. Luke would never turn."

"Anybody can turn."

I chunked the paper onto the dying coals. The banquet had ended, and the afternoon was waning. We helped clean up the tables then told each other our final goodbyes. Little League baseball was done forever. I followed Mother to the parking lot and gave her my trophy. I said I wanted to walk up and watch Jack play his game at the Legion field. Mother said okay, and I told Sally goodbye.

After they left, I strolled up the creek and passed the springhouse to the hill cut in half by the wall. I leaned against its tree

42

on top and watched Jill's house. The night the guys and I raided Sandra's sleepover, Jill had told me to drop by sometime, and that she'd help me with something I was missing. Since then, though, I'd never found the time. Instead, I made excuses to myself like I had to work in the yard, or my little sister needed tending, or that I'd ultimately see Jill someplace such as the pool. Now as I stood in the distance, I knew that I should take the chance and go over and knock. I imagined the door opening, followed by the appearance of her face and cordial smile, but I had no idea what drama might unfold next—a romance or a tragedy. I stayed there a long time, hoping that she might miraculously appear, but nothing happened. She'd probably left to visit her family in Tennessee, I told myself. I turned and walked away.

After leaving, I headed along the park's winding road. I first walked by a fenced-in WWII fighter plane that had teeth and eyes painted on it, strolled by the park's pool and small zoo, then arrived at the Legion field where teenagers played their summer baseball.

At the game, a sparse crowd had gathered in the roomy covered stands, but I chose a patch of grass near the dugout to watch. On second base stood a baserunner whom I recognized as my brother. He had blackout smeared on his cheeks and dirt all over his uniform. While the pitcher waited for his signal, Jack took a big lead off the bag as he clapped his hands and chattered.

"How's the game going?" I asked another kid near me.

"Jack just cleared the bases with a double," he said. "They're one run away."

UNDER THE LIGHT OF FIREFLIES

Checking the scoreboard, I saw that Jack's team led by nine runs in the bottom of the 8th inning. One more score prompted the mercy rule, and the game would end. I went to the foul line and leaned over the fence, seeing Jack's buddy Keith getting ready to face the pitcher. He stared at his bat as if burning his own name into it, then stepped into the batter's box where he wind-milled the club and banged it on the plate.

The pitcher got his signal from the catcher and checked my brother at second. He looked again to home plate, bobbed his head a few times, then reached back and brought the heat. Keith stepped forward with a big swing whereafter a crack rang out.

"Whoo-wee," an old timer behind me crowed.

The ball zoomed off the bat, flew over the third baseman's glove, then landed inside the line. Fair ball. Barking and pumping his fist while the team roared, my brother rounded third base in front of his dugout, headed for home. He scored the run with ease, and they won the game.

The players stormed off the benches and swarmed Keith and my brother who got slapped and shoved around. After a good mauling, Jack emerged from the scrum all grins, and in that moment he reminded me of dad.

Our dad. If only he could've only been there, he would have loved every second of it. He'd been a man ready made for baseball or barbecues. He loved jokes, and he was always willing to lend a hand. One time, we were on the way to his league bowling final when we passed some college kids stranded on the road. He pulled over and worked on their car for a whole hour so they could get back to school, even though it meant missing his match. I'd watched him from the eyes of a son, emulating

44

him, abiding under his wing, hoping to make him proud. He was never coming home.

I stood in the gate as the team bagged the equipment. I could hear them talking about the game and how they'd baited a pitch, or fooled a runner, or stole a signal. After tidying the dugout, the team sat in a ring on the outfield grass where their coach addressed them with the undying sermon of effort and teamwork. My brother noticed me and gave a salute. I nodded back. When the coach finished his talk, the boys slapped fives, and Jack trotted over.

"Good game," I told him as he came up.

"Meh. Those guys were easy. We should've finished them off sooner."

It was warm. Summer had come. The concession was changing shifts and the stands sat empty except for tossed popcorn bags and paper cups.

"What's wrong, little man?" he asked as we walked.

"Nothing."

"Don't pull that on me. I'm your brother."

He nudged me, so I stopped and took a breath.

"Remember what happened to Barry Vaughn?" I asked.

"He got ripped off. He should've been out here playing today. Why?"

"Say hello to the new Barry," I said and pointed at my chest. "I didn't make the team."

We looked at each other the only way that brothers can, then he jerked his head and spit. "Damnit," he said.

He looked at me again, this time with a tinge of pity, and it stung me. I didn't want my brother's pity. I wanted my brother

UNDER THE LIGHT OF FIREFLIES

to see me the same way that I saw him—with pride and maybe a hint of jealousy. We walked with his arm across my shoulder as his spikes clicked upon the pavement. The lights flipped on early for the late game while in the parking lot Jack's friends chatted at their vehicles, some of them with their girlfriends leaning against them.

"Where are you going tonight?" I asked him.

"I'm supposed to meet some folks at the Circle."

"Sounds like fun."

"It's the same old people and the same old deal." Then seeing my head hanging, he added, "But you know what? I can do that anytime. Why don't you and me take a ride together?"

"Don't worry about it."

"Come on," he said with another nudge. "We'll go to the river bottoms by the farms. I'll let you drive the car just like Dad used to do."

"That's okay."

"I'm serious."

"Are you sure your friends won't miss you?"

"They'll be fine. After our drive, I'll take you for a milkshake. You in?"

"I'm in if you're in," I said.

Jack told his friends bye then changed out of his spikes into some sneakers. We jumped into the car, and with the radio playing, we embarked upon our ride into the country. The road we took was heavily populated by trees which blotted out the late sun, but after several minutes we turned onto a long bend, coasted down a hill, and then emerged upon the wide roaming spaces called the Shuffle.

46

Rich swaths of farmland emerged, scattered with swampy bayous and rows of oak and pecan trees running into the distance. For many miles the steamy earth drank in the dripping sunlight, bringing up wheat, soybeans, or cotton. Occasionally, a wooden cross appeared on the roadside where some unfortunate soul had rolled off the embankment to their fate. We put down the windows and smelled the loamy summer air which had grown thick from the river.

We turned off and pulled up a dirt road that ran like a tunnel through wild overgrowth, then arrived at a dilapidated bridge rising forty feet above a creek. The bridge was narrow with no rails, supported by a skeleton frame underneath, while on each side, the creek's banks plunged straight down.

I'd ridden across this bridge before, but only when my dad was at the wheel. My brother could drive fine, and the bridge seemed simple enough to maneuver, but still there remained that fear of falling. More than a few folks had lost their lives at this very place.

"Sit tight, buddy," Jack said. "We'll be all right."

"Okay. Just don't go too fast."

Jack turned down the radio, lined the tires up, and drove us onto the tracks. The wooden planks sounded off clickety-clack as we rolled high above the crooked stream. From the other side, tree limbs stretched towards us, their trunks clinging to the bank, while strewn along the creek bed laid the bodies of their friends who hadn't hung on. The sun was hidden, and Jack had to hit the headlights to see the weathered tracks better. From the other side, a murder of crows cawed at our approach, lifted, then swooped down into the ravine. At

UNDER THE LIGHT OF FIREFLIES

last, I heard the crunch of the gravel road, and I relaxed. We pulled to a spot on the side where Jack stopped.

"Are you ready to drive?" he asked.

"I'm too big now to sit in your lap."

"Can you work the pedals?"

"Yeah, I can do it."

"The right one is the gas, and the left is the brake."

"I know."

"Go easy with it. If you see another car then pull to the side."

"Will there be trouble if we get caught?"

"Not out here."

I was smiling ear to ear as Jack moved the seat up and switched places with me. I could barely see over the steering wheel and my feet strained for the pedals, but I managed. Jack coached me as I got going, and though it was a little wobbly at first, I soon was putting down the road on my first real drive. Jack settled back and together we rode, man to man. It felt grown-up to be trusted. All my other problems went away. Twice a truck appeared in front of us, and I pulled over and waited. Each time, the farmer simply waved and plodded on past. Jack let me go a mile or so before we switched places again, then he drove us to the end of the road.

"Let's walk from here," he said and we got out.

On the left stretched decayed flatland with no crop planted, while on the other side stood a wild orchard with black nuts and dead leaves littering the ground. In the middle of the trees, a brick fire-pit had crumbled in half, and farther away huddled a tired farmhouse, dirty and forlorn. I'd heard that an old hermit lived there, but nobody ever saw him.

48

As we walked on, the specter of the Red River rose into view. She flowed wide and strong, the color of rust from the clay and sand that had washed off the endless miles of North Texas plains. We made it to the bank's edge where far below the water gurgled, smacked the chalky earth, then swirled back the other way. *This bank won't last for long,* I thought. Across the river stretched a long beach where ducks flocked to munch grit. Further down, shrubs and yellow grass clung to a sand bar as backwater churned around its side.

"Right over there was where it happened," Jack said gloomily.

"On that bank over there?"

My brother took a seat in some grass and pulled his knees up. I sat next to him and watched the river.

"That's where Dad and Gary Donald went hunting," he said. "At that bend is where he went under."

Jack sighed deeply. We didn't say anything for a while. We watched where our dad had drowned and felt the darkness of that memory. Before us, the river yawned while logs and branches bobbed along its heavy current, headed for the ocean. My heart ached at the thought of my father falling into that russet water with its sucking eddies and drifts of sand beneath.

"Tell me how it happened," I said.

"Details are sketchy," he replied. "All we know is that he went to the edge and fell in."

"But how could he fall in?"

"I think he must've been on a steep bank."

"You think? That doesn't explain it. What did Mr. Donald say?"

"He didn't see it happen."

"Dad wasn't dumb. He had to know where he was going."

"I thought that too."

"So there has to be a reason."

"I wish there was. I really do."

"Are you hiding something? Just tell me."

"I told you everything I could."

"All you said was that he fell in. That's the same thing I heard before."

"I can't change it."

"What are you leaving out?"

He tightened his mouth but refused to look at me.

"What you say doesn't make sense," I insisted. "How did it happen?!"

"*I don't know*," he replied then stood and paced around. "I thought you were ready to come here. I come by myself all the time and just sit and watch this dreary river. I know how you feel. I think about Dad every time I walk in the house, every time we eat supper, every time I look at you or Sally. I wish to heaven things were different."

I didn't know why or how our father had died, and it appeared I never would. I remembered when it happened, and how our mother wept. We got the call from the Sheriff, and I heard her quick sharp cries from the kitchen, almost like yelps, before they deepened into a tormented groan. I knew right away it was about Dad. After she told Jack and me that he was missing and probably had drowned, I thought of how wrong everybody was. That soon he would reappear alive and that there would be an explanation for it all. Later on when I

50

saw Sally, that's when it hit me. She would never see our dad or share his laughter again. At the river, I reached for a rock and threw it over the bank where it disappeared without a sound.

"God, how I miss him," Jack said.

"So do I."

The sun was hanging low, and the air smelled of dank earth. Somewhere downriver stood a bridge with a highway stretching over the water, but here the current flowed barren and uncrossable. After a minute, Jack pulled me up and we walked away.

"This is the last time I come here," he said. "Don't look back."

At the car, we started up and headed past the barren fields towards the wooden bridge. We drove onto the planks and over the creek where the water had turned black, the same color as the crows mingling on its banks. We passed on the far side through the growth until we came again to the Shuffle. As we turned onto the road, the last vestige of sun smoldered, painting the western sky a dying blaze of orange. In the bottoms, a wooded ridge stretched beneath newborn twilight as the sultry bayou receded into darkness.

Our windows were still down but the radio was off. We were deep in our thoughts. After a few minutes, Jack turned onto a dirt road which we bumped down for a couple of miles before veering onto a sturdy highway. I didn't know where we were anymore. After a while, we drove up a long rise where a glow came booming into sight. We crossed the interstate and the life of my hometown rushed upon us, belying the solitude of the farmland we'd just left behind.

State Line was a boulevard of light, and the heart of everything for miles around. It divided Texas on the west and Arkansas on the east. The thoroughfare ran five miles south before reaching an imperial federal courthouse straddling both states. Beyond that huddled the hollow remnant of a once bustling downtown, crying about a glittery past to which no one listened.

State Line still bustled, though. Since Texas was a dry county, shops and food joints stood mainly on that side, while Arkansas was dotted with liquor stores and bars. On summer nights, the road stayed busy with cars full of young adults and teenagers from all over, cruising the line for some action.

Jack and I were from Texas. Our high school was called Texas High while the other was named Arkansas High. We'd been rivals since the beginning. During our annual football game, the rivalry reached its pitch. The town called it Hell Week. For seven days a year, caravans of brave souls crossed into enemy territory, but heaven help those souls who got caught behind the lines. Eggs were the main weapon of choice. Countless cars—under no provocation of their own—got barraged simply because their license tags said the wrong state. Many times, though, things went too far. Teenagers got hung up or trapped in a parking lot or an alley, and a frenzy of rocks and bottles would ensue. Fights were commonplace, and every year a few people ended up in the hospital. Before the game that past year, a kid from Arkansas had stolen our tiger statuette off the school marquee. Though we'd won the game and the tiger eventually reappeared, in everybody's eyes, the score remained unsettled.

LEE SANDERS

Diggs Burgers was a drive-up joint on the Texas side and one of the stops for teenagers. We wheeled into a bay, and through an intercom, Jack ordered a couple of milkshakes. Minutes later, a cute waitress named Veronica skated up and dropped off our order.

"Hi there," she said, biting her lip. "Y'all sure you don't want something else?"

"Go ahead and get us a few cheeseburgers," Jack replied.

"Sure thing, darlin'."

"Hey Jack!" somebody called from a shiny red car behind us. I saw it had Arkansas plates and was full of guys drinking and smoking.

"Rip! What's up?" Jack replied.

"Same old deal, man," the guy said with a smooth grin. "What you got going tonight?"

"I haven't decided. I'm with my little bro right now."

"Here's a little inside info. Brandy's folks are out of town and she's having some people over. If you want to, come on by. Just keep a lid on it."

"Thanks, bud. I might do that."

The guy gave a two-finger wave and chugged off.

"Who's that dude?" I asked.

"Doug Ripley."

"I didn't know you hung out with Arkansas folks."

"They're all right," he said with a wry smile. "As long as they don't mess with our chicks."

"What about Lisa?"

"What about her?" he replied and fiddled with the radio.

"Are you still dating her?"

53

UNDER THE LIGHT OF FIREFLIES

"I'm taking a break right now."

"What's wrong?"

"Nothing."

"Is that why you wouldn't talk with her the other day?"

"You ask a lot of questions, don't you?"

"I'm your brother."

He found a station, paused, then turned it off. "Look..." he began, "you're going to learn that after you've been dating awhile, girls can sort of lose their independence. It's like they always have to be around. I just want some space right now."

"But you've been going out for a whole year. Do you want to quit after all of that?"

"She's a good girl. It's complicated."

"Will you ever get back with her?"

"The general idea is when you break up, you stay broken up."

"But she's so pretty and nice. Aren't you afraid she'll go out with other guys?"

"That's something you've got to accept."

"Why accept it? She's the one."

He let out a breath but didn't answer.

"Well, I always thought you and Lisa were really good together," I said.

Jack wouldn't say anything else about it. After we ate, he paid Veronica who chatted with him a minute, then he drove us back home and stopped at the curb.

"Aren't you coming inside?" I asked.

"Nope. Just tell Mother that I went out."

"What time should I say you'll be back?"

54

"It doesn't matter."

"You're going to the other side of town to that party, aren't you?"

"Don't worry about it."

"You've still got on your uniform. It says Texas."

"I'll be all right."

"Okay. Well, thanks for taking me out today. I really enjoyed it."

"My pleasure, little brother. We'll do it again sometime soon."

"You promise?"

"Absolutely."

We both smiled, and I got out and went to the front door. After I opened it, I looked back and watched my brother slowly disappear around the bend.

CHAPTER FOUR

It was a sparkling summer day at the park swimming pool where kids were having a lively time splashing, playing ping-pong, and chowing down on hot dogs and hamburgers. Sam, however, did not have his dollar to get inside. He was hoping that another kid named Alex would be there. Alex had made a bet with Sam in paper football the week before, and Sam actually won. Sam, who wasn't exactly accustomed to winning, got so ecstatic that afterward Alex couldn't find his dollar. Alex's life would have been a lot easier if he had, though, because he'd now have to endure Sam stalking him for the rest of his life. While we waited by the fence, a girl named Jamie from my old homeroom came up with a sly look on her face.

"What are you doing out there?" she asked me.

"Trying to get some money for Sam."

"Have you seen Jill lately?"

"Uhhh..." I mumbled, wondering what this was about. "I think she's gone."

"Where'd she go?"

"Tennessee."

"Why Tennessee?"

"Her family lives there."

"I see. And for how long?"

"I wouldn't know."

"Sure you wouldn't."

Her comments unsettled me, but I didn't pursue it because I had no idea where it might lead. Jamie was odd. Normally a girl with rich auburn hair and a pretty face would have had lots of friends and attention, but not her. It was because she did bizarre things like speaking in strange accents or prancing down the hall as if it were a red carpet. Everyone ignored her.

"Could you find Alex for us, please?" I asked.

"That's going to cost you something."

"I only have enough money to get inside."

"How about if you promise to lay your towel next to mine?"

"Noah would love that," said Dusty. "Maybe you could rub oil on each other too."

Her eyes lit up with an inviting smile.

"He was only kidding, Jamie," I said.

She kept the idea on the table for a few seconds, but when she saw that I wasn't interested, she huffed and stomped away.

"In an odd turn of events," Dusty mused, "Jamie is a looker whose personality actually does matter."

"Junior high should work out well for her."

"I saw her riding her bike around Glenwood the other day on the other side of 40th."

"Was she alone?"

UNDER THE LIGHT OF FIREFLIES

"As always."

"In a way, I feel sorry for her."

"Yeah, but what can you do?"

"Alex won't come over," Sam said and moaned. "What a welsher."

"You're going to have to beat it out of him," Dusty told him.

"I'm no fighter."

It was evident that Sam wouldn't have the funds to get in, and Dusty and I had already covered him twice before. If we didn't do something with him, though, he'd be forced to return home to his parents' smoke-filled cavern or sit outside and watch us rollick in the pool.

"I know what," he said. "We can go to the zoo. It's free for the first two weeks of summer, so we've still got time."

"The zoo is lame," I said. "We've seen everything a hundred times."

"Nuh uh. They just got a new tiger."

"They already have lions, and all they do is lie around."

"I'll go with you," Dusty said.

"Really?" I asked. "When did you start liking the zoo?"

"You know how I feel about the word free. Let's go see the new tiger."

"Nice!" said Sam.

"All right," I agreed. "I've got nothing better to do."

Our city zoo was a sad excuse for a zoo, and an even sadder existence for the animals. It was tiny, it stunk, and for the wildlife, it was hopeless. A few exotics did live there, but we didn't think much about them since we lived so close. At night, we could open our windows and listen to the woeful serenades of

58

the earth's mightiest beasts.

The first exhibit actually was the lions. To no surprise, the two females laid sleeping spread eagle on the concrete flat, paying no attention to anything. We next moved to the biggest cage of all which had been empty for as long as I could remember. Posted in front stood a new brass placard with the inscription: *Bengal Tiger, Male, West India*. Yet the tiger wasn't there, or at least it wasn't visible. The pen had a recess in the back, and after adjusting our eyes to the darkness, an outline of the tiger's white chest momentarily appeared.

"He doesn't want to come out right now," said a burly man with a walrus-like mustache. He wore denim jeans and a khaki shirt with a name tag that read "Dale Kippinger—Parks Director."

"He's a big boy, though," he added as he wiped a handkerchief across his pink face. "512 pounds."

"That's as big as a car!" Sam exclaimed.

"Not quite, son. But he can eat as many chickens as our coop'll hold."

"Are they alive when you feed him?" I asked.

"Yes sir. That's the only thing that makes 'im happy."

"Does he ever come out?"

"Not much during the daytime. He's brand new and isn't used to people yet. He'll get better in the next week or so."

Our shoulders sagged. Though I didn't admit it, I wanted to see him too. Inside that darkness, though, we could tell he was watching us. Then a low guttural growl drifted from the chamber, making our bodies stiffen as the snarl rose before ending in a muffled snort.

UNDER THE LIGHT OF FIREFLIES

"Whoa," said Dusty. "That's some serious throat power."

"He's the king," I said.

"Let's come back later in the week," said Sam.

"We'll see."

We next went by the monkeys who were awake, acting like hooligans as they worked the crowd for peanuts. A teenager flicked in a cigarette and a monkey laid back and smoked it. At the end were peacocks, ducks, a few scroungy deer, and some other animals we didn't care about. We made the turn where living at the backside under the bright sun in a blue pool awaited my favorites. The seals.

I spent a lot of time watching them when I was little. Always playful, it seemed impossible for a seal to be unhappy. When we got there, though, we found the pool empty. Its floor was faded and peeled, and grass had grown in the cracks. The nameplate remained, but otherwise it bided lonely and abandoned.

"They took them away," said a strange voice from the rear.

I swung around where next to me stood a slight man with a weathered face and high cheekbones. His eyebrows grew thick and dark, and deep wrinkles coursed his sun-browned neck. He wore a gray work suit with a withered tag that read "Henry." We knew him as the Russian. It was the first time I'd ever heard him talk.

"Where'd they take them?" I asked.

"Someplace else," he said with a shrug. "They do not tell me these things."

His slouched demeanor resembled that of a peasant, though his thoughtful eyes and rich voice hinted at either wisdom, or a life filled with experience. The story was that he'd bailed

60

from a Soviet vessel years before in a gulf harbor, then later a government agency gave him a job in our town. As kids, we knew very well that the Russians were our enemy. So, having a certified commie in our park brought a certain level of intrigue.

"They were my favorites," I said.

"Mine too," he replied with a nod.

We both looked again at the pool and remembered happier days when the seals were still there. He coughed into a handkerchief, smiled kindly, then walked away.

After leaving the zoo, the guys and I pedaled lazily through the neighborhood under the midday sun. Blotches of shadows doused the yards while heat waves floated off the white streets. Between two rows of backyards ran a long concrete gulch which sat mostly dry. We dropped down and followed it along, splashing across its dying trickle until we arrived at a tunnel that cut underneath Summerhill Road. On the other side stood a corner store called Bookout's. Sam, though, wasn't allowed beyond this point.

"I guess you have to wait here," I said to him.

"I know. What are you getting?"

"Something cold to drink."

"Don't take too long, please."

"It's okay, Sammie," Dusty said. "We'll get you something too."

Dusty and I steered through the tunnel to the other side where we hiked our bikes up a small bank to a hotel parking lot. On the far side, a hulking figure was cruising alone on his bicycle. When he turned, we saw that it was Connor Strait. Afraid to be spotted, we quickly hopped back on our bikes,

UNDER THE LIGHT OF FIREFLIES

zoomed across the lot, then raced each other inside the store.

"Hellooo, Noah Ellis," crooned the owner as he glanced up from his newspaper. "You are here, no doubt, for a comb and a pint of Old Harper."

Mr. Reef was a tall man with a bulbous nose and thinning hair slicked straight back. He and my dad had attended the Rotary Club together. Although somewhat severe in appearance, he also possessed a dry wit, and he'd always liked me.

"Good afternoon, Mr. Reef," I replied. "Just here for a soda."

"Nothing like an orange pop for a little afternoon refreshment. We keep them ice cold for that very occasion."

We strolled down the aisle to the floor cooler, and while we did, my eyes wandered as always to the back magazine rack. Its shelves were stacked with the usual choices such as gardening, automobiles, or sports; but on the top shelf hidden behind the others sat the seductive dirty magazines. Although I'd never risk looking for fear of being caught, just seeing the covers sent thoughts through my mind. As I wavered there in a half-trance, I was awakened by the front door bursting open.

"What did I tell you boys about coming in here?" Mr. Reef demanded and stood up.

It was Fenton, Billy, and Tyler. The last guys I wanted to see.

"Don't get in a twist, dude," Fenton responded, his hair bunched in curls.. "We just came here to buy some Driftwood."

"Of course, you want chewing tobacco. You're too young for tobacco."

"Fun Pak sells it to us all the time."

"Then I suggest you get back on your bicycles and ride over there."

62

"Why do you always have to be so hard?" Billy scoffed with a dark glare.

"Because every time you come in here, I end up short an item. The last time it was a cigarette lighter."

"I've got a hundred lighters, old man. Why would I want to steal yours?"

"Can't we at least get some sodas?" Tyler asked and simpered facetiously. "It's hot outside, and my dad would be ticked off if we couldn't even have a drink."

"Your *dad*," Mr. Reef responded with a head shake. "Give me the money."

They handed it over, and he directed them to wait outside. He then marched to the cooler, grabbed three colas, and took them their drinks and change. Afterward, he came back in and sat down with a scowl. Respectfully, Dusty and I approached the counter with our sodas.

"You need an ID for that," he said.

"Sorry," I replied. "My ID got washed away in a flood."

He peeked over his newspaper, gave a wink, then rang us up.

"I appreciate your business," he said straightly.

"Yes sir."

When we got to our bikes beside the store, we found the boys loitering while sipping their drinks. My first inclination was to get away as fast as possible, but that was easier said than done. It wouldn't look too cool, besides. Looking cool and playing it cool was an important factor of boyhood, especially if you were concerned with your future fate at the junior high playground.

"Say Dusty," Tyler said. "When does your practice start?"

UNDER THE LIGHT OF FIREFLIES

"The first one's in an hour," he responded.

Dusty had made the all-stars just like he deserved. I didn't begrudge him for it, but I was certainly jealous.

"Are you pitching?"

"Coach said I would."

"Get ready to run some laps," Fenton said then belched rudely.

"Oh, coach will make you run," I agreed with a laugh.

"Did you make the team too, Noah?"

"Not this year."

"You mean not any year. I bet you got a little team trophy with your name on it, though."

"We made second place at least."

"Second place? Only losers care about second place."

"It's better than your team did."

With that, Fenton calmly set down his drink, walked over, and stood nose to nose with me.

"Maybe, but I can still whip your skinny butt," he said and poked my chest with his chunky finger.

"Hey man, I'm not trying to start anything."

"*Hey man, I'm not trying to start anything.*' Shut up, wimp."

This time he shoved me. I stumbled backward a few steps and remained there. This was the part where I had to play it cool. Contrary to popular belief, there was no medal for standing your ground in a parking lot and getting pummeled. A fight is the only event on earth where people love to watch a loser. Usually it happens when a kid gets badgered until he finds the wrong courage, then it unfolds slowly and for everyone to see. Only after it begins does the poor sap realize that he's in no

64

way prepared for it. The crowd isn't any help. Hell, watching an ass whooping is what they came for. News spreads fast afterward, and unless that kid finds some redemption later, he'll always be remembered for the day he got whooped. Nobody cares that he stood up, and nobody ever forgets a fight. While Fenton stewed over what to do with me, the ring-ring of a small bell sounded out from behind us. We looked over and found Connor rolling up on his massive bicycle.

Connor Strait wasn't part of the regular crowd. He wore cutoff fatigues for shorts and a tee-shirt with the words "Taxi Driver" stitched across the front. He had sweat bands on his wrists, a Bowie knife strapped to his belt, and a disturbed look on his face like he was dealing with a busted radiator. He whirled up and skidded to a stop, then leaned his burly body on one foot as he slowly surveyed the scene.

"You like pushing around smaller guys, don't ya?" he asked with a thumb pointed at Fenton.

Fenton's arms fell by his side, then he peeked at Tyler and Billy who said nothing.

"What are you doing here?" Fenton asked.

"Looking for you."

Fenton licked his lips and stepped back.

"You ain't supposed to be talking to us," he said, scratching the back of his hand.

"Or what? You gonna call the cops on me for talking?"

At that, Billy slid next to Fenton and stood there as if bored.

"What are you looking at, punk?" Connor said to him.

"There's three of us," Billy replied.

Without hesitation, Connor dropped his bike and strode

UNDER THE LIGHT OF FIREFLIES

directly into Billy's face. Billy was almost as tall, but Connor was a beast, and there wasn't much doubt that he meant business. Everything got still.

"*Come on with it then*," Connor said with his finger almost touching Billy's eyeball.

Billy worked hard not to blink. Connor lurked before him, the perfect picture of menace. Dusty and I stayed as quiet as mice. Fenton then braved a step to flank Connor, but it did not go unheeded.

"One more move," Connor said to Fenton but with his gaze still planted on Billy, "and I swear by my dead ma that I'll gut Spanky here like a fish."

Connor moved his hand to his knife and popped the strap.

"You're not serious," Tyler said nervously with his hand raised. "You'd go straight to jail."

"And Laddie here'll go to the morgue."

"He's only bluffing, Tye," Fenton said.

"Tell that to your boy," Connor replied then unsheathed his knife and swung the blade between him and Billy.

Texarkana was a town of many standoffs. Trash talk abounded, and for lots of folks that could not go unchecked. Even at my age, I'd seen plenty of showdowns. Sometimes, the threats ended up being hot air. Other times, they did not. This didn't feel like Connor was bluffing. Every breath streaming past his lips seemed to convince Billy that he might've met someone as crazy as himself. Connor searched Billy's eyes, daring him to make a move.

Billy stared back in silent hatred. He wasn't as big or strong as Connor, but inside him dwelled a mechanism that generated a kind of crooked energy that shielded his conscience from feelings of sin or guilt. Any other kid standing before Billy would have wilted. Connor, though, appeared fiercely aroused by Billy's ventured toughness, as if this was the exact moment he'd been praying for. Dusty and I did not utter a breath. To judge from our reaction, those guys could've been hanging from a cliff. At the road, a car approached then wheeled into the store lot and parked. The driver got out with an uneasy expression as he legged it into the store. Billy shot a side glance at the new witness and thought this would be the end to the standoff. Connor, however, stayed put with his knife still brandished like he owned the place. After a few tense moments, Billy slowly backed away with Fenton at his side. While they went, Connor peeled his eyes wide and clicked his teeth.

"This ain't over," he said with his blade aimed their way. "Not by a long shot."

They didn't respond. Tyler mounted his hundred-dollar bike and attempted his pretty boy smile, but it came across contrived and weak. Billy and Fenton let him pass, then each followed. At the embankment they dipped down to the creek, and with a last glance Connor's way, they disappeared into the tunnel. After they'd gone, Dusty and I tip-toed to our own bikes and delicately got on to leave.

"Where are you going?" Connor asked.

"Who, us?" I responded.

"Who else would I be talking to?"

"Umm... we're just going home."

"Home is good," Dusty agreed.

"You ain't gonna thank me?"

UNDER THE LIGHT OF FIREFLIES

"Sorry," I replied. "Thanks."

"What are you sorry about?"

"I didn't mean that. I meant...I don't know what I meant."

"Why'd you let that punk push you around?"

"Fenton? Because he's a year older. He's bigger. Plus, there were three of them."

"So?"

I had no idea how to respond.

"Check this," he said and waved his blade back and forth. "A good knife and a strong chin will get you far in life."

Again, I had nothing.

"Well?" he said.

"Well...you're a lot bigger than those guys, and you're the oldest."

"But you said there's three of them. Remember?"

"You weren't really going to use that knife. Were you?"

Connor regarded me a second like he was judging a cut of meat. After re-holstering his knife, he grabbed his bike and walked over with an amused look. "You wanna go for a ride?" he asked.

"What do you mean?"

"You don't understand?"

I massaged the back of my neck and looked to Dusty for help, but he was giving the silent treatment. "Where would we go?" I asked.

"Waterworks."

Waterworks Lake was across the interstate towards the Shuffle. My dad had taken me fishing there when I was younger, but it was a long way to go on a bicycle. I didn't know any kids from my neighborhood who'd ever done it.

"I don't know," I replied. "Dusty, what do you think?"

"Can't do it," he readily answered. "I've got baseball practice."

My jealousy deepened. *I shouldn't have asked Dusty anyway,* I thought. *I should've just told Connor no at the beginning and taken my chances with a stabbing.*

"That's a pretty far ride," I said.

"No it ain't," Connor replied. "I know a back way. It'll save us five miles."

"I never heard of any backway."

"You saying I'm lying?"

"No, no, no. I mean, if it's true then..."

"Then you'll do it," he said and clapped my shoulder. Hard. I was stuck. To back out would lose me respect, if I ever had any to begin with. In junior high, respect from one's peers stood paramount, especially from the wild-eyed knife wielding kind.

"I need to be back by supper," I told him.

"Great. What's Mom cooking us?"

I searched for a response while he just sat there with a sorry look on his face.

"I can read every thought in your pea-sized brain," Connor said. "Not that you're very hard to read."

Across the road, I saw Sam watching us with his hands clasped like a worried mother. I couldn't help but chuckle. I turned to Dusty who offered me the bro handshake.

"I'll give Sammie a kiss for ya," he said and pumped my hand.

"If I should die, tell everybody that I lived."

UNDER THE LIGHT OF FIREFLIES

With me in the back, Connor and I got moving, first over the access road and then onto the interstate bridge. Cars crowded on the top while a knee-high railing separated us from a twenty-foot drop below where trucks and cars barreled along. I was very scared of heights and the sight below made my skin crawl. Besides falling, I also worried that somebody would recognize me and call my mother. We made it across, however, without issue.

A mile later, Summerhill Road turned into a two-lane with no shoulder. Heading to the countryside, it ran over tree-covered hills that rose and fell like the spine of a dragon. A painted white line marked the edge of the road, and we did our best to stay on that line, but over the back slopes of hills, we were blind to any traffic coming behind us.

Connor never wavered for one breath. The sun was high and glaring, and after a few more miles I got thirsty. The soda that I'd drank earlier apparently hadn't done the trick. I didn't want Connor to think I wasn't able, but not long afterward, I knew that I would have to find some water.

"Connor," I said. "Sorry to say it, but I'm bad thirsty."

"Stop saying you're sorry. Follow me."

Without a thought, Connor turned left down a narrow-shaded road, over a hill, then through a turn towards a random gray house in some trees. Once there, Connor got off his bike and stomped right up the sidewalk towards the front door.

"What are we doing?" I asked. "Do you know these people?"

"Give me a few seconds."

At the door, he rang the bell and waited patiently. Then he rang it again. I was spying the side of the house for a water

70

faucet when the door opened and a housewife answered.

"Can I help you?" she asked.

"Hello ma'am," he said. "I'm Connor Strait and this here's Noah Ellis. We've been out biking today and ended up a long way from home. Could we please have a drink of water?"

"Well, of course!" she said. "You boys just come right inside and I'll fix you a glass."

She then stood aside and let us pass. Inside, it was cozy with natural light illuminating the rooms which stretched open and broad. She led us into her kitchen to a table set with yellow place mats and a vase filled with wildflowers. She poured two glasses full of ice water and placed them on the mats in front of us. We gulped them down greedily, and afterward she poured us one more. When we'd finished, she showed us back to the front door.

"You boys can come by anytime," she said.

"Thank you so much," I replied.

She gave a friendly nod and shut the door. As we rode off, I realized that I never got her name.

"Cheryl," Connor told me.

"How do you know that?"

"There was an embroidery with her name on it."

"I didn't expect something like that to happen."

"All you have to do is ask."

"You also have to knock."

"That's very true," Connor said, rapping his knuckles against his noggin. "You're starting to get it."

He made it sound simple. For me, though, it was never simple getting the things that I wanted. And I wanted so much.

UNDER THE LIGHT OF FIREFLIES

Finishing this trip would mean something at least. For a bonus, I got to witness Connor back down the "Wandering Stars." Now I had a story to tell.

As we continued on our journey, fields soon stretched out before us and the sky opened up. At the end of the road, Connor turned onto a dirt path that had a fence draped with honeysuckle and roses. We rode it up until we reached an abandoned cemetery sitting wild and overgrown with a black tree overhanging its entrance.

"Where are we?" I asked.

"This must be an old cemetery for early settlers or outlaws," he said. "The grave markers don't have any names."

We crested a rise overlooking far sloping meadows. In the midst stood a worn-out shack, sun bleached and peeled. Next to it sat a crumbling barn with its cracked doors hanging open. The shack appeared to have been an old bunkhouse. We stopped and peeked through the dirty windows, hoping for treasure, but there was no hope in that place. Inside, an empty kitchen sat covered in dust, papers laid strewn about the floor, and a stack of forlorn toys were thrown into a corner. In the main room, some chairs were arranged in a circle, like a secret meeting had just adjourned, and a shiver went through my bones. I grabbed my bike and hurried down past the barn.

"At that distant ridge of pine trees, there's a trail." Connor pointed out as he came along. "It takes us straight to Waterworks."

Through high swells of grass, we rode down a hill until we hit a tiny path and disappeared into the woods. The trees were dense, and the ground sat covered in leaves. Ivy grew all

72

around while spider webs glinted here and there in rare spots of sunlight. After a half-mile, we came to the edge of the woods where the dark waters of the lake appeared, lapping onto a gray shoreline. We followed that until it stopped near the dam.

"This is it," Connor said.

We got off our bikes and walked up to lean on a thick concrete wall. Reaching to the other side rose the dam's small spillway. Water splashed over its top and dribbled down to a small secondary dam and then to the basin floor that was coated in black moss. In different places, thick clumps of earth had caked up with weeds growing out of them. Near the back of the basin, a stout bridge stood. I saw that its top had never been built, leaving a naked frame exposed. For supports, blunt concrete pillars had been spaced many feet apart, with each one connected to the other by steel beams hanging a few stories high. From end to end, the bridge's length spanned about thirty yards.

"Have you ever ridden the rails?" Connor asked.

"Ridden the rails? What is that?"

"Have you walked across the bridge?"

Looking at it, the beams seemed too skinny and the pillars too far apart. If a person slipped, they'd fall twenty feet onto slime covered concrete. To cross over would be a scary affair, but half of what boys did was to prove it wasn't.

"No," I replied softly. "I never tried."

"Let's check it out," he said and backhanded my arm.

Against my better judgment, I clambered down with Connor to the landing. At the end of the basin, water trickled to the edge then dropped into a putrid swamp from which

73

UNDER THE LIGHT OF FIREFLIES

mosquitos and a fetid smell emanated. On the opposite side of the bridge hunched a line of white diseased trees, grouped together like a chorus of vultures. I couldn't imagine what this bridge could've been for. No road existed.

"Does it scare you?" Connor asked.

"No."

"Perfect answer."

I shouldn't have lied. Connor acted as if he knew the ending to a movie that I'd only started watching.

"If you cross right now," he said, "then you'll never have to prove yourself again."

"But what if I slip?"

"It'd be a bad scene. Rewards do have their risks, though."

It was true that I didn't do noteworthy things. I didn't make the all-stars. I'd never won a ribbon. I never kissed a girl. That day at mini-golf, those boys called me a loser. How appropriate. The edge, though, didn't seem to mind. Indeed, the edge held no prejudice towards anybody, be it a debutante or a degenerate, a preacher or a prostitute. Take a step, it whispered. Results were guaranteed.

"I could probably do it," I said, trying to convince myself.

Connor kept reading me. When he saw that I was serious, he changed to cold silence. I couldn't figure him out. It was useless to try. Instead, I measured the distance to the bottom, telling myself that it wasn't so far that I would die if I fell. Maybe I wouldn't even get hurt. Then I studied the beams and found them slightly wider than my foot. If they were suspended only a few feet above ground, it would be no problem. The more I thought about it, the more I convinced myself it

74

was merely a matter of perspective.

Fighting my apprehension, I cautiously stepped forward and inched my toes over the fringe until they touched the beam. It felt stable and sure. So, I put my whole foot on it while my other remained on the landing. Everything seemed fine. I felt almost calm. Concentrating on my balance, I took a breath and told myself it would be okay. Stay steady, and I'd show this guy what I was made of.

After wiping the sweat from my eyes, I put my full weight forward and brought my other leg around. As soon as I stepped out, though, my perspective instantly changed. Without the safety of the landing, it didn't seem so simple now. Falling became a real possibility. That was twenty feet down. With this new reality, my legs began to twitch and my body to shake. Taking a glance at the opposite side, which laid a hundred paces away, I utterly regretted my decision. My face furrowed into a deep frown, and I began to jitter frantically.

The next instant, I felt a hard smack against my back. A shock rippled through me. My ankle gave, my knee buckled, and I veered uncontrollably sidewards. As I flapped my arms in a fury to regain balance, my shirt tightened around my chest. In the next instant, I was yanked backward off the bridge and sent flying through the pine straw.

"Don't be an idiot!" Connor shouted at me.

I slid to a stop and gripped the clayish dirt in my hands, feeling the good earth.

"Are you for real?" I exclaimed, hardly believing what'd just happened.

"Don't risk your life just to prove something, Noah. It only proves you're stupid."

"Where in the world did you come from, man?"

"A mountain town in the Ouachitas. Hot Springs."

"Can anything good come from Arkansas?"

"Ha! I've heard that one before."

He helped me back up, and after dusting myself off, we crept to the edge and looked over. On the other side, the vultures remained unmoved, the mossy basin undisturbed, and I was okay. I blew out a deep breath. We left and made our way back up to the shoreline. At the top, we sat down and watched a boat gunning it across the lake.

"I never knew this trail existed," I said. "How'd you find the way?"

"I discovered it."

"When?"

"I went to the other side of the dam to fish when I first moved here. I found the bridge, crossed over, then followed this trail leading to those fields. The rest I researched on a map."

"You crossed the bridge? Alone?"

"Yeah."

I laughed and shook my head. Nothing surprised me anymore.

"I wish we had some fishing poles right now," I said.

"So, you're a fisherman too."

"My dad used to take me here. It's been a while though."

"Why'd you stop?"

I was going to answer, but words couldn't say. I breathed in the lake air and watched the boat skimming over the water. My mind went back to the times that my dad had taken me here. Mother always packed us a basket, and Dad and I would eat breakfast on the water. I caught my first fish here. My eyes welled up with tears. Connor quit analyzing me and turned aside.

"I've been there," he said then threw a rock into the water with a plunk.

Going back to the trail, we took our bikes into the woods then reemerged and crossed the field. We rode past the abandoned bunkhouse, then the cemetery, and at last made the shady road but without stopping this time. After the long ride back on Summerhill, we passed over the interstate bridge and took a turn into our neighborhood.

I felt like broadcasting where we'd been, but nobody was around to hear it. We coasted down a side street full of sleepy houses with gardens full of azaleas and roses. Onward we continued past street signs and gulches until we arrived in the park, that old concession we returned to if only because she was always waiting.

I'd called Connor trash because I never knew him. He wasn't involved with sports or even the band. Instead, he took woodshop, dressed wrong, and was a loner. That's how I judged him. I knew that if I was spotted with him, then the others would judge me too. The others made it hard to do the right thing. For once, though, I could see the truth. I could see that Connor was just as good as they were and maybe even better.

In the park, we first rode by the zoo where fresh tire ruts had been dug up across the lawn and a sign was smashed over. *Teenagers*, I thought. We continued past the old WWII fighter plane with the eyes and fangs painted on, then headed to the

UNDER THE LIGHT OF FIREFLIES

springhouse where cold water gushed into the creek and pond. Crossing over the bridge, we coasted through the playground to the two stone lookouts at the entrance, jumped off, and climbed the ladders inside. It was warm and smelled of urine, so we got down and walked our bikes to the swings. There we took a seat, and I turned my eyes near the entrance to watch Jill's house.

"Who lives there?" Connor asked.

"Which one?"

"The one you keep staring at."

"I'm not staring."

"You've been watching it since we got here."

"No, I haven't."

"I see. So, it's a girl that lives there."

I pretended that I didn't know what he was talking about, but it was useless. "Yeah," I admitted. "A girl does live there. Jill Newcastle."

"And you like her."

"Yep."

"Have you asked her out?" he asked.

"Nope."

"Why not?"

"Because I don't know what she'd say. You're the only one who knows about it anyway."

"You think so, huh?"

"It doesn't matter. She's gone for most of the summer."

"Have you liked her for long?"

"Since the first day of school."

He sat there and watched the house too.

78

"Aren't you going to tell me that I'm chicken?" I asked. "That I should've made a move already?"

"Nah. There's no sense in pushing people into something they're unsure of. They just get tense and screw it up."

"I'm pretty good at that."

"Who knows, though. Maybe she can tell that you like her, and maybe she likes you too. Girls pick up on stuff like that. Dudes, though, are blind."

The sun had dipped low behind the trees. The sky's glow was receding deeper into dusk.

"I have to leave," I said. "I'm probably late for supper already."

"You don't want to miss that."

"What about you?"

"TV dinners are waiting in the freezer. The enchiladas have a nice greasy film that isn't half bad."

I sat there thinking it over, twisting side to side on the swing. "Do you want to come to my house and eat?" I asked.

"I wasn't serious about that earlier."

"I know. You can still come."

"Maybe another time."

Ducks swam across the pond towards the island. In the lush grass, frogs croaked and crickets chirped. Along the creek, fireflies had appeared, looking like strings of Christmas lights as they blinked around the bridge and along the banks.

"That's really beautiful," Connor said.

I was surprised he said that, but he was right. We watched them as they bobbed down the creek towards the pond, reflecting their golden light in the water.

79

"Can I ask you a question?"

"I'm not the innocent type," he answered.

"I didn't ask yet."

"I can read your thoughts, remember?" He got off the swing and leaned against the poll next to me. "I was there that night, but it's not how you think."

I dropped my head, disappointed.

"What do you care?" he asked.

"I don't know. I was hoping that maybe..."

"That maybe I'd run for student council? Give me a break. The funny thing is, I'm okay with school if it's done right. I just can't stand some idiot teacher babbling on about his glory days, or his favorite chili recipe, or whatever. The same goes for any jerk principal eyeballing me in the halls."

"You stashed a teacher's edition in your locker. Why?"

"If I was to steal something, do I look fool enough to leave it in my locker?"

"Then why'd they send you to Lincoln Street?"

"It's not that hard to figure out, bud. I'm the new guy. They don't like the way I look or my attitude. To them, I'm just another piece of white trash. They would've thrown me out and made me repeat a grade, but my father wouldn't let the bastards do it. So, they sent me off campus."

"Where will you be next year?"

"Pine Street. Ninth grade. You'll be there too, although I doubt we'll talk."

"Don't say that."

"You're angling for one of those slots with the popular crowd. Folks like you and me don't mix."

"You're wrong this time," I said.

"You sure about that?"

"I can't stand the same people you can't. Plus, we've gotten to know each other."

"Do you need a protector?"

"Why do you have to be so sarcastic?"

"Because people are predictable."

"You can be wrong sometimes too."

He didn't respond. Instead, he'd taken a sharp look behind me and now stood there rigid. Something in the distance had caught his attention. I turned sideways to see what it was.

"What's going on?" I asked.

"Shhh... Don't make any fast movements."

His eyes were fixed far away. The shadows had grown long, and the air hung still. My ears were tuned to every sound. Beyond the monkey bars, hiding behind the spinner, there appeared to be someone or something watching us. I couldn't completely make it out, but a shudder went through me.

"What are you looking at?" I asked, pulling Connor's shirt.

He didn't answer, but I could hear him breathing. His chest rose and fell rapidly, which made me even more worried.

"Tell me, Connor."

"Something ain't right."

"What is it?"

"I don't know, but something's stalking us."

"Stop kidding around."

"It's watching. Whatever you do, don't move."

Inside my head, though, a voice told me that moving was exactly what we should be doing. Sitting still made us sitting

UNDER THE LIGHT OF FIREFLIES

ducks. Then a face quickly appeared and dipped out of sight. Soon after, a figure the same color as the pine straw crept to the side of the spinner. It next slunk behind a slope where it laid flat with its eyes peeking over the top. In short order, it began crawling forward inch by inch. Against Connor's advice, I slowly rose from the swing. When I did, my trembling hands rattled the chain and the thing stopped.

"Stay still," Connor said.

"We should run for the water. It can't get us in the water."

"You'll never make it."

"We've got to try."

"It wants us to do that. Wait and maybe a car will drive up."

I let go of the chain, my hand jittering wildly. As I refocused my sight, the creature rose and moved into the open. I couldn't believe my eyes. Emerging from the shadows, as gently as a ghost, was the unmistakable form of a tiger.

It was huge. From what I could tell, the tiger must've measured eight or nine feet long. Its body was smooth and sleek. Its paws were like baseball mitts. Then there were these eyes, glowing black amber, fastened laser-like on Connor and me. We stood unable to move.

With quick guarded steps, it lurched forward then stopped. It snuck another few feet and stopped again behind a bench. My head was swimming. *There must be a remedy*, I said to myself. Someone—anyone—had to jump out and say not to worry. All this was a bad mistake and things were under control. But that didn't happen. There was no zookeeper, no police, not even a stranger. Only us three.

"It's a tiger," I said desperately. "We can't just stand around."

Connor didn't answer. He stood there still.

"Come on, Connor. We've got to go. We've got to go now."

"It's only watching us. So we wait."

"Wait for what?"

"Someone will come along. You've got to believe."

"Believe?"

"It's not doing anything."

"Yes, it is. We've got to run for it."

"No. Don't make it chase you, man."

But it was too late. Terror had seized complete control of my senses, and I could restrain myself no longer. I had to go. I had to go right then. As I turned to leave, I jerked Connor's shirt with one last desperate plea, but he didn't respond. Left to escape alone, I made a mad dash for the pond.

My feet scrambled feverishly across the loose gravel while involuntary cries emitted from my throat. I ran with all my strength. My heart pounded fiercely inside my chest. But each step I took was like that dream where your feet stick to the ground and it's impossible to move. It was surreal beyond reason. The water's edge actually seemed to recede before me like a mirage to a thirsty man.

The tiger did not betray itself with sound. About fifteen steps in, the sharp sensation of ripping flesh was what told me that I'd lost the race. Its claw tore down my left ribs. Tendons and sinew popped like banjo strings. The stunning force knocked me flat on my face while the tiger tumbled over my head.

The taste of dirt filled my mouth as dust flew up my nostrils. Blood instantly gushed from my wounds like a sieve, soaking my shirt through. I felt ill. I listened to the tiger snorting after which came a low clucking growl. I rolled over and there it was—a tiger—with its lustrous amber eyes staring at me with murder. Fate never spoke so clearly. There would be no escape.

A rush of roars burst forth. Exquisite pain pierced my eardrums. Its snout curled back to expose stiletto-like fangs, followed by a seething growl. I peered into its black throat while coppery breath filled the air. All the contempt and rage over its capture was expressed in that single moment.

It came closer. My shoes scuffled weakly through the bloody gravel as I raised a trembling hand for mercy. I knew it was futile. In that moment, every dream ended. There would be no game winning hit. No first kiss. No new story to tell. My stomach turned violently at the knowledge of how this would end. The tiger crouched for the kill, contorted its face grotesquely, and then everything cut to black.

CHAPTER FIVE

When I finally woke up, I was lying inside crisp white sheets on a bed that had steel rails running down its sides. Next to me, a bag of solution hung from a stand with a tube leading into my arm. A sanitary scent filled the room which sat completely dark save for a few streaks of sunlight peeking around the curtains. My body ached as if my bones had been scraped with an iron rake., and I couldn't move an inch without pain surging over my entire left side. I hadn't a clue where I was, and I didn't understand how, but one thing I knew for sure was that something was dreadfully wrong.

Across the room, a woman laid curled up, sleeping on a short sofa. I coughed weakly a few times and called out to her. She roused and blinked drowsily, wiped the sleep from her eyes, then arose and came softly to my bedside. Her clothes were rumpled, her hair fastened with a beret, while behind her smile simmered a weary travail.

"How are you feeling, darling?" she asked, stroking my hair.

"What's going on?" I replied drearily. "Where am I?"

"You're in a hospital. You've been sleeping again. Don't you remember speaking earlier?"

I didn't remember that at all. My mind was filled with haze and patches of fog, and I had trouble assembling thoughts into any particular order. I tried reasoning how we could've talked earlier, but that thought just spun round and round like a hamster on a wheel, and I began to panic. This woman, though, I knew her. So I reached for that.

"Mother," I said. "I don't understand. What are we doing here?"

She didn't answer, instead pulling up my covers with her eyebrows wrinkled. As I laid there terrified, I could feel I'd been torn apart in some unknown way, and I realized this was why I was in the hospital. Suddenly, I just wanted out.

"Help me up," I pleaded, leaning forward. "We've got to get away from this place. We've got to go."

"No, son," she said calmly. "You have to stay here. You have to rest."

"But I don't want to rest. We've got to go. Please help me. Mother, please."

She strained to keep her emotions in check as she gently held me down. She told me everything would be all right. Still, the terrible sensation that I'd been ripped to pieces—and I didn't know how—kept crawling through my panicked mind. In that outstretched state, though, exhaustion came quickly, and I soon relented in a gasp for breath. Mother pressed a red button attached to the bed. I figured this must be a device to call for help, which was a good thing. Yes, that device meant that somebody official would come and explain. It would be the third time somebody official had come and explained.

First a nurse arrived to look me over, and noting I was still alive, she left to fetch the doctor. It took him some time to get there, but when he did, he was very doctorly indeed with his starched white coat and versed manner.

"Noah Ellis," he said with raised eyebrows as he strode into the room. "I'm Doctor Cooper. I'll be the one watching you for the next several hours."

He didn't ask how I felt. Instead, he snapped the chart from the end of my bed and flipped through the pages until he stopped at a certain spot and read attentively.

"Has he remembered anything yet?" he asked Mother.

She shook her head no.

"But he knows who you are?"

Mother nodded yes. The doctor chewed on that thought and slapped a few more pages backward. He then popped out a pen, scribbled, and hooked the chart back on the bed.

"All right then, Noah," he said as he returned the pen and shoved his hands into his white pockets. "You were in a bad accident. As I'm sure you can probably tell, your back was torn all the way down your left rib cage. It's a pretty serious injury, but here's the good news: surgeons operated and sewed you up successfully, with over a thousand stitches no less, and you're going to be just fine. You'll be sore as heck for a while, but your faculties should return intact. All right?"

I blinked as I tried to catch his words flitting around my brain.

"Stitches will do what again?" I asked.

UNDER THE LIGHT OF FIREFLIES

He observed my words like guideposts as he put his knuckles to his mouth. He checked on Mother, then came back to me.

"The reason you're having trouble understanding is because your mind is suffering from a case of amnesia. It means you can't remember certain things. Usually that happens when someone hits their head, but you didn't hit your head. Instead, you..." He paused as he scrolled his mind for his doctor words. "You suffered massive blood loss and heavy trauma, which can do the same thing. The memories should come back sooner or later, though. At least we think they should. But for now, there's nothing to do but rest and get better."

"What happened to me?" I asked. "Why am I here?"

"Here's the rub. We can't tell you right now. If we go too fast, it could prompt a negative response or even a nervous breakdown. That's not good for anybody. Your mind needs to heal, and then you will remember on your own. So, you'll have to wait. Mmm kay?"

Mother and I stared at him without comment. He shrugged his shoulders.

"Anything else?" he asked.

"That's nice," I said. "But I should probably head to my game. Where's my uniform?"

He squinted his eyes like I'd asked some existential riddle, then Mother intervened.

"Noah," she said and patted my hand. "We're staying here for a few days. The doctors need to watch you, and the hospital has everything you need."

"Yeah, they have a big TV. Can you open the drapes now?"

"We don't need the glare."

88

The doctor tapped his lips as he continued to squint at me.

"Where's Sally?!" I exclaimed and bolted upright, sending pain curling down my ribs. "Mother! Oh no! We left Sally at the park."

"Sally is fine, son," she replied, and along with the doctor they pushed me back against my pillow. "Try not to think too much right now."

"But Sally. Where is she?"

"She's at home with Jack, your brother. Everyone is perfectly safe."

The words drifted through my ears like a boat without a rudder.

"Where again?"

"At home."

"Okay," I replied and yawned. "I'm tired. I'm really really tired."

"You should get some sleep," Doctor Cooper advised. "Rest is the best remedy."

"That's a great jacket, doc," I said then laid against the pillow and dozed off.

Several days later, I got released. At home Mother let me stay in her bed since it was big and soft. She played the steady nurse, tromping up and down the stairs every time I needed something to eat, or a trip to the bathroom, or some other request. I wouldn't say that I was too needy, but I was definitely bored, which took its toll on us both. As the days passed, I recovered most of my memory, but only up until that fateful day. From there, it was a complete mystery, and nobody would tell me anything. I knew it was bad. I had plans to find out, though.

After a week, the pain subsided enough to start some light physical therapy which consisted mainly of stretching. I had my first bath, which felt great except the water made my body feel like a stitched saddlebag. Afterward, I put on a fresh shirt and shorts, and I never thought that being clean could feel so wonderful. With my arm in a sling, I carefully crept down the stairs under Mother's watchful eyes and then was left alone. Quietness filled the house. After looking out the windows at the bright summer day, I walked down the hall to my father's old study.

Nothing had changed since he died. A sailboat's brass compass rested on his credenza. Gold satin curtains hung over the French doors where an oak drafting table and a globe stood nearby. His desk remained clean and polished, arranged with paper weights and personalized pens sitting unused. Behind the desk, a glass cabinet displayed a baseball autographed by Joe DiMaggio, along with pictures of him and his father whom I never knew. On a bookshelf, an old mantel-clock sat biding the time. I pulled it down and set it on the desk. On its back hung a teeny brass handle. After tugging it, the back popped open where inside laid a hidden key.

"What are you doing in here, sport?" I heard from behind me.

My brother leaned against the doorjamb with a friendly face. His face had been very friendly ever since I came home.

"Sport?" I responded. "Only Dad ever called me that."

"I know. I was quoting him."

I removed the key, unlocked the glass cabinet, then took

out the autographed baseball as Jack watched. Though faded a light yellow, it otherwise remained in mint condition. I rolled it in my hands and felt the smooth leather and stitched seams, imagining the day when DiMaggio himself had slung it into the stands where our grandad plucked it from the air. I turned to Jack, and with my good arm I tossed him the ball.

"I always wanted to take that baseball to school," I told him. "Dad wouldn't let me."

"Of course not. What if it got lost or stolen?"

"Nobody ever believes me when I tell them about it."

"Well, you're not taking it to school."

"But if others could see, then they would believe."

"That still isn't a good idea."

"What's the use in keeping it hidden in here?"

"It reminded him of Grandad."

"How do you know?"

"Because there's nothing else except this and those pictures."

"Throw me the ball back," I said.

"Promise that you'll never take it from this house."

"Just give it here."

He didn't do it at first. He wanted a better reassurance, but that would mean he didn't trust me, so he tossed it back and I put it up. At the bottom of the glass case, I pulled open a slim drawer and removed a lavender box with gold trim that contained our father's Purple Heart. I opened it and checked the detail of Washington's image below the shield of stripes and stars.

"How'd you find the key?" Jack asked.

"The same way you did."

UNDER THE LIGHT OF FIREFLIES

"Dad never showed me."

"Me either."

"Mother's taking you to Grand'Mere's cabin tomorrow. Are you cool with that?"

"I can't fish with one arm, and I can't paddle the canoe."

"You can still hike. Plus, other kids will be there. It'll be good for you."

"Are you coming down?"

"I'm sticking around here. I have a tournament to finish up."

I knew that would last only a few days. I wanted to ask him to come and visit, but I figured he'd just make an excuse. He'd denied me three times already.

"I looked outside earlier and it's empty," I said. "Where is everyone?"

Jack shrugged his shoulders and looked at the Purple Heart in my hand.

"What number are you batting tonight?" I asked.

"I haven't seen the lineup."

"Who's pitching?"

"John."

"So you'll be batting leadoff as usual."

"Looks like it."

I placed the Purple Heart back in the drawer, locked the case, then returned the key and clock to the shelf.

"Will you hit a home run?" I asked him.

Jack smirked and replied, "I'm a bit overdue. So, why not?"

I gave him the thumbs up. He patted my good shoulder and together we walked out.

92

The next morning, Mother packed us up as Sally followed her from room to room, excited. If anyone ever loved their grandmother, it was Sally. Every two minutes she asked if Grand'Mere had anything planned for us and if we were leaving soon. Mother gave the same answers again and again, occasionally stopping to remember what we needed while Sally talked and talked. When it was finally time to go, a knock came at the front door. Mother asked me to answer it. I opened it and there, as tall and tan as ever, stood Dusty.

"Dusty!" I exclaimed. "Where have you been?"

"Hello, Noah," he responded, using my real name. "That's quite a get-up you have on. How do you feel?"

"I'm getting better, but I'm still plenty sore. I hope you didn't come here to dance."

A light flickered across his face. "Aww, Rosie. You never could dance anyway."

We came together and hugged. After seeing my family watching us, we quickly parted.

"Why don't you boys go to the back porch and talk?" Mother said. "We can wait a minute."

Upon hearing that, Sally sat down and clutched her Teddy bear wistfully, wondering if we'd ever get to Grand'Mere's. I led Dusty through the kitchen and onto our back porch in view of my treehouse, home of the "SLP Loafers," a place where I couldn't go because I was unable to climb.

"Man, are you going to be all right?" Dusty asked.

"I'll be fine, but I'm tired of staying inside."

"You couldn't have gone outside anyway. I mean, you know, because you're not healed up."

UNDER THE LIGHT OF FIREFLIES

"I understand. That's what I'm tired of."

We sat there blankly, wondering what to say. The elephant was in the room, something I'd never had a taste for, so I just said it. "Look. I have no idea what happened to me. They won't tell me."

"Yeah, I know." Dusty sighed.

"What does that mean?"

"It means that I know that you don't know."

"But you know what happened, right?"

"Of course. For the most part."

"So? Are you going to tell me or what?"

"I can't," he said and slumped forward.

"What do you mean you can't?"

"My dad's being really serious about it. If I tell you, then I'll have my privileges taken away."

"Privileges? What, do you have a butler now?"

"I'm not kidding, Noah. He said not to talk about it. It could break your brain."

"Your dad said that?"

"You know what I mean."

I was vexed. My thoughts fixated on what everyone was hiding, and the harder I tried for answers, the less I got. Even my brother was a dead end. About the only person I hadn't asked was Sally because she wouldn't have known anyway. Sally was too little to know. So, I spent my time trying to remember something about myself that everyone else chose to hide. Seconds, minutes, and hours ticked away. It was maddening.

"By the way," Dusty said, "we all think you got ripped off with the all-stars, even if you can't play. Donovan told Coach

94

Pritchett about it and everyone overheard."

"Donovan isn't afraid to speak his mind."

"He has a voice."

"Being a coach's son like Brian is the real privilege."

"And the parking is good too."

"How's the team doing anyway?"

"We've had some delays, but we're winning."

"I can't remember it raining that much," I said.

"Amnesia is a peculiar condition."

"Like you'd know."

"I read about it in a book," he said.

"What kind of book?"

"A dictionary."

"You couldn't find a bigger book?"

"No, this dictionary was huge."

We both laughed. I'd tried my best, but I wasn't getting anywhere with Dusty. I knew that if he wouldn't tell me, then nobody would. It was a lonesome feeling. Mother poked her head out and said it was time to leave, so we got up and went inside. At the front door, Dusty leaned in for a last hug, but I held out my hand instead.

"I can smell you just fine from here," I said.

"You old honey dripper," Dusty replied and squeezed my neck.

To Sally's delight, we finally got to leave. Mother loaded her into the front seat with her Teddy firmly in her grasp. In the back, Mother had arranged pillows so that I could kick up my legs and relax. Jack helped me in and told us goodbye. Mother sternly warned him not to throw a party, to which he returned

UNDER THE LIGHT OF FIREFLIES

his sincerest assurance. She started the wagon, backed out, and onwards we went.

For an hour and a half, we traveled down snug East Texas highways cut through the piney woods. It was a drive that I'd always enjoyed as we passed by churches, barns, and barbecue joints. We made our usual stop at a variety shop where we bought a writing tablet, some mason jars, and peanut brittle. The people inside remembered us from the times before but respectfully didn't ask about my appearance. We left and got back on the road.

Underneath Caddo Lake, outside the town of Uncertain, dwelled a small camp named Roanoke Village. We turned onto its gravel drive that ran from the camp's entrance between two long rows of cabins before it reached the lodge at the far end. One row stood in the hills while the opposite row rested on a slope that dropped down to the lake. Our grandmother, whom we called Grand'Mere because she was from France, lived in a cabin on the lakeside.

We pulled into the driveway under her colossal dogwood tree where she stood waiting for us with arms spread wide like an angel. Sally instantly broke into a fit of glee and opened the door to embrace her while I wrestled myself out of the car. After Sally let her go, Grand'Mere approached me with a solemn gaze and held my chin in her hand.

"My blessed child," she said. "I am so glad you are alive."

I tried to respond but a frog had jumped into my throat. She slid her arm around my waist and led me up the back deck.

"We always have wonderful adventures, don't we, you and I?" she said. "Today we can take a nice ride in the canoe, or go on a hike, or shoot my bow and arrow."

"I don't think I can shoot your bow, Grammy," I replied.

"Well, who said anything about you shooting? You can watch me. You know, I was the champion at the Wildflower Festival back in..."

"1942. It was the same year you got pregnant with Mother."

"I was only testing your memory. Maybe I enjoy the recognition too. Ha ha."

Much like her laugh, Grand'Mere was lovely. Her accent was steeped in charm, and with a lithe figure and silvery hair pulled into a bun, she breezed through life like a ballerina. She'd rather be cooking or hiking than wearing a dress, and though she was a widow, I never remembered her acting lonely.

The inside of her cabin was decked with hardwood on both the floors and walls. It had wide bay windows that looked onto the lake where Cypress trees dripped with moss. Plants sat arranged upon stands or in sills with spools of ivy coiling down, while paintings of Paris and the French countryside hung from the walls. The kitchen, where Grand'Mere seemed to exist half the time, had been painted mint green with an island generally covered in flour.

"In case you're wondering," she said, "I will be baking a cake at some point. We'll eat lunch here, but tonight we can either go to the lodge, or I can make us a nice roast and some gougères to snack on."

"I want a strawberry cake!" Sally cried.

"Of course you do, my dear, because you are a strawberry. If you like, tomorrow morning we'll go hunting for some."

Sally broke into another fit of joy, then she and Grand'Mere

UNDER THE LIGHT OF FIREFLIES

hopped outside to help Mother with the luggage, a duty which I'd mercifully been relieved of. After they carried everything inside, Mother called me to my room.

"It might be too much for you to carry luggage, but you can still put up your clothes," she told me with a kiss. "So go ahead and get it over with."

While she left, I heard a dog bark followed by Sally breaking into more laughter. Bosco was a big fat chocolate Labrador who spent most of his time soliciting other cabins for snacks or belly rubs. He had now directed his exuberance upon Sally, so I quickly shut the door before he directed it upon me.

I laid my clothes in the chest of drawers above which hung our family pictures that had been there forever. There was one of my great-grandfather in a French military uniform from WWI; then my grandfather in an American one from WWII; and another of my dad wearing his in Vietnam. Grand'Mere was pictured as a child on a famous bridge in France with her parents kneeling beside her. In another, Mother twirled a baton. My favorite photo was of her and Dad at their wedding reception. They looked so young as they held each other, dancing and bursting in laughter. Dad's brilliant smile was no rarity. I asked him once what they were laughing about, but he couldn't remember.

I heard a polite knock on the door and in came Sally.

"We're about to take a canoe ride," she said. "Do want to come?"

"No thanks," I replied and sat on the bed. "I'll just stick around here."

"But you said you would. Please?"

98

"I'm really tired. Can I rest for a bit?"

Snorting and huffing sounds came barreling down the hall whereafter Bosco busted through the door and jumped on my bedside. I greeted him the best I could, then Grand'Mere appeared and scolded him out of the room.

"Bosco has arthritis," she said. "He's still a trooper, albeit not the valiant knight he once was. Chivalry, however, must carry on."

After they left, I relaxed on the soft bed with its twill coverlet and fresh pillows. The lace curtains let in a hazy glow, and the room was very quiet and very safe and I drifted off to a very sound sleep. I did not awake until early evening.

When I finally came to, I was greatly refreshed and my back even felt better. I stumbled to the den where I found my family sitting quietly as Sally played with some old dolls.

"Hello, child," said Grand'Mere as she put aside her knitting. "I hope you had a wonderful rest."

"How long was I down?"

"Five whole hours. We didn't want to disturb you, so instead of starting supper here, we thought that we'd eat at the lodge. I'm sure you're hungry."

"Why don't you wash your face and hands," Mother said. "They begin serving soon."

Roanoke Village stretched green and wide, spotted with lilies in the waters, lush glades on the land, and wild herbs covering the trails. We walked to the end of the drive where a lawn unfurled with a dry creek cutting across. Swing-sets rested on one side and a croquet course on the other. A ranch style lodge stained with age sat in the back while in front hung a large bell

UNDER THE LIGHT OF FIREFLIES

to announce dinner and events.

We entered the mess hall as rowdy scores of villagers gabbed and ate at bench style tables. We waited in line and were served a healthy portion of Salisbury steak, sweet potatoes, fried okra, and peach cobbler. As we sat at the table and tried to convince Sally to eat her food, I caught a glance from a curly-headed girl who quickly turned away. I didn't think much of it at first, but she kept peeking over. Girls really didn't look at me, so I figured it was my sling that had brought her attention. We told Sally that if she at least ate her dinner roll, then she could have a cookie when we got home. In her clever way, she promised that she'd eat it along the walk back.

After we finished eating, Grand'Mere stopped to speak with a few villagers at their tables. I wasn't sure if any of them had heard what happened to me, but I moved ahead anyway. Their cringy, banal sympathies was what I longed to avoid. I refused to give them the chance. When I got to the door, I caught the curly-headed girl's eye yet again. Now it seemed like something was there, though I still felt compelled to leave. I hopped down the porch steps outside, glad to be free of any encumbrances, when somebody immediately called my name.

"Noah, Noah, Noah!"

I turned to see a young kid running out the front door after me.

"Noah, hey!" he said, excited, as he came alongside me. "It's great to see you."

"Same to you, Elliot."

"Wow. What happened to you?"

"I wish I knew."

"What do you mean?"

"It's a long story."

"You've got bandages bulging under your shirt."

"Really. I hadn't noticed."

Elliot was two years younger and a meticulous kid who always wore his shirts tucked in and his socks pulled up. He was a child of many interests, most of which I didn't care about, like identifying the makes of cars, or rare birds, or bugs. His mind and his hands were always busy with something, and he usually wanted to include me. His family's cabin stood across the drive from us. I had known him since he was a toddler.

"I'm building a fort," he informed me.

"Okay. Go ahead and explain."

"I collected a stack of branches which I've stripped and cleaned for posts. I found some twine to string them up with. For the roof, I'll use more branches, unstripped of course, though pruned perhaps. There's a crate for the back door. I have a rough sketch if you'd like to look at it."

"No, I trust you."

"Do you want to help me with it tomorrow?"

"It'd have to be in the afternoon."

"I can wait."

I checked on Mother and Grand'Mere, and I could see that they were both discreetly excited that I was interested in doing boy things again.

"Why not?" I said.

"That's terrific news. A plus. I'll see you tomorrow then." And with a quick bow, he took off back inside.

When my family and I made it back to the cabin, Mother

UNDER THE LIGHT OF FIREFLIES

and Grand'Mere paused under her dogwood tree to talk about something in private. Inside, Sally and Bosco both went directly to bed without complaint. After I brushed my teeth, Mother came in and cleaned my wounds and changed my bandages, all the while enduring my nightly pleas to tell me what happened. Later, Grand'Mere appeared in my room to say goodnight, and I asked her about a set of painted portraits which hung opposite the photographs.

"They're our distant ancestors," she said. "This portrait here is one of your very great-grandfathers. His name was James Fredericke Dansereau."

"They sure dressed fancy back then. What is that ribbon and medal for?"

"The Ordre de la Croix de Juillet," she said in her perfect accent. "It was an accolade for helping to overthrow a tyrant, a king, Charles X."

"A king? Do you have the medal?"

"No. Either some far relative would have it, or it's lost."

"That's too bad."

"There are more important things."

"What were you talking about outside with Mother?"

"Something about my dogwood tree."

"What about it?"

"They'd like to cut it down."

"Who is 'they?'"

"The tyrants here at Roanoke. They want to install new electric lines, and they say my tree's in the way."

"But you won't let them."

"No. I'll try to reason with them."

102

I sat there thinking about it when she said, "Don't worry about the tree. It's getting late now. Have a good rest, darling."

She pressed her cheek to mine and retired to her room. After she was gone, I examined my ancestor's portrait once more and tried to picture the scene, him conquering a king and later receiving honor, but like all things from long ago, the images came through in black and white. In the mirror, I checked my own portrait void of any medal or ribbon. I crawled into my very safe bed where I started my nightly search for my wayward memories as the eyes of my fathers looked on.

CHAPTER SIX

On the village hillside ran a path called the Dewberry Trail which spanned the length of the camp before disappearing into the woods for a dozen miles, leading to a fire tower. About thirty minutes down the path between two ridges rested a sleepy glen sunbathing in the breeze. In shaded places patches of berries grew, some of them in abundance. Our trail took its name from the ubiquitous dewberries, but this bright dell also had strawberries, blackberries, and even nuts from pecan trees. It was a refuge of flora and fauna, and this is where our Grand'Mere took us to pick fruit.

In the cool of the morning under an arch of blue sky we departed, each of us with our own small bucket, including Sally who was taking this very seriously. We'd hoped that the strawberries were still in bloom, and we found we were in luck. The spring and summer had been unusually mild but with plenty of rain. The result was a jackpot. As soon as we arrived, Mother made an instant discovery, and Sally and Grand'Mere tip-toed over to check out the goods.

"I see 'em! I see 'em!" Sally shouted as Mother pulled back the high grass, exposing the plump riches beneath.

"You must be careful," Grand'Mere instructed. "We don't want to squish them, and we always preserve the shoot."

Sally followed her instructions to the letter, delicately handling each strawberry as if it were a baby bird. After that first discovery, our collective motivation mounted and each of us fanned out to find the next score. And we found plenty. The glen was gorged with raspberries, boysenberries, every kind of berry, along with an array of flowers so the bees could suck nectar for their bulging hive.

"We got the biggest strawberries ever!" Sally cried. "We're going to make piles of cakes."

"We'll stack them all the way to the ceiling." Grand'Mere gestured with an arm wave.

"All the way to the sky!"

"To the moon and beyond."

"Oh Grammy. You're the best."

"And what about me?" Mother asked.

"Mommy, please. You already know that I love you."

Even I laughed. So we carried on, filling our buckets until we could fill no more, afterward being sorry that the hunt must end. With bounty in hand, we returned to the trail and followed it back as it curved in and out of the woods through a verdant landscape bristling with butterflies, birds, and bees. About halfway to the village, Mother stopped and cautiously crouched to the side, then motioned us to do the same.

"Be quiet," she said and pointed. "Do you see them?"

UNDER THE LIGHT OF FIREFLIES

"See what?" Sally asked. "What is it, Mommy?"

"Look beyond the path. In the woods. By that fallen tree."

We all pulled in tighter and followed her finger. At first all I saw was thick woodland, but then in a dark recess, I could finally tell what she was talking about.

"It's a fox," Mother whispered. "And she's with her pups."

Sally gasped, and we all sat there motionless. The foxes were the color of the crimson sun, blending in perfectly with the forest floor. The mother fox had made a home in a log's hollow and was busy putting her pups to bed. Every tiny movement she performed, every step she took, she did with perfect care. The sight of them was like a precious gem.

Then something inside of me clicked as if a forgotten thought had flashed by. I'd experienced this already when small things came to me just after the accident. So I instantly began reaching, seeking, straining for the memory, but this time it stayed suspended from view.

"*Look*," Grand'Mere then whispered.

The fox was now sitting up and checking the air with her nose. Then with quick leery eyes, she peered in our direction. After confirming her suspicions, she ducked and nimbly darted behind the log.

"What's she doing?" Sally asked.

"She's found us," Mother replied.

"Did she go into the tree with her babies?"

"She's keeping an eye on us. I doubt we'll see her again."

"Are we safe?" I suddenly blurted out. "I mean, do you think she'll come after us?"

Grand'Mere winced, then kindly nodded no.

106

LEE SANDERS

"Foxes are wary of people, dear," she said. "She would never leave her pups."

As I sat heaving, Mother laid her hand on my neck and soothed me.

"Don't worry, son," she assured me. "We're all safe."

Fear does its best work when there are no other options at hand. Only a single path to the village existed, and that path ran past the foxes' home. The thought of walking that direction filled me with dread, although I couldn't understand why. Overhead the sun had ascended, so I raised my face to feel its light, hoping the warmth would settle me down. After some time, it seemed to be working. Sally laid her little hand on my back, and that's when I reckoned I'd be all right. Mother helped me up, checking first how I looked, then off we hiked arm in arm.

My eyes remained fixed in the trees, searching for any sign of danger, but the animals had vanished. Although it made sense that we were more of a menace to them than they were to us, I still felt unnerved. We passed the foxes' part of the forest at a brisk pace with no sign of them. After a twitchy twenty minutes, we descended to the final clearing where the lodge popped into view. At last, I felt at ease. After we made it to the edge of camp, I took one last look behind us. There at the top of rise, staring directly into my eyes, stood the red fox.

"The fox!" cried Sally. "She's followed us here."

"That's not a she," Grand'Mere said. "That's the father."

The fox surveyed us for a moment longer and put his nose in the air. After taking a last furtive glance our way, he swung around and skulked back into the forest.

107

At his cabin, I found Elliot dressed in an ironed bronze shirt tucked into his equally ironed khaki shorts. He had a wagon filled with an array of tools, including a hammer, wood saw, tape measure, shears, a spade, and a host of other items. He'd even brought an I-beam. I supposed that making the fort precisely level was a duty that could not go neglected.

After stashing everything at the site, we towed the wagon to fetch wood when I decided to shed my sling. It was one less question that I'd have to deal with from other folks. Elliot being the exception, of course.

"You said that you don't know what happened to your arm," he said.

"It's my shoulder and back. But no, I don't."

"How could you not know?"

"Because my mind shut it out."

"How can your mind shut something out?"

"It just does."

"That sounds like you forgot on purpose."

"I guess so. The doctors think I should remember on my own. They won't tell me anything."

"Gosh, it must have been something extraordinarily terrible."

We walked to the village center where a pile of crusty boards laid behind the lodge. We sorted through the stack and picked out the best ones we could find, then loaded the wagon and went back to the site where we commenced the project from the ground up. A big necessity for any great fort was concealment, so we scoured around until we found a spot behind some bushes away from the trail.

We dug the postholes and planted the limbs which Elliot had so scrupulously trimmed. We connected the corners with long boards and twine, laid vines across the top, and the shell of a large crate served as the entryway. The work took several hours, with us hitting the deck every time we spotted a hiker, but no one saw us. Once finished, we examined our creation and found that from the trail it looked practically invisible.

"What do we do now?" Elliot asked.

"I guess we wait."

"Wait for what?"

"For hikers."

"What do we do when they come?"

"We prank them."

"How do you mean?"

"We could set some kind of a trap for them, then watch it from here."

"*Pranks,*" Elliot then said with a devilish grin. "Of course. People are so stupid. It's the perfect crime."

As he paced back and forth and marveled at the notion, I searched my imagination for a plan. I thought of digging a pitfall and covering it with brush, or maybe twisting a branch backward to whack somebody with, but those ideas were too detailed and could take hours to build. The main purpose was simply to make somebody look dumb.

"I've got it!" Elliot said with a snap of his fingers. "I have a rubber snake at the cabin we could use."

"Now that's a pretty good idea."

"We can lay it on the trail to scare them. And I could rub some oil on it to give it a slimy sheen. You know, to make it look more real."

"You do that, buddy," I said. "Wherever we lay it, though, we don't want it to be too obvious."

"We could cover it with pine straw and have its tail poking out."

"Showing the snake's tail blows the gag. We should first make a sign to lure hikers. Then we lay the sign over the snake."

"What would we say?" he asked.

"*Free Prizes Here.*"

"Too obvious. How's about this. *Mystery Treasure Awaits.*"

"That's corny, bro."

"It's no different than yours. Plus, people like treasure. Especially the mystery kind."

"I know what," I said. "Let's do rock-paper-scissors. Whoever wins, then they get to make the sign."

I figured that Elliot was too clever for his own good and would assume that I'd throw the rock sign. For young kids, the rock was invincible. So we counted to three, and like I expected, he flashed the paper sign to beat rock. I threw scissors instead which then sent his brain into a spasm. After watching him cycle through a series of blinks, I shook him out of it, and he left to retrieve the fake snake.

It took him a while to return, but when he did, he'd wiped the snake down thoroughly with oil just like he suggested. It didn't look bad, though. At first sight, it appeared exactly like a real snake. For cover we used a paper sack, and I took a magic marker and wrote the catch phrase.

"Where do you think we should place it?" Elliot asked.

"Lay it to the side of the path."

"But what if they walk past it?"

"It's better to make it subtle. If it's too obvious, they won't fall for it."

"We should inspect the trail."

"Inspect away, Inspector."

He did his inspection and found a depression to the side where gravel had washed out at the top of an embankment. There we positioned the snake near a boulder and propped the sign over it. For practical reasons, Elliot marched down the trail and back again in the manner of an unsuspecting hiker, testing the prank's viability, then nodded with token approval.

We went to the fort to hide and watched through the aperture. It was cozy and dark inside which made us feel exactly like spies. The wait was longer than we'd anticipated, though. After twenty long minutes, some villagers came by. Two men were going along and talking busily, but neither looked down. Then a group of children rambled past playing chase. Still nothing. After another group missed, we were reconsidering our strategy when two girls casually strolled up. As they got closer, one of them spotted our sign and then pointed it out to her friend. Elliot and I did not twitch a muscle.

"Take the bait," I whispered.

"They won't go for it."

"Just give it time."

"I predict we used the wrong slogan."

"You're killing me with optimism."

"Sorry. I just think it's a lemon."

"Shhh..."

After peering at the note, one girl spun around and sus-

UNDER THE LIGHT OF FIREFLIES

piciously checked the scene. Elliot snorted obnoxiously and pressed his hand over his mouth. Then the other one checked behind her too, and it happened to be the very girl with curls who'd looked at me the night before. Though plain in appearance, she was still decent enough, or at least I thought so. But they were acting unsure. I worried that our prank would fail.

After a small discussion with her friend, the one with curls shrugged her shoulders, bravely crouched forward, then yanked off the sign. Bingo. The snake suddenly appeared, which resulted in two hysterical shrieks reverberating through the quiet forest. Stomping their feet together as they frightfully clutched each other, they turned and dashed away like rabbits. At the sight of that, Elliot lost it and collapsed in unmitigated laughter.

"Ahh ha ha ha!" he cackled. "Did you see those morons? Did you see that? Ha ha ha."

"Calm down," I said. "They stopped up the trail and we don't want to get caught."

But he couldn't help himself. Covering his mouth this time with his arm, he rhythmically wheezed and huffed, so much so that I wondered if the poor kid had ever pulled a prank at all. Meanwhile, the girls had recovered and were returning to the scene. They paused at a distance, checking for any movement, then cautiously inched towards the prank as they held each other. Next, a surprise idea popped in my head.

"I'm heading down there," I told Elliot. "I'll grab the snake for those girls."

"But why?" Elliot asked, recovering from his episode.

"I think that one with the curls likes me."

"How do you know that?"

112

"She stared at me at dinner."

Then he indicated my arm.

"So? I'm not the first guy who had a bum arm."

"It's something else," he said.

"Like what?"

"I heard some folks talking about you."

"About me?"

"It was grownups."

"What'd they say?"

He sat up and hung his head in shame.

"Well??" I demanded. "Give me the news."

"It was something about finding you..." He paused as if scared to tell me. "Something about finding you in a lake. They had to pull you from the water. You were messed up real bad."

"I got pulled out of a lake? What was I doing in a lake?"

"They didn't say."

"What else did you hear?"

"Nothing. They noticed me listening, so I left."

It had to be about my accident. But how? I thought for sure that I'd been drug around by a car or a truck or a train. How in the world did I get shredded to pieces, end up in a lake, and not drown?

"Maybe I got run over by a boat and then was rescued," I said.

"That might be it."

"Except I don't know anyone with a boat."

"Could be a problem."

"And I haven't been to a lake since...well, it's been a long time."

UNDER THE LIGHT OF FIREFLIES

"It's a puzzle. A riddle. A knot that can't be..."

"Please be cool."

"Sorry."

I tried to sort out the scenarios spewing wildly through my mind, but the dots didn't connect, and my frustration deepened even more than before.

"What does it all mean?" I asked and ran my fingers through my hair.

Back at the trail, our victims had figured that something didn't add up. With a long stick in hand, the curly haired girl was slowly advancing on the phony serpent. After a conference with her friend, she gingerly poked it and retreated. Seeing that the snake hadn't responded, she repeated the process again to the same results. She finally resolved to leave the stick behind, and mustering great courage, she stepped forward and frightfully picked up the snake as she bounced on her toes. With blushing faces, the girls examined the specimen and grazed their fingers along its greasy skin. Realizing someone might be watching, they glanced about for pranksters, but our fort did not betray us.

Next, though, a surprising thing happened. Instead of stealing our prank or chucking it in the woods, the girls replaced the snake to its original position and then put the sign back on top. Afterward, they looked at each other, giggled, and scampered away with their hands covering their grins.

"They replaced the whole setup," I remarked.

"They don't want to be the only suckers."

"That's pretty cool."

"I've never seen a girl be cool before."

114

LEE SANDERS

"My brother says they're a different species. You have to learn their language."

"And flatter them. That's how you boat the big bass."

"Have you ever tried it?" I asked.

"Once."

"What'd you say?"

"I told a girl that her dress had intriguing flower patterns."

"Whoa, that must've floored her."

"She wasn't insulted."

"Did you ask her to go with you?"

"I'm taking my time with it."

"How long's it been?"

He looked down and drew his knees under his arms.

"Don't worry about it," I told him. "It takes a while to catch the right one."

As the day wore on, a few more hikers came and went intermittently, but only one other person fell for it. With blue hair chicly accenting a pink muumuu, an obese older lady halted at the sign and immediately took a stance, leery from the very start. No fooling this one, we figured. But we soon found out how wrong we were.

Instead of a slow developing scene, the blue hair marched straight to the sign as though insulted by the pathetic attempt at guile. As soon as she plucked the sign off, though, she jolted backward with a throaty wail and grabbed her chest as if kicked by a mule. Elliot and I almost died right there, but it was just getting started.

After recovering from the initial shock, she prowled before our ruse with gritted teeth and furious eyes. Then with alarm-

115

UNDER THE LIGHT OF FIREFLIES

ing alacrity, she seized the prank and commenced to whip and whale the rubber reptile about as if it were possessed by demon forces. After the snake did not respond to her provocations, she inspected it in her clutched fist for a contentious moment. Next, she bent down, grunted, and snatched up our sign too.

When she returned from the squatting position, however, she took a bad step on the washout which then shifted under her weight. In response, she unconsciously kicked up her other leg which now left her teetering on sifting sand. With eyes peeled wide, she held suspended for a timeless moment, arms and snake whirling about spectacularly, then toppled backwards into a crash straight down the bank.

Flailing and ripping up plants the whole way down, she rolled head over heels like an unhinged tractor tire, flab flying everywhere as she grunted and cursed the gods above. At the bottom, she slammed to a stop in a mighty plume of dust, followed by a period of morose and bitter silence.

About half a minute later, she blaringly revived with tremendous bawls and barks. After regaining her feet proved impossible, she determined to crawl back up the bank on her hands and knees. It took great effort, and all the while she pleaded in that throaty wail of hers to some unseen companion. "Branston!! Haaalp!! Haaalp me, Branston!!" Branston, however, did not respond.

As for Elliot and me, we were doubled up in hysterics, suffering to keep quiet. It wasn't over yet. In a dogged struggle, blue hair clawed and snorted her way upward—fake snake clinched in her teeth the entire way—until at long last she reached the top. Once there, she collapsed onto the trail with

116

her chest heaving feverishly, the sweaty muumuu clinging like shrink wrap to her unholy carriage.

Upon catching her breath, she found a small tree and proceeded to mangle the poor thing in a battle for her feet. Finally, she stood upright in haughty triumph as the innocent sapling slouched sideways, its bark shorn clean from the abuse of her testy claws.

She spent a minute to brush the debris and cobwebs off, then scanned the woods for onlookers. Elliot and I ducked for cover. After her search, she cocked her head proudly and limped away, leaves and pine-bark stuck to her back, the rubber snake dangling lifelessly from her grubby fingers.

Elliot and I laughed very hard for a very long time. So hard, in fact, that we couldn't speak. Elliot reacted almost violently, ejecting snot and spit to the point of hyperventilation. I couldn't help him, though. I was fighting for my own air. It was the greatest prank I ever saw, but the fun was over. The blue hair had absconded with our fake snake.

After giving her plenty of time to clear out, Elliot and I packed the wagon and rolled away with Elliot battling spasms of giggles the whole way. We unloaded at his cabin, and as I was about to leave, we noticed far back on the trail the pink muumuu. The blue hair had returned to the trail with another woman. Pointing up and down as she waved the snake about, blue hair jabbered furiously while the other lady nodded with her arms crossed over a clipboard.

"Uh oh," Elliot said. "She's back and she looks mad."

"Good luck catching us, though."

"As long as they don't find the fort, you mean."

UNDER THE LIGHT OF FIREFLIES

"It's invisible. Besides, the fort doesn't prove anything."

"It's pretty obvious the prankster would be watching from there. It could point to us."

"How's that?"

"Because we took those boards from behind the lodge."

"So?"

"Somebody could've seen us."

"They're not tracing those boards to us."

Elliot bit his nails as we both sat there thinking it through.

"Let's tear it down," he said.

"Right now? She'll be watching."

"No, later. But I can't go tonight. We'll have to do it in the morning."

"You don't think you're overreacting?"

"Do you like getting caught?"

No, I thought. *I hate getting caught.* I also hated to agree with Elliot, as paranoid as he was. In the end, though, I decided it was better to be safe.

"Fine," I said. "We'll do it in the morning."

"Daybreak."

"You've got to be joking."

"It's the best part of the day. Plus, there will be nobody around."

"You're a strange, strange bird. But whatever."

"Terrific. See you at sunrise."

At 5:45 a.m., the annoying clang of my alarm clock sounded. I'd been sleeping hard. What a chore this was, all because an old hag couldn't find the humor in barreling headlong down an embankment.

From the night's sleep, my scars were now tweaked as tight as baling wire. I sat up, hung my arms over, and stretched. The pain throbbed into the base of my skull and my skin felt like a scuba suit, but eventually I loosened up enough that I could slide on my shorts and shirt. After a big drink of juice, I splashed my face, put on my shoes, and slipped outside. I crossed over to Elliot's driveway. As soon as I walked up, he appeared from the carport in his perfect wrinkle-free get-up.

"I hope I'm not late," I said. "I'd hate for the birds to beat us there."

"We've still got twilight, but it's going away fast."

"It's dark, dude. Nobody is up."

"I normally go to the mess hall for breakfast. Trust me, people are up."

"What time does the mess open?"

"Right now."

The eastern horizon was turning lighter, but under the cover of the forest everything took on a bluish-green hue. The trail smelled of honeysuckle, and trees and bushes hovered around like dark sentinels. With a single flashlight, we were having trouble finding landmarks until finally we came upon the poor sapling old blue hair had so eloquently disfigured. I took my post there so Elliot could go check the fort, but just then a separate pair of flashlights crested the rise ahead.

"What'll we do?" Elliot asked.

"Walk on," I said. "We don't want to get noticed at the crime scene. We'll come back in a minute."

We started towards the two flashlights coming at us. When we got close, a small glow revealed two men in work clothes

119

with a shovel and an ax. They looked at as us and nodded.

"Good morning, Elliot," one of them said.

"Good morning, Branston," he responded.

None of us stopped but kept on our way. After we got over the back of the rise, I asked Elliot who those men were.

"They're the maintenance guys," he said.

"Aren't they up awful early?"

"They always start work this early. It's funny they're all the way over here, though."

"Why's that?"

"They're usually loading ice or cleaning the pool."

We waited for a few minutes, then started slowly back with our flashlight off. As we returned over the rise, we came to a stretch of bushes and stopped. Just around the corner, we heard snapping and rustling sounds. Elliot and I both looked at each other. The breaking and popping kept on, so we peeked over the bushes.

In the dark light, we could make out shadowy figures busily cutting and pulling things apart. An axe rose and came crashing down through a limb. Vines were ripped out. Boards clunked as they got stacked. It was no mistake. The maintenance guys had come to tear down our fort.

"How'd they know?" Elliot asked.

"I guess the old mare found it."

"You mean Beatrice Lively."

"How do you know her name?"

"After dinner last night, I followed her to her cabin."

"You stalked her?"

"No. I watched from a distance as I pursued her. I then

located her cabin number in the directory."

"You're a sneaky Pete," I told him.

"I watch *Rockford Files*."

"Well, I never saw her until this summer."

"In the book, it says she works here. She's some kind of planner. A hard lady, I heard."

"She's about as pretty as a wart hog, I can tell you that."

"She had a serious fall. She's not going to cool off until she catches somebody."

"Was it worth it?" I asked. "The answer must indubitably be yes."

"We should go eat breakfast."

"My Grand'Mere makes a fabulous omelet if you can wait a bit."

"The maintenance guys already saw me going towards the mess hall. They know I eat there every day."

"Do they check your schedule?"

"I'm also hungry. Please?"

The men continued to work on the fort, banging and splitting and slashing.

"It's free," he added.

"Free? I guess they do make a decent breakfast. Let's go."

While we left, the morning sun broke across the treetops. The greens and rust of the forest came up as birds chirped and fluttered around. The stillness and the first light created a calm that would stay only a small while before it passed away. Elliot had been right. This was indeed the best part of the day.

After five minutes of hiking, we made it to the mess hall. Out front, old timers chatted with one another on porch

UNDER THE LIGHT OF FIREFLIES

benches. As we passed by, they gave a friendly nod and that was all. Inside, it smelled of bacon, biscuits, and coffee. Only a handful of people were eating, and all spoke in low tones. We got eggs and pancakes then found a table away from everyone.

Just as we started to eat, though, I looked across the room and detected the blue hair herself, Beatrice Lively, staring right at us. My appetite ceased. I was instantly mad at myself for letting Elliot convince me to come along. After her rodent-like eyes made contact with mine, she promptly rose and marched straight towards our table.

Elliot gulped hard as if watching the approach of a zombie, but I tried to stay casual. When she arrived, she stood with her shoulders arched back while her hands rested comfortably upon her robust paunch.

"Good morning, boys," she said and smiled, exposing a line of filmy teeth. "I don't think I've met you two yet. I'm Beatrice Lively, the new project director. Who are you?"

"I'm Noah Ellis," I answered and smiled.

"Elliot Gifford here," he said in a frail whisper.

"I know your grandmother, Noah," she said. "I'm so glad you're here to enjoy all our new improvements. I haven't seen you at the pool yet, though. Won't you come by today for a visit?"

She stood freshly bathed and powdered while donning a new muumuu, this one cobalt blue. Unlike the final condition of her last gown, this one hung mercifully loose over her bloated corpus. Except for the cuts and scratches layered upon her neck and ears, it would have been impossible to picture her clearing half a forest on a colossal dive into childhood lore. I

122

was certain she was putting on an act. Instead of deflecting, though, I decided it was best to take a more assertive approach.

"My back got torn up in an accident and the chlorine makes my scars burn," I told her. "So I can't go." Then after exchanging an unspoken look of contempt with her, I added, "But thank you for the invitation."

She sat there with her scaly lips half-parted and studied me several long seconds. She didn't like my response, although she had no choice but to accept it.

"You can still sit in the concession area," she said, maintaining court.

"Yes ma'am."

"And I have a question for you," she then said, turning to Elliot.

His eyes bulged and his shoulders sagged, and I feared he would give up the ghost before ever a question was asked.

"Okay," he murmured.

"What precisely did you do yesterday afternoon?"

"Yesterday afternoon?" he said, blood receding from his face.

Silence hung over the table as he laced his fingers behind his neck. He looked bad. No, he looked terrible. I couldn't understand how such a simple question could turn him into the bowl of gelatin I now watched in disgust. But then with wide eyes, Elliot swiftly sprang up and raised his finger.

"The Dewberry Trail," he said. "That's precisely where I was yesterday afternoon. I was on the Dewberry Trail."

"Is that so?" Lively responded with a wriggle of her shoulders. "And exactly who were you with?"

"With me," I interjected. "We went hiking together. Boy,

UNDER THE LIGHT OF FIREFLIES

what good times that turned out to be. Right, Elliot?"

Lively's eyes darted back and forth between this dubious duo, inspecting for any shade of a lie.

"Was there somewhere special you went?" she asked.

"Oh yeah," I said. "That meadow with the giant beehive and all the berries. It's like a Norman Rockwell painting."

"Lots of flowers," Elliot added. "Intriguing patterns."

"And you were there all afternoon long, were you?"

"Yes ma'am," I answered. "We were trying to make it to the fire-tower, but we got thirsty and had to stop. We saw a family of foxes, though. They live in a big fat log."

I nodded shrewdly at Elliot who nodded shrewdly back. Yes indeed, we'd seen beehives and flowers and foxes. It painted a most impressive picture. She watched us very closely as the new sun sparkled through the window and alighted upon her prodigious frame, casting a shadow across the floor like the silhouette of Sasquatch. She was the most grotesque creature I ever saw. She could also cause my Grand'Mere a lot of grief, though, if she ever discovered that it was our prank that had caused her rumble down the mountain.

The mess hall's door opened and the two maintenance workers from the trail walked in, sweaty and dirty. Lively noticed them right off and turned to us one last time.

"I'll be sure to speak with you later," she said curtly. "I have important business to tend to for now."

She then left and stomped over to the men. In a rush, Elliot and I raced and scraped our plates into the trash and hustled out the door.

"Do you think Miss Lively is suspicious?" Elliot asked as we

124

bolted down the steps.

"I think she's a bigfoot."

"We put on a good act, though, don't you think?"

"A-plus terrific, Elliot."

"I hope she doesn't figure it out."

"As far as we know, nobody saw anything. So whatever you do, hold the line."

"I'll hold it."

CHAPTER SEVEN

Once a week after sundown, Roanoke put on a musical ensemble that the whole camp would come and watch. The amphitheater was a century old, fashioned out of the natural landscape where the land sloped down and flattened. At the bottom, an inlaid stone floor served as the stage, and from there backless pews spread upwards in semicircles. In the aisles and on the stage, torches burned while lights and shadows danced about the theater. Sally's eyes sparkled as a troupe of musicians with guitars and a lone violin undraped their somber homily, the notes hovering over the audience like stardust. When the last note played, silence engulfed us, and we were left to ponder how lovely everything could be if it were only this simple.

After the performance, we all filed out to the main area where villagers mingled and chatted. As we tarried, that same curly-headed girl appeared again, and we shared another look. She had a round face with her hair parted and pulled behind her ears. Wearing a cornflower blue dress, she appeared plain enough, though she also conveyed a fairness that could be called pretty to the right eye.

I felt a tug on my shorts. Sally stood next to me with her Teddy bear cuddled close, looking up with her big eyes while Bosco waited faithfully at her side.

"I have to go to the bathroom," she said.

"Did you ask Mommy?"

"She's talking with a bunch of strangers."

"You can go up to her. She doesn't mind."

"Can you take me, please?"

I looked over, and standing in a large group were Mother and Grand'Mere engaged in a lively discussion. I didn't care to interrupt either.

"Come on then," I said. "I'll take you."

Minding her Teddy, she wrapped her little hand around my fingers as Bosco waddled alongside us. The restrooms were located behind the lodge in a tan brick structure. When we arrived, I took Sally to the men's side so I could go in with her, but she protested.

"There's no choice," I said. "I can't go into the ladies room."

"But I can. Bosco will protect me."

"They only have the big potty chairs here."

"I'll be just fine," she said with the flip of her hand as if the subject was beneath her. Bosco fell in line and into the bathroom they went, Teddy and all.

I wasn't the kind of dude that loitered indiscreetly around women's latrines, so I walked to the side and waited in the shadows. While I did, a group of girls approached the building chattering excitedly with the curly-headed girl in the lead.

127

UNDER THE LIGHT OF FIREFLIES

Right as they made the bathroom, Beatrice Lively herself came lumbering outside like a gorilla. The girls stood aside and let her pass. As soon as Lively had gone away, a couple of them burst into laughter and rushed inside.

The bathrooms had been constructed with walls about a foot lower than the roof to provide ventilation. Since the floors and ceiling were both made of concrete, anyone rightly positioned outside could hear every word that echoed inside. With this knowledge, I slipped beside the wall and turned up an ear.

"That's the old lady," I heard a first girl say. "Beatrice Lively."

"The one who fell down the hill?"

"Yes! Oh my gosh. Can you imagine her rolling and rolling with dirt and leaves flying everywhere? It was actually pretty sad, and I did feel a bit guilty."

"It serves her right. She's the one trying to chop down our trees. Nobody likes her except her only friend, Betsy Wilcox."

"I have to admit, though, that we did laugh our heads off when it happened."

"Did you ever figure out who made up the prank?" asked another.

"No, but I have an idea," replied the first girl.

"Who do you think?"

"It's that boy. You know, the one that I talked about."

"Oh, the boy who got mauled. I heard about that."

"That's wild that he's actually at our village!" a different girl said. "Who does he stay with?"

"His grandmother," the first one answered. "She's lived here forever. Her cabin's on the lakeside not far from where

128

Lively crashed."

"Have you talked to him?"

"Not yet, but I've caught his eye several times."

"He wouldn't come over?"

"No. He's painfully shy."

"Do you think he's cute?"

"Hold on," the first one said. The she whispered, "That little girl there came here with him tonight."

Silence.

"So, do you think he's cute or not?" the other girl asked again.

"Shhh... I don't want her to hear," the first girl replied.

"She doesn't know."

"Children have ears. You'd be surprised at what they pick up on."

Then a longer silence.

"She's gone now. Why all the worry?"

"That was almost a really bad situation," the first one answered.

"What do you mean?"

"Because I came this close to calling her brother a freak."

"Oh my gosh! That would've been terrible."

Then they laughed and laughed, and the life went out of my body. I had to press against the wall to keep steady. When their laughter wouldn't stop, I dropped to a knee and covered my ears so I wouldn't hear them anymore. After they'd left, I trudged around front to where Sally stood looking for me. Once she saw me, she came solemnly to my side and wrapped both her hands around my fingers. Vacantly, I led her and the

UNDER THE LIGHT OF FIREFLIES

dog through the muttering crowd.

Near the bell, I found Mother and Grand'Mere waiting, and together we headed back to the cabin. Along the way, Mother picked up Sally who laid her head on mother's shoulders and wrapped her arms around mother's neck. The night was filled with the sounds of the bayou. This usually brought me to quiet reflection, but what kept ringing in my ears was that single word I'd heard earlier. Freak. I never wanted to see that curly-headed girl again.

At the cabin, I faced the bathroom sink and mirror as Mother stood behind me. She did her nightly duty of cleaning my wounds, which were mostly mended. Mother still wouldn't explain what happened, though, and the excuses were running thin.

"We've been through this, darling," she told me. "You're still too sensitive."

"No, I'm not. I swear. I just can't remember is all."

"That means you're not ready."

"That's not true."

"You shouldn't be in such a hurry."

"But it's been weeks."

"Just wait a little longer."

"That's easy for you to say. Everyday I'm trying my best to remember but nothing happens. I just..." Then my lip quivered. "I'm tired of people staring at me like I'm weird."

"I think people want the best for you, son. You're not weird."

"Yes, I am."

"Why would you think that?"

130

"Because I heard a girl say it tonight."

"What do you mean?"

"She said it."

Mother laid down the swab and looked at me in the mirror.

"What did she say to you?"

"She didn't say anything to me."

"But you overheard her."

"Yes."

I held onto the sink and thought about that word.

"You can tell me, Noah."

"She called me...she called me a freak."

"Oh no, honey. No. That's not true."

"Yes it is."

"Listen to me. You are not a freak."

"You're my mother. You have to say that."

"And kids say careless things. They don't mean it. They don't understand."

"Everyone laughed. They said I'd been mauled, and they all laughed at me. And the other day, Elliot heard a grownup talking. A man said that I was pulled from a lake half-dead. Everyone is talking about me, and I don't know what any of it means."

My breathing became choppy and I paused. Since Dad died, us kids had taught ourselves to be strong. I had to be strong. From the mirror, I saw tears brimming in Mother's eyes.

"Mother, don't cry," I said and turned around. "Please don't cry."

"I don't want to see you hurt, son. I want to do the right thing."

UNDER THE LIGHT OF FIREFLIES

"But everybody knows except for me. Folks act like I'm on the TV. If you told me, then maybe I would remember. I'd know who I am."

Mother peered her strained eyes into mine. She shut her eyelids tightly. At last, she nodded. She moved her hands underneath my own, squarely looked me in the face, and with a clear and steady voice, she told me.

"It's true that you were mauled," she said. "Not by a person, though, by an animal. That day, that terrible day, you'd been out with Dusty and Sam when you ran into an older boy named Connor Strait. He suggested a bike ride to Waterworks Lake. You agreed to go with him alone. You stopped by a house for a drink of water, but that's all we know about your trip.

"It was later that it happened. Around sundown, you made it to the park when you were attacked by something." She stalled and squeezed her eyes shut, battling with herself. "An animal had escaped from the zoo. It was a tiger that did this to you. It's unconscionable to imagine, but it's true."

Stunned at the revelation, I couldn't make a reaction. I didn't budge an inch. Mother searched my face, but there was nothing there because what she'd told me sounded impossible. Finally hearing the truth that I'd feverishly wanted, it turned out so strange that it came across artificial and dry, like an old show coming over an antique radio.

"We don't know how, but you made it into the pond," she said. "You waded to that little island. They searched for you everywhere, but it wasn't until midnight that by God's grace a man spotted your legs in the grass. His name is Derreck Mayfly. He rescued you."

132

Staring blankly, I tried to process what she was saying. It was too big, too confusing, and nothing would register. In my mind, there was no light, no epiphany. Instead, the wheels spun round and round.

"I was frantic," Mother continued, her hand gesturing aimlessly. "But I had to stay calm. Thank goodness your brother was there. Finally, after what seemed an eternity, a knock came to our door. I was afraid to answer it because of what I might hear..."

She gasped and her hand went to her mouth. The memory was still raw.

"It was the police," she resumed. "They told me you were alive, but barely. I was so relieved you'd been found, but there was still the chance you might die. I had to see you. I asked your brother to watch after Sally—whom we've never told anything—and I rode with the police to the hospital."

She breathed out and smiled tiredly, wiping the tears from her cheeks.

"You fought, though. You were torn apart and lost a lot of blood, but you lived."

I felt that I should've been reacting or exhibiting some sort of emotion. But there was nothing. Instead, a kaleidoscope had formed in my head where thoughts and feelings collapsed inward then resurfaced on the edge. Scenes, revelations, and reality all appeared inside a device for viewing but with no attachment.

"When did I wake up?" I asked, the words tasting like paper.

"Over a day later. At first, you couldn't remember being awake from one minute to the next. Finally, you came out of it.

UNDER THE LIGHT OF FIREFLIES

It's been horrible seeing you this way, honey, but the doctors said that I shouldn't tell you. I only wanted what was best."

"How'd the tiger get out?"

"Do you know that old man, the foreigner who works at the zoo?"

"You mean the Russian?"

"They call him Henry. He was supposed to have fixed the pen's lock that day, but it didn't happen. The cage door was faulty, and the tiger got out. Then the back gate was left open too. It's beyond imagination."

"And Connor Strait?"

Her face tightened as she pulled in a breath, glancing at me in that nervous motherly way.

"What happened?" I asked again.

"He didn't make it."

"No?"

"No."

He didn't make it. In an instant, those four words were forever branded onto my brain. Without explaining, Mother had just told me that Connor was dead, and not any normal kind of dead, but the getting eaten by a monster kind of dead. Then something inside me cracked. The whole thing was so acutely ironic that it hit me like a bad joke. I understood I should've been relieved that I'd survived—but then again—why should I be? Connor wasn't relieved. Unless cadavers had started feeling relief without my knowledge. I chuckled. Then I giggled. After that I slid into wild laughter, veering towards the edge of hysterics. As I reeled and cackled at the absurdity of it all, a splash of cold water hit me in the face. I stopped and there was

134

Mother, staring.

"*Get control of yourself,*" she said. "You can't allow yourself to slip."

Blinking, I nodded okay.

"And keep respect for the dead. Now, do you want to see?"

I nodded again. From her purse, she grabbed a mirror and angled it over my shoulder. Reflected in the other mirror behind me, I could see my entire back. From my shoulder to the base of my ribs streaked four clean lines, fleshy and bright. The skin was swollen and bubbled where it had been shorn and stitched, looking like pink rubber. The tiger had left its mark on me forever.

At last, I felt something.

"Why didn't it kill me?"

"We don't know," she said. "Perhaps you dove for the water, and the tiger decided not to follow. Nobody knows for sure."

"So, the only way to know is for me to remember."

"It appears that way."

"Do you think I'll ever remember?"

"The doctors think so."

"I didn't ask that."

"I think you should be happy you're alive. Try not to stress yourself."

"How's Connor's family?"

"His dad is shocked and grief stricken, of course. Connor was his only child."

"What about his mother?"

"She died when Connor was little."

This was bad. It was so bad that my mind began to feel

UNDER THE LIGHT OF FIREFLIES

unstable, so I stopped thinking about it. Mother finished cleaning my back, I put a shirt on, and that night we did away with the dressings for good. When we opened the door, Sally was standing there rubbing her eyes.

"Sally," said Mother as she stooped down. "Why are you up?"

"There's something outside," Sally answered. "Lights. Lots of them."

"Lights?"

"They're blinking."

Mother glanced at me confused, but I knew what Sally was talking about.

"Come with me, Sally," I said. "I'll show you what it is."

Hand in hand, we went to the den where we pulled back the drapes and looked through the bay windows. Outside, a million fireflies had descended over our deck and filled the darkness with blooms of light. Sally stood frozen, mesmerized by the sight. Telling her to stay there, I ran to the kitchen and found a mason jar, then opened the back door.

"Do you want to see?" I asked.

"Is it okay?"

"Sure it is. They won't hurt us."

She came outside and wandered into the fireflies, gazing all around. They were everywhere. Catching one in my hand, I showed it to her as it crawled harmlessly across my palm.

"They really don't sting?" she asked.

"No ma'am."

I dropped it into the jar and closed the lid. We took a seat on a lounger and watched as the insect crawled around and

136

blinked its golden light. Such a small thing, so gentle and benign, it blinked and blinked without thought or emotion. It blinked because that's what it was here to do. It tried to fly, clinking lightly into the glass, then fell to the bottom where it searched around some more.

"Noah," Sally said faintly. "Can we let him go?"

"You don't want to keep him?"

"No. He wants to be with his friends."

"Okay."

Opening the lid, we watched the bug continue along the glass until it discovered the rim. Once there it stopped, stretched its wings, and flew away to join the rest. Afterward, Sally and I reclined with her head resting upon my chest.

"I can hear your heartbeat," she said.

It was a windless night, quiet and dark, hung with a low crescent moon. We sat there under the light of fireflies as if stars had dropped in for a visit, filling our minds with visions and dreams. Sally dozed off, and I could feel the rhythm of her breathing, innocent and sweet. Soon after, I became drowsy as well. As much as I hated to do it, I forced myself to rouse her. As I slid off the seat, she reached around my neck and clung to me. For the first time in a long time I carried her, and the pain didn't matter.

"Will you stay with me tonight?" she asked me in her room.

"Okay," I replied and delicately crawled into the bed.

Sally scooted against me and laid her head once more over my heart, then let out a long breath and squeezed my hand. Through the gauzy drapes, cloudy figures of light zoomed past our window. As we faded towards sleep, Sally squeezed my

UNDER THE LIGHT OF FIREFLIES

hand one last time and said sorrowfully, "That mean old tiger."

Our next morning was our last, but before we left, Mother and I embarked upon our annual canoe trip. Although only my one arm worked well, I decided it was better to go than to miss out on our tradition. We pushed off from land and paddled over the placid waters of the bayou. It was warm, and the sounds of bullfrogs had quieted from the night before, which only seemed to increase the stillness. Cypress and tupelos sprung marvelously from the lake's bottom, and inside the watery maze appeared passages like intersections through a prehistoric landscape.

"Did you know that a canoe ride was the first date your father and I ever went on?"

"A canoe ride?" I said, turning to face her. "But I thought your first date was at the Yamboree."

"Officially, yes. But we'd met once before when I was sixteen."

"Here at Roanoke?"

"It was our little secret."

"Did he kiss you?"

"Ha! Is that all you kids think about?"

"Answer the question."

Stiffening slightly, she laid her paddle down and touched her hair.

"If you must know," she said. "Yes."

"It was your first?"

Blushing, she nodded another yes.

"That's pretty gross," I said.

138

"Ha! That's the last secret I ever tell you."

We paddled through the murky narrows as the morning ebbed towards day. When we made the open lake, we turned towards home, and after a while the lagoon reemerged. Waiting on the far bank stood Sally, arms curled around Grand'Mere's legs. Upon seeing us, she stamped her feet back and forth as if to propel us faster. We coasted to land and pulled ashore where Sally was weeping.

"Darling!" Mother said as Sally lunged into her arms. "What on earth has happened?"

"It's Teddy! It's Teddy!" she cried, clutching Mother tightly.

Confused, Mother smoothed Sally's hair from her face and asked, "What happened? Did you lose him?"

"No. I had him last night but now he's gone."

Grand'Mere and Mother exchanged quick glances. They didn't remember her coming home from vespers with her Teddy.

"Let's check inside," Mother said.

"We already have," Sally moaned before turning on Bosco. "You took him somewhere, didn't you? Bad dog! Bad dog!"

"Now, now," Grand'Mere soothed. "Bosco wouldn't hurt your Teddy."

"I know," she said and hugged the dog. "I'm sorry, Bosco. It's not your fault."

Bosco accepted the hug, whimpering at all the anguish. We went inside and turned the place upside down, but no Teddy was found. Inconsolable, Sally refused even ice cream and left to go fret. Next, a knock came to the door. I opened it and

UNDER THE LIGHT OF FIREFLIES

found Elliot who'd come to say so long.

"Ever hear from that old bag?" I asked as I stepped outside.

"Not personally."

"See, I told you."

"I still think she believes we did it."

"Yeah, but she can't prove it, which makes it all the more sweet."

"She actually took that rubber snake to the pool and shook it around, demanding to know whose it was. It upset the children."

"Did she wear a swimsuit?"

"No."

"Then they got off easy."

"It was a good time this year. The best cabin trip yet!"

"At least now you understand how to set up a proper prank."

"I've already got more ideas. Would you like to hear them?"

"Save it for next time," I said and smiled. "Have a fun summer. I'll see you next year."

"See you next year." We shook hands and he left.

Inside the cabin, we did one more sweep to appease Sally, but found nothing. She lay on the couch, defeated, as Mother stroked her back and finally convinced her that it was time to go. Outside, we gave our final goodbyes and hugs.

"I hope you find Sally's Teddy," I said to Grand'Mere.

"I'll put out an APB immediately."

She gave me a kiss on my cheek, and I climbed into the car. As we pulled onto the gravel road, Bosco hopped in place beside Grand'Mere who waved and smiled goodbye, her gorgeous dogwood tree spread above her with its white flowers reflecting the sunlight, its future uncertain. Mother drove us away, and I peeked one last time at the lagoon with its dripping trees before the last cabin disappeared. At the end of the lane we came to a sign that read, 'Roanoke Village.' We pulled onto the highway and were gone.

CHAPTER EIGHT

Judge Caraway's office was big and bright with tall columns of windows casting sunlight over a polished floor. Banners from his outfit in the last world war hung on the wall, and there were too many acknowledgments, certificates, and degrees to count. Behind his desk stood the Texas and American flags bordered with yellow tassels, and a nameplate stenciled "Honorable Whitaker Caraway" rested prominently on the front of his large square desk.

Sitting open in front of him was a package I'd received the previous day in the mail. Wearing his reading glasses, the judge reclined in his roomy chair and studied its contents. The sender of the package had been Henry the maintenance worker—the Russian who'd allowed the tiger to escape. A lowly man, he sat in a wooden chair near a wall with his hands placed reverently on his lap. He wore a buttoned-up shirt, a secondhand tie, and a tweed jacket that hung raggedly upon his thin shoulders. His timid eyes stared at the floor from a sun parched face that'd been chiseled with sharp Scandinavian features.

Standing proudly on his flank was the hotshot defense attorney from Tyler. Diamonds flashed from his rings, and alligator boots jutted beneath his silk pants. Stringy, crinkled hair was combed across his thinning scalp, contrasting an otherwise handsome face. He carried an easy cockiness about him, like he already knew the answer to any question you could ask. He'd lost his very first case fresh out of law school, and then never lost again. So, he couldn't say he was undefeated, but he didn't mind saying he was unbeatable.

Off to the other side sat the prosecutors with their backs mostly to me. They wore department store suits and dusty black shoes. The older one had a big body, flat face, and bland disposition. The younger one was short with a receding hairline and a plucky attitude like an auctioneer on too much caffeine. A battered briefcase shoved full of files laid between them through which they sifted for papers, speaking to each other in hushed tones.

Henry had been charged with negligent manslaughter for Connor Strait's death. Judge Caraway was overseeing the case. Without telling anyone beforehand, Henry had done an outrageous thing and mailed me, the only witness, a package which included a letter and a family heirloom. When the surprise parcel arrived, Mother straightway contacted the judge who had no choice but to hold a deliberation in his chambers.

Up until then, Mother had successfully sheltered me. It was inevitable, though, that I should be exposed. In my sleepy town of about fifty thousand people, things moved slowly, and life there was simple and sedate. So, when news of the tiger attack came out, the story went predictably haywire. Our local paper, the *Texarkana Gazette*, covered it like a rat does cheese, and although the national media never personally showed up, the story was picked off the wire by papers far and wide. Meanwhile, the townsfolk went into a tsunami of gossip and intrigue. People love to gossip, and this was certainly a subject worth gossiping about. *How in the world could a tiger have gotten loose? Will little Noah Ellis ever use that arm again? I heard that dead boy's father is a nutcase.* After a long while, when everyone had talked all they could talk, the gossip ebbed into a trickle and tiger mania fell quiet. That is, until one day when out of the clear sky, a canary yellow Cadillac came rolling into town ridden by that notorious defense attorney, trimmed in gold and cowboy swagger. When the town saw that, the story blew sky high once again.

Clive Longbranch. Only thirty-five years old, he'd already cleared a serial bank robber, a crooked state-congressman, and, most notoriously, Jeb Strahan—the brigand who'd stood down the Texas Rangers at his Fort Griffin ranch for three days. Always seeking the spotlight, Clive scheduled a press conference to announce that he was taking Henry's case pro bono for the sake of justice, then boldly predicted that before Labor Day, his client would be acquitted. The defense didn't ask for much time, and the trial had begun just that week; but now, because of the package, the proceedings were drawn into recess.

Judge Caraway's steely eyes flashed with intelligence as he rolled a pen between his fingers and scrutinized Henry's missive. Judge was the type of man who could perceive intent seemingly from the curves of pen strokes. Upon finishing, he removed his glasses and nodded to the other attorneys in an unspoken language I wasn't privy to. He laid the paper aside and put his elbows on the desk with his long fingers interlaced.

"So how's that arm doing, son?" he asked me warmly.

"It's good," I replied, aware of the other men as they listened.

"It's not fun what happened to you, but at least it wasn't on your throwing side, isn't that so?"

"Yes sir."

The judge was a widower who occasionally attended my church with his daughter and grandkids. He'd always loomed large, but now in the halls of justice, his presence commanded an aura of respect, if not a little fear. There was a perceived dominance around him, like by the force of his will he could collapse any argument, cure any debate, or solve any riddle. Criminals shrank before him and attorneys obeyed. Even Mr. Longbranch seemed appreciative as he leaned casually against the wall and handled a nickel lighter.

"I know what it's like for you, Noah," the judge told me. "In the war, my plane got shot all to hell, and I laid bleeding in a kraut hayfield for two days until the good guys arrived. What I'm telling you is that if my wounds healed, so will yours."

"Yes sir."

"Noah," he continued with a long breath, his eyes deepening. "I'm sure you know that this man, Hendrik Magi, is on trial for the terrible tragedy that occurred. Recently, though, he mailed you this package with a letter. You didn't get to read it, but that's not important. We do need to clear a few things up, however. I want you to tell me how you know this man, this maintenance worker from the park."

UNDER THE LIGHT OF FIREFLIES

Everyone waited quietly with their ears tuned to my response.

"Well, I don't know him," I said.

I glanced at Henry, but his eyes remained downturned, his presence without note save for a meek smile on his face. The judge's own countenance towered. He nodded at me in a way that said I was safe with him.

"I would see him sometimes at the zoo," I added. "Everybody knows he's from Russia."

"Did he ever speak to you?" the judge asked.

"No sir."

"Are you sure?"

"I can't remember us ever talking."

There was hesitation while the prosecutors fidgeted and looked back and forth between themselves and then at the judge.

"So just for clarity, son," the judge delicately pressed, "you can't remember seeing or speaking with the accused, 'Henry' as he's known, on the day in question?"

"No. Am I supposed to?"

The judge thought about how to answer.

"Because if you told me," I added, "then maybe it could help me to remember."

The judge exhaled through his nose as my mother shifted uneasily.

"We understand that Mr. Magi indeed spoke to you in the zoo," the judge told me. "On the day in question, at the former exhibit for the seals."

"What happened?" I asked.

146

LEE SANDERS

"As I stated,, you and Mr. Magi allegedly spoke."

"No. You said the 'former' exhibit. What happened to the seals?"

That gave him pause. Everyone waited.

"The zoo is shut down," the judge told me. "The animals are no longer there."

"So, the seals are gone?"

"I'm afraid so."

"Forever?"

"I'd guess so."

"But why?"

"Because of what happened, son."

The room sat quietly and respected this new reality I'd learned, and that reality was that there would be no more woeful serenades from mighty beasts coming through my windows. No more maniacal court. The pool would remain empty because the seals had been taken away. Wherever they'd gone, I only hoped they were still happy.

"This is enough," the judge said. "As long as there's no objection, then Noah and his mother may leave."

"Your honor," the flat-faced prosecutor whispered. "The family should be made aware that we might need the boy's testimony later. Only if his memory returns, of course."

"Mr. Prosecutor," the judge answered, "we'll cross that bridge when we get there."

"I may also remind you, the accused blatantly tampered with a witness. The implications..."

"Counselor."

"This boy is not a witness," Mr. Longbranch then inter-

147

UNDER THE LIGHT OF FIREFLIES

vened. "He can't remember a thing. He didn't read that letter. My client is a modest, uneducated man whose intentions were harmless. Either way, the letter contains no admissions or pleas. It's inconsequential."

"That's an awful poignant letter from a man who's uneducated," said the younger plucky attorney. "Poignant timing too. It's very consequential."

Longbranch's back straightened, and then Judge Caraway said in a low tone, "Gentlemen, mind your manners."

"The defense moves to waive the letter," Longbranch submitted with a pass of his hand.

"What a ridiculous motion," the plucky attorney snorted. "It shouldn't even be discussed."

"You're just aching to put that child on the stand, ain't ya?"

"I'm not aching. But if his memory returns then perhaps, respectfully, we would ask for his testimony."

"Cheap tears and cheap points. You're a real class act, Bickford."

"Class act? You've defended bank robbers and fugitives. You'd take Judas Iscariot for a client if it earned you a headline."

"I set men free," Longbranch growled and started forward. "How many innocent men have you thrown behind bars and smiled about it?"

"I don't call criminals 'friends' if that's what you mean!"

"And who do you call friends, you little hick?!"

"Counselors!" Judge Caraway thundered and rose from his chair. "I'm not going to have it. Not in the courtroom, not in my chambers, and certainly not in front of this family."

As he stood tall over his desk, I became fully aware that this was a man's game and that I was not a man. The prosecutor relented and Longbranch slowly backpedaled, each one eyeballing the other like mortal enemies.

"We'll reconvene in twenty minutes," the judge said. "You will return with hats in hand, or you will regret it. Now get out."

Everyone got up to leave, especially me, but Judge Caraway told Mother and me to wait. As the attorneys exited, the judge shut the door and gently pulled up a wooden chair.

"Sorry for the drama," he said and sat down. "This is a unique situation, though, if I may say so. To be direct, your mind is still delicate, Noah, and I'm keen to that. However, that man sent you a package during his trial. It is very irregular to say the least, and now I have to decide what to do about it. I'll try my best to keep you off that stand, but I also have to do the right thing. Do you understand?"

"We understand, Judge," Mother answered. "We only ask to be treated fairly. Noah is innocent."

"It's a consideration I take with gravity, Lauren. You did the right thing coming to me. If something else arises, call me directly. That means a surly journalist, prank callers, anything that comes your way."

He then took a business card off his desk, scrawled a number, and handed it to Mother. She dropped it into her billfold, then the judge showed us to the door.

"How long will the trial be?" I asked him before we left.

"Those things determine themselves," he answered.

"It won't last very long, I bet."

"Why is that?"

UNDER THE LIGHT OF FIREFLIES

"Because he's a commie. I mean, everyone knows he's guilty, right?"

The judge glanced at Mother, then back to me, and replied, "That verdict is presently undetermined and precisely what this trial is for. I won't discuss the matter any further."

He then opened the door, and we politely said our good-byes and left. In the sunny hallway, the prosecutors sat on long benches reviewing papers and writing notes. I jerked Mother's sleeve, but she swatted me away and held her finger to her lips. Outside, it was more of the same until we made it inside the vehicle.

"So that's it?" I asked.

"What's it?"

"I can't read the letter?"

"Noah," she replied as she started the engine. "Can't we just let that go for now?"

"Why? He mailed it to me, didn't he? Explain what it said."

"It's not to be discussed."

"But I won't tell anybody."

"Are you going to battle me on every little thing?"

"This isn't a little thing. I'm not a little boy."

"But you're not a man either. At least I don't want you to be. Not yet."

She pulled the wagon out and drove away. The radio was playing a song that she'd loved years before. She flipped it off and stared ahead for a long while, thinking.

"That letter was written in perfect English," she began as she rubbed her temple. "It's surprising if you consider where's he's from. He wrote about his own life, which seems to have been one long catastrophe. He said that he was sorry for you. There's another part as well, but I'm not going there. That's it."

"Did he say he was innocent?"

"He didn't mention it."

"Because he's guilty."

"Maybe he felt no need to say it. It's as if the truth didn't need explaining."

"Those two men know he's guilty," I said.

"They don't know it. It's their job to prosecute."

"They don't go after people who aren't guilty first."

"It's the jury who decides. One day you'll understand."

"But that man *is* guilty."

"Guilt is a strong word. We should wait until the trial is over."

"Do you believe he's *not* guilty?"

"Possibly," she said.

"But that's not how you felt before."

"I hadn't read the letter before."

"But the letter can't prove he's innocent."

"That man doesn't have to prove he's innocent. They have to prove he's guilty."

"Why are you switching sides?"

She drove a few blocks without speaking. She had to know that I'd eventually hear the details or read them in the papers, so she decided right there to tell me.

"There was a work order for the cage's lock to be fixed," she said. "This man, Hendrik, claims that he went to fix it, but that it couldn't be fixed. He waited a very long time for his

151

UNDER THE LIGHT OF FIREFLIES

boss to return. When he didn't come back, Hendrik wrote a note explaining the situation and left. The other side claims he never wrote any note, but instead abandoned his post. At the end of the day, the park director and another worker showed up together and moved the tiger from the holding pen back into its cage with the glitchy lock. Then it got out. Either way, it's impossible that Hendrik could've been the one who left the back gate open if he wasn't the last person there."

"So then the director and his assistant went home and left the gate open? That's hard to believe."

"They never went home. At least one of them didn't."

"What do you mean?"

A hand shot back to her temple as she strained her eyes. "I mean that the park director was killed too," she said.

"What?!! You mean someone *else died*??"

"Yes. Inside the zoo. His name was Dale Kippinger."

"Why didn't you tell me?"

"You've experienced a lot of trauma."

"But you still could've told me."

"I'm telling you now."

Unreal. I couldn't believe another person had been slain, the park director himself. I morbidly pictured his pink face and walrus like mustache resting six feet under. As I tried to absorb it, I stared at the drab outline of downtown with its smokestacks rising over the trainyard.

"Were there any more deaths?" I asked.

"No."

"Did that man die the same way as Connor?"

"Yes."

152

Silence.

"What happened to the other worker?" I asked. "The one who lived."

"He was outside at his vehicle when the tiger got loose. He saw it and raced away for help."

He saw the tiger. What a sight that must've been. I wondered how I'd reacted when I first saw it. Did I freeze? Did I run? Another person had seen the same things I had, though, which made for strange company. Connor had strange company too, but his was different than mine.

"So will this Russian get off?" I asked.

"He is Estonian."

"What's the difference?"

"The Soviet Union invaded his country in the second world war and took him as an orphan prisoner. He was your age. That's the difference. But to answer your question, I don't know if he'll get off. He does have a good attorney, though."

A good attorney meant he had a chance. Even I knew that. Every time I heard that somebody had a good attorney, that person got off scot-free. I compared it to rich people and how they got away with everything, or how coaches' sons always made the all-stars, but now even a commie? I decided then that justice wasn't a virtue. Justice wasn't for everybody. Justice was a system, and it was for those who knew how to work it. The rest of us had to sit and watch.

During that period, Mother kept the phones mostly off the hook because of the endless inquiries and condolences, plus the pathetic calls of intrigue. As a result, we heard from nobody. So,

UNDER THE LIGHT OF FIREFLIES

when I could finally ride my bike, my first visit became Sam's house. It was either there or Dusty's, but the all-star team was having great success and had made it all the way to the Dixie World Series in Georgia, therefore Dusty wasn't around.

As Sam's father opened the door, I noticed a couple of shotguns in the foyer, which surprised me because I never took Mr. Wooderson for a gun advocate. Then again, guns and the paranoid did make good bed partners. He wore a tight polo shirt with a pack of cigarettes in the pocket, his shorts were very short, and his socks rode up to his knees. He looked ready to play a round of tennis which was funny because a tennis court was the last place I'd expect to see him, unless barfing up a lung was his latest thing. At the sight of me, his face lit up with surprise.

"Noah!" he cried out. "I can't believe it! You're here!"

"Hi, Mr. Wooderson," I said shyly. "Is Sam home today?"

"Sam? Why, no. He's not. He's staying with his cousins in Henderson."

My hopes fell. Since I'd returned home, I hadn't played at all, and the streets were deserted.

"Do you know when he'll be back?" I asked.

"Not for a while, I'm afraid. With all the things that have happened. Well, I don't need to tell you. You understand."

"I understand. So long then."

"Wait," he said and stepped onto the porch. "Tell me. How are you feeling?"

"I'm getting better. I can ride my bicycle now."

"That's great! That's great!" Then, with his eyes shifting around, he asked, "Are you out alone?"

154

"Yes, sir. Dusty's gone, and the park is empty. Do you know why they closed the pool?"

"The pool in the park? Because it went into disuse and then got parasites. They closed it for the summer."

Closed for the summer. A phrase every kid hated to hear. Not that I was eager to have a crowd of people staring at me, but the words themselves were depressing. I couldn't imagine how the park pool could have ever fallen into disuse.

"Okay," I said. "If you talk to Sam, tell him hello."

"Noah," he said, stopping me once more. "I'm glad you're okay. Truly. We're all glad you're alive. Please be safe out there."

"Thanks, Mr. Wooderson. I will."

The day was blistering hot, being nothing new in Texas, but in the East we had our own brand of hot where the humidity magnified the suffering. On empty streets, I biked into the park where I headed to check out the zoo. I wasn't sure what to expect. Maybe an answer or a clue. When I got there, the gates were locked and the zoo stood empty. Over the lawn, the grass had grown into two tire-ruts that led to a pothole filled with gravel. A chain-link fence encircled the zoo with notices saying it was condemned. Where the sounds of pandemonium once reigned, not a single animal was heard. Even the owls had joined the seals as a memory of better times.

Passing the old fighter plane, I cruised up to the pool but it was just as Mr. Wooderson described. The water was drained, the grass uncut, and a silver lock hung on the gate. I gripped the fence in both hands and thought about the times I'd spent there. The roar of summer's watery frolic had fallen into an impossible silence.

155

UNDER THE LIGHT OF FIREFLIES

As I pedaled towards the springhouse and playground, I grew cagey. I felt that my return to the crime scene would almost certainly trigger the memory, and thereafter the horrible event would unfold in my mind. I stopped on the drive with sweat beading on my body as I looked down on the playground. I rode on and braced for what was coming. Nearing the bridge, my breath quickened and my heart pumped loudly. I was ready. As I crossed the bridge to the playground, though, nothing happened. No jolt. No sudden influx of memories. No answer. It remained just another bike ride. The waiting continued.

At the swing sets, I sat down and tried to picture the scene, but the attempt was a waste. I walked to the water's edge and looked to the little island where a stranger had rescued me. I never even knew the water was shallow enough to wade through. For the first time since it happened, I felt lucky to be alive. Reaching into the pond, I let the wetness cover my hand, squeezed the soft mud at the bottom, then stood and turned away.

I took my bike into the shade by the park entrance. Jill's house sat on the opposite side. How far away she seemed now. I imagined her in Tennessee going on hikes, or making new friends, or even kissing a boy. I thought that inevitably someone else would see what I saw in her, and then she'd be snatched away forever, probably by a punk or a pretty boy. It burned me so badly that I hung my head. Then I heard my name called and it startled me. I turned to look but no one was there.

"Hello?" I called back. "Who said my name?"

"Over here!" a girl's voice responded.

My heart jumped. I scanned the playground but saw nothing. Over at Jill's house, the porch sat empty. A car passed on the park road. Then finally a girl's hand waved from behind one of the little stone towers. With my hopes surging, I dashed over to see who it was.

As I arrived, a face popped out from behind, but to my disappointment it wasn't Jill. It was Jamie, the odd girl from school I'd seen at the pool on that fateful day. She waltzed around wearing an orange tube top and brown shorts. Since I last saw her, the sun had painted her skin a smooth bronze and her hair a goldish auburn. As she slipped over, a sly grin spread over her face.

"Well, hi there, stranger," she giggled. "It's been a long time."

"What were you doing over there?"

"Spying on you."

"What for?"

"It's something to do. This park is dead."

"I know. Where is everybody?"

"Probably on vacation. Probably forever."

"Forever?"

"You know. They're still scared, although not nearly as much as before."

"Scared of what?"

She chuckled at me as if I'd made a joke, but after checking my face she saw that I was serious.

"You really don't know?" she asked.

"No. Tell me."

"Why, good sire," she answered in a hackneyed English accent, "they're all scare't of the tiger, of course."

"Why would they be scared of the tiger?"

157

UNDER THE LIGHT OF FIREFLIES

"You're going to love this. They never caught the thing, old chap!"

I jumped back in disbelief. It couldn't be true. When I saw she wasn't joking, I reflexively spun around and scanned the playground for danger, which evoked from her a hearty laugh and a clap. I spun back, but she just stood there biting her lip.

"People are silly," she said. "That tiger is long gone. But I guess since it did eat two people and cripple a third, folks would naturally be afraid."

"I'm not crippled," I snapped.

"I'm sorry. Although you have to admit, that tiger did do a number on you."

"At least I'm not a weirdo like you," I said and stormed away.

"Hey wait," she said and ran alongside me. "I might not be in the 'cool crowd' per se, but I'm not a weirdo."

"How about a thief?"

"What does that mean?"

"You stole from Nancy Thomas."

"What are you talking about?"

"She sold raffle tickets. You ripped off her bag."

"No, I didn't."

"That's not what everyone else says."

"Would you please stop a sec?" she asked and grabbed my arm.

I halted and turned towards her. She had a concerned look on her face. "They can say whatever they want, but it doesn't make it true. I didn't steal anything. I swear."

"You should tell that to Nancy then."

"I will."

158

"Sure you will."

"Watch and see."

She seemed sincere, but who knew if she was telling the truth.

"Just don't include me in your conversation," I said. "I've got enough to deal with."

"I would never rat you out, Noah. Don't you know that I think you're the coolest kid in school?"

"Yeah right. How am I cool?"

"Because you're so genuine."

I didn't know what to think of that word. She pulled her head back and gazed through the treetops, then blew out a long breath and came forward again.

"Look, Noah. I know that you like Jill."

"What? No! That's a non sequitur thingy. Or whatever."

"Oh yeah? You stared at her house longer than you did that island where they rescued you. Plus, I saw what you wrote in her yearbook."

I blushed so hard I had to turn my head. *The stupid yearbook*, I thought. That thing would be the end of me.

"Don't be embarrassed," she said and touched my arm. "I thought it was funny."

"No, it wasn't. It was dumb."

"Jill's got a sense of humor. She'll get it."

"Is it that obvious I have a thing for her?"

"I don't know. I just have a really good eye."

She stood there relaxed as if she understood all things and all people, yet was puzzled how others couldn't do the same with her. Her face was indeed appealing. To be fair, she was probably

UNDER THE LIGHT OF FIREFLIES

the prettiest girl in school. I'd never trusted her, though, and yet here she was making me feel better about my deepest secret. Maybe Jamie had improved. I could sense her reading me.

"Come on," she whispered. "I'll show you something."

She took me by the hand, and grudgingly I followed her to the lookout tower where she pulled me into the small chamber. The saccharine scent of pee hung in the air, and it was muggy and warm. Jamie stood still and gazed into my eyes.

"What are we doing here?" I asked.

"What boys and girls are supposed to do."

"Are you kidding?"

"I never kid about romance."

"Jamie, listen. You're all right, but I'm not interested."

"Are you sure about that?"

She continued her gaze. Even in that musty chamber, her physical beauty was real. I'd always known it. I had even thought about her in some of my most private moments, but I never considered making a move because she was unpopular. Now that we were alone and unseen, though, I could feel myself being drawn to her like a magnet.

"Are you scared?" she asked.

"No."

"Is this your first time?"

I nodded no, an obvious lie, but she didn't call me on it.

"Don't worry about it," she whispered. "I don't kiss and tell."

"It's not that."

"Then what is it?"

I had nothing. My bullets were dry. In the gap she moved in closer and put her hands on my shoulders. I could feel some-

160

LEE SANDERS

thing soft about her. Something I'd never known. I gave pause
and then, unexpectedly, she did it. She pressed her lips against
mine and moved her arms around my neck. There was no struggle, and after a few seconds, we parted. She looked into my eyes.

"Jamie," I said weakly. "I... I shouldn't be here."

"What's your problem? It's not like this makes us
boyfriend-girlfriend."

"It's something else."

"Is it because you have a crush on Jill? Or because everyone
thinks I'm weird? Or is it a combination of both?"

"I just don't want you to get the wrong idea."

"It's only a kiss, Noah. Can't you just deal with it?"

I couldn't respond, but stood there instead and grimaced.

"I'm telling you, *dahling*," she now said in a Southern drawl.
"I can keep a secret."

Then she pulled me forward and we kissed again. My emotions raged against each other. I told myself that everything
about this was wrong, though underneath it laid something undeniably splendid and new, and I was a victim to its allure. The
kiss didn't last long. The room was overbearing with its heat
and stench, and so we stopped. Once outside, my eyes adjusted
to the light then darted around for anyone looking. I felt guilty.

"Oh, stop it," she said. "Nobody saw us."

"I know. I was just checking."

She sighed loudly as she smelled her hair for any residue.

"Look," she said. "I've got to go to my aunt's now. Are you
okay?"

"I'm okay if you're okay."

"I'm always okay. I'll see you another time?"

161

UNDER THE LIGHT OF FIREFLIES

"I guess. There's nobody else in town, right?"

"Don't worry, Noah. There's no tiger in town either."

Batting her eyes, she squeezed my hand and waltzed away. When she was gone, I went and sat on a swing and looked at Jill's house on the corner. The day was bright and the heat hung in the air like steam. A truck came rattling through the entrance. My first kiss had not been how I envisioned it. Nothing was how I envisioned it. I picked up my bike and left the park.

CHAPTER NINE

40th Avenue was a mile-long drive that ran from Summerhill Road and ended at Texas Boulevard. On each side of the avenue sat a neighborhood, the park on one side and Glenwood on the other. Although kids from both places went to the same schools, on the streets we ran with our own crews. It was common to explore each other's turf, but things like treehouses and forts were kept off limits. I normally didn't venture far from the park, but the time had grown so dull that I had to do something, so I headed south and crossed over.

Glenwood resided the same as my neighborhood, peaceful with tree-spotted lawns and lazy sun-drenched streets. As I was riding through, I passed by some younger kids in their front yard spraying each other with water hoses. When they saw me, though, they stopped playing and stared blankly as I rolled by. After checking a few houses I knew without luck, I descended around a bend onto a side street flanked with unkempt bushes and weeds. A concrete culvert ran beside it,

UNDER THE LIGHT OF FIREFLIES

and at the dead end, some young teenagers were loitering and playing yo-yos. Just like the kids from before, they quit everything upon catching sight of me.

As I drew closer, I saw that three of the guys happened to be Fenton, Tyler, and Billy—the most loathsome troupe that I could've ever hoped to stumble upon. I felt like turning around and leaving, but there was no cool way to pull that off. As I came to a stop, they stared at me like I'd just walked out from the grave. I debated whether I should talk, get off my bike, or shut up and stay still. While I sat there fidgeting, an older teenager whom I'd never met before popped his head back with a nod.

"You're Jack Ellis's little bro, ain't ya?" he asked.

"I am."

"He flies them planes in the park meadows."

"Sure. My dad used to build them. Jack's making his first one right now."

"What are y'all talking about?" Fenton asked.

"They got these wooden planes about three feet long with engines," the guy said. "They fly 'em in the park with remote controls. You should check it out, man. It's wicked."

Fenton listened, then returned to spinning tricks with his yo-yo. Tyler leisurely leaned on his handlebars, looking me over, while Billy brooded in silence behind them both. *No telling what those guys had been into that summer*, I thought, *but I knew it was no good.*

"Bring a plane over so we can see," Billy said.

"I can't," I replied. "My brother won't let me."

I wished I hadn't said that. It made me sound little. Then the older guy stepped over and held out his hand.

164

"Call me Ringo," he said.

With dirty blonde hair parted in wings, Ringo sported a bad teenage mustache and bell-bottom jeans, even on a smoldering day like that. I shook his hand. Then he winked at me as he pulled from his hip pocket a bright yellow tin with a blue outline.

"You got the stuff?" he asked another teenager who handed over a strip of notebook paper and a lighter.

Ringo wadded the paper into a ball, stuck it on a ball-point pen, then drizzled fluid from the yellow tin over it. Next, he placed the spout between his lips and squeezed a long time as the other boys snickered. After tossing the tin aside, he flicked his lighter and lit the paper on fire. Swishing his mouth a second, he cocked his head backward, calculated, then lurched forward and spewed the fluid onto the burning paper.

A giant flame suddenly exploded from the wadded ball with a small roar, arching several feet as it cast a yellow glow over the happy onlookers. For an instant we could all feel the heat from the fire. Then it was over. The other guys hooted and applauded as Ringo stamped out the burning paper.

"I saw that at a concert three weeks ago," said Ringo.

"We did too, man," Fenton replied. "We were on the fifteenth row."

"That was one live gig."

"My ears rang for hours."

Then Ringo turned to me and asked, "Say man, were you there too?"

"No," I answered uncertainly. "I was at... I was out of town."

Unconsciously, I scratched my shoulder, which they all

UNDER THE LIGHT OF FIREFLIES

noticed, and I quickly returned my hand to my handlebar.

"Sorry, dude," Ringo said. "I wasn't thinking."

"Don't worry about it," I replied.

Tyler's gaze met with mine whereafter he blinked and looked away. Then he turned back with a smirk as he rocked back on the seat of his dazzling bicycle, posing like an ad in *Tiger Beat*.

"Well, if it isn't Noah the tiger boy," he said. "Tell us the tale, dude. How'd that whole thing go down?"

"There's nothing to tell," I answered with a shrug. "My mind's a blank."

"That's what I heard. Does that mean you're some kind of schizo now?"

The others laughed under their breath at Tyler's bravado, but I kept my cool.

"No, man," I replied. "Getting attacked by a tiger and losing half your blood makes you forget stuff. I'm just glad I made it to that island."

A hush ensued.

"Connor got eaten alive," Billy said under a dark stare. "And you can't remember what happened?"

Without a word, I eased off my bike, stepped to the middle, and lifted up my shirt. After I showed them my back, I turned and said, "That's what happened."

They all seemed mildly impressed, though Billy's eyes showed no response. A flash of fool's gold glittered somewhere in there, but he never cared about normal things such as grades, clothes, or even popularity, although popularity still graced him in good measure. His disregard for people, property, or other's opinions only served to boost his reputation. He was the right guy to have on your team if you didn't care how you won.

Ringo and his buddy broke the lull. They said goodbye and parted for the culvert while the others mounted their bikes. They filed slowly by me, and after they'd passed, Fenton whispered something to Tyler and Billy and they stopped.

"Are you strong enough to ride?" Fenton asked me.

"I can handle it."

"We're going to the store if you want to come with us."

"Sounds good."

"But if you fall behind, we'll leave your gimpy butt."

Riding with the enemy wasn't my normal course of action, of course, and I felt a measure of guilt knowing what my friends would think. My excuse would be that there was nothing else going on, but just as importantly, it would be unwise to say no to these guys. If I could impress them even in a small way, it would be a major positive. Junior High awaited like a stormy sea, and these sharks would be swimming in it every day.

"I heard you crashed Sandra Prince's slumber party earlier this summer," Fenton said as we rode.

"We did," I replied. "Sam knocked over a bunch of trash cans. It was funny."

"Sam Wooderson?" Tyler cried. "That little buster? How many bones did the baby break?"

I avoided the question, saying instead, "Mrs. Prince came out in a short night gown. She looked fine."

"Mrs. Prince?" Tyler then laughed. "She's got to be forty years old, boy."

"What kind of gown?" Billy asked.

UNDER THE LIGHT OF FIREFLIES

"Red lace."

"Could you see through it?"

"Sure," I lied. "She was soused too, and everything was bouncing around."

"Look at that!" Tyler quipped. "Noah's into *mommies*."

"Cade Brooks' mom is fine too," Fenton said.

"She lays out at the club pool in a bikini," Tyler had to agree. "Totally fine."

We ruminated on hot moms as we crossed over 40th Avenue into the park. I stayed in the back and tried to act nonchalant.

"Isn't Shur Pak the other way?" I then asked after several blocks.

"Yeah," Tyler said. "But that wop is working the register."

"A wop is an Italian," Billy said.

"So?"

"I'm half-Italian."

"Sorry, dude," Tyler said. "It's just that he always comes around and stares at me."

"That's because you're too obvious," Fenton said. "You haven't mastered the art of the five-finger discount like my man Billy."

"Bookout's is better," said Billy.

"Wafer-brain Reef works there," Fenton cracked. "He's afraid of us."

"My dad loaned him the money for that store."

They all laughed, and I wished I hadn't come. There was no doubt in my mind they would hassle, or even worse, steal from Mr. Reef, my dad's old Rotary Club buddy. He'd wonder why I was riding with these hoods. I wasn't sure what to do. I could either peel off now and become a permanent wimp, or go inside with them and suffer Mr. Reef's disappointed stare. Letting people down was something that nagged at me, so I desperately searched my mind for a solution. After we'd made it through the tunnel under Summerhill, a wild idea popped into my mind.

"Say fellas," I said, "Can I go in first while you wait outside a few minutes?"

"Why would we do that?" Fenton asked.

"Because he's scared to be seen with us," Tyler said.

"I have an idea," I said. "You'll thank me later. Trust me."

"Trust you?" Fenton responded, crossing his thick arms. "You've only been around for fifteen minutes."

"I need cover, so just let me do my thing after you come inside."

"What are you doing?"

"You'll see."

"This better be good, tiger boy," Billy said and poked my bad shoulder.

After we made it up the bank and arrived at the store, they waited in the side lot as I rode around front. At the door I paused to ask myself how in the world I was going to pull this off, but it was too late to quit. I took a gulp, pushed the handle, and slipped inside. At the counter, Mr. Reef peeked over his newspaper and immediately his eyes brightened. Putting the paper down, he stood up and strode around the counter.

"Noah Ellis," he said and took hold of my hand. "It's very good to see you. How are you feeling, son?"

169

UNDER THE LIGHT OF FIREFLIES

"Fine," I replied bashfully. "Thanks for asking."

"Is there anything I can do for you?"

"One pint of Old Harper, please."

"Ha ha! I'll tell you what, your orange soda and whatever else you'd like are on the house today."

"That's okay."

"No, I mean it," he said and put a hand on my good shoulder. "It's my pleasure."

Then the front door opened, and I saw the other guys were already coming inside. Mr. Reef watched with his hands on his hips as he shook his head in contempt. I prayed they wouldn't say my name.

"You boys just don't listen, do you?"

"What's your deal?" Fenton replied. "We're not gonna rob you."

"I know you're not because I'm standing right here."

"We give you business all the time and all you do is hassle us," Billy sneered.

"Hassle you? Hassling would be turning you over to the cops for all the snuff cans you've pilfered."

"We don't dip snuff, old man. We chew."

"What do you want?"

"Same deal as always," Fenton said. "Three sodas and..."

"And that's it. You're not getting any chew."

"I was gonna say a bag of chips. *Pretty please?*"

As they debated, I moved surreptitiously to the back of the candy aisle, still praying the guys wouldn't address me. Mr. Reef took their money and said to wait in the lot. He then went to the cooler, collected their stuff, and took it outside.

170

When the coast was clear, I quickly jumped to the magazine rack in the corner.

Since I'd last visited, the racks had been fitted with risers to conceal the covers of the lewder versions, so I had to stand on my toes to reach over. As I frantically fumbled around, my ears stayed perked for the front door. Getting caught would mean more than simply receiving a stern lecture beneath Mr. Reef's glowering façade. It would also mean a humiliating phone call to my mother to inform her that not only was I a thief, but a smarmy, debauched, girly-mag thief. The shame would be unbearable.

After several strained moments, the greasy laminate of a magazine cover finally grazed my fingertips, and I blindly ripped it out. With cringy trepidation, I spun around, fully expecting the grave figure of Mr. Reef to be looming behind me, but all I found was an empty room.

With loot in hand, I hastily stuffed the magazine down the back of my shorts. My belt was too tight, though. While I wrestled with that, the front door opened and in came Mr. Reef. As he paused to shout something in parting at the boys, I scampered behind the end of a row and undid my belt. I was so terrified that I considered tossing the contraband, but there would be nowhere to ditch it except bare floor, making me an idiot on top of a thief.

When Mr. Reef came inside, he unexpectedly turned down my aisle as I gasped and emitted tiny squeaks. I had managed to finagle the magazine halfway into my shorts, but there was still the issue of zipping up and fastening my belt. His steps drew closer. I contemplated what level of dignity I was willing

UNDER THE LIGHT OF FIREFLIES

to sacrifice for mercy. But then he simply stopped, turned sideways, and arranged some cans on a shelf. Once he was done, he left and went back to his post.

Revived with hope, I secured the magazine in the back of my shorts, cinched my belt, and pulled my shirt over. Taking a breath, I slithered daintily to the fridge where I rolled back the top and coolly reached inside for a soda. Afterward, I waddled to the counter, looking the whole time like someone had kicked me in the rear. From the register, Mr. Reef watched me with a narrow stare until I arrived and nodded. Leaning forward, he tapped a thumb on the counter, his unblinking eyes upon me.

"What's going on with your shorts?" he asked.

"Shorts?" I gulped. "What about my shorts?"

"XYZ."

"Say again?"

"Your zipper is undone."

I looked down, and tragically, my fly hung wide open. Then I turned my head up and found Mr. Reef's disapproving eyes locked onto mine. He had to know. The air slowly went out of me in a rueful groan. Giving myself a ten-percent chance of survival, I fixed my zipper and slumped my head for the final judgment.

"I guess I won't be joining the Pharaohs," I uttered with a regrettable laugh.

He lingered there for several seconds as he drummed his fingers over the counter.

"You know, Noah," he said. "I don't get upset very often. I feel like I'm a fair man. So when I say something, it's not

172

in vain. I'm telling you right now, loud and clear. Those boys outside are *punks*," he said and pointed at the window. "Spoiled rotten punks. They come in here with their sticky fingers and snide remarks, disrespecting property and elders alike, with no thought of courtesy or even the law. I hope you're smart enough not to run around with boys like that."

"Me run around with those guys? No. Never. Well, actually, I was biking earlier when they saw me..."

He leaned forward with his bulbous nose hanging over the counter.

"Are they picking on you?" he asked.

"Oh no. They don't pick on me. Not really. Not like usual."

"If they are, I can do something about it."

"Don't worry about it, Mr. Reef. They've been nice to me ever since, well, since what happened to me."

That statement was the showstopper. Although I couldn't remember it myself, Mr. Reef was undoubtedly aware I'd been at his store on that tragic day. It was in his parking lot where I'd met Connor for the first time. With a small nod, he turned to his cash register.

"You have one free soda and one free...what else did you get?"

"Nothing. I'm good."

He looked at me like I wasn't right. Kids don't turn down free stuff. Then the magazine slipped and I had to jerk sideways, making Mr. Reef even more perplexed. To deflect his attention, I hastily reached beneath the counter, randomly grabbed an item, and slammed it on the counter.

"One snowball?" I remarked dubiously.

UNDER THE LIGHT OF FIREFLIES

Mr. Reef glanced at the coconut poof with uncertainty and said, "I've never seen you buy one of those before."

"Pink marshmallow balls? Oh yeah. They'll set you on fire, man."

His eyebrows flew up, then a smile slowly emerged.

"On fire, eh?" he said. "Sort of like a swig of Old Harper, right?"

"That's right!" I agreed and slapped the counter.

He rang up the items, pulled the lever, then shut the register without charge. Licking his fingers, he snapped open a paper sack and bagged my items. After handing them to me, I backed off slowly, thanking him as he curiously watched me go. When at last I felt the door on my backside, I eased outside nice and slow. In the lot, I continued to shuffle sideways until I got to my bicycle as Mr. Reef watched me the entire way.

When I finally made it around back, I stumbled over my bike in a small crash and let out a big sigh of relief. Saying nothing, the other guys mildly munched their chips as I groped and rolled off. After regaining my feet, I smiled, whipped out the magazine, and held it up. The boys didn't react with any surprise, though. Instead, they leaned forward with squinted eyes.

"*Biker Babes*," Fenton said. "What is that?"

"Say what?" I replied.

Flipping the magazine around, I found on its cover a platinum blonde lady lavishly spread across a motorcycle as if she were the dessert of the day. Clad in a black leather bikini, one set of her crimson fingernails tugged at the throttle while the other tugged at her equally crimson lips.

"I stole this," I said. "It's supposed to be a dirty magazine."

174

"What?" Billy said. "Give that thing here."

He strode over and snatched the book from my hands, then zipped past pages and scanned for the goods. At a place near the middle he stopped, turned it sideways, then unfolded the spread. The boys nodded and shrugged.

"It's only a half-nude mag," Fenton said. "But I guess it's better than nothing."

"Half-nude?" I replied. "Can I see?"

Billy handed it to me and there was that same blonde—red fingernails and all—sitting topless upon a Harley as she rolled towards some half-naked utopia.

"Nice try, tiger boy," Tyler snickered. "You don't get the touchdown, but a field goal is good for you."

"Tiger man," I retorted and glared at him. "If you're going to call me a stupid name, then call me tiger man."

They all stopped, amused at the novelty of my response. I stuck out my chest, and Tyler rolled his eyes and dropped a glance at Fenton who did nothing. Billy took back the magazine and put his face in it.

"Fine," Tyler said. "Tiger man it is."

"Fine."

"We're keeping the magazine, though," Fenton told me. "We'll add it to our collection at the club. Maybe one day we'll let you come and see."

"You mean your treehouse?" I asked.

"It's more than a treehouse."

"It's a church," said Billy.

175

CHAPTER TEN

In the garage on the big workbench laid the beginnings of the model airplane, untouched for the better part of a month. Jack was staring at its instruction manual which could have been written in Chinese for all I knew. Page after page contained directions to tiny strips, spines, and brackets that would one day become an airplane. At the end of the project, a miniature engine would then be dropped into the body and paired with a remote, all with the assurance that the thing would fly if Jack hadn't screwed up somewhere. It was an impossible task, and one that I wondered how my father had ever gotten mixed up in knowing that his sons would ultimately try themselves and be tortured by it.

As I observed Jack's progress, which was close to zero, tailpipes came rumbling down our street. A red sports car with a shiny chrome grill and Arkansas plates then appeared and pulled into our driveway, parked, and cut the engine. It was Rip, the same guy my brother had spoken with that night at Digg's burgers.

He had a girl with him, and I saw that it was the temptress, Desaray. With her bikini exposed beneath a denim shirt, she emerged with the confidence of a lioness, her pitch-black hair flowing back from that gorgeous face and eyes glowing like the high beams on a semi.

Rip himself had loose locks hanging below his ears and around his eyes. He was skinny but lean, and he had a casual style about him like there was never any rush. He wore a tight tee-shirt with shorts and sandals, and he slunk as much as he walked.

Relieved for an excuse to quit, Jack dropped his work and went outside as Rip and Desaray leaned on the front of the car.

"What you got going in there?" Rip asked.

"It's a model airplane," Jack said. "The high-end kind. My dad started this one but never finished. I'm just messing with it."

At the mention of my father, Rip and Desaray respectfully bowed their heads.

"How long before you're done?" asked Desaray after a moment.

"Around a lifetime at this pace," Jack replied.

They laughed lightly and then stayed there staring at the ground. They seemed out of place, like something was eating at them.

"Say Noah," Jack said to me. "Why don't you run inside and check on Sally? You can come back out in a minute."

"Can I get anybody something?" I offered. "A soda or some tea?"

177

Hoping that Desaray might speak to me directly, she instead raised her eyebrows and glanced away like the question didn't concern her.

"I'm cool," Rip said.

"Go on," Jack told me. "You can bring some tea later."

I trudged into the garage then glanced back from the door. Rip laid his hands on the hood as he talked and then brought them up in a gesture of some significance. Desaray reached into her purse for a cigarette and eyed Jack. Rip said something surprising to which Jack's head snapped back and his arms went out. Rip watched without emotion but with his ears tuned closely to Jack's words. Something was up.

After going reluctantly inside, I looked around for Sally but didn't see her. First checking upstairs, I came down again and found her in the study sitting in dad's leather chair as she peeked through a desk drawer. When I entered, she quickly shut the drawer and placed her hands delicately on the desk.

"It's okay," I told her. "You can look through the drawers."

"I won't hurt anything."

"I know."

I stood in front of the desk while she remained there self-conscious.

"I like to come in here too," I said. "It's like a secret getaway."

"I know! There's lots of neat things in here. This was Dad's quiet place."

"Yep. He liked to come in here and doodle."

"Doodle," Sally repeated with a giggle.

We gazed over the room with its clocks and globes and mounted fish on the walls.

178

"Daddy used to bounce me around in here," she continued. "He'd throw me all the way up to the ceiling!"

"Remember how he chased you around this desk?"

"He did?"

"Sure. This desk right here," I said and rapped my knuckles on the top. "Around and around. You'd scream and giggle every time he caught you."

She leaned forward with a smile, but her eyes were absent. She'd only been three-and-a-half when dad died. That was a bad time. For several days after he went missing, we said nothing to her. Mother wanted to be certain Dad wasn't coming back. Then they found him down-river, so she had to tell her. From then until the funeral, Sally curled her arms around herself for long stretches and stared into nothingness. Mother would hold her and hum songs as Sally quietly lay there confused at how her father, who'd been so vivid and full of life, could possibly be dead. The house became empty of his presence. The laughter went away. The day after we buried him, Sally suddenly brightened and spoke the same thing again and again, almost as a message of assurance.

"Daddy went far away with the angels," she said as she rocked in his leather chair.

I looked at her sweet face as she repeated those words from memory, her same memory which now held only the fading face of our father, his wonderful laughter an echo chasing across her soul. She laid her head on his desk and rubbed its edge with her finger.

"It was time for him to go," she said. "He couldn't stay any longer."

"Do you need anything?" I asked her.

"No. I just want to stay in here."

I walked around and hugged my little sister for a long moment, both of us being quiet. Afterward, I left and went back to the den. Through the window, I could see Jack and the others still talking. In the kitchen, I poured a glass of iced tea, then moved into the garage. Outside on the driveway, Jack had his hand on the back of his neck as Desaray talked. I stepped to the edge of the driveway to listen.

"I don't know what to tell you, Dez," Jack said. "I was out with Veronica last night. Nobody's said anything to me."

"Veronica Rochelle?" Desaray asked. "Why her? She's a sophomore at Liberty Eylau, right?"

"I saw her one night at Diggs. We know some of the same people."

"And where did you take her, specifically?"

At that, Jack dropped his arms and his demeanor changed. He tapped his foot several times impatiently but didn't speak. Dez smoked the last of her cigarette then flicked it in the street and crossed her arms.

"What's wrong?" she asked.

"I'm not going to answer that question," Jack said.

Her eyelids and shoulders dropped as she let out a sigh.

"Don't get mad," she said. "I didn't mean anything by it."

"Fine," Jack responded. "Then I'll say it straight because I know why you're here. I didn't steal the thing, and I don't know who did."

"No, no, no," Rip said with a raised hand. "We're not saying that you took it, cuz."

180

"Good, because I didn't. If you want to find out, then Dez can ask *her* friends."

"I grew up on the Arkansas side," she said. "I haven't been here even a year. Nobody's telling me anything."

"Then what do you want from me?" Jack asked.

At that, Rip dropped his head and slapped his hands on the grill. After another second, he stood up.

"It's all good, Jack," he said. "I was just in the area and thought I'd swing by. Maybe I'll see you around later."

"Maybe."

"Bye."

They both stayed quiet and got into the car. As the engine roared to life, I saw Desaray snicker through the window. The car reversed out of the drive and then sped away down the street. Jack stayed until they were out of sight, then headed back to the garage as he rubbed the corners of his mouth.

"I brought your tea," I said and held out the drink.

He pulled down his hand and there I saw a long happy grin. He then clapped his hands and did a quick jig.

"Whoa-ho-ho!" he exclaimed. "I can't believe it! They did it!"

"Who did what?" I asked as he took the tea.

"Somebody's getting a gold star."

"Gold star? Why are you so happy?"

He danced into the garage and did a slide. "Remember last year when somebody stole the tiger off our marquee at Texas High?" he asked.

"Yeah. So what?"

"Last night somebody stole their hog from Arkansas High.

It's gone. Texas strikes back!"

"No kidding!" I said and followed him to the workbench. "Did you and your buddies do it?"

He shot me a side look which meant no.

"Okay," I said. "Who did then?"

"That's what Rip and Dez were wondering. I don't know yet, but I plan to find out."

The previous summer when Arkansas had ripped off the painted tiger atop our school's marquee, prank callers tormented the Texas side folks for months before it finally turned up in the school's breezeway the first morning of school. The guys who stole it were never caught. Of course everyone found out, making Brian Duchamp and his buddies eternal legends. So now their own mascot was missing, and this time they'd have to hear it from us all summer.

"So, who do you think did it?" I asked.

"There's only about a hundred guys I can think of."

My mind poured over all the actors on the teenage stage. Football players, stoners, preppies, rednecks. They all had a motive.

"Didn't Tim Blaylock swear revenge after his Camaro's windows were smashed out during Hell Week?" I asked.

"Don't forget that Arnold got twenty stitches. He's an animal."

"So what was Desaray's problem?" I asked.

"Dez is her own problem. She thinks she can play both sides."

"But she's a Texas girl now."

"No, she's not. She *had* to move here."

182

"What made her do that?"

Jack sipped his tea and pondered that for a moment. Then he picked up the instructions for the airplane and put them back into their cubby hole.

"What if there was a little incident," he said, "that may or may not have occurred between a certain cheerleader and a certain football coach over there?"

I gawked and sucked in a breath.

"So that was Desaray who hooked up with Coach Harris?" I whispered.

"We don't know that, but that coach isn't there anymore and neither is she. Though don't ever say you heard it from me."

"Never," I responded. I thought of all the implications and then asked, "So why was she riding with Lisa that last day of school?"

"They're related. They never really hung out, though, until Dez moved here."

"So, does Rip think you'd tell him who stole it?"

"I doubt it."

"Why was he here then?"

"Rip's not a bad dude. He knows everybody's going to find out anyway. So, he just wound up on my street."

"Then he had to try."

"Had to."

"Then he can keep trying."

"Listen up," Jack said and turned to me. "Even if I knew who stole that thing, I still wouldn't tell. There's three things you never do. You never rat out your own kin, and you never rat out your own countryman. Or hook up with your buddy's girl.

183

UNDER THE LIGHT OF FIREFLIES

That's the code. Got it?"

"Got it."

We left what little we'd done, and I went inside to grab some chips and watch TV. Mother had recently allowed us to put the telephones back on the hook so the outside world could reach us, and the phone rang before Jack could start spreading the news.

"Hello?" I answered.

"Tiger man. What's up?"

"Who's this?"

"Fenton. What're you doing?"

"Watching TV. What's going on?"

"Me and the fellas want to head to the go-cart track. You interested?"

I was surprised. With the dirty magazine trick, I'd only hoped to score enough points to keep from getting dogpiled at school, but here was another chance to increase my status. The question was whether my arm would hold up riding go-carts. Every day it felt stronger, but the doctor had said not to push it. Mother constantly monitored me. However, she wasn't home at that particular moment. Therefore, the answer was yes.

"What time would we leave?" I asked.

"Soon. Just head to my house and come around back."

"See you in a bit."

I put down the phone and ran up the stairs to my piggy bank. The pickings were slim, but I had managed to save a few bucks from the lawns I'd mowed earlier that spring. I grabbed my only dollars, then went and stuck my head in my brother's room where he was already on the phone, gossiping.

184

LEE SANDERS

"Jack, I'm heading out," I said.

He threw a wave without looking.

"Can you check on Sally?"

He squinted his eyes and shooed me off. I peeked in Sally's room, but she was still in Dad's office. I left the house and pedaled down the street.

After I crossed back into their neighborhood, I rode to a hidden lane tucked into the far back. At the very end next to the concrete culvert stood Fenton's house, hidden in the front by an eight-foot-tall fence. The property had a gate and a gravel driveway shielded by tall bushes and overgrowth, making it almost like going into a cave.

As I entered, his house appeared in the center of a lot nestled under tall hardwoods. It was built mid-century style with a slanted roof, big pane-less windows, and a second story rising on the backside. The roomy lot contained maybe three acres, and it opened in the rear to a grass lawn. On the far side of the house ran the culvert with small trees and brush growing along its bank. Away from that stood an enormous red oak stretching upward with big sturdy boughs. A treehouse rested in its heights. Someone had painted the heavenly bodies on the outside along with shooting stars trailing from corner to corner. The year 1959 was conspicuously written on its façade with the motto inscribed in lustrous silver, "To thine oaths be true"—which admittedly sounded more poetic than my treehouse club's motto, "Once a loafer, always a loafer."

Fenton and the guys barged out the back door without a greeting and told me to follow. We walked to the end of the gravel driveway towards a metal shack. Paneled and rusted, the

185

shack stood semi-covered with ivy and had random stacks of scrap iron and old lawn equipment piled on the side. Fenton strode to the door and banged on it.

"Yeah, who's there?" a man's voice yelled.

"It's Fenton. I'm with friends."

A few seconds later, we heard a lock unlatch. A man opened the door then stalked away. Fenton entered and spoke with him and afterward motioned us to come inside too.

The shop was a large single room with a concrete floor smudged with oil and the faint smell of gasoline wafting through the air. The walls were covered with steel scabbards and all kinds of tools including drills, picks, and chainsaws. In the back, a pool table sat before a security door that had an air conditioner rattling beside it. On the far wall, a tool chest was rolled away from a storage-closet stretching the length of the wall. Its door hung open, and on the side were steel levers that looked like the workings of a safe.

In the middle of the room stood a brawny man with a set jaw and thick blonde hair combed back in waves. He wore a sleeveless flannel shirt, and his blue jeans had a chain hanging from the belt to the hip pocket. Against the rear wall leaned an aluminum frame which he grabbed, carried over, and dropped into a stripped-out boat shell resting on supports. He then took a rubber mallet and tapped the frame into place.

"Get me that sander," he ordered Fenton.

Fenton grabbed a strip of sandpaper and a hand pad.

"Always leaving your crap around," he said.

The man gave him a dull look and snatched the sandpaper. He then tamped the hand pad and walked around inspecting the hull.

"Now bring me my beer and smoke."

Fenton dutifully went back again and got an ash tray and a golden can of beer.

"How's the boat coming?" Billy asked.

The man stooped down, sanded several spots, then ran his fingers over it. Grabbing the smoke from Fenton, he pulled a deep drag then crunched it out in the tray.

"She's coming," he said and sipped his beer. "You boys break anything today?"

"Not today," Billy responded.

The man gave a light smile as he set down the beer and hand pad, then wiped his hands with a rag.

"You watch your asses," he said. "I don't need no call from downtown, or some cop snooping around here 'cause you got dumb."

"We ain't in trouble," Fenton said.

"Do you need money?"

"I always need money."

"What for?"

"The go-cart track."

"Is Sloan taking you?"

"I didn't ask."

"In case you hadn't noticed, that grass outside ain't growing any shorter."

"I'll cut it later. I promise."

The man then walked to the giant metal closet and disappeared inside. A moment later he reappeared with a rifle and closed the heavy door. On the outside was a combination lock

UNDER THE LIGHT OF FIREFLIES

which he spun, pulled a lever, and turned a key. After tossing its oval key ring on his workbench, he took a seat at his workbench and broke down the rifle.

"Who's the new boy?" he asked.

"This here's Noah," Fenton said. "He lives by the park."

"Crossing the tracks, eh?" he said then turned to face me. "Renegade."

He sat with his back straight and a fist planted on his knee. Sinew covered his shoulders and neck, a few tattoos streaked his arms, and dog tags hung on his chest. He had sideburns, two deep wrinkles across his forehead, and eyes that said they'd seen a lot of things.

"What's your full name, son?"

"My name is Noah Ellis, sir," I replied.

His cheek twitched as he observed me for a second.

"I knew it was," he said. "You come to see that treehouse?"

"No sir," I answered correctly. I hadn't been invited yet.

He nodded and contorted his back until it cracked. "How's your momma doing?"

"She's fine."

"Is she working?"

"No sir."

He watched me for another second as I held his eye, then he reached into a rusted coffee can and pulled out a deck of playing cards whereafter the boys bristled and nudged each other. The man stretched his fingers, popped and strummed the cards, then from the bottom of the deck, he showed a Jack of Diamonds. After a few more shuffles on his knee, he pulled a random card and flung it skyward. We followed it up to where

188

it hit the ceiling, but it stopped and didn't come down. It stayed stuck there. The Jack of Diamonds. I didn't understand, then I noticed a few dozen other cards stuck to the ceiling in the same way.

"That's so boss," Billy said with a curled lip.

The man grinned, showing a blaze of silver from his teeth. I didn't know whether I was more impressed with the card trick or that an emotion had been evoked from Billy.

"You wanna see another trick?" the man asked.

"Who, me?" I replied.

"You're the one I'm looking at."

"Yes sir. That'd be great."

He grabbed another deck, fanned the cards out, and nodded at me.

"Pick one. But don't show me. Show the others."

I stepped to him, feeling the eyes of the room upon me as if I were the trick. I carefully pulled a card out and showed it to the others. Two of Hearts.

"Put it back in the deck," the man said.

I gently slid the card back. He then clapped the deck together and reshuffled it.

"Tap it twice," he said and held it out.

I tapped the deck twice. After that he turned to the worktable, spread them out, then picked one up and showed it.

"Is this the card?" he asked me, holding up the Three of Clubs.

"No sir," I said.

"What?"

"Sorry. That wasn't it."

UNDER THE LIGHT OF FIREFLIES

I looked at the others, but they had no reaction.

"Let me try this again."

He mixed and reshuffled, laid out more cards, then picked up another, being a Six of Spades.

"This is gotta be it," he said.

"No sir," I replied.

He suddenly slammed the deck on the table with a loud bang and stared around the room. Nobody moved. I didn't understand his reaction, so I stepped to a safer distance while he bounced his clinched fist on his leg.

"I *know* that was the card," he growled.

I didn't respond but stayed in place, waiting to see what he would do. As he rocked on his chair, he next started to snort and breathe unevenly. He coughed loudly and soon afterward his face turned red. Raising his hands, he began to clutch his throat and beat his chest with loud thumps.

I worriedly looked to the other guys, but they didn't do anything. The man hacked and hacked, banging on the table as the veins in his neck protruded. I was tempted to go and smack him on his back to help out, but then he let out one last cough and a wad popped out of his mouth onto the worktable. After catching his breath with a head shake, he picked up the wad and examined it like he was confused. Then little by little, he unfolded the paper ball until it was fully opened, and next he showed it to me.

"Is this your card?" he asked.

There in his hand laid the very playing card I had picked out, the Two of Hearts. I sat dumbfounded for a few moments.

"Yes, sir," I finally replied in disbelief.

190

"I didn't hear ya?"

"Yes sir!" I responded and looked towards the other guys who broke into stitches.

The man flashed that silver smile again then got up and strode to the fridge while I sat in a state of awe.

"You can say you saw something today," he said.

"Yes sir, I can."

The fellas pointed and laughed at me while I held up my hands with a bewildered smile. I walked over where Fenton gave me five and pushed me. The man came back and set another beer on the workbench then followed his silver chain to his hip and pulled out a stuffed wallet. He thumbed through, snapped out a twenty, and held it up. Everyone got quiet.

"Go-carts are on me, boys," he said.

"Right on!" Tyler exclaimed.

"Fenton, you ask your brother if he can drive you. Then you fill up his tank and pay for everybody's rounds. If that grass ain't cut by lunch tomorrow, you'll be paying me, and it won't be with dollars."

"Thanks, Pop."

"Now go on. I got work to do."

We all ambled happily to the door. Before I got there, though, I stopped and went back to the work bench.

"Thanks for spotting us the go-carts, Mr. Felcher," I said and reached out to shake. "And thanks for the neat trick."

He looked at my hand, then stood up and faced me.

"Call me Marshall," he said and shook my hand.

I blushed because I'd never called a grownup by their first name. He reached behind and grabbed the Two of Hearts.

After drying it off good with a rag, he handed it to me.

"Here. Stick this in your pocket and remember it."

"Yes sir."

He regarded me for a few long seconds before nodding.

"You look like Walt," he said.

I blinked and bowed my head.

"You go on now and have some fun. Don't get into trouble."

"I will. Thanks again."

He then showed me the door where I went outside and joined the others.

CHAPTER ELEVEN

Many miles down the interstate in an area called Pleasant Grove, a go-cart track sat hunkered on a sunbeaten tract of land paved over with asphalt. Although Fenton's dad had told him otherwise, we ended up biking there anyway because Fenton refused to ask for a ride. Paying to fill up his brother's gas tank wasn't exactly Fenton's style, neither was any thought for how far we all had to pedal in dripping sweat so he could keep that extra cash. When we arrived, we dropped our bikes at the fence and went inside the coolness of the concession building where Fenton approached the counter. I stayed to the side with the others, hoping he would cover my fee too, but I didn't count on it. I wasn't one of them. After he paid, he handed Tyler and Billy their tickets and they each left to grab a cart. Disappointed, I made for the counter myself, but then Fenton took a step back.

"Here ya go, dude," he said holding out a ticket. "Merry Christmas."

UNDER THE LIGHT OF FIREFLIES

Outside at the track, the go-carts were queued in the pit while a group of customers waited for the previous drivers to exit. Without pause, Fenton muscled right through the line towards a homely-looking ticket girl standing at the gate. After a few words, she sparked a grin then waved us up where we were allowed to pick out go-carts while the other customers had to watch.

"I get number six!" Fenton shouted. "Stay away from six."

Tyler found it and said, "You can have it, but only because your pop paid our fare."

"Thanks, sweetie," Fenton responded and pushed him aside. "Enjoy eating my dust."

Tyler and Billy found the next best carts, and I simply grabbed the nearest one and hopped in. We finished and the ticket girl dropped the rope to let the other customers inside. When everyone was strapped in, the girl told us to start our engines and drive to a column with a red blinking light. After we got lined up, the red light dropped through a series of colors until it reached green where we then hit the gas and the race was on. It took a few moments to get up to speed, but soon enough, we were running inside the thunder of engines and fumes while tiny rubber specks from the tires bounced off our faces.

The track had been designed like an hourglass with a hairpin turn on the top end and an elongated arch at the bottom. Before the end of the second lap, my arm started to throb, so until it loosened up, I chose to stay inside the pack and go with the flow. Not so with the other guys. They banged heavy and hard through the crowd without any regard, chasing the lead like wolves after a fawn.

194

The ride was anything but smooth with the steering wheel jittering like a buzz saw, but I did all right. I'd visited that track dozens of times and learned how to master the turns. After halfway, the pain became somewhat bearable, and so I climbed up the board past the slower drivers and little kids. After several laps, I managed to make it all the way into fourth place behind only Fenton, Billy, and Tyler, though Fenton had gained an insurmountable lead and even threatened to lap the slowest drivers.

Tyler and Billy were busy bobbing back and forth as they jockeyed each other for second place. Tyler was behind, weaving from side to side while Billy guarded him off. Then on a straightaway, Billy got a little wide which allowed Tyler to nose inside. When they hit the long turn, Billy was forced out, and while he fought to regain the lead, his back-end skirted sideways and Tyler zipped past. As Billy continued to drift, an opening appeared for me too. I decided to go for it. Billy shot a ferocious glare my way, but I disregarded it and managed to inch ahead by a hair.

The next turn was the hairpin, being impossible to take at full speed. So, mindful of my injury, I braked slowly into the turn. I hadn't pulled halfway through, though, when a loud blow sounded off as I got slammed from the rear. My head banged backwards off the stiff headrest, stunning me while needles of pain spider-webbed through my wounds. That could've only been Billy. He was after my head.

When he slammed me the second time, the pain effectively turned my arm into rubber. I somehow recovered, though, and managed to keep my lead through the backside and around the

UNDER THE LIGHT OF FIREFLIES

long turn, refusing to cede my place to Billy no matter how badly it hurt. At the check point on the straightaway, the ticket girl waved a yellow flag and shouted, "Final lap!" My left hand was done for, laying on my lap like a dead monkey's paw, but the contest would not be delayed. The hairpin was upon us.

I dreaded the blow that Billy lusted to deliver. So at the turn I passed on using my brakes, flying into it at full speed which sent me into a wild horsetail that allowed Billy to cut under. As I whipped side to side, I accidentally veered into his lane where once again he whacked me. Instead of knocking me into a spin, though, the effect sent me swerving towards the boundary which had been lined with tires. As I came within inches of clipping an edge, I jerked the steering wheel over and swooped blindly back onto the track. By sheer luck the lane was clear. I was able to regain control, but several drivers had scurried by me with Billy several lengths ahead.

As I was working back to full speed, a lone kid zoomed outside at the big turn where together we arced around the bend onto the last straightaway. Neck and neck, the two of us raced towards the finish line while bystanders mingled and watched. I saw that the other driver was a younger boy with a gritty face and crew-cut. He looked as determined as I was to finish ahead.

I had my foot all the way on the floor, but that's as fast as my rig would go. The kid crawled beside me. His cart was faster than mine, that much was clear. I knew that unless I took matters into my own hands, I'd lose. Normally I wouldn't have done what I was about to do, but I wasn't letting that boy beat me in front of the others.

Creeping closer to him, I turned my cart into his and nudged

196

the tires. The kid shot me a surprised look as I leered back, but he wouldn't brake. Thundering towards the finish, I jerked the wheel harder this time. The bang of our steel frames rang out. Iron railing zipped past his shoulder. Now he was sitting upright, a sallow look coming over him. Once more I swerved and popped him yet another time. Terrified, the boy finally let off the gas and backed down before he got knocked off the track. The finish line appeared, and I crossed over ahead.

Relived I hadn't lost to a child, I coasted down the lane and slowed to a stop at the end of the pit. My body was killing me. I had to wrestle my seatbelt off with the use of only one arm. After tumbling out of the cart, I dropped my helmet onto the rack and took a long breath. I was glad it was over.

Dazed from all the jittering, I walked through the pit while my arm dangled like a noodle. A man then appeared from the crowd with sharp, piercing eyes. He looked mad as he worked against the flow of people until he freed himself, then found me and stormed straight over.

"Who do you think you are, you little brat?!" he shouted.

All the bystanders stopped to listen while the man loomed in front of me, seething.

"I saw what you did!!" he cried with spit flying. "You tried to wreck my boy just so you could finish first, didn't you??"

I didn't answer, too stunned for a response.

"He could have slammed into the rails or flown into the crowd," he carried on, gesturing wildly. "He could've been killed for crying out loud!!"

His face had turned the color of deep crimson and his lips shivered. Behind him, I could see the boy with the crew-cut

UNDER THE LIGHT OF FIREFLIES

wearing a shameful frown.

"I wasn't going to wreck him," I replied with caution. "It was just a race. That's all."

The man scowled and ground his jaw. I thought for sure he'd collar me and report everything to a manager, or worse. But after noticing the gawking crowd, his color lightened, his face relaxed, and he blew a hard breath through his nostrils.

"A race," he said. "Was it really a race? My son's nine years old. I brought him here to have some good clean fun. But you bullies have to ruin it every time, don't you?"

I dropped my eyes and didn't look back up. I'd never been called a bully before, a title that I personally reserved for vermin. It didn't feel good. The man wanted to lecture me, probably worse than that, but the boy was embarrassed enough as he waited under the eyes of the onlookers. After a prolonged silence, the man backed away and left without another word, putting his arm around his boy as they walked off. The other guys loved it, of course, and snickered while the father and son passed by. All I could think about was how everything that man had told me was true.

"The tiger man..." Fenton said while I walked up. "Culling out the weak ones. That's cool."

"His dad sure freaked out," I said.

"Forget that jerk," Billy replied.

"If that boy can't hang," Tyler said smugly, "then he can keep his wimpy butt at home. Right, guys?"

"Fer sho' right," agreed Fenton. "You can either run with the big dogs," then in unison they all bellowed, "*or sit on the porch with the puppies! Whoof! Whoof! Whoof!*"

The crowd stopped and looked again, holding us in the same regard that all loudmouths are held.

"I guess I didn't come in last place at least," I said.

"You still got whooped, though," Fenton teased.

"Next time, I get the good cart," Tyler said.

"That horsey-looking ticket girl likes me. I've got a permanent reservation."

We biked back the same way we came with my dead arm slowly regaining life, giving me hope that perhaps I hadn't ruined it. When we got near my neighborhood, I was unsure if I should go home or continue on with them. So I hung back, waiting to get sent away, but they said nothing.

Once we'd crossed into their neighborhood, we cruised down Fenton's drive and disappeared through the brush onto his property. At his house, Fenton took us into the kitchen and gave us each a cola from the fridge. After drinking it, we went back outside to the big red oak where they climbed up some nailed-on boards which served as the ladder to the treehouse. As the other guys made their way to the top, I remained at the bottom, still uninvited. Tyler was the last to climb up. When he'd made it inside, the trap door slammed shut behind him. That was that. I trudged to my bicycle, ready to leave, when I heard my name called. I looked up and saw Fenton sitting in a window.

"What are you doing, dude?" he asked.

I shrugged my shoulders.

"Is your arm too busted to climb up?" he asked.

"No. I can make it."

"Good, because nobody's gonna carry you."

199

UNDER THE LIGHT OF FIREFLIES

Then he left the window open. That was the invitation, I supposed. So, I went to the tree and looked at the job. His treehouse was a lot higher than mine. There were nine rungs leading to the door, all spaced a few feet apart. My left arm felt better, though still not strong, but being invited into their inner sanctum was a big deal. Once again, I felt compelled to go.

It was rough climbing since I only had the use of one good hand. A whole minute passed before I made it to the last rung. I stopped and looked to the ground almost twenty feet below. My stomach quivered. To knock on the door meant I had to bang it with my good hand while I balanced precariously with my body flat against the trunk.

"Yo!" I yelled. "Open the door! Open up!"

I heard some folks mumble, but nothing happened. So I banged some more. More mumbles. Finally, I shouted loudly, "Hey, man!!! I've only got one arm! Open the door!"

At last, someone stomped over and pulled up the hatch.

"Well, that only took a half a century," Fenton said as he lurched over me. "You're gonna have fun getting back down."

"I'll need help getting inside first."

"And if I don't help?" he asked.

"Come on, man."

After pausing a second, he took mercy on me. Without thinking, he reached down and jerked my weak arm, causing me to flinch.

"Not that one, bro," I groaned. "That's my bad arm."

"What the hell?" he said and reached for my other hand then pulled me up with a grunt.

200

LEE SANDERS

Ungraceful yet indifferent, he dragged and scraped me inside with the same delicacy he'd give a hooked tuna. The other guys watched with mild pity. Once I got all the way in, I rolled onto my knees and brushed the dirt and bark off.

"I thought tigers could climb," Billy remarked.

"Does our club let people inside who can't even make it up the tree?" Tyler asked.

I didn't humor them. Instead, I found a piece of floor to sit on and checked out the joint. It was a lot bigger than my treehouse and had the trunk going right through the middle. They'd decked the place with candles in wine bottles that had wax dribbling down their sides. Against a wall sat a small table with knives sticking around a skull-ashtray. Posters of rock bands and old movie stars hung on the walls. There were chintzy sheets for curtains, beanbags for chairs, a jambox, a stop sign, swords stacked in a corner, and glittery stars strewn across the plywood ceiling.

Fenton got comfortable in one of the beanbags and they all regarded my presence within their hallowed space. Billy slapped a chest and opened it. Reaching inside, he pulled out a magazine and tossed it over. That was the only generosity he ever showed me.

"That's from *our* stash," he said.

It was a magazine whose cover I remembered from the corner store sitting on that forbidden rack. As I opened and flipped through its pages, women appeared. Naked women. Now this was a real intrigue. I'd only seen a dirty magazine twice before. Once was at Dusty's house when we got caught by his dad before we ever got going; and another time was in

201

UNDER THE LIGHT OF FIREFLIES

the woods, but the pictures had been mud-stained and faded. This one, though, remained in pristine condition, and I had license to examine it page by page which I proceeded to do. Then I heard a snort.

"What's so funny?" I asked.

"Your eyes are glued to that mag," Fenton said.

"Yeah, it's like he's never seen one before," Tyler quipped. "Does it make you blush?"

Slightly embarrassed, I closed the cover, not wanting to appear impressed, but which proved precisely the opposite. Then other voices came from under the treehouse followed by a loud bang on the door. I jerked upright and quickly pushed the magazine aside before the hatch flung up. An older teenager next appeared and pulled himself into the room.

"What's up, hooligans?" he asked.

Wagging his eyebrows, he turned back to the door and took hold of a dainty hand that had reached through. A girl's face followed, and with some help she made it inside too. Afterward, the guy went around to slap five with the others, laughing and poking them as he did. When he made it to me, he paused and cordially held out his hand.

"Greetings," he said. "I'm Sloan Felcher. And that's my girl, Crystal."

"Hi," I responded and shook his hand. "I'm Noah Ellis."

One of his eyebrows cocked as he held my hand.

"Welcome to the clubhouse," he said. "It's good having you here."

Sloan sported curly blonde hair and a clean shave. He was handsome with smooth, clear skin and a smile like a set

202

of pearls. The sleeves had been cut out of his shirt much like Marshall's, though his build was thinner, and he wore cutoff green fatigues. His eyes drooped slightly at the corners from a face that came across forever clever and cool. Although his girl was cute, she had pallid skin with dark circles under her eyes like she never saw the sun, and she donned a black concert tee tied into a ball at the bottom. After the two of them eased onto some pillows against the wall, she reached into her purse and pulled out a long cigarette, lit it, then fiddled with a strand of her hair.

"Ain't I seen this boy before?" she asked Sloan, smacking her gum.

"Maybe," Sloan replied. "You like hanging with the Little Leaguers, right?"

The others laughed.

"I know I've seen him somewhere," she said and eyed me closely.

Sloan sat there a moment, waiting for her realization which did not come, then he scratched behind his ear.

"This here's the kid brother of Jack Ellis," he said to her plainly. "Jack drives that Monte Carlo."

Her face lightened and her eyes spread wide as she now understood. Then she took a quick drag and fiddled with her hair some more.

"His dad and my pop played ball together back in the day," Sloan added with a side look at me. "I hear Noah's a baller himself."

I drew my eyes away because of the false recognition. He'd obviously not heard that I didn't make the all-stars. Glancing

203

away, I noticed the dirty magazine beside me, and I tensed, not wanting to be connected with such an unsavory item after such a hospitable welcome.

"Noah almost killed a pip squeak at the go-cart track today," said Fenton.

"He didn't want to lose that sixth-place spot," Tyler added.

Sloan drew his mouth down and nodded in approval. "You drove the whole race with that bum arm?" he asked.

I nodded yes and said, "I could've done better, though."

"You can always do that. Just don't let these boys push you too hard. They're jackals."

I looked at Billy who rested his head against the wall without the slightest expression. I questioned what went on inside his head.

"So, Mr. Fenton," Sloan then began with his hands hanging off his knees. "You and me got some business to tend to."

"No, we don't," Fenton said with his arms crossed, looking away.

"Oh yeah, we do. You were supposed to fill up my gas tank."

"Nuh uh. You didn't give me a ride."

"And you didn't come to ask."

"The deal was that you had to give me a ride."

"No sir," said Sloan and tapped his finger on the floor. "You didn't follow orders, little bro. So, cough up a ten-spot right now."

"I don't have it."

"Then you better find it."

"Let's throw the dice."

"Boy, if we throw the dice then it's gonna be double or

LEE SANDERS

nothing, and I know you don't have *that*."

Instead of owing Sloan ten bucks, it would be twenty, and that was a bad bet for Fenton. Although Fenton's big brother had just graduated, he was already a legend. In high school, Sloan hosted massive keg parties with set-ups for poker games. He even built his own felt craps table. I heard that he'd cleared five hundred bucks one night being the house. Upon turning eighteen during his senior year, he went straight to hustling pool at the bars in Arkansas. It was rumored that one night he was shooting at a place called Mother's on State Line when he got called out. Some trucker was sick of getting duped by a squirrelly teenager. After a particularly degrading loss, he decided to destroy Sloan. That didn't meet with much resistance from the Mother's crowd. In fact, a bartender helped pull him into the back. Sloan was about to make a visit to the hospital or worse, but he forfeited back his winnings and sweet talked his way out of it. He later smoothed it over with the owner who let him come back, and Sloan continued to gamble. During the summers, he always worked for his dad at their trucking yard. Now he'd graduated high school, that job went full time. No college for Sloan. With that in mind, money wasn't the issue with his little brother. It was about principle.

"Pop just gave you a promotion," Fenton argued. "And a raise."

"You're right. I'm filthy rich. But I did a favor for Dad, and he owed me. Now you owe me. So, fork it over or roll the dice."

Sloan was done with arguing, and little brother knew it. Fenton stalled a moment for the sake of defiance, then jumped to his feet with his arms swung wide. Sloan watched with drab

UNDER THE LIGHT OF FIREFLIES

curiosity. After his half-cocked show of prowess, Fenton pulled out his wallet and flicked a ten onto the floor several feet away. Sloan responded with that beautiful smile of his.

"You did the right thing, little bro," he said. "You don't want to throw dice with a fox like me."

He then motioned to his girl who scooted forward and snatched the bill. After she handed it over, Sloan kissed the money with a loud smack and grinned at Fenton.

"Thanks for the cash, kiddo," he said. "My tank's already full. Enjoy mowing that yard."

The other guys turned their heads in muffled laughter as Fenton balled his fists, incensed that there was nothing he could do. The next instant, though, another knock came at the hatch, this one much quieter than before. Everyone paused. Sloan glanced at his little brother dubiously with a thumb pointed at the hatch.

"You expecting somebody?" Sloan asked.

"No," Fenton replied as he marched past. "But we do have our admirers."

He pulled up the door, looked, then spoke with cheerful surprise. Next, another girl's hand appeared. Fenton helped her up, but with much more consideration than he'd given me. As I wondered who it could be, a shock of light auburn hair soon appeared that I vaguely recognized. After she got farther inside, my suspicion deepened, and I told myself *no*. It couldn't be. Then her full body pulled into view. My suspicions were right. There was my first ever kiss, Jamie Jimmer, coming right through the door as sure as the sunrise. My blood turned to ice.

Straining and wiggling until she made it fully inside, she sat

206

on the edge of the hatch and checked her nails. Billy and Tyler passed a sarcastic glance while I turned my face the other way. I knew it was inevitable she would see me. I only hoped that after she did, she wouldn't come and sit beside me. As it was, though, Fenton moved another bean bag next to his and told her to sit there. She said a polite hello to everyone and took a seat. Then it got quiet. Real quiet.

I kept my face down, but I could feel her eyes upon me, wondering why I was there, which is exactly what I was wondering about her. Everybody knew that she and I went to school together. They waited to hear what we would say, but we stayed quiet.

When I finally did turn to her, she was leaning forward with an unblinking stare planted firmly upon me. To her, it was all too obvious. She understood what I wanted without even asking. What I wanted was her secrecy and her pretense. For her to play dumb and keep her mouth shut. Though she said she didn't kiss and tell, I knew that she didn't care one iota if the whole world should learn about our little dalliance. She was impervious to shame, fully aware she was a pariah, but took pleasure where she could find it. It was true I'd tasted the fruit and even liked it. But unlike her, I needed to hide it. She knew every bit of that. I was her hostage.

"Hello, Jamie," I offered with a hard swallow.

"Hiiiii Noaaahhh," she replied in a long croak.

We didn't say anything else, but just sat there. I could feel the seconds ticking off as everyone watched us.

"You two are in the same grade," Tyler said and wriggled his fingers. "Do y'all play together at recess?"

UNDER THE LIGHT OF FIREFLIES

Jamie leaned back and flipped her hair before answering, "Noah sat in front of me in homeroom."

"Ooohh, anything naughty we should know about?"

It was warm in the treehouse. Warmer still as blood flushed my face while sweat formed on my brow. Jamie sat carelessly, though, wearing another tube top with short shorts to expose her tan. She passed on a response. Feeling compelled to answer, I made a clumsy mistake and attempted a jest.

"I've had a huge crush on Jamie ever since the fourth grade," I said. "But she won't even give me the time of day. Heh."

No one laughed. Not one person smiled. Trying to give it some juice, I jokingly raised my hands and wagged my shoulders. It was the most awkward silence I'd ever known. I felt like crawling away.

"Ha ha!!" Jamie then burst out. "You're such a little liar. Why would you even say that?"

I coughed a few times and ran my fingers through my hair, wanting nothing more than to jump out the window.

"It was only a joke, Jamie," I said.

"I know but it was stupid."

Tyler giggled at that. He loved insults.

"Fine," I said back to her. "I'll remember that next time you need an answer with your vocabulary quiz."

"Oh, please," she replied with an eye roll. "I don't need your silly help in vocabulary."

"Now who's the liar?"

Then a cackle sounded out as Sloan clapped his hands. He elbowed Crystal who gave a shallow grin and flicked her ash.

"Ahhh, the tangled affairs of elementary school," Sloan said

208

philosophically. "So many memories."

Fenton squinted, clearly annoyed.

"Just drop it, Noah," he said. "Nobody cares about your sixth-grade bull crap."

"I didn't do anything."

"I said drop it."

"Fine."

Then something happened I didn't expect. Fenton turned to Jamie and rubbed her back in front of everybody. They exchanged guilty smiles, and she moved closer. He left his hand there, and that's when it occurred to me. They were seeing each other. Fenton and Jamie had become a thing. And suddenly, right before me, she transformed. Her beauty deepened. A sultry glow seemed to hover around her now, and her cryptic allure became an electric magnet. It reminded me of the first day of school when Jill had breezed into class wearing a bright yellow dress. Something I'd never noticed instantly blossomed right before me. Here it was happening again, except this time with a girl who'd had a crush on me. Where I once thought she was strange, she now seemed exotic. A tinge of jealousy pricked my heart.

"Sooo..." she said with her hands placed primly on her knees. "Have you heard the big news?"

"No," Fenton replied as he gazed at her. "Tell us."

"Well, remember last year when someone from Arkansas stole our tiger?"

Everyone nodded.

"Guess what? Last night, somebody stole their hog away from them!"

UNDER THE LIGHT OF FIREFLIES

"What?!" Fenton exclaimed. "Are you positive?"

"I'm very positive. They don't have a clue who did it. I thought you all might know. Do you?"

The guys all checked each other and said no. Sloan and Crystal whispered as intrigue swept the room.

"I can't wait to see what they do with it," she added. "Hopefully they don't get busted."

Everyone chattered and discussed the news. Even Billy himself seemed interested. After all, thievery was of the highest virtues.

"Well, that calls for a little party," Fenton said and rubbed his hands together. "Sloan, did you bring your stash?"

Then the room settled down and waited on the answer.

"What you talking about, boy?" Sloan responded with a hard look.

"You know what I mean." There was a long pause, then he asked, "What's the problem?"

Sloan held him with a death glare, but Fenton sat puzzled. Sloan gave a slight nod towards me. Fenton glanced my way then back to his brother with the same mystified expression.

"Stars," Sloan commanded. "We've got a call to order. It's time for some church."

"Right now?" Fenton asked incredibly.

"You heard me." Then to Jamie and me he said, "I don't mean to be rude, kids, but you've got to go."

Jamie checked with Fenton, but he didn't contest his brother this time. I felt relieved and marched straight for the door without thinking about the magazine, but nobody said anything. Jamie stood and exchanged a few words with Fenton,

210

then followed me to the hatch.

I pulled it open and peered at the roots below. My head felt light. It was a long way down. Plus, the first rung wasn't easy to reach without the use of both arms, but Sloan came over to assist.

He grabbed a handful of my shirt and told me not to worry. I took a breath and felt around with my toes until I found the first rung. Gripping the trunk with my good arm, I scraped painfully down to the next rung, then the next, and at last to the bottom. Once there, I waited on Jamie to make sure she got down safely. I offered my hand to help her, but she didn't take it.

"Are you okay?" I asked as she scooted past.

"Of course I am. It's not my arm that doesn't work."

"Where are you going?"

"Wherever."

She moved at a brisk pace to her bicycle. Once there she quickly jumped on, got straight into gear, and in the next instant she'd disappeared through the gate. After wrangling with my own bike, I eventually got it going and raced away to catch her. Once outside the property, I located her far up the street and I hit the pedals to chase her down.

"You're sure in a hurry to get out of there," I said as I finally caught her, breathing heavily.

"You don't want to be seen with me anyway. Remember?"

"I never said that."

She kept riding without regard, the early evening turning her brown eyes into shades of amber.

"So..." I asked casually. "What's up with you and Fenton?"

UNDER THE LIGHT OF FIREFLIES

"He's a boy and I'm a girl."

"I know that, but is he your boyfriend now?"

"I couldn't say. Why, are you jealous?"

"No."

"Good for you. Let's just leave it at that."

"That's not why I'm asking. I'm just looking out for you."

"Give me a break."

"I'm being serious."

"Please. I told you that you and I weren't boyfriend-girlfriend. I thought you'd kissed a girl before."

As always, Jamie didn't mince words. She knew the truth. Still, I had to play the game.

"I know we're not boyfriend-girlfriend," I said. "What are we, though?"

"We could've been friends if you weren't so stuck up."

"I'm not stuck up."

"Yes, you are."

"I've always been friendly to you."

"You've been polite. There's a difference." Then she sighed. "Look, just forget about it. It doesn't matter anyway."

I never thought I'd want Jamie. That was before I'd seen her affection with Fenton. Even though I chose to hide it, I felt a fondness from our first kiss. Now, even that was spoiled.

"You'd better watch out for Fenton," I warned her.

"Stop it. You sound desperate."

"I mean it."

"Why do you even care?"

"You're not in their club. They're only loyal to each other. They'll betray you."

"That's not how they are with me," she said.

"You'll get hurt."

"You're such a pest."

"Fenton doesn't like you."

"Go away!!"

"Everyone there thinks you're a freak."

That did it. Her eyelids fluttered and her chin crinkled up. Turning away so I couldn't see, she moved her hand to her face and trembled. All of this from a lie. I'd never heard those guys say she was a freak. It was a word that I knew could cause pain. Now, I felt guilty. I wanted us to stop so I could explain, so I could start over, but she kept onward with her wobbly legs straining to turn the pedals.

"I'm sorry," I said. "I didn't mean that. It's just that those guys... They're a hard bunch. They don't care about other people's feelings."

After a few moments she turned back. Her cheeks were wet, and her eyes soft. My arrow had struck its target.

"I know what people think of me," she said. "But I can't help it."

"You're okay, Jamie. You're just ahead of your time."

"That's what my mother says," she said with a head shake. Then she turned to me as we slowly rode and asked, "Why are you hanging out with them? So you can look at dirty magazines?"

"No," I said with a touch of embarrassment. "I was visiting because there's nobody else to hang with."

"I know what that's like. What happened to Dusty?"

"He's still playing baseball. His all-star team made it all the way to the championship in Georgia."

213

UNDER THE LIGHT OF FIREFLIES

"And Sam?"

"He went to stay with his cousins. His dad's still afraid of the tiger. Probably still afraid of polio too."

She laughed. It made me feel better that she had laughed.

We crossed into our neighborhood and glided down a shadowy street full of pines. The sun had fallen behind the trees, and the thrum of crickets and cicadas was all around. On a porch, some folks were visiting and drinking iced tea while smoke billowed from a barbecue grill.

"Noah," she said, unsure. "I've been wanting to tell you something, but I haven't because I don't believe in going behind other people's backs. Plus, I know that you and Dusty are best friends. And I know how much you like Jill."

My head shot sideways, but she showed no expression.

"What are you talking about?" I asked.

"Like I said, I don't like being a snitch."

She slowed to a stop, and I did too. Her eyes were red from tears, but her face was very serious. My pulse quickened while I waited for what she would say next.

"Tell me," I said. "What is it?"

She took a breath and blew it out, then crossed her arms.

"You know how Jill, Dusty, and I attended the ARC program on Fridays?" she asked.

"Yeah. So?"

"We sat at lab tables over there. Dusty, Jill, and I shared the same table all year. They sat next to each other. You knew that, right?"

No, I didn't know that. Immediately, I became confused why I didn't. Every Friday for the whole year, Dusty and

214

Jill had sat next to each other at an off-campus program? My guts churned.

"Go on," I moaned.

"Just so you'll know, Noah, I'm not trying..."

"Save the sympathy and get on with it!"

She put her hands up, taken aback, and then slowly continued.

"Okay," she said. "Dusty flirted and teased with Jill every time we got to class. It never stopped. He was constantly joking and tickling her."

"Tickling?" I asked, my voice tightening. "Did Jill push him off? Did she get mad at him?"

"No. She didn't. She played along. I figured they had a thing for each other."

A thing for each other? *No, not that,* I thought. Please, anything but that. How could this be? Dusty had never flirted with Jill in front of me, and Jill never appeared to like him in the slightest. No rumors existed about them at school. No mention of romance. Not one clue. Those facts, though, didn't allay my quickening dread. Whether Jamie's interpretation was true or not, the poison had entered my veins. Twisted ideas started to form inside my head. Like maybe they'd always been a thing and were only keeping it secret because they knew I had a crush on her. Probably the whole town knew. They were laughing. The thought of it pierced my soul and the air went out of me.

"Noah, are you okay?" Jamie asked and put her hand on my back.

"I don't understand."

UNDER THE LIGHT OF FIREFLIES

I held onto the bike frame. My head swam with a thousand sick thoughts, my reality shaken, and my hope torn.

"Does anybody else know?" I asked.

"I couldn't tell you."

"Why not?"

"Nobody speaks to me, Noah."

I sat there wincing from the images of those two together.

The thoughts of my best friend with the girl I loved tightened like a rope around my heart. There had to be a reason. They couldn't betray me. That was conspiracy.

"I shouldn't have told you," Jamie said.

I straightened up and tried to settle my emotions. "It's okay," I said.

"Are you sure?"

"It's better that you did."

"The truth isn't always friendly."

"Sometimes you get what you ask for."

"It's only because you're so decent."

I looked at her, but she had no expression. I couldn't get a read. We sat there a moment in the lull before dusk. I gazed blankly into the distance. I didn't know what to do.

"I've got to go," she said. "It's getting late."

"Okay."

"I hope you'll be all right."

"I'll try."

With a smile of pity, she got on her pedals and left. I stayed in the street, confused, wondering what to do. At the house beside me, neighbors visited and laughed while the smell of smoke swirled all around. I rode away with no direction in mind.

CHAPTER TWELVE

The sad eyes of the Hotel Grim stood watch over downtown Texarkana like a ghost living in a graveyard. The sparkle and hope which once resonated in them had now faded to black, leaving only empty windows staring into the past. Their departed majesty still held a flicker, though, and I could picture a dapper young man standing next to a grand staircase while he waited for his bride to descend. They would cross to the rail station happy and excited, board the train for New Orleans, and disappear down the tracks, speaking only of the golden days which lay ahead of them and nothing of what they'd left behind.

"Did you know that Bonnie and Clyde once stopped by that hotel?" Mr. Roundtree asked as he pointed his scissors towards the plate glass window.

"You mean the gangsters?" I replied.

"You bet," he said with a wink as he snipped my hair. "They happened to stop by the hotel restaurant for lunch. Bonnie ordered a sandwich. Didn't get to finish it, though. She was spotted right off, and they had to high tail it out of there."

"Did the police catch them?"

"No, sir. They slipped away."

"Why's the hotel so run down now?"

"Folks stopped riding the train, and it's not like this town is Shangri-La. It was too expensive to keep up, so they closed down. It's condemned now."

Since as far back as I could remember, I'd gone downtown for my haircut at a barber shop called Hank's. When my dad was alive, he'd take me there for a trim and then afterward we'd grab breakfast and explore the sidewalks in that empty old district. All that remained were a few scattered shops, bailbonds offices, and the bi-state justice center. Nevertheless, a type of romance still lingered in those tired gray streets with their abandoned buildings and storefronts. It was like walking through an old photograph, and something that I missed doing with my father.

Just then the bells on the front door jangled as someone came in. With my head tilted downward, I was unable to see who it was, but Mr. Roundtree let out a grunt when the door closed. He didn't greet the man. Instead, he told him to take a seat in the corner.

"I'll just grab a shoeshine while I wait," the man replied.

"Suit yourself."

Mr. Roundtree spun me away from the front of the store. I now faced an adjacent barber chair which sat empty, save for a newspaper resting on its seat. I didn't think much of it at first, but as I eyed the paper, the headline caught my attention:

Manslaughter Case Dropped Against Russian.

I sat puzzled by the pronouncement and strained to read the story, but it was too far away. Something dramatic had happened, though, because headlines didn't lie. Manslaughter case dropped. Did they simply let that Russian man, Henry, go free? Judge Caraway would never allow that. Someone had to pay the price. That's the way it was supposed to work, just like on television. Still, I remembered Mother saying that the man could be innocent. Her words carried weight, but it still seemed impossible to me that two people could die, another could get mauled, and it would all go unpunished. Deep inside, though, I suspected it was true.

After the barber finished, he powdered my neck and brushed the hair off. Letting me check my look in the mirror, he then whisked off the gown and I climbed out. As he escorted me towards the front, he began to ask me a lot of questions about the new school year which I hadn't thought about since my summer was only halfway over. Mother had given me five dollars to pay with. As we made it to the register, though, Mr. Roundtree politely refused the money.

"But I'm supposed to tip," I said and stopped.

"This one's on the house, son," he replied, trying to pull me to the door. "I insist."

"Then can you make change for the soda machine?"

He seemed in a quandary over my request, but just then I looked to the shoe-shine chair and caught the gleam of freshly polished boots. The man wearing them planted his feet on the floorboard and stood up. A fancy silk suit brushed his boot tops, his fingers flashed with diamonds, and a heavy gold watch hung on his wrist. With a sculpted jaw and cutting eyes, his handsome face belied the wiry hair that swept across his scalp. He deposed himself with an air of self-awareness and swagger, and when he stepped down, his head lolled casually from side to side. With all that, he also transmitted a great deal of respect and appreciation as if barbers, shoe-shine men, and common folk were members of his own guild. He was Clive Longbranch, the defense attorney. He pulled out his wallet, paid, then dropped a generous tip into the jar.

Mr. Roundtree tried again to pull me towards the door, but it was too late. Mr. Longbranch and I had already met eyes. The attorney's face fell and his brows slowly bunched together while he wrestled with what he should say. It would take more than words could ever do, though. All activity in the shop had stopped too, and the somber faces of the barbers stood there like the faces of the one true jury. I drew close to Mr. Roundtree who put his hand upon my shoulder. Since I was a boy, I was strictly taught never to say anything bold or rude to an adult, and I didn't have the courage to start then, but standing before me was a very bad man. A man who'd gotten that commie off the hook—that commie who'd been responsible for making me the way I was, and for the way Connor was not.

Before anyone could say a word, I suddenly broke away and rushed through the door, the bells jangling behind me. Mr. Roundtree followed outside and called after me. I didn't look back. While Mother and Sally sat in a bakery window and ate pastry, I bolted past and ran deeper into the slate streets of Texarkana, a ghost-town etched out of concrete where nothing happened, and whatever had happened was sucked

LEE SANDERS

backward into its own beginning. Frozen in a final gasp, a gallery of boarded storefronts stood idly by as I vaulted the transom into the null. Up above, the lonely eyes of the Hotel Grim watched me tread those empty sidewalks with only my shadow next to me, following the path of a million footsteps from which no memory remained.

Mother found me sitting before the federal courthouse and post office—the entrance and exit to downtown. The bench was a novelty place for photos where the border of Texas and Arkansas joined in the middle, allowing the visitor to sit in two states at once. Through revolving doors, folks milled in and out of the ashen granite building as they tended their ceaseless routines.

The sun was hot while I sat there with a newspaper I'd bought. Sally, normally so cute and lively, sensed that something was wrong and came and sat respectfully next to me. I handed the paper to my mother. After reading the headline, she set it quietly on the bench and laid her arm over my shoulders. We stayed a moment as cars circled around and around the building while the glass doors opened and closed.

"What do you say we grab an ice cream cone?" Mother asked.

Sally liked that idea and looked hopefully at me.

"That's okay," I said. "Could you drop me off at the bowling alley instead?"

"Are you meeting someone there?"

"No. I want to play some pinball."

"Just promise not to bowl."

"I bowl with my good arm."

221

UNDER THE LIGHT OF FIREFLIES

"I still don't want you to push it."

"Sure."

College Bowl was a windowless world of cool air filled with the smell of lane-oil and the clatter of ten-pins. After I arrived, I went to get quarters at the back counter where the normal coterie of thugs shot pool and drank beer. Beside them stood a table for juniors, and playing a game with a friend hulked a big black kid with an afro.

With pensive, searching eyes, he lined up his shot and knocked the ball into the pocket. He was Donovan Johnson, my old teammate. His buddy had his back to me, but as he moved down the table to give Donovan another shot, I recognized that long-limbed figure right away. He turned to the side, and sure enough, there stood Dusty.

After getting my change, I went over. With a squint and a long smile, Donovan observed my approach like a painting had come to life. He laid his stick down and strode over to greet me.

"Check it out!" he said. "Noah Ellis! My man. Best center fielder in the city."

"What's up, Donovan?"

Dusty walked over with a big smile on his face too.

"Old Rosie," he said and nudged me. "Where've you been hiding?"

"I've been at the house for a few weeks," I replied.

He and Donovan both nodded.

"Was the cabin fun?" Dusty asked.

"It was okay."

"How's your grandma?"

"We call her *Grand'Mere*. She's alive and well."

"Were any girls down there?"

"A few."

"Did you meet one?"

I didn't answer right away. Instead, I tried to read Dusty to see if it was possible what Jamie had told me about Jill and him was true, but I couldn't tell. That didn't dispel any anguish. On the contrary, the thought of it stung me bitterly.

"No," I said.

"Not even one??"

I shook my head no.

"Why are you here bowling?" I asked Donovan.

"Coach Pritchett," he replied and pointed across the lobby. "He brought us here as a last get together for the team."

Pritchett, the Judas head coach. At a few of the bowling lanes, about a dozen kids from the all-star team were eating popcorn and banging balls down the alley.

"So the tournament's over," I said.

"We finished a few days ago," Donovan replied. "We got home yesterday evening after driving all day and night. I didn't think we'd ever make it."

"How'd it go?"

"We got gypped. During the semis, an outfielder for Tennessee dropped the ball and rolled over it, but the umps missed it and called us out. We still made third place, though."

"Did you hit any home runs?"

"I got three. Dusty got one too! He won a game for us."

My face burned at the report.

"We all thought you got gypped too, bro," Donovan told

UNDER THE LIGHT OF FIREFLIES

me. "You deserved to be there instead of all those coaches' kids. Ain't that right, Dusty?"

"Absolutely," he said then gave me another prod. "Everybody knows it."

I stared at the ground a moment longer, trying to let the blood flow out of my face.

"Do you want to say hello to the other guys?" Donovan asked. "They'd love to see you."

"Yeah, man," Dusty said. "I bet Coach would even let you bowl a game."

"Thanks, but no thanks," I said.

"So, what are you going to do?"

"Play some other games."

A roar erupted from the lanes. One of the kids must have hit a strike. Dusty and Donovan turned to look.

"Let's talk in a few," Dusty said afterward. "I'll check with you before we leave."

They left to go bowl, and I left towards the toilet. A little hallway ran between the foot lockers and the bathrooms. At the end of it stood a steel door for an exit. I passed by the men's room, hit the door, and marched straight outside.

Behind the building flowed a wide creek filled with weeds and scattered trash. A tree grew on its bank. I sat down in the shade to spy the parking lot. After a half hour, I saw the team walk outside and pile into the back of the coach's truck. Dusty and Donovan took a spot against the cab. After they drove off, I rose and headed back inside the alley with a pocketful of change.

In the game room sat an assortment of video games and

224

pinball machines. There was one pinball machine in particular called Sling Shot that was the only game I'd ever mastered, and I'd spent plenty of time and money to figure it out. Pumping quarters into these machines was where a lot of my allowance and lawn-mowing money ended up. As I walked in, however, my machine was already taken by a bulky young teenager. He had his ball cap turned backwards while he worked the flippers and kicked the game in disgust. I knew this guy, but I was surprised to see him there alone.

"How's it going, Fenton?" I asked as I walked up.

He glanced at me but didn't answer and kept playing. On the game, he'd made it to the third stage where a player could win an extra ball or even a new round. He banged it off some bumpers with a cha-ching and scored a bonus. He was getting close to a big payoff when he caught the pinball and held it in place. He aimed and took his shot. It missed the target, though, then banged around the top and ricocheted down the middle past his flippers. Game over.

"No!!" Fenton hollered and smacked the machine. "I can't ever get past this stupid level."

I'd never known Fenton to be anything but an expert at whatever he was doing. He was an exceptional athlete and smart too, even if he didn't make good grades. He was the sort of student who did well on tests but didn't see the purpose in homework.

"It's not easy," I said. "But did you know that left bumper turns into triple bonus when you make it to five-thousand?

"Oh yeah?"

"Yep. So what you do is just tag the bumper as many times

as you can until the shields pop up at the top. If you knock those down and land it in the bowl, you'll get a triple on everything. Before you know it, you've won an extra game."

"But the chute is an easier bonus," he said.

"I know, but if you miss and hit that top rail, the ball kicks down and rolls right past you."

After considering my words a moment, he stepped aside with an open arm and said, "All right then, hot-shot. Let's see you do it."

His challenge was not unexpected. I stepped forward and slid my quarter in, then waited as the machine charged up with bells and whistles. After the ball popped into place, I pulled the plunger and sent it flying onto the board. Just my luck, though, because before I'd scored hardly any points, the ball kicked down and zipped into the trap. Then the exact same thing happened on the second ball.

"Great shooting, dude," Fenton said. "You're not even gonna make it to five-thousand."

"It'll be all right. It can't happen three times in a row."

This was my last turn. I shot the ball again, but this time it missed the rail and rolled down softly to my flipper. I tagged the bumpers and hit a few targets up top for some solid scores. Then the ball luckily rolled into a loaded seat which triggered two thousand free points. Just like that I was at five thousand, ready for the big numbers.

The ball kicked perfectly to me again, and now I began hitting the bonus bumper. The recoil on it was weak, sending the ball directly back to me each time, or sometimes it dropped on the backside where it would rapid-fire for more easy points.

I knocked that bumper again and again like a punching bag. The scoring sound of ding-ding-ding blasted out with spinning lights and sirens. The shields were now raised, ready to give a triple-score on the total. So I lined up, rolled the pinball safely to the tip of the flipper, then hit the button and sent a long-shot flying up the board. At the top, the pinball knocked down the shields and landed safely in the bowl.

Sounds erupted as the machine rang up triple everything and the register rolled over and over. My score suddenly went from seven grand all the way to over twenty thousand. I continued on this strategy until, for the heck of it, I took a shot up the chute and hit the double bonus. My score climbed to forty thousand. Finally, after I'd assassinated the board, the ball drifted past my flippers into the trap and the game finally ended. With one ball, I'd made enough points for two free games.

"Whoa!" Fenton shouted as he thumbed my ribs. "That's got to be the all-time high, boy!"

"I don't know. It's my personal best, though."

"So, you got a couple of free games, eh?"

"I owe you from the go-carts. Let's bust this joint up."

Fenton immediately took to my strategy like a duck to water. We jammed on that machine for the rest of the afternoon as sirens and gizmos rang out score after score. We won more games than we could play, and Fenton giggled devilishly every time we racked the board. At some point a group of kids crowded to watch us punish the record with over ten free rounds. It was like a circus. Alas, the manager appeared and told us we'd had enough fun. The poor guy had only earned two quarters for the entire afternoon. Fenton was about to let

227

UNDER THE LIGHT OF FIREFLIES

him have it, but I needed to leave, so he relented.

"Where's your bike?" he asked when we got outside.

"Oh, I forgot. I need to call home for a ride."

"Don't sweat it, man. You can ride pump with me."

"Are you sure? You've got to go up that hill."

"That ain't nothing."

Fenton was a strong dude. He had thick brawny legs and his shoulders bulged with muscle. Undeniably a brute, he'd proved his mettle many times on the playground and in the arena. He was a guy that had total respect, even from older boys, and he was apt to put a person down if they didn't show it. Though I would've never admitted it out loud, it felt good to have the toughest kid around being charitable to me.

After I climbed aboard, he hit the pedals and off we went. Right at first, he had to bike up a hill on College Drive which took a lot of effort, but he never stopped. Halfway to the top, we cruised into a neighborhood then took a quick trail though some woods before emerging at Kennedy Lane across from Texas High. After we went over, we found the gates open. We rode inside and coasted down the long, cavernous sidewalks.

The school was a complex of short parallel hallways with an overhanging roof that stretched above the lockers and sidewalk, both which sat outdoors. It was always strange visiting an empty school, like there was something inherently wrong with the absence of voices. *One day I would be here*, I thought, *a teenager old enough to drive, to play ball under the lights, and hopefully cool enough to have a girl waiting on me after the game.* Fenton slowed the bike and stopped near the classrooms at the far end.

"Let's check and see if the doors are open," he said.

Down the sidewalk stood sets of double doors, which entered short hallways, three classrooms on each side. We tried a few, but they were locked, and the classrooms sat closed and dark. We rummaged through a bunch of lockers though all we found were papers and trash. Because it was off-limits, we explored the girls' bathroom. We didn't find much difference from the boys' room except the girls had stalls only. Back outside, we tried a few more lockers where we ominously discovered two empty glass bottles. Grabbing them, Fenton checked around to make sure nobody was watching, then we marched across the yard towards a brick wall jutting across.

"Here you go," he said and handed one to me.

"Shouldn't we do this somewhere else?"

"Nobody's gonna see. Don't be a wuss."

We'd barely crossed the lawn when as easy as you'd like, Fenton reached back and hurled his bottle. It sailed through the air end over end towards its target where, in an almost casual manner, it struck the bricks and smashed everywhere. Then all was quiet again. I quickly looked around, but we were still alone.

Next, Fenton calmly stepped aside and waited on me like it was my turn at the water cooler. He didn't press me. He didn't suggest. He simply stayed there because he knew I'd do it. And for once, I wanted to do it. I wanted to break something and get away with it. To feel like a rebel. So as simply as he'd done, I reached back and chucked my bottle.

It flew as gracefully as a dove before connecting seconds later in the center of the wall with the sound of shattering

UNDER THE LIGHT OF FIREFLIES

glass. Then silence yet again. It felt odd. Our schools still operated under the old method of corporal punishment— including paddling—for violating any speck of the conduct code. Yet for busting two bottles on sacred ground, silence was the only response. It felt marvelous, powerful, like we owned the place.

"Good throw," Fenton said as he strolled past and whistled.

Back at the causeway, he picked up his bike, and without any sense of urgency, we walked past the last set of lockers towards the north gate. Then behind us we heard words. We turned and saw at the far end of the sidewalk a black man wearing square framed glasses and a button-down shirt. He held a giant key-ring in his hand and carried that official demeanor which screamed that he was a principal or an administrator.

"Hey you!" he yelled as he stalked our way. "Stop right there!!"

My senses froze. As easy as the throws we'd made, this man had caught us. We'd trespassed and vandalized the school. We were in serious trouble. When I looked at Fenton, though, he carelessly regarded the man like a fly on a wall.

"Screw this," Fenton said. "Let's skate."

"But he sees us."

"I know he does. That's why we're leaving."

"What if he finds out who we are?"

"Then I guess we better give up now and beg for mercy. Listen up, bud. My pop would be super ticked if we stuck around. He doesn't deal well with calls from the principal's office. Especially during summertime."

I swallowed hard. We were in trouble, yes, but we did have

a chance to escape. If we got caught running, though, then it would be twice as bad.

"Stop thinking!" Fenton shouted. "If you get busted and rat me out, I'll freaking kill you."

He poked me in the chest. The man in the distance had started to trot and was getting closer.

"Let's just get out of here," I said.

"That's what I was saying."

We hustled through the gate while behind us the man yelled threats. He next broke into a run. Outside, a treeless lawn stretched over long open spaces towards practice fields. We ran to the sidewalk, jumped on the bike, and got into action.

It was slow going at first. After several turns of the pedals, though, Fenton had us at full speed. Racing down the path to the students' parking lot, I realized there was no way that man had the speed or the stamina to catch us. He'd have to return to the office and call the cops. We rode across the lot until we made it to Summerhill. Once there, we stopped and checked behind us. The back gate stood empty, and the sidewalk and lawn were barren.

"I guess he's gone back," I said.

"He doesn't want to look stupid, but he is. Freaking principals think they're so righteous."

We didn't waste any time chatting. Instead, we crossed the road onto a street that entered my neighborhood. The whole way I looked for a car to come chasing us, but none did. Winding through the streets, Fenton biked us for several blocks until we arrived at my house. Inside the garage, my brother was sitting in a lawn chair and hanging out with

UNDER THE LIGHT OF FIREFLIES

a few of his buddies.

"Hey, do you want to check out my treehouse?" I asked after I got off.

"No. I got something else going on."

"We sure killed it in pinball today."

"Your quarter paid out pretty good."

"The manager certainly didn't appreciate it."

"It was illegal for him to kick us off that game. Next time we'll stay as long as we want."

"You better keep your eyes peeled for cops."

"I've said it before and I'll say it again, the cops ain't ever catching me."

"Well, thanks again for the ride."

Then Fenton tugged my shirt as I was about to leave, and I stopped. He had a troubled look on his face.

"What's going on?" I asked.

He looked hard into my eyes and then said, "You and Jamie. I know what's up with you two."

I sucked in a quick breath and stood there still. He stayed seated with a furrowed brow.

"I swear I didn't know you were going with her," I said. "I would've never done something like that."

"You wouldn't have, huh?"

"That kiss only lasted two seconds, I swear."

Fenton glanced at the garage where my brother and his friends sat, then he dubiously shook his head. "You just played your cards all wrong, dude," he said.

"It was only a peck, man. Believe me. It didn't mean anything."

232

"That's not it. What I'm saying is that you just spilled the beans. You gave over the goose too easy. See, Jamie's never told me a thing. But I could sense something was up by the way y'all acted in the treehouse."

Of course, Jamie had never said a word. With zero resistance, I'd freely given myself up in little more than a microsecond. I couldn't have felt more stupid. "I don't know what to say," I said.

"You can do way better."

"I know."

"Tell me something, though. What'd you think about it?"

"The thing with Jamie?" I replied, uncertain if this was a trap. "We were inside one of those stone lookouts at the park. It was hot and it smelled like pee. So, it wasn't that great."

Fenton spun a pedal a few times as he listened.

"Are you going to bring it up to Jamie?" I asked.

"I haven't decided."

"Just don't get mad at her because of me."

"I don't really like her. But she's real good looking. I'll let her hang around until school starts, then I'll cut her loose. If I were you, I'd stay out of the way."

A black car pulled around the corner. We stopped talking. It slowly approached my house, creeping along, but it turned out to be an elderly lady. Fenton pulled his bike off the driveway and got ready to leave.

"We've got an excursion planned in a few nights," he said. "But it won't be any panty party. I'll let you know when and where we'll meet."

"Sounds good."

233

"Before I leave, here's one piece of advice."

"What's that?"

"You can rat out a girl whenever you want, but don't ever rat out a bro. Especially a Wandering Star. You'll be sorry for the day you did."

"I won't."

"Then it's cool."

He turned his bike into the street and rode away. Stuck in my thoughts, I walked directly into my house without speaking a word to my brother. I was thinking of Jamie.

CHAPTER THIRTEEN

There is an old Hindu proverb which says that a tiger does not need to boast it is a tiger. The tiger is the king. Tigers don't have a natural fear of man. Call it more of an aversion. Attacks on humans are rare, but they do happen, and those tigers are then labeled maneaters. Scientists characterize maneaters as opportunistic, meaning that the predator is too old, too sick, or suffers from an injury which keeps them from successfully hunting their natural prey. So, if one or more of these conditions exist, and a human population lives close by, tigers will hunt people. In the nineteenth century, a lot of those conditions must have existed. Over one hundred thousand men, women, and children were killed as human populations exploded and encroached upon the tigers' habitat. It seems the only reason death ever abated was because the tigers' numbers themselves eroded from half-a-million to less than ten thousand. Though dismissed as fiction by pundits, legends abounded of tigers that developed a lust for human flesh. A lust that started with the

UNDER THE LIGHT OF FIREFLIES

first kill and grew evermore unquenched, resulting in stalkers which singlehandedly slayed dozens of people or more. Every time a maneater struck, the reaction was the same. Abject terror and superstition. Those same pundits have also said that this is the normal response in the absence of true knowledge and wisdom. To the dwellers who are subject to the tigers, however, the only true knowledge and wisdom is this: the jungle has but one king, and it is the king with whom the keys of death reside.

Such was the substance of my fascination ever since the tiger had attacked Connor and me. The frustration over my inability to remember the attack swung back and forth between dull acceptance to acute obsession. The fact that I did survive added mystery to the equation, and that mystery was where my imagination festered.

A tiger's swipe will pack up to a few hundred pounds per square inch, and its claws can grow four inches long. Indeed, the claws had sliced my flesh so cleanly that the doctors said it could have been made from a razor. They sewed me up nicely enough, and the good news was that my shoulder and ribs had not shattered, but the scars were shocking. And I was the fortunate one.

The fact that I'd survived, and Connor had not, should have provoked an emotional response within me which simply wasn't there. And I wanted it to be there. It was cold and inhuman to feel no compassion or sympathy. I couldn't remember the attack, though, and I'd never known Connor.

So, I sought knowledge. To be sure, I read our dusty encyclopedia until everything about tigers was registered into my mind. When that no longer satisfied, I rode my bike to the

LEE SANDERS

library and searched out more books and more stories—the grizzlier the better—but no matter how much I read, knowledge could not substitute for the memory. Every day that I didn't remember, I feared I might never remember, and that a part me of would be lost forever. So late into the night, I would sit at my desk and voraciously consume books, hoping for some sentence, some passage to trip up a memory that would not come.

As a result, I learned everything about the tiger—its instincts, its zoology, its mind. Did people understand that tigers have the best memory of any animal alive? A single male's range might span a thousand square miles. Their stripes appear upon their very skin. They can grow ten feet long, weigh up to 700 pounds, and leap over a basket ball goal. Among cats, they are the champion swimmers. The best piece of advice is that if a tiger is ever encountered, *do not run*. That's the cardinal rule. They dislike being spotted and might leave without attacking, but they will engage the chase every time. Sitting still and looking them in the eye, ironically, is the best course of action.

As the nights of my study wore on, I began to gain a strange appreciation for the beast. I realized that a tiger couldn't help being a tiger any more than I could help being a boy. I learned to recognize and admire its perfection. The immaculate killer. Soon, I was reading so much that many times I awoke with my head on a book and drool running over its pages. I'd become obsessed, and the more I obsessed about it, the more I ached for the truth. In time, I began to lose hope and a grimness crept into me. I felt like it would never come. That I'd be stuck forever in this empty state. What I couldn't know was that in a

237

few more days all the memories would come rushing back in a moment when I least expected it, but needed it the most.

One morning as I slept on my desk, Sally nudged me and asked if I was getting up. I had told her the day before that I would fly a kite with her, a promise not forgotten, and she wondered if we could leave soon. Sally was impossible to say no to, so I pulled myself off my chair, splashed my face with water, then went downstairs where I was dutifully led outside.

The north end of the park opened to big sweeping meadows which every autumn became the Four States Fairgrounds. At the bottom near the pool sat the toothy fighter plane inside a chain-linked fence. Taking our spot there, Sally and I watched our tethered diamond take flight, its green tapestry and tail of yellow banners contrasting with the puffy clouds and blue skies. I stayed behind Sally, guiding her hands while she listened carefully to my instructions to never let go.

"How high will it fly?" she asked.

"Twice as high if you let out all the string."

"That's almost to the moon."

"Not quite."

"I don't want it to go too far."

"Why not?"

"I'm afraid the string will break, and it won't ever come back."

"We'll keep it close."

The wind blew steadily and the kite behaved fine. Sally enjoyed it beyond words, though she tried a few. Her unaffected giggles described it better. As we sat there watching, a sound of wheels rolled up followed by a bicycle plopping down. A second later Dusty appeared next to me, his eyes fixed upon the kite as he sipped on a can of soda.

"Dusty," I said. "What are you doing here?"

"I'm watching you fly a kite."

"Well, duh."

"I went by your house and your mom told me where you were."

"You should've called first."

"The line was busy."

"People like talking."

"They won't shut up."

We gave each other a side glance and smirked. Whenever I saw Dusty, even if it had been a long time, we always picked up right where we'd left off as if neither time nor space had passed between us. Now, I had other leanings. Whatever excitement I first felt upon seeing him, thoughts about him and Jill took over. Whether it was true or not, I'd avoided Dusty ever since, even leaving our secret walkie-talkies turned off. Now that Dusty stood next to me, my suspicion became unclear. He was, after all, my best friend.

"You ought to let out more line," Dusty said.

"Sally doesn't want to."

"But that's the whole point of flying, to go as high up as possible."

Sally frowned and didn't say a word.

"You can fly it however you want," I told her.

Dusty heard me and quietly took another sip. "So how's your injury coming along?"

"I'll be all right."

UNDER THE LIGHT OF FIREFLIES

"Does it hurt still?"

"I'm sore but I can do most things now."

"Most things like what?"

"Like anything."

"Like riding go-carts?" he asked with a raised eyebrow.

"Where'd you hear that?"

"I've got long ears."

"Everyone's been away, man. I ran across Fenton one day and he invited me along."

"He invited you?"

"Yeah."

"So, you're friends now?"

"I didn't say that."

"Have you been by his treehouse?"

"Once."

"Are you kidding me?"

"It was no big deal. There were even girls there."

"What kind of girls?"

"His brother's chick, and...and some other girl."

"But you're one of us. You're a Loafer."

"Whatever. It's not like I was cheating on you."

Sally looked at me, curious. Aware that I was aware of her, she went back to watching the kite. I took a breath and changed the subject.

"What about Sandra Prince?" I asked. "Have you seen her since you got back?"

"We're going to the movies tomorrow night."

"Who else is going?"

"Some guys from the all-stars. Sandra is bringing friends

240

too. You can come along if you like."

"I can come along? What a privilege. I get to hang out with your team while you're on a date. No thanks."

"I said there'd be other girls too."

"Far be it from me to crash your party."

"Hey, it's not like I'm cheating on you."

We sat there and simmered. Never before had any derision existed between us, but circumstances were changed. Dusty made it on the all-stars who later achieved great feats of glory, whereas I'd been ripped off by my head coach himself and replaced with his younger son. Then there was the bigger deal. His thing with Jill.

"I'm sorry," he said.

"It's cool."

I didn't care to talk, so I asked Sally if she wanted to go home, and she replied yes. I helped her reel in the kite and we disassembled it.

"We're leaving now," I told Dusty after I gathered it up. "I can't let her go alone."

Dusty nodded, threw his soda in the trash, then got on his bicycle. "I'm riding by Sandra's," he said with a grin.

"Don't let her dad shoot you."

"I'm too good looking to get shot," he said with a laugh. I did not laugh.

"Say hello to her for me. And to Jill too if you see her there."

"Jill's not in town," he replied, looking away. "Let me know if you change your mind about the movies."

Sally and I walked home where I went to the garage and put up the kite. Jack was at the workbench messing with the

241

UNDER THE LIGHT OF FIREFLIES

airplane again. He'd finally made some progress. I glanced briefly at his work then passed without talking.

"Where are you going?" he asked.

"To my room."

"You've been spending a lot of time up there."

"I've been reading. I don't have a lot of friends right now."

"Is that so?"

"Yep. See you later."

"Then what about that Felcher kid?" he asked. "Fenton's his name."

I was astounded. Had somebody advertised my business with Fenton? Anonymity was a quality I began to appreciate.

"I'm not riding with Fenton," I said.

"Stop it. I saw him drop you off the other day."

"He brought me back from the bowling alley. I didn't have a way home."

"So you did ride with him."

"It's not the same thing. I didn't plan to see him."

"Listen up, bro," he said. "The Felchers are bad news. They'll just use you and get you in trouble."

"I know that. Except they never actually get in trouble."

"Yes, they do. They just never get caught."

"I got it under control."

"You don't know them like I know them."

"I've known Fenton forever."

"Like I've known Sloan. You don't remember it, but they used to come here when you were little."

"What do you mean?"

"There are things you don't understand."

242

"Like what?"

"Dad and Mr. Felcher were friends once."

I did a double take, but my brother was serious. "It doesn't mean anything now," he said.

"But how was Dad ever friends with Marshall?"

"Who?"

"Mr. Felcher," I corrected myself.

"You really don't remember, do you? We used to go to each other's birthday parties and cookouts. You probably were three years old when we stopped."

"Why'd we stop?"

"Dad and Mr. Felcher had a falling out. I don't know what it was about. It just ended."

"This sounds so crazy."

"They knew each other as kids and made a club. They called themselves the 'Stars.' It was a silly thing. Several years back, Sloan revived the club and acted like it was some hallowed society."

I'd never heard anything about this. It was difficult to picture. Something bad must have caused the rift between my dad and Marshall, though, because I never knew Dad to lose a friend.

"So you'll know," I told him. "Fenton's not that bad of a guy."

"Don't do it."

"Seriously. People just don't know him."

"Don't go there."

"What's your problem? I see you running around with Arkansas folks all the time. What happened to Keith and your other buddies?"

"They were here the other day."

"Do they know you're hanging with what's his name, Rip? And his girlfriend, Desaray?"

"Nobody cares, Noah. Just because Rip's from Arkansas doesn't mean he can't be cool."

"But they stole our tiger."

"And we stole their hog."

"They stole ours first. Plus, he wanted you to rat on your friends."

"You really don't get it, man."

"So how come I don't get it, but you do?"

Jack tossed a rag and took a step towards me.

"Rip makes perfect grades," he said. "That might sound geeky to you, but he comes from good stock. Now look at Fenton's brother, Sloan. He seems like a cool guy as long as the beer's flowing, but you turn your back and he'll stick the knife in. He'll work for his dad forever at that shipping company, then hustle pool until he's seventy. That's not how you and I are raised."

"La-di-da. I guess you're too good for regular people now."

"Don't get smart, Noah. If I tell you something, it's for your own good. So do what I say."

Then he thumped my chest. *Who does he think he is?* I asked myself. *He isn't Dad.* Suddenly a rage welled inside me and I rushed forward, swung, and hit him in the shoulder. It caught him by surprise and he fell back. Without a retort, I rushed in with an onslaught, flailing fists everywhere, and he dodged to the side then wrapped his arms around me. Now I was angry. I writhed and kicked, screaming at him to let me go, but he held on all the more. My arm was too weak to fight, and that made me even madder.

"Settle down!" Jack said. "You'll hurt yourself."

"Let me go!!"

"Calm down and I will."

But calm down I would not do. I wanted to be released on my terms, not his. Then the back door flung open, and Mother rushed into the garage asking what in the world was happening.

"Noah's freaking out," Jack said.

"No, you're freaking out!"

"Both of you stop it right now!" Mother ordered. "Jack, let him go."

Jack hesitated, but Mother pulled at his fingers and implored him. Finally, he jerked his hands away and stepped back.

"I'll get you for this!" I hissed and wheeled around. "You've got no right!"

"What is the problem?" Mother demanded. She stood between us, exasperated, but we both just stayed pat without speaking. "Please," she tried. "Tell me what you're fighting about."

We remained still.

"Oh, I get it," she said and threw up her hands. "I'm your mother and this is the honor code. Let me tell you two something right now. Things are starting to fray. You're both staying up all night and sleeping till noon. Nobody cares about their chores or getting to dinner on time. All you want to do is run, but I'm the one who runs things around here. Jack, get home at a decent hour starting tonight. Noah, I'm sorry what

245

happened, but it's time to move on. We're halfway through summer. Now quit fighting and shake hands."

Jack and I looked at her quizzically. Had our mother ordered us to shake hands? That's what they did in the Boy Scouts.

"I am serious," she repeated. "Shake hands right now."

Jack started laughing. I did too. We both swayed as we thought about it, amused at the notion, then Jack stuck out his hand.

"Put her there, tiger," he said, then his face suddenly went white. "Whoa. That came out wrong. Noah, I'm sorry. Mother. I didn't mean anything by that."

Mother put her hands on her hips, crossed her arms, then put her hands back on her hips. I had an opening. I could act insulted and go back on the attack, but there was a better way. The best way to win was to forgive. That way he could never tell me what to do again.

"It's all right," I said and reached out.

He reached out too and cautiously shook my hand. With that, Mother let out a sigh and pulled us in tight. She rubbed both of our backs with a mother's hope, and I could feel for the first time how tired she was. Then the back door opened again and Sally appeared with a letter in her hand.

"Mommy?" she said.

Mother released us and touched our faces.

"Mommy?"

"Yes, dear?" Mother answered.

"Why does this letter have my name on it?"

"Your name? Can I see?"

Sally hopped over and gave Mother the envelope. Sally's

LEE SANDERS

name had been addressed on it in colored crayons.

"It's a letter sent to you," Mother said. "Should we open it?"

"Yes yes yes!!!" Sally cried.

Mother went to a chair then tore open the envelope. Inside, there was a polaroid picture. Mother took the photo and handed it to Sally.

"It's a picture of Teddy!" she exclaimed. "And he's all dressed up!"

In the picture, her Teddy donned a tourist's outfit, replete with Hawaiian shirt and hat as if he was having a grand vacation.

"There's something else," Mother said. "He wrote you a letter."

"Read it, Mommy, read it! Please?"

Sally snuggled onto her lap while Mother started the letter.

"'Dear Sally, How is everything back home? I've missed you so much since you left, but don't fret! Grand'Mere has kept me busy with lots of canoe trips and hikes. Yesterday we saw a deer! We've baked lots of cookies too. So many that we can't eat them all. I do miss you and I can't wait to sleep in our bed again. See you soon and lots and lots of love, Teddy, XoXoXo'"

Sally's face glowed. She took the letter and the picture and held them to her heart, then laid back against Mother and stayed still.

"I wish Teddy could be here now," she said sadly.

"I know, dear," Mother replied and kissed her head. "He'll be back before you know it."

"Do you promise?"

"I promise."

247

UNDER THE LIGHT OF FIREFLIES

That night, I sat on my bed looking through a comic book, but my mind was fixed on Dusty. I couldn't stop thinking about what Jamie had said. I hoped she was wrong. Still, I'd never known her to lie, so perhaps she misinterpreted the situation. I decided to turn my walkie-talkie back on with the vague thought that I'd buzz Dusty. As soon as I did, though, it crackled to life on its own.

"Apollo to earth. Apollo to earth. Come in, Houston."

I pulled the receiver off the cradle, hesitated, but went ahead with it. "Apollo, this is Houston. We read you."

"What are you doing?" Dusty asked.

"Nothing. I don't want to sleep."

"Sleep is overrated."

"And yet everyone does it."

"So, have you changed your mind about the movies tomorrow night?"

"I don't think I have the money," I answered.

"Ask your mom."

"I haven't done chores in weeks."

"I owe you from the golf match and I have a few extra bucks. So it's all good."

I paused to think about it, but instead found an excuse. "I'm not ready to stand in a crowd," I said. "Maybe another time."

"Okay. But hey. Would you want to go to a Rangers' baseball game next week? Nobody would know you over there."

"You're heading to Dallas?"

"My Uncle Ned has a van. He said me and my cousin could both ask a friend. We'll stay for a night and then go to the amusement park too."

248

"I'd love to go!" I replied.

"Of course you would."

"How much will it cost?"

"I'm talking about free."

"Free is the word. I'll have to ask my mom first, though."

"She's a cool chick. You're in."

I was excited for an adventure, but my thoughts were eating me up. I could no longer put it off. It had been close to a year since my crush began with Jill, and I'd never told Dusty. I'd never told anyone except for Jamie.

"I want to ask you a question," I said.

"I'm not teaching you any of my dance moves."

"I asked you one time what you thought about Jill. You said she was like a sister."

Silence from the other end.

"Did you mean that?" I asked.

"Yes. I meant that. She doesn't do it for me."

"You never felt *anything* for her?"

Another silence.

"Did you hear me?" I asked again.

"I don't know what you mean."

"It's a simple question. Did you ever think she was cute?"

"Yeah. For a bookworm."

"Did you ever call her or go out with her?"

"Like where?"

"Like anywhere."

Now another silence which wasn't good. I sat there kicking my heels on the bed, praying that he'd say the right things. "Look, bro," he began faintly. "Something happened that you

249

UNDER THE LIGHT OF FIREFLIES

should probably know about."

"What's that?" I asked, my mind racing.

"It's not a big deal, okay?"

"Don't do that. Just tell me."

"You know how Jill and I were in the ARC program, right? We sat at the same lab table with Jamie and Joey. One week, we took a field trip to Murfreesboro to dig for diamonds, and afterward we went to some decrepit old museum. For the ride, the teacher had assigned us bus seats by lab tables. I got assigned to sit with Jill."

"Keep going."

"On the ride home, it got late. It was real dark on the bus. Jill and I were all the way in the back, talking to each other. The next thing you know, we accidentally knocked heads. It hurt so bad that we started laughing. We laughed so much that we couldn't stop. Then the teacher came back and shushed us. So after she left, we had to lean in close and whisper."

His voice trailed off and he quit speaking.

"Then what?" I demanded.

"Seriously, it's no big deal."

"Tell me."

"Look man, I didn't know that you liked her."

"Tell me what happened."

After a long moment, he finally said it. "We kissed."

A bomb went off inside my head. My heart felt like it'd been ripped out and thrown against the wall. The worst thing I could have imagined was now true. My best friend had kissed the girl I pined for, and then they both hid it from me. All the pent-up hope, anxiety, and energy suddenly went out of me. I laid there like a burst balloon, useless and wilted.

"Right after we did it, we felt weird," he explained. "Nothing else happened, I swear. That's why I said she's like a sister. It didn't mean anything."

I limply held onto the walkie talkie as lifeless as a corpse. It didn't mean anything to him, he said. I wished that I could've known how a moment so significant could mean so little. But I wasn't significant. Those things weren't for me. They were for the big and the beautiful.

"I think my grandmother is visiting next week," I said in a broken voice.

"Don't you mean your Grand'Mere?"

"I can't go on the trip. I've got to hang up now."

"Jill and I never liked each other, Noah. It was an accident. Please believe me."

"Whatever you say."

"Don't be mad. Please don't be mad."

"I've gotta go."

I placed the receiver back on its cradle and turned it off for good. Then I laid on my back and stared at the ceiling, my hopes shattered, my spirit turned to black. I hated everything in my mind, from the truths I did know, to the memories I didn't. I wanted to trade one for the other, the unknown for the truth, but that wasn't possible. How I wished the cosmic dealer would deal me all the cards so at least I could know everything. Hadn't I earned that much? But dealers only deal the cards, they do not choose. Another sleepless night would be my hand. I couldn't do anything about it, so I did what I could. I pulled myself out of bed, sat at my desk, and began to read about the king.

251

CHAPTER FOURTEEN

"We're going to church," Mother insisted as she hovered over the breakfast table and poured my juice. "I realize that you're shy and embarrassed still, but you have to start sometime."

Sally fiddled with her pancake, not really eating as much as making a piece of art with it. She didn't mind church so much. Sally really didn't mind anything. Even if she did, she always agreed because she chose the path of peace. For me, it was more complicated.

"Please can we stay home this one last time?" I asked. "I promise I'll go next week."

"That's what you said last week," Mother responded. "So then next week will become just like this week, and then it will be the same thing over and over again. I know how this goes, son. Believe me when I tell you that facing the crowd will be good for you. You'll have to do it sooner or later, so you might as well get it over with."

Mother was taking a stand. I tried to think of an argument,

but I knew I couldn't win. On top of missing church, I hadn't been pulling my weight around the house. I didn't take out the trash like I was supposed to, I didn't vacuum or dust, and my room was turning into a dirty-clothes depot. So, now I had to walk the line. I set down my fork, scraped back my chair, then trudged towards the stairs.

"I love you, son," Mother called as I left the kitchen. I didn't respond.

In my room, I changed into my itchy church clothes, clipped on a tie, then combed down my hair. Before I left, I paused at my desk to grab a few illicit items from my desk and shoved them in my pockets. Back downstairs, Mother and Sally sat on the couch with their Sunday dresses on. I noticed there weren't any other males present.

"Where's Jack?"

"He got in very late," Mother replied and stood up. "He had a tournament down in Lufkin."

"They didn't get in that late," I said.

"He told me it was after 1:00 a.m."

"Sure..."

"That's pretty darn late, son."

"I was awake then too."

"Why were you awake?"

"Because I couldn't sleep."

"And what were you doing?"

"Reading."

"Uh huh," she said and tapped her lip. "That's what we call a *personal* choice. I've warned you about staying up so late."

"But it's still the same thing."

UNDER THE LIGHT OF FIREFLIES

"Jack played three games yesterday, rode a bus for four hours, and has to lifeguard at the pool today. It's not the same thing."

She believed that. What she didn't know was that Jack didn't play any *three* games the day before, and he didn't ride on a bus until 1:00 a.m. I had his schedule put to memory. He played a double-header that started mid-morning, meaning he would've finished sometime in the afternoon. After stopping for a meal, that bus should have made it back no later than 9:00 or 10:00 p.m. Jack got to town then went somewhere else, probably a party, and came home late with Mother none the wiser. When the sun came up and it was time to go to church, Jack naturally complained about the toil of life on the road. Perfect. I couldn't tell Mother about it, obviously. The whole honor-code system that she had questioned before was true, established, unbreakable—unless I wanted to face the shame from ratting my own brother out, not to mention the consequences of torture. To be plain, I was jealous.

"Poor little Jack," I said. "Let's just go."

We piled into the car and off we went. My anxiousness rose as I counted house after house and block after block that I'd traveled past hundreds of times. I imagined the gawking onlookers at church, the framed grins, and the same platitudes again and again.

"Time heals everything."

"What doesn't kill you only makes you stronger."

I knew everyone meant well, but I didn't care. I wanted to stay home.

Behind the church, Mother parked in some grass. I slowly slid out the door. From across the lot, the first boy I saw

254

LEE SANDERS

instantly stopped to watch me as I walked over. When I got close enough, I stuck my tongue out which elicited the desired reaction, and he went away.

Entering the side door near the classrooms, I found the foyer mercifully void of people. When we turned into the hall, though, we saw some men drinking coffee and talking, one of them being Judge Caraway. He noticed us and left his conversation to step over and speak to us.

"How are you all doing?" he asked.

"We're doing well, Whit," Mother said.

"That's good to hear," he replied then looked down at us kids. "Sally, I've never seen a more beautiful dress. Is green your favorite color?"

"No, pink is. And yellow. And green too."

"That's a lot of favorite colors."

"I like all the colors, really."

"They look swell on you," he said and pinched her cheek. Then looking to me, he asked sedately, "How's that arm holding up, son?"

"Good."

"Are you getting outside any?"

"Yes sir."

"It's good to see you at church."

"Thank you."

He could tell my unhappiness. He had let the Russian off the hook, and he knew that I knew, but he didn't have the compunction or need to explain it. He was a judge. We said our goodbyes and left. As we approached my classroom, Sally put her arm through mine and escorted me as if I were heading

255

to the gallows. Mother walked on the other side, shoulder to shoulder, her chin high.

Suddenly, a group of children spilled out of a room, slapping each other and laughing, then halted with mouths agape as I passed by. Mother couldn't help but notice their reaction, meaning she'd witnessed firsthand my cringy circumstance. Her resolve, however, didn't allow her to turn back. Instead, she carried on with quiet dignity. Soon enough, we made it to my Sunday School class where I paused at the door.

"It'll be over before you know it," Mother said.

I gave her a short glance, turned the knob, then pushed open the door. Inside, the class chattered busily before they turned to see who it was. Then all talking stopped. To me, their shock seemed ridiculous considering that most of us had known each other since we were babies. I supposed that in many ways these reactions wouldn't cease until everyone had seen and inspected the freak for themselves, and that's exactly what they did.

As I entered, their greedy eyes crawled over every inch of me, searching for any hint of a scar, or pain, or derangement, irresistibly picturing that crystalline moment where the tiger had attacked me and then ripped Connor apart. It was plain to see what they were thinking. For the favor, I returned them no expression, no greeting, no nothing.

With clenched jaws and fists, I stiffly tramped past the eyeballs towards the only person I could possibly stand, the only one whom I knew would treat me no differently than before— my pudgy baseball teammate, Joey. He sat on the back row watching indifferently. To my relief, a chair was open next to him and so I plopped down and crossed my arms. The other kids each had their head turned around, staring at me as if I were a blinking neon sign. I checked side to side where they rudely continued without the slightest consideration.

"Why don't you take a damn picture," I said. "It'll last longer."

Cursing in Sunday school was a major no-no, and more than enough to shake them out of their trance. A few winced, others blinked, but they all complied and turned around.

"Well done," said Joey.

His eyes were stuck on a *Star Wars* figurine he'd brought with him just like at our baseball banquet. That was the same day we watched Connor biking across the park. It's also where I learned about the teacher's editions found in Connor's locker that got him suspended. Apparently, I'd learned much more because I became the only person ever known to have ridden with Connor. *How could I have gotten chummy with that guy?* I asked myself. It seemed totally implausible.

Our teacher, Mrs. Scott, primly entered our classroom with her dress shoes clicking across the tile floor. She arranged that day's lesson on her desk then closely inspected the room. Her eyes fell on me and hesitated as if she might say something, but she passed on the idea, then turned to the chalkboard to write the title of the day's lesson. *When life gets you down.*

The lesson that morning centered around the setbacks in our lives, and how we should still count our blessings and go forward. I chuckled. It never failed that whatever happened in my life, somehow it got addressed in church the next Sunday. On and on, Mrs. Scott talked about how much harder life was in Bible times and how they still got through it being thankful.

UNDER THE LIGHT OF FIREFLIES

I tried to listen and think about the lesson, but it was hard to do. So, I ended up doing my usual exercise. Daydreaming.

Outside there wasn't a cloud in the sky, and I thought about heaven. If heaven was true like I'd been taught, then my father had to be there. That meant the only way for me to see him again would be to get there myself. I was told that only good people went there. I wondered if I was good enough. Being good wasn't always so easy, but I also knew it was my choice. I told myself I'd do better. After all, I had plenty of time. Then my name was called.

"I'm sorry, what?"

"Please give us your thoughts on the lesson," Mrs. Scott said.

Entering class, I'd felt fairly safe that Mrs. Scott wouldn't draw attention to me, considering my condition, but that wasn't Mrs. Scott's style. She had to prove she was different and superior all at once. I hadn't heard the original question, or, even worse, the lesson. So after reviewing the title scribbled across the chalkboard, I concluded to venture with an uncontestable response.

"Life can get you down sometimes," I said. "But like the good book says, you win some and you lose some. We should still be thankful for what we've got."

That should cover just about everything, I thought, and sat there smugly. However, Mrs. Scott's reaction didn't match mine, and, incredulous, she waited for me to continue. I had nothing else to add, so I dropped my smugness and instead switched to the role of poor victim. Though she was a tough lady and didn't buy my act, she decided it was better not to pursue the matter. At least not that Sunday. Beside me, Joey laughed under his breath and gave me the thumbs up. It was the first time anybody had slipped one past Mrs. Scott.

As she continued class, I reached into my pocket and pulled out my elicit pack of gum and offered Joey a piece, which he accepted. I took one myself, then put the gum back and brought out the other item. I held out my hand for Joey to see. In my palm sat the black figurine of Darth Vader. Joey's face flashed with surprise, and he checked to see if I was serious. I gave him an affirmative nod. He gave me another thumbs up, this one more emphatic.

Class eventually ended, and I found Mother and Sally in the hallway. I rushed us to the sanctuary, scooting past gazing churchgoers before they could collar me. At my request, we sat in the enclave on the far side where I remained with my head down and awaited another lesson, this time from our preacher. In classic old-Protestant form, we stood and sat a half-dozen times, chanted creeds, and sang hymns. I never understood why we had to go through all the motions but figured it was probably to keep the men from falling asleep, although that didn't seem to work so well either.

After another bout of daydreams, we made it through the service. Following the benediction, at my behest, we bounded for the back door where we managed to encounter only about fifty people. I'd known them all my life. They were wonderful folks, but as expected, they acted more like sad admirers than friends. When we got to the car, I'd never been more relieved to get out of a place in my life. I wasn't so sure if the trip had been good for me or not.

"Isn't today the day we landed on the moon?" I asked as we

259

UNDER THE LIGHT OF FIREFLIES

drove past the same blocks and houses once again.

"Not quite," Mother answered. "That's on the twentieth."

"We always had a cookout."

"We usually did, yes. Your father liked that day."

"Tell me about it."

"Your dad was funny. He thought of that day as a complement to the Fourth of July. Our founders first landed on the shores in the new world, made a country, and centuries later we landed on the moon. To Walter, it seemed like an affirmation of the great experiment called America. I always said that it was his summer holiday season, sort of like Christmas and New Year's is for winter."

"Who would we invite to the cookout?"

"Lots of people. You should remember. Your dad was quite the host."

Mother tugged her earlobe while viewing the memory clearly in her mind. Sally sat between us and listened. She was proud of Dad and loved to hear about him.

"Daddy made big fires," she said cheerfully. "He always cooked lots of food on the fire."

She declared the words like a newsboy reciting the latest headlines.

"He never turned anyone away," she added.

My angle had been to probe about Marshall. I could have plainly asked about dad's relationship with the man, but it felt taboo. Mother might get suspicious why I asked. Jack was already suspicious of my dealings with the Felchers. I decided then that silence made a better companion. I had plans for the night.

260

LEE SANDERS

At the intersection where 40th Avenue ended at Texas Boulevard, a giant white Victorian mansion dwelled for the whole world to see. It climbed three stories high with Roman columns in front and black shutters around the windows. In its yard were equally giant pine trees that stood as fat as grain silos and almost as tall. It was there I'd been instructed to meet the Wandering Stars.

Mother had gone to a late movie after putting Sally to bed, and when she left, I asked my brother if he could stay home a few hours while I went out. I could tell he wanted to say no because that's what Mother would've said. This request flew right in the face of her recent demands. Due to our latest spat, though, Jack acted self-conscious about ordering me to do anything. He reluctantly said yes on the grounds that I promised to be home before Mother returned. If she came back and found me missing, he'd be in as much hot water as me. I assured him there was nothing to worry about then fetched my bike and rode away, marveling at how well that whole forgiveness thing had worked out.

After crossing over Texas Boulevard, I took a dark sidestreet bordering the mansion to a corner in the back. The guys were waiting for me outside a halo of streetlight. Fenton played tricks with his yo-yo while Billy whittled on a long stick. To the side, Tyler sat by himself, posturing as always.

"Well, if it isn't the little scooter," he said. "I didn't think you'd show."

"I made it on time."

"But are you ready for tonight?"

261

UNDER THE LIGHT OF FIREFLIES

"I can ride just fine."

"We'll see."

I glanced about and saw that Billy had shaped one end of the stick into a sharp point which he tested with his finger. He then folded his knife and dropped it and the stick inside his backpack with the tip poking out. Fenton did one last trick with his yo-yo before sitting up and checking me out.

"Have you heard of any slumber parties tonight?" he asked.

"Not tonight."

"So what was that chick's name, the one who had the slumber party before?"

"Sandra Prince."

"That's the one. Her old lady is fine like wine, right?" The others laughed. "Maybe we should go spy on her place."

I remembered that night and how Dusty, Sam, and I had scared Mrs. Prince. Instead of getting mad, though, she was cool about it and let us talk to the girls. That was probably the only success which had ever garnered our club any repute. It seemed like a long time ago.

"You all want to check out the zoo?" I asked.

They paused and turned towards me, their smiles wiped clean. June bugs zipped through the light as I waited on their answer.

"Zoo's closed, son," Tyler said.

"We could still get inside," I replied. "There's only a chain link fence guarding it."

"Aren't you scared of going back there?"

"Nothing happened to me at the zoo."

Tyler asked Fenton a question out of my hearing while

262

Billy's eyes twinkled in the dark. They weren't used to having a challenge issued to them, which is basically how they took it. It was Billy who answered.

"We'll do it," he said.

"All right by me too," Fenton agreed. "Maybe we'll find that Russian camped out there."

"You go inside first," Tyler told me. "And don't chicken out once we get there."

"Let's go then."

After riding a few blocks and crossing the boulevard, we took a street above a stretch of land where another school stood with a cemetery looming across from it. I halfway figured that we'd stop at one of these spots to explore, or do something worse, but we coasted right past to a short trail, cut through some brush, and hopped over a set of railroad tracks. Once we were through, we stood directly in front of the park entrance where the two small towers stood like stone soldiers. To the right of them sat Jill's house without a light on. When we rolled through the entrance, the boys looked back at me. Beneath our tires was the very spot where Connor had been slain. Though it was now washed off, I figured the guys had searched the ground for blood stains. I knew I had.

"Let's go to the pond," Billy said.

We turned off the street, passed by the slides and swings, then went to the water's edge. No wind blew, and the sultry air draped us like a cloak. The sky hung low with clouds glowing faintly from the dull light of the moon.

"There's the island where they found you," Tyler said as if I didn't know.

UNDER THE LIGHT OF FIREFLIES

They all observed me, waiting for words. It felt like theater, but that was nothing new to me.

"The man who found me," I said. "He's an expert hunter. He goes alone in the Rockies for weeks."

"Derek Mayfly," Fenton said. "He served with special forces in Vietnam, just like my pop did. He spotlighted you. Your legs were sticking out."

The island sat all alone in the murky water. Bullfrogs croaked in the night. Nothing else made a sound or moved, not even a duck.

"Do you think you'll ever remember?" asked Tyler.

That was the million-dollar question, and the one I suffered with. I didn't care to discuss it in that place, though, so I gave no answer.

"You didn't get killed anyway," he added.

"Connor did," Billy said. "If you ever do remember, I want to hear all the gory details."

Billy surveyed the dim scene with those coal black eyes. His spirit seemed like a ghost caught in a machine. Whether he'd been born that way or forged by some malign force, I could not tell. It was evident, though, that his thoughts drifted on a lower plane.

"Just so you know," he said. "We let Connor off the hook that day at Bookout's. He's lucky we decided to leave."

The other boys shuffled anxiously.

"I don't know what you're talking about," I said.

"What? You can't even remember being at the store?"

"No."

Out of all things, Billy found that most amazing. They all

stood in a line facing me.

"We shouldn't talk that other stuff," Fenton said.

"I didn't say anything about that other stuff," Billy replied and spat. "You think that I'd give us up?"

"Easy. I'm just reminding."

"It don't matter anyway. It's all over with now." Then he turned his doll's eyes upon me and said, "I'm glad Connor's dead."

On a trail under the lofty pines, we biked past forlorn park benches and cold barbecue grills. It was so dark that we had trouble keeping on the path. After we came out, we crossed the park lane and went up to the zoo which sat as mirthless in the night as a carnival ride in winter. The only sound of anything was the electric buzz of a streetlamp.

In front of the zoo spread a chain-link fence slouching over like a drunk. We laid down our bikes, and at the bottom we ripped back an opening where I crawled through first and the others followed. The front gate was around waist high, and before Tyler could make a wisecrack, I'd already jumped over. They all dutifully jumped over too, and we were in.

The zoo was deserted. The cages sat black and hollow behind a lawn which had grown wild from neglect. Where monkeys once held their lunatic court, nary a creature moved. I bent under the railing and walked beside the cages, running my fingers along the steel bars. The boys stayed in the back, poking their heads around to see if anyone or anything was alive.

"Come on over," I said. "Don't you want to check it out?"

"There's nothing to see," said Tyler. "Plus, I don't want to

UNDER THE LIGHT OF FIREFLIES

get burrs from the weeds."

"There's no burrs," I laughed.

He laughed back in mockery.

"Whatchya gonna do then, tiger man?" Fenton asked.

I curled my lips back and clicked my teeth while they watched with grim eyes.

"EOWWW!!!" I suddenly howled. "Oww!! Oww!!"

The other guys didn't move except for a headshake or two.

"Why don't you act like you've been somewhere before?" Tyler said.

"I have been somewhere. I just can't remember."

I walked past the lions' dens to my main destination, the tiger cage. This is where the escaped beast had lived for a single day. That beast was long gone. It was a certified maneater, though. I wondered if it would ever eat another person. Then I heard a scraping sound from inside the bars. The guys were talking, and I told them to quiet down.

"Don't shush us," Billy said.

I cupped my hand to my ear for them to listen. Then another scrape came followed by a quick rustle of leaves.

"Bring me the light," I whispered. "Something's moving in there."

"There's nothing there," Tyler said. "He's just kidding."

"Don't you hear it?"

Perturbed, Billy himself crawled under the rail, slung off his backpack, and pulled out a flashlight.

"Over in that back corner," I told him. "There's a rustle."

After a disapproving look, he flicked on the light and pointed it inside the cage. We didn't see anything at first except

266

scattered debris and a mound of leaves in the back. Then something behind it moved that caught our attention. It sounded like shuffling or shagging. The light rolled back and forth when at once a filthy brindled body emerged, and a revulsion seized me. Billy kept the light on it while the thing hunched around, working on something in the pile. When finished, its face turned to us. Green eyes eerily appeared, glowing in the light, and a slow lifeless hiss emitted from of its mouth.

"What the hell is that?" Tyler asked from behind us.

"It's a possum," I replied.

The creature humped to the other end of the pile, rummaged in the leaves with its draggled arms, and picked something up. Next, we saw another set of green eyes, smaller this time, glaring at us from the creature's clutches.

"Oh gross," Tyler said. "It's got a baby."

The mother blew another hiss before placing its joey back into the dugout. After it was tucked away, the mother swiftly turned and slashed across the floor directly at us.

"Whoa!!" I yelled and jumped back. "That thing's coming straight for us!"

But Billy didn't move. With one hand he kept his flashlight on the possum, and with the other, he gripped his sharpened stick as if he were a centurion with his sword. Right as it reached the pen's rails, the creature quit its rush. Now exposed, it cowered backwards and drew in its shoulders. In the dim light, tiny fangs hung down from its black lips.

"Bring it on," Billy told the creature. "Just a little closer and I'll ram this spike right through your black heart."

267

UNDER THE LIGHT OF FIREFLIES

His hand held steady with his light continually shining on the grungy rodent. But the possum wouldn't come. Instead, it retreated a few feet, flattened on its back, and stopped breathing. From behind the pile, the baby possum stayed quiet too. Billy stood his ground, though it wasn't to prove his courage. He didn't care about proving anything. He wanted to plunge his spear into that animal. As we sat there watching and waiting, we unexpectedly heard a set of tires rolling across the parking lot. Billy turned off his flashlight.

"*Someone's here,*" Fenton said.

We all crouched down and listened as the vehicle parked and cut the engine. A door slowly opened and slammed shut. Footsteps scuffed across the asphalt towards the back gate, keys jangled, and a squeaky lock turned.

"Who could that be?" Tyler whispered.

"The cops?" I wondered.

"What would they be doing here?"

The gate creaked open and a flashlight combed along the side wall. We heard more footsteps, this time shuffling around the back storage bin. Afterward, the light bounced further along the wall until it came into the breezeway beside the zoo.

"We've got to jet," I said. "Like right now."

The other guys sat frozen. I waited a few seconds. They still wouldn't budge. Maybe they were hoping the stranger was there to check on something in back, but I didn't care to wait and find out.

"Did you hear me?" I said to them. "We've got to get out of here before he comes around."

I yanked on Fenton's shirt, but unlike that day at the school,

268

he refused to move. Billy listened intently. Tyler's face drooped like he'd heard a ghost. I didn't know what had gotten into them, but I couldn't sit around without trying to escape. I gave them one more moment then told them to forget about me, I was leaving. That's when they finally woke up. Jumping to our feet, we left in unison and bolted across the yard towards the entrance.

I got to the gate first where I jumped and clumsily scraped over, hitting the ground in a pile as dull pain coursed through my shoulder. The other guys followed right behind me, with Fenton in the rear barking to go faster. At the back of the zoo, the stranger turned the corner. He held a flashlight in one hand and a liquor bottle in the other. Upon hearing us, he quickly shined the flashlight our way. Fenton's face lit up, his curly hair prominently visible. At the sight of us, the man hastily threw aside his bottle and rushed straight towards us.

"Don't you move!!!" he hollered. "*I'm gonna get ya!*"

"Damn damn damn!" Fenton groaned as he spun over and fell to the concrete. "Let's get out of here!"

We sprinted for the fence where each of us squirted under like rabbits. The galloping stranger arrived at the gate, turned the knob, and simply went straight through. I felt dumb for not trying that myself, but I didn't have time to harp on it.

We dashed to our bicycles, hopped on, then took off posthaste. At the fence, the stranger was now crawling underneath like an animal. Tyler was the last to get on his bike and whined fearfully for us not to leave him. For Billy and Fenton, though, it was every man for himself. They took off like their pants were on fire.

UNDER THE LIGHT OF FIREFLIES

It was I who slowed down for Tyler as the stranger pounded the pavement, grunting and charging like a deranged ape. Tyler pumped the pedals with all his might, but he was losing ground. The stranger got ever closer. I yelled at Tyler to go faster as the madman strained ahead. One step away, he reached and grazed the fringe of Tyler's shirt. Tyler's eyes bulged. He pedaled harder. With a last emphatic surge, the stranger lunged forward and took a mighty swipe. But Tyler, who'd never taken his gaze off the stampeding psycho, ducked just in time. After his failed attempt, the man faltered and stumbled a step behind while Tyler, biking furiously, managed to pull away. At last he made it beside me, and together we clicked into high gear and didn't slow down until we'd sailed into a grove where Billy and Fenton sat waiting. After skidding to a stop, we turned to look behind us.

There at the edge of a streetlight, with his fists balled and chest heaving, stood the silhouetted figure of a complete unknown. Who was this man? What was his intention? Though his face was darkened, we sat there looking at each other, and I could still feel his stare. Chills ran over my body. Then the stranger strode towards us like a robot, a sight I'll never forget, but we didn't wait around this time.

We jumped back into gear and gunned it to the end of the park. When we looked back again, though, the figure had disappeared. I thought he must be hiding behind a tree, or perhaps he'd turned back to get his truck. Either way, I was convinced the guy must be a homicidal maniac, and right there a new policy was forever established. Never break into a condemned zoo. Our most imperative task, though, was to get

270

out of the park before that lunatic came in his vehicle to kill us.

As we made it to the park road, I suggested that we cross to the empty field where the trail cut through to the dead end of my lane. The others agreed, and I led us onto the path. We zipped through high grass overgrown with cattails then splashed across a shallow creek. At the end of the trail appeared a gate where we hurtled through and came onto my lane. After a block or two, we felt safe enough to stop and take a rest.

"That had to be the Russian," Fenton said.

"They should've given that man the electric chair," Tyler added.

"That wasn't him," I told them.

"Like you'd know."

"I do know."

"How do you know the Russian?"

"He's not Russian."

"Are you taking up for that commie, you little twit?" Billy asked.

"No. I just happened to have seen him a few times. He's shy. He wasn't crazy like that man."

"It could be that other idiot assistant," Tyler said. "Dude drove five miles that day before he found a cop."

"Which assistant?"

"The man who got away from the tiger."

"Where exactly did he drive to?"

"You really don't know jack, do you?" Fenton said. "While the director was inside the zoo getting chomped, the assistant was outside at his truck looking for cigarettes. He was so drunk, though, that he fell asleep in his cab. When he came to, he

271

UNDER THE LIGHT OF FIREFLIES

looked through his windshield and saw the tiger in the back gate, just flicking its tail."

"He saw the tiger. What happened next?"

"The guy first locked himself in his truck. He claimed he wanted to wait and see if his boss would reappear, but seeing how the tiger's face was drenched in blood, he figured his boss must've been supper. He started up the engine to leave, and then the tiger made a move his way. Dude completely freaked out. He spun backwards across the lawn, smashed a signpost, and knocked it out of the ground. He sped away with his bumper hanging off and didn't stop until State Line. By the time he found the cops, you and Connor were already in the park."

He stopped there. Even I knew the rest of the story. A somber courtesy fell over the others, the first time they'd ever acted that way. With nothing more said, we started up my lane. After a few more blocks, my house came into view. It was time to part.

We came to a cross street and I told them goodnight. They were about to leave when Fenton stopped the others and spoke with them in low tones. I heard Fenton mention something about his pop and the war, but I couldn't understand what that was about. Tyler started to argue. After they'd debated a few moments, they agreed to something.

"Say, man," Fenton said as they came over. "You want to drop back by my house tomorrow?"

"Sure. What's up?"

"You'll see when you get there. Just come by around lunch."

I nodded and started to leave.

"And bring a personal item," Fenton added.

272

"Personal? What do you mean?"

"Something valuable. Something special."

"I don't understand."

"Like the most important thing you own."

"What's it for?"

"Don't ask questions. Just remember that it has to be important." As he was about to leave, he said, "Nobody's forcing you to bring it, by the way. It's your choice."

They pedaled around the corner and went away to their own world. There was no telling what they had left on their agenda, or what innocent property lay at risk merely for lying in their path. I was happy my night was over. As I contemplated, a car pulled down my lane and turned into my driveway. It was Mother. She'd made it home, and now I was in trouble.

While she got out of the car, a man appeared from the other side who then escorted her to the front door. I'd never seen this man before. They stopped there to say a few words and squeezed each other's hands, smiling. The man said goodbye and walked back. Mother made it inside, and the car pulled out and drove away.

I dreaded what was awaiting me, and I tried to think of excuses. As I walked closer, the light went off in the living room. A few seconds later my brother stormed outside, slammed the door shut, jumped in his car and peeled away. I went around the end of the garage and found the side door thankfully unlocked. Inside, I set my bike against the wall and crept to the kitchen door. Turning the knob with care, I softly slipped into the house.

Everything was still. I removed my shoes and tip-toed

UNDER THE LIGHT OF FIREFLIES

across the floor, hoping to get up the stairs undetected, when curiously I heard music from the far end of the house. In our dining room, a piano was playing. Notes floated through the air sorrowful and melancholy, like a song about a lost love. Torn over whether to inspect the sound or to sneak towards my room, I decided to go down the hall.

I walked quietly into the dining room where Mother sat at the piano under a dim glow from the streetlights shining through the window. The song was sad. I'd never heard her play it before. As I stood in the doorway, I saw a cigarette burning in an ash tray with a wine glass beside it. Mother took a sip and returned to playing the tune. The melody moved in the shadows like the sound of a tarnished music box, its ballerina dancing the same dance again and again.

I came to the edge of the dining table to listen. Mother's fingers were long and lovely. They pressed the keys without effort, unconsciously producing sound as if guided by a spirit. She was always an excellent pianist. Her playing, though, had been absent for a long while. She stopped and sat there still.

"Hello Noah," she said without turning.

"That was nice. What's the name of it?"

"It doesn't have a name."

"I haven't heard you play in a long time."

"You quit taking your lessons."

"I'll start again soon."

She gave me a glance but didn't comment.

"It's dark in here," I said.

"Yes."

I stepped closer and stood at the piano. Mother took another

274

sip of wine as her hand lightly drug across the keys and made a small phrase. She then stopped and reached for her cigarette.

"Why are you smoking?" I asked.

"It's an old habit."

"But you quit a long time ago."

"It's not permanent."

"I'm sorry I went out."

"You're sorry," she said blandly. "It doesn't seem to matter, though, does it? We all do what we want around here."

"I'm sorry."

Thoughts flashed across her eyes for a second. They were thoughts of the weeks and months passing us by.

"You two boys..." she said. "You stay out late. Jack throws parties while we're out of town. And little Sally, she's always so worried that one day I'll be..."

She trailed off. The words were too delicate to speak.

"I've been upset," I said. "I feel trapped sometimes in this house. I just wanted to get outside for a bit."

She smoked her cigarette and put it out. Then squeezing her hands together, she shook her head.

"That doesn't cut it," she said. "You're allowed to be upset, but you still need structure."

The streetlamps shone dull and gray through the curtains. Everything in the room was black. Mother's hands now rested again on the keys as she turned her head downward, but she didn't play.

"It won't happen again, Mother. I swear."

She sat there thinking. She wanted to believe me. She was tired.

"This is fair warning," she spoke in a low voice. "Obey the rules of this house, or suffer the consequences."

"I will."

She exhaled and finished her wine. I tried to hug her, but she only sat there.

"I'm going to bed," she said at last and rose to leave. She made it to the door where she stopped for one last thing. "Life is a choice, son. It can be as hard or as easy as we choose it to be."

"Yes ma'am."

She left and went up the stairs to her room. As I stepped into the hall, many thoughts came into my mind. I knew I hadn't been at my best lately, but I promised myself that things would get better. I'd fix it. I just needed time. Then my thoughts turned to the man who'd escorted her home. Who was he? I'd never heard her mention another man. Was she hiding things from me?

In my father's office, I clicked on the reading light over his desk. As always, the surface was shiny and clean. From the shelf, I pulled down the mantel clock, popped open its back, and took out the key. I unlocked the glass cabinet where inside awaited the autographed baseball signed by Joe DiMaggio. It was a treasure, and one that had been passed down from a grandfather I'd never known to his son who was now dead. I knew that it would go to my older brother and not me. I slipped my hand past that and instead pulled open the slender drawer at the bottom. I found the dark lavender case with gold trim. I took it out and flipped it open. There laid my father's Purple Heart. I ran my fingers over it, feeling the shape of the golden profile, examining the perfect craftsmanship. Closing the case, I dropped it into my pocket, re-locked the cabinet, and returned the key. I crept upstairs to my bedroom, hearing the breath of my mother and Sally as they slept in her bed. Once in my room, I closed the door quietly and then hid the medal in my nightstand. After changing into my night clothes, I crawled under the covers, clicked off the light, and stared into nothingness.

CHAPTER FIFTEEN

That night I had a dream. In this dream appeared Connor, Henry the Russian, and me. We'd gathered on the side of the park where the fighter plane sat rusting inside its cage. Along the cage's fence, white Christmas lights had been strung which blinked off and on. I was looking intently at the plane's nose with the painted-on tiger teeth, but the teeth had grown into real fangs and the nose had turned into a tiger's snout. The tiger itself, though, lay cradled in my arms, as passive as a house cat.

The plane's engine cranked, coughed, and burst alive, followed by the thunder of whirling propellors. Inside the cockpit, Connor piloted the plane with one arm on the wheel as the other dangled weirdly by his side. After takeoff, he circled the plane inside its cage, searching for a way out, but there was none. The plane kept going faster and faster, scraping the fence and sending sparks everywhere as the wings wobbled erratically. I desperately needed to signal Connor. He had to eject or else he'd crash, but I couldn't let go of the tiger.

I turned and there stood Henry. From his pocket, he produced a shiny silver key and held it before his face, expressionless. The blinking lights grew brighter and brighter. The tiger became heavier and heavier. I yelled at Connor to eject, but the engine was too loud. The plane spun out of control. Connor violently jerked the wheel to maintain flight, his dead arm flopping side to side, but his efforts were useless. In a single flash, I saw my father's face before the plane caromed off, rolled over, and slowly nosedived towards oblivion. Then without words, Henry walked to the front of the cage where a silver lock hung on the door. He took it in his hand, inserted the key, and turned the lock. Then my eyes opened.

It was close. It was so very close. I could feel it. I'd been waiting a long time, and I was so tired of this misery, straining day after day to remember, yet I could never give up, no matter how miserable it might be. I had thought plenty about it, though. Giving up.

I'd reasoned out everything to justify why it wouldn't matter if I never remembered. What is the stuff of memories anyway, I asked myself. If they can fade or disappear, doesn't that make all our actions meaningless? There must be something more that makes our hearts beat. I was constantly seeking to reassure myself that I'd be all right if the memory never came, but it was a ruse. I had to know the truth. My scars ran too deep.

Henry wrote me a letter. The morning after my dream, I awoke to find that Mother had finally handed over the package which Henry mailed to me during his trial. She'd told me I needed to get past the tragedy, and if she meant that, then she had to

UNDER THE LIGHT OF FIREFLIES

do her part too and treat me like a man, hoping that if she did then maybe, just maybe, I could be a boy once more.

Along with the letter, the package included a personal item. A locket that contained tiny pictures of Henry's father, Boris, and his mother, Astrid. Both sat reposed in the early twentieth century manner—father in a tall, starched collar and tie, and mother in a velvet and lace dress. In the photo, she wore the very locket conferred upon me. It must have been Henry's only surviving memento of them, and I marveled.

As for the letter, it was personal. In fact, it disarmed me. The man was a stranger, so confiding his life's story to me, a twelve-year-old boy no less, was difficult to wrap my mind around. When I first learned about the letter without having read it, I figured it was written for the sake of conscience. Somewhere inside, Henry needed absolution for what he'd done. But as I read, his words spoke not from a man begging for forgiveness, but from a man who had learned how to forget. It wasn't written to plead his case, or because of a desperate need to tell his story to someone, even if it was a boy. What he was telling me was not to lose heart.

The letter described his childhood, first the beauty, and later the darker realities. He mentioned his three-year-old brother, Juri, and their charming hometown of Narva, Estonia. He framed it so perfectly that it seemed impossible that in an instant it could've been swept away into smoke and rubble. The only indiscretion Henry's family had been guilty of was living in a country bordering Russia. The Red Army arrived with fire, and a bomb blew apart Henry's home. He later awoke half-buried in rubble, feverish, and deaf in one ear. In his hand he

280

found his mother's locket, but he did not find her, nor would he ever find her again. He was twelve years old.

He became an orphan prisoner—first to the Russians, then to the Nazis after their invasion, and finally to the Russians again when they reconquered. Each time, Henry would explain to the guards how he'd lost his family, asking if there was a way he could find them. No one listened. Henry never knew tenderness again. Eventually, he got deported to the Arctic town of Murmansk. As an adult he became a mechanic on a Russian vessel traveling the provinces. It was that vessel which received a rare command to ship a load of ore to America.

One day at twilight in the Houston harbor, Henry took his fate into his own hands. Before the spotlights came on, he jumped onto a dark conveyor belt and was deposited on a dirt heap. He clambered down to a utility road and later managed to wave down a truck. The first American he ever met was decent, for it was that man who smuggled Henry to freedom.

Concerning his trial for manslaughter, Henry was unconcerned. The only thing he wrote about it was that he would accept, without appeal, whichever verdict the foreman read. If that notion truly existed, I initially believed that it was the sort of surrender which had been conditioned into him by communism.

It was only later when a deeper truth came to me. What Henry was really talking about was his unfailing desire to be free. A desire which had burned in him since he was my age. For if that same dark power which had taken his freedom over there were to take it yet again, this time in America, then Henry had already discovered the greatest freedom of all. The freedom of letting go.

Clive Longbranch ultimately got the case dismissed. As he put it, Henry was free to go as he pleased. There was no welcome mat for that man anywhere in my town, so go is exactly what Henry did. After the ordeal, I asked several adults if anybody knew where he went. They usually returned my question with a puzzled look or a head shake. No one knew and no one cared. Most of them told me that I shouldn't care either. So, I stopped asking.

Later on, I had another dream. In this dream, Henry was living happily on a warm beach. The ocean stood vast, clear, and the color of emeralds, undulating and flowing like the breathing of a soul. Near the end of the dream, Henry walked into the waves and swam away from shore. There were no ships sailing, no buoys bobbing, not a single person to be found anywhere—only Henry and the seals—and in that one wonderful moment, he became free.

I put the package back on my desk and climbed downstairs in a stringy bathrobe. On the couch, I heard Mother explaining to Sally the subtle differences between alligators and crocodiles. It was a very important subject to which Sally listened with her usual devotion. A moment later, the doorbell began ringing spastically. In a state of perplexity, Mother wondered aloud who that could possibly be? Mother then asked Sally if she would like to find out. Sensing something, Sally giggled and skipped to the front door. She opened it up, and waiting there dressed in the same Hawaiian costume as in the polaroid sat her Teddy bear.

Sally erupted with glee as she cried, "Teddy! Teddy! Teddy!"

and scooped him into her arms, hugging and swinging him in perfect bliss. "What took you so long?" she asked as she petted him. "Did you miss me?"

"Well, I suppose I could have brought him sooner," said a familiar voice from outside, "but he was such a good companion, I was afraid to let him go."

Then an older lady in a sun hat and sandals stepped into the entrance, smiling with her arms open. It was Grand'Mere. Sally cried out her name too, almost as loud as Teddy's, and leapt forward into her arms. Mother stood aside and watched the reunion, her face aglow. After a bounty of hugs, Grand'Mere knelt and reached into her tote bag.

"These are the cookies that Teddy and I baked together," she said. "They're so yummy. What do you say we take them inside and have a little tea party?"

"Oh, Grand'Mere!" Sally answered with a grin. "You're always full of surprises."

She grabbed the bag along with Teddy and danced to the kitchen. Grand'Mere came into the den and gave Mother a greeting. Seeing me, she waltzed over and reached her hands out to mine.

"Well, Noah," she said as she looked me over. "You're always dressing up for the wrong occasions."

She laughed her lovely laugh and embraced me.

"You look as fit as a fiddle," she whispered in my ear as we walked to the kitchen with her arm tucked under mine. "I believe you're almost healed up, am I right?"

"I feel like a hundred bucks."

At Sally's orders, Mother pulled out some saucers and

UNDER THE LIGHT OF FIREFLIES

then served the cookies with teacups filled with milk. We got acquainted as we ate the snack, all of us brightened by Grand'Mere's presence. After a few minutes, she peered over my shoulder towards the den, clasped her hands over her heart, and let out a quiet gasp.

"Jack-a-roo-boy," she said in a low voice. "My darling, come here and say hello."

As she rose, Jack stumbled in with his hair mussed from a hard night's sleep.

"I thought I heard a Frenchie down here," he said.

"Jackie, you are as bronze as a marron glacé," she told him with a hug. "The sun has always agreed with you."

"I've been working at the pool all summer. I'm like that grasshopper in the kid's story."

"Store your wares for the cold, my son. Winter has its season as well."

The chairs were all filled now, and Sally sat in Mother's lap while we chatted. Grand'Mere always had a way of filling the house with sparkle, and Sally never took her eyes off her.

"So tell us what happened with your dogwood tree," I said.

Grand'Mere's eyebrows rose as she took in a long breath and placed her hands flat on the table.

"Well, that was quite the ordeal," she began. "As you know, the administration arbitrarily declared that we needed new electricity. The project council, led by the newbie Beatrice Lively, decided to cut down our trees without so much as a discussion."

"Is she the old lady with blue hair?"

"I suppose it is blue, darling," she said with a laugh. "She and her cohort, Betsy Wilcox, think they're the dynamic duo

284

when it comes to decision making. It turns out that I wasn't the only native of Roanoke who'd had it with the bullying and the senseless proclamations. So after a few get-togethers, we assembled a coterie of cadres who decided to rise and resist the council's untamed tyranny," she declared with a raised fist. Then she shrugged and added, "In the end, our trees were saved. All of them."

We gave a cheer as she shrugged.

"How'd you do that, Grammy?" Jack asked.

"It was simple. The original settlers were granted certain rights, so we forced a quorum and designated our trees as landmarks. And that's that."

Everyone listened as she tapped her fingers on the table.

"Plus, we threatened to fire them," she finished with a pirate's sneer. "Just to show them who's boss."

"Wow," Sally said with wide eyes. "Don't mess around with Grammy."

It was always good having the family together. Not surprisingly, Mother began pulling plates from the cabinets to prepare a lunch. It was impossible for her to avoid hosting. She was her mother's daughter.

Mother first required Jack and me to change into decent clothes, and then the meal was served. It was sandwiches with potato salad, and as we lingered afterward, I suddenly remembered that I had somewhere to be. Shooting a glance at the clock, I saw it was past noon. I was due at Fenton's.

I excused myself, dropped my dishes into the dishwasher, then bolted upstairs. Grabbing the Purple Heart from the nightstand drawer, I shoved it in my pocket and ran back

UNDER THE LIGHT OF FIREFLIES

downstairs. In the kitchen I told everyone goodbye.

"Where are you going in such a hurry?" Mother asked. "Melinda called and invited us over for a swim. I thought we could all go together."

I frowned and indicated my shoulder.

"You don't have to get in the pool, son," she said. "You can sit with us and be good company."

That wasn't possible. I couldn't back out on Fenton. I had a goal in mind. Grand'Mere, who had no idea of the discussion the night before, intervened.

"Noah," Grand'Mere said. "Do as you please. I'll stay a few nights. Only, be back for dinner, okay?"

I looked at Mother who sat there anxiously.

"Be home by six," she said with a point. "And stay out of trouble."

"I will."

I hugged all the ladies then slipped to the garage for my bike. Getting on, I jetted at top speed to the end of our lane, and then back through the field with the cattails. After the park, I crossed over 40th and raced through the neighborhood until I made it to Fenton's street and ducked onto his property. As I got there, I saw the boys with their bikes about to leave. I rolled up and stopped as Fenton watched me in a perturbed way.

"I thought I told you to be here by lunch," Fenton said.

"It is lunch. I had a surprise visitor."

"This ain't summer camp, boy. Let me see what you brought."

I reached in my pocket then produced the purple and gold box.

286

LEE SANDERS

"We don't take costume jewelry," he said.

"It's not jewelry."

They all looked at me, then he opened the box. At first, it felt like I hadn't brought the right thing. They all stood there quietly and stared at my dad's Purple Heart.

"You're not going to keep it, right?" I asked. "It's important I get it back."

"I'll let you know," Fenton said. "We have to decide if this'll do."

Then he turned around and walked to his pop's workshop. Everyone followed, though at the door I was told to wait. They stayed inside for a good five minutes. I wondered what they could be debating. That was a valid Purple Heart my father got when he was only twenty-one years old. He'd ended up in the war because when Mother was pregnant with Jack, the military offered to pay for his college. So, he joined. Not too long afterward, though, the president decided to send American boys to Vietnam. My father was one of the first to go. About halfway through his tour, he got shot in an ambush. The bullet had imbedded so deeply into his femur that the doctors chose to leave it in there. That ended the war for him. He later received the Purple Heart and dropped it in a drawer. Other than a few comments, I never heard him talk about his time over there.

The shed door opened, and the boys came out with Fenton's older brother, Sloan, leading the way. He walked up to me with the box in hand.

"Are you sure that you want to hand over your pop's Purple Heart?" he asked me.

"Isn't it good enough?"

287

UNDER THE LIGHT OF FIREFLIES

"You don't have anything else?"

"The only other thing is a baseball autographed by Joe DiMaggio, but my brother would kill me if he found it gone."

Sloan considered it a minute as he scratched his chin.

"If that's what you want," he said. "Fine. This is the deal. You can only answer 'yes' or 'no.' There is no other answer. Got it?"

"Yes."

"Did you come here by your own choice?"

"Yes."

"You weren't forced?"

"No."

"On the chance we ask, would you be willing to go through a test to join our club?"

"Yes."

Sloan looked back and forth between his brother and the other guys, then proceeded.

"You are officially invited to take the test, but that's it. It doesn't guarantee you'll be invited to join the illustrious 'Wandering Stars,' these stars who wander to and fro. I'll now teach you the first rule: Stars are loyal to each other first and at all costs. We come to a brother's aid anytime, anyplace. We never leave a brother behind, and we never rat a brother out. Right, fellas?"

"Stars for Stars," the others answered.

"If you pass the test," Sloan continued, "then you go on probation. If you don't screw up, we'll take a vote on whether to make you a member. Do you understand what I said?"

"I understand."

288

LEE SANDERS

"*Yes or no.*"

"Yes."

"Do you still want to take the test?"

"Yes."

"You're sure?"

"Yes."

"Hold out your hand."

I reached out, and in my palm he laid an oval patch with a silver star stitched across it, but the club's name was missing.

"This is your first token," he told me. "Do not lose it. You must present the patch when we ask for it. Whatever happens, you must give this patch back. Then you'll get your second token, and we'll tell you what to do from there. Are you square with that?"

"When will I get my dad's Purple Heart back?" I asked.

"Are you deaf?!" he replied sharply. "I ask the questions around here."

"Yes, sir."

He pulled out a cigarette and lit it.

"Do you understand everything I said, yes or no?" he asked.

"Yes."

He blew smoke through his nostrils and flicked the ash before checking with each of the others.

"It's all right, man," he then said. "What you gotta know is that this ain't no pretend thing or some kid's club. It's for real, and it's for life. Now, stick out your fist."

I put out my fist. With a solemn look, he raised his own fist and gave mine a knock. In formation, the other guys filed behind him, each of them knocking my fist in order. When it

289

UNDER THE LIGHT OF FIREFLIES

was done, we all stood there quietly a moment before Fenton spoke up.

"Are you ready to ride?" he asked me.

"I'm always...I mean....yes."

"You don't have to keep answering 'yes,'" Fenton said. "Just be cool."

"You can't be scared, Noah," Sloan added. "When the door opens, you gotta go through it. That's the key."

"Got it."

Sloan strolled back into the shop, and we departed. We rode out the same way we'd gone the night before, crossing Texas Boulevard to the street between the cemetery and the school. In the sky, thick puffy clouds had bloomed, floating along a steady breeze. The air was thick and sultry, making my body sticky. It hadn't rained in a few weeks, but it felt that with the right provocation a storm could flare up anytime.

Crossing at the cut-through and back over the tracks, we came out again at the park entrance. Instead of going through the park this time, though, we went north onto the park road. Farther on, it ran underneath the interstate and then curved for a few miles before meeting up with Summerhill Road towards the Shuffle.

"Where are we going?" I asked.

Fenton swerved his bike in a figure eight, then sniped the back wheel and sent a rock flying.

"Don't ask so many questions," he said.

They rode in front and stopped talking to me. I figured this was the part where they treated me like a plebe. We still hadn't hung out a lot, and we didn't treat each other like friends yet.

290

I was surprised that I'd been invited to take the test, although the gravity of what I was doing hadn't dawned upon me yet. I only knew that I would be called a "Star," just like my father had. He'd had a falling out with an old friend, and they parted ways for reasons unknown. I felt, though, that if my dad was alive, he'd have eventually patched things up with Marshall. That's how Dad was. So, I would carry his torch.

As we came to the stop sign at Summerhill Road, something startling happened. A thought clicked in my head, and a flash raced through my mind. It flickered in front of me, almost in reach, and I felt my body flinch and my skin crawl. I shriveled with dread for I had no clue what memory might come next.

"This is gonna be sweet," Fenton said.

"Little buster doesn't even know what's in store for him," Billy added.

They talked and laughed, but Tyler wasn't smiling. He acted grave.

"Are you sure you can you find the back way?" Tyler asked.

"Don't doubt me," Billy replied.

"So you think he can actually do it?"

Fenton shot a disapproving glare at Tyler and snorted.

"We are talking about the bridge," Tyler pressed. "Right?"

"Quit your bellyaching," said Billy. "We already decided this at church. You see, if anyone can ride the rails, surely a tiger man can."

CHAPTER SIXTEEN

Near the end of a winding road, we took a turn onto a dirt lane where honeysuckle and wild roses grew over a barbed wire fence. The puffy clouds from before had since grown dark underbellies, and a thick haze smeared the sky in a veil of gray. We came to an abandoned cemetery where a wretched black oak stood guard. I noticed the tombstones had no names. While I was pondering that, my mind suddenly winked, followed by another flash. Words echoed in my ears. Then, like the opening of a curtain, I saw him.

Connor was sitting in front of the cemetery where he told me that the departed were probably settlers or maybe outlaws. The next instant, time was pulled backwards to our bike ride. We got a drink from a lady in a gray house. Then further back it went to the convenience store. I saw the standoff between Connor and the guys. Burning between them all was a kind of contempt and familiarity that I wasn't privy to. Connor pulled his blade which caused Billy, Fenton, and Tyler to stand

LEE SANDERS

down and leave.

And that was it. To my disappointment, the recall would only go backwards, and I didn't get to see what happened to us later in the park. As the memories swirled, though, I became more and more anxious. Something about this trip began to feel very dangerous.

"Hey, Ellis!" Fenton barked at me. "Get your head out. We've got riding to do."

I'd stopped to brace myself for the full recollection, but Fenton's interruption halted everything. As I got back in line, my body started to tingle. I feared the inevitable rupture that was coming and the horror it would reveal; yet I had no way of controlling it. In that moment, all I wanted to do was stop and get control. But that wasn't possible. We were on a mission whose end felt as inevitable as it did uncertain.

We crested the hill and below us sprawled long grass fields running towards a neck of woods. Before that, we came upon a sun-bleached shack and a weathered barn that seemed strangely familiar. These worthless structures naturally grabbed the attention of the others, particularly Billy who'd dropped his bike to peer through the dirty windows. In quick order, he was working the door's rusty knob when the bolt popped with a bang. The handle snapped off, and the door cracked open. Billy pulled and wrestled with it until a sharp crunch sounded whereafter he jerked back in pain. A splinter had stabbed into the meat of his palm. In return, he erupted in a flurry of kicks and screams at the door.

"I've got a knife," Fenton told him. "You should cut that splinter out."

293

UNDER THE LIGHT OF FIREFLIES

"Give it here," Billy replied.

After rifling his backpack, Fenton found the knife and handed it over. Opening the blade, Billy stuck it into the swollen nipple and dug around before extracting the splinter. He then snapped shut the knife and held up the black sliver as blood creased down his arm.

"Wash up, dude," Fenton told him and pulled out a water bottle.

Billy grabbed it and poured the bottle empty over his hand. He chucked the bottle at the house and stared at the cut as if he'd been betrayed. From there a black mood fell over him.

"Let's get where we're going," he said grimly. "I want to see what the tiger boy can do."

My hands trembled on the handlebars as we descended through the tall grass towards the woods and the unknown thing beyond. I knew about Waterworks Lake, but only because my father had taken me there when he was alive. I'd caught my very first fish with him there. I hadn't been back since he died, and I'd never visited from this side of the lake.

"Do you think we'll find the trail?" Tyler asked.

"Zip it, Tyler," Billy said.

We came to the forest where tree after tree stood in formation. Patrolling the line, the others scanned the woods methodically until they noticed a small deer run which they agreed to take. We cut onto a narrow trail and crept through a shadowy interior of broken limbs, poison ivy, and cobwebs. I could smell the lake.

The farther we rode, the more I dreaded what was in store for me, but I still couldn't leave. After a while, we arrived at a gray shoreline scattered with bullrushes and willow grass. On the water, I saw a boat full of people fishing. How I wished that I could've been with them instead of with these hoods.

"So...we're really doing this," Tyler said.

"Shut up," Billy said, this time more sternly.

We stopped, and Billy's mouth was drawn at the corners as he crawled off his bike like a sullen monkey. I got off last and cautiously followed the others to a concrete bulwark. There, we looked at a spillway with murky water dribbling down its side. Slick moss and scattered clumps of earth covered the basin floor. A sickly swamp scent polluted the air. At the backside stood a half-finished bridge with no road on the top. Exposed beams stretched to the other side where a mass of dead trees was grouped. I had no idea what they had in mind for me, and my trembling hand had not abated.

"Remember what we talked about," Tyler said.

"Shut up, Tyler!"

It was Fenton who said it this time. *Why are they hating on Tyler?* I wondered. They weren't treating him much like a brother. Billy rubbed his palm where the splinter had been. The blood had stopped, but his flesh was swollen purple. His face simmered. Staying quiet, we hiked beside a concrete wall down to a landing. We arrived at the bridge, stripped and naked, when words suddenly popped in my head like a distant echo. It was Connor.

Does it scare you?

"Are you man enough to do it, boy?" Billy asked.

Fenton watched with a sardonic grin while Tyler stood to the side.

UNDER THE LIGHT OF FIREFLIES

"Man enough for what?" I asked.

"You agreed to take the test," Billy answered. "So here it is."

"I'm not sure what you mean."

"Get out there on the rails, boy!"

"Out there?" I asked and pointed at the bridge. "You mean you want me to cross that?"

"What do you think you're doing here?"

I looked out. I couldn't believe this was the test. The rails were too skinny. The fall too steep. If I failed, I'd bust my skull and maybe even die.

"It's way high up," I said. "What if I get stranded on the rail?"

"You won't pass the test," Bill replied.

"But I could fall."

"Gee, that'd break our hearts."

"Is this really the test?"

"You don't ask the questions here, punk!"

You'll never have to prove yourself again.

"Hold on," I said. "Please. Give me a second."

Billy saw I was afraid, and the fear thrilled him. His eyes twinkled, and I could feel electricity stream out of him like sparks off a car battery. Still, I wavered. My legs stood frozen to the spot. Billy saw my uncertainty, that I was in danger of cowering out, so he decided on a new approach.

"You can do this, tiger man," he coaxed. "Cross that bridge and you'll be a Star forever, exactly like us. We've all had to do it. Just take that first baby step. After that, it gets easy. I swear."

Their eyes burned. I felt I had no choice but to step to the edge. Once there, I looked down and my my body flinched while my head swam. If only I could remember that day with

296

LEE SANDERS

Connor, I'd know what to do. Every second I wavered, Billy's patience grew shorter, his face uglier. He had no desire to coax me. No goodwill existed. At last, he lost all control and waded into me.

"*You pathetic momma's boy!!*" he yelled. "Coward! Cross that bridge right now or you'll be sorry for the day you met me!"

Fenton stood beside him with a vile smirk.

"We got your dad's Purple Heart, boy," he said breathing into my ear. "You'll never see it again unless you go right now."

My loyal and decent father. A man who would've never have gotten within a thousand miles of this situation. I'd betrayed him. I'd dishonored him. I looked at the edge. The step was so close, it was so ready. Somewhere there had to be hope. Faintly visible, in the far reaches of my soul, I still looked to the promise that one day I would know the truth.

Don't be an idiot.

Then came a voice. Everyone stopped to listen. It came again. We searched the landing and the trail but found nothing. Then on the far side of the spillway where the dam was, we discovered someone leaning over a buttress, watching us. He was a Black man and very old with a white beard. He wore denim overalls and held a fishing pole in his hand. He grimaced with perplexity, like he couldn't understand what he was looking at.

"What in the world is going on over there?!" he hollered. "What do you boys think you're doing??"

His words cracked the atmosphere like an icepick. At once, I felt released. I stepped away from the bridge, timid of what they might do, but no one said a word. Fenton blinked as if woken from a trance, while a worried expression covered Tyler's face. Billy rubbed his swollen palm with his venomous eyes stuck to the old man. Nobody gave a response.

"There's a deputy parked right at the end of this dam!" the old man said and pointed. "So, you better do what's right and go on back to where you came from. Go on now!"

Billy hesitated several moments longer, searching for that malignant force which had empowered him, but it was gone. He stepped away, giving me a hateful glare, then trudged back up the embankment where we followed him to the top. From the other side, the old man remained with his fishing pole in hand and watched us. I wanted to wave to him, to say thank you, but his ancient face made me silent.

I've been there.

I found my bicycle and followed the others back into the woods. I felt incredibly relieved, but they acted as if they'd been slapped in the face. My thoughts went to Connor and how different he'd turned out to be than I imagined. When I was thirsty, he found me a drink. When I tempted fate, he saved me from the bridge. The first pangs of guilt began to gnaw at me. I wished I could remember more. *How extraordinarily terrible it must be,* I thought, *that my mind wouldn't let the recollection out of its cage.*

Billy's black mood had now turned much blacker. Fenton brooded like a deprived child. Tyler rode behind them, somewhat despondent, his routine smugness gone. We came to a spot in the woods where Billy slowed down and stopped.

"You're a dirty little rat," he said after I came up. "You ain't no Star. And you never will be."

He'd picked a spot where no one else on earth could see us. We were completely blocked from sunlight. Only the skinny pines bore any witness. I remained quiet while the others scowled at me.

"What you just did was bunk," Fenton said and spat. "You didn't take the test, boy."

"But that man caught us," I replied.

"He didn't catch nothing. You chickened out."

"What about the deputy?"

"There ain't no deputy!"

Fenton knew better, but he didn't care. Whatever trust I ever placed in him had vanished. To deceive Jamie, I'd told her that he would turn on her. Now, that statement had become ironically prophetic. Fenton was trash.

"Look here, crip," Billy said. "You failed. We don't need you, and we especially don't want you. I might just have to kick your ass right here."

"Of course, we don't want him." Tyler finally spoke, figuring it was safe for him to join in. "He can't even remember being attacked by a tiger. I mean, what kind of brain-dead freak do you have to be..."

"I KNOW I CAN'T REMEMBER!!!" I screamed with all my force. Tyler stopped and blinked several times. Fenton and Billy watched. "I already know that, and I don't need you to tell me! You think it's funny, don't you? How would you like everybody staring at you like you're some deformed nut, and you don't even know what happened? Every day and every night, I try as hard as I can to remember. I want to remember more than anything. But it won't come. It just won't. So, if

UNDER THE LIGHT OF FIREFLIES

anybody knows that I can't remember, it's me."

Tyler didn't respond. None of them did. Fenton adjusted his backpack and put his foot on a pedal, wondering what to do. Billy's dark eyes twitched. Though these guys didn't express any true empathy, the whole idea about me being mauled by a tiger where another boy died had finally dawned on them. So, they laid off.

"We'll have church when we get home," Fenton said. "You can follow along if you want, but you aren't allowed at my house. So just stay in the back and keep your mouth shut."

"Don't even cross into our 'hood," Billy warned.

I reached into my pocket and felt the patch they'd given me. I wanted to offer it right there for the Purple Heart, but I knew it would be a mistake. They'd only take the patch and scorn me or even slap me around. I had to let this play out. The only thing I cared about anymore was getting my dad's medal back, and it made me sick to think how I'd handed over something so precious with such ease to such fiends.

Billy faced forward and started back through the woods. The sky had darkened significantly, and the pitter-pat of rain-drops fell through the treetops. After we emerged, a slight drizzle started as low rumblings of thunder echoed in the clouds. I could smell the coming storm.

We climbed through the grass and again came to the barn and shack. Ignoring the looming skies, Billy jumped off his bike like the real mission had only just begun. He went to Fenton, took the backpack, then stalked to the cracked door.

To protect himself against splinters this time, Billy gripped the door using the pack and yanked it back and forth violently.

The door squeaked and cracked as it bent further and further until a long split sounded out, the hinges snapped, and the thing came crashing down. Billy pushed it away and proceeded inside with Fenton and Tyler close behind. It was important for me to play the part, so against my better judgment, I once again followed, praying nothing too terrible would happen.

Inside the house sat a creepy circle of chairs while in the corner laid a pile of forgotten dolls. Against the rear wall stood a bunk bed with tick mattresses. Debris and leaves scattered the premises. The walls had grown so parched that the wood was peeled with hair-like splinters sticking out. In random spots on the floor, water had begun to drip from the rain plunking off the roof.

Billy dismally surveyed the scene then went opening drawers and cabinets in the kitchen. He found no treasure. I wished there was some because maybe that would slake his grim thirst. A troubled feeling came over me for I could see a darkness growing inside Billy that would only lead to a bad end. Tyler, who'd been tiptoeing around like a brushed housecat, made an ominous discovery on the other side of a partition.

"Whoa, check it out!" he said.

"What is it?" asked Fenton.

"This is the biggest wasp nest I've ever seen."

"Where?" Billy demanded and marched around.

The partition had a door and a bay window, and through that, I watched their eyes comb the ceiling to a corner where they stopped and stood in awe. Then Billy set to work. He searched around until he found some newspaper which he wadded up as he walked out the front door. When he came back

UNDER THE LIGHT OF FIREFLIES

inside, he was holding a bright yellow tin with a blue outline. I recognized that right off, and my blood ran cold.

"What are you doing?" Fenton asked with goofy excitement.

"Fire-bombing some wasps," Billy replied.

"Are you kidding me?" Tyler said. "You'd better use a lot. There must be a million of those things."

"Don't worry. I will."

Eager with anticipation, Fenton and Tyler scooted in closer and grinned. I knew this was a very bad idea, but I didn't dare say it, and instead forced myself to step around for a look. When I did, hanging in a far crook of the ceiling appeared a gargantuan wasp nest. It was bloated to the size of a beach ball and teeming with insects. Outfitted with crimson bodies and jet-black wings, the tiny creatures toiled hungrily over the nest's bubbled surface like a miser over his gold. They were guardians of the womb, weaponized, and they did not play around. The very sight of them normally caused a quick retreat. I'd been stung before. It was not a pleasant experience.

Billy stuck the paper-ball onto a pencil and doused it with fluid, filling the air with the pungent scent of fuel. He next put the tip in his mouth and squeezed the tin empty, tossed it aside, and produced a lighter. Strangely, the wasps seemed aware that something was awry. All the while Billy prepped, the faster they crawled and bustled. Fenton and Tyler acted like schoolchildren at a fireworks show, both of them bouncing on their toes with excitement. I, on the other hand, was not so jazzed. I moved back a step while contemplating the various outcomes—none of them good—and measured the path to the door.

Billy flicked the lighter and touched the paper ball, which

302

sprung into flames. At the sight of fire, the wasps instantly stopped all activity and raised their wings at full guard. Billy slowly stepped closer with the flaming ball before him. When he got within a few feet, the first wasps took flight just as he blew out a long spray of fluid. Then *POOF!!!* Fire exploded onto the nest.

What happened next had not been calculated. The entire force of wasps suddenly erupted from the nest and charged into direct attack. They darted for Billy and Fenton first, then onto Tyler who immediately began screeching like a schoolgirl. Not me, though, because I was ten steps to the door before the first wave got started.

At the threshold, I stopped and had to look back. At the other end of the shack, hundreds of wasps had completely flooded the building, some of them actually on fire, zipping and zooming in a swirling cloud. The boys rushed in wild circles, trying to swat the little demons away. But the little demons wouldn't go away. They had transformed in a black and red fury.

The boys cried and twirled around blindly, and then came a crackling sound. Next, the flaming nest broke off the ceiling, fell onto a tuft of straw, and caught on fire. The spray from Billy's mouth had also splattered the wall which was now equally ablaze. As the boys gyrated and fought the wasps, the flames quickly spread over the desiccated paneling and to the debris covering the floor. No one paid attention. They were too confused as they spun and batted at the assaulting throng.

"FIRE!!!" I hollered as they fought the attack. "Can't you see?! Tyler!! Fenton!! Billy!! You've got to get out of there!!!"

UNDER THE LIGHT OF FIREFLIES

It was Fenton and Billy who first took notice. When they saw the place ablaze, they ducked their heads and bolted towards my voice, their hands flailing everywhere. After banging past some boxes and chairs, they made it to the door where they rushed into a steady rain. I'd gone outside too, pressing myself flat against the building. As if guided by radar, a batch of wasps raced by and continued their raging attack on Billy and Fenton who zig-zagged through the grass.

I stayed and waited by the door for Tyler, but he didn't come. After a few moments longer and still nothing, I went and checked through the windows. The flames were growing second by the second, like a spawning tornado. Yet, there was no sight of him. I ran to the front door and peeked inside, but the shack had filled with smoke and made it hard to see. He wasn't in the kitchen nor in the den. Finally at the end of the house, trapped in a corner beneath the bunk beds, I saw Tyler helplessly drawn into a ball. The floor around him sat covered with leaves and trash. I knew that soon the fire would be all over him.

"Tyler!!!" I shouted through cupped hands. "You've got to run! This is the only way!"

"I can't see," he cried. "Don't leave me, Noah. Please don't leave me."

Against a far wall, the blaze had found a pile of newspapers which now bellowed like a bubble from the deep. Where the nest had fallen, fire sprawled from floor to ceiling. It wouldn't be long before this whole place was done for.

"Help me," Tyler bawled. "My eyes are stinging."

I could hear the terror in his voice through the crackling fire.

304

There existed only two options. I had to choose one. I thought about my little sister and what it would mean for her to lose me too, and I almost quit. *Yet there's still hope*, I told myself. The fire hadn't won yet. I silently asked Sally for forgiveness, wrapped my wet shirt around my head, then dashed into the room.

As fast as I was able, I sprinted past the blaze and slid like a baseball runner to the bunk. Though mostly dispersed by fire and smoke, some wasps still remained, and they wasted no opportunity for another attack.

"Come on, man," I said and pulled on Tyler's arms. "You've got to come out now."

My lungs quickly filled with dirty smoke, and my first thought was how we wouldn't last long in this trap. The wasps had formed a line on my body where they now stung me. The blaze yawned and groaned as it grew. A sharp acrid smell stung my nose. Time was running out fast, but Tyler sat paralyzed. Like before at the zoo, he wouldn't move.

"We're going to die, Tyler," I pleaded with him, hacking and swatting at wasps. "I'm serious, man. You've got to come now."

Still, he wouldn't budge. The flames had grown so much that the heat was now touching my skin where the wasps mercilessly pricked me. The pain was exquisite. With no other options, I finally grabbed Tyler by the hair and dragged his body from under the bunk. As he whimpered, I rolled him over and slapped him in the face. He looked at me with a stunned moronic stare. I slapped him once more. Still, nothing. So, I slapped him again and again. At last he woke up, clambered to his feet, and wiped his eyes.

"Look!!!" he exclaimed and pointed.

The conflagration had swollen into a blazing leviathan—torrid, flaming, alive—and it was there for one purpose alone. To burn it all to the ground. The flames poured over the floor and ceiling and now reached for us. I felt dizzy with smoke to the point of fainting, and I had to fight to stay alert.

"Let's get out of here," I coughed.

Tyler steadied himself, and with whatever energy we could muster, we stumbled along the wall and crossed past the blaze. As we went, I felt sizzling tongues lick my skin while oxygen was stolen from my throat. We bungled through fire and smoke towards the front where we clumsily tripped over a chair. Half-witted, I pulled Tyler and me up as a blind wasp bounced off my chest. With hearts pounding, we hurtled towards the door. With one last push, we crashed outside into the glorious summer rain.

Scraping and crawling like beaten dogs, we spasmodically coughed and hacked up smoke to the point that I thought I'd lose my breath forever. My scorched lungs felt like they'd been seared in an overn; my swollen tongue caked with black soot. I continued to choke and wheeze for several minutes until finally my convulsions eased, my delirium abated, and I was able to catch my breath. When my senses had recovered, I pulled the shirt off my head and felt around my scalp. The hair hadn't burned off at least, although my backside had blisters, and my arms were dotted with stings.

Tyler, though, didn't look so prime. His once beautiful coiffure now sat smoldering like a pile of wet burning leaves. Milky white welts from the wasp stings covered his entire face.

His cheek was swollen purple from where I'd smacked him. After checking around, we found that Fenton and Billy had split the scene. Their bikes were gone. *So that's how it is*, I thought. Tyler's mates, his fellow "Stars" who swore of never turning a back on a brother, those same brothers had just left Tyler for dead.

"Are you all right?" I asked and squeezed his shoulder.

He sat blanched and drained of blood but nodded yes as he gingerly touched his stings. Tears coursed down his face with the rain. He'd just escaped death, but his courage had failed him. It mortified him. He couldn't even say thanks.

Behind the dirty windows, the inferno raged on. The mighty rumpus had arrived. The open door fed in sweet oxygen as the fire reveled and raged. Faintly, faces and eyes seemed to dance in the flames, causing my guts to twist. Those eyes— I'd seen them before. Then I felt something sinister moving inside me, a monstrous reality on the warpath, and I braced myself for the horror. As soon as it came near, though, it passed by yet again, leaving me to shake in fear. Tyler said my name. I looked up and he was standing with our bikes.

"We've got to go before the cops come," he said.

A crunching sound came, and when I glanced over, I saw the roof collapse. After a calamitous crash, the massive fire reached upward and collided with water, its ancient enemy, causing steamed smoke to billow skyward in a radiant silver. The column would be seen for miles. Outside the door on the lawn, I saw that Fenton had left his backpack with his name stenciled across the top. That was a rather important item. So, I ran over and snatched it away, feeling the incredible heat wafting from

UNDER THE LIGHT OF FIREFLIES

the fire while it roared its destructive carol. Without another moment's pause, Tyler and I mounted our bicycles, stood on the pedals, and bolted towards the cemetery while in the distance sirens rang out.

CHAPTER SEVENTEEN

Down a tree covered lane spotted by sleepy houses with long yards, Tyler and I hid in a ravine while fire trucks blew past on their way to the blaze. It was perfunctory, I supposed, that the city should send its entire fleet to douse a bunkhouse. Then again, the rain had turned the smoke into a glaring pillar which could be seen from all points on the horizon.

After the parade of sirens ended, we felt safe enough to come out. We still wanted to stay out of sight, so we ducked down a side street where we randomly discovered a trail that carried us into the woods. After a few miles, we came upon a different neighborhood we vaguely recognized. Having no other choice, we took to the streets but avoided major roads.

The entire way, Tyler rode slouched over his handlebars while his thoughts haunted him. He'd almost died a coward, his friends had left him behind, and then there was still the possibility of us getting fingered for burning down a house. It was a bad day for old Tyler, even if he should've been happy to

UNDER THE LIGHT OF FIREFLIES

be alive. I knew I was.

With peals of thunder, the rain pounded relentlessly for a while, which raised my hopes that if the shack was done for, then at least the barn and the fields could be spared. As I looked behind me, the smoke continued to pour into the sky.

"Lightning," I said to Tyler. "That has to be what caused the fire."

Tyler avoided speaking. He rode with his head down.

"Check this out, man," I continued. "Lightning is the cause of more fires than all other sources combined. I actually learned that in earth science. Did you ever have Mrs. Dent? Kooky Mrs. Dent? That lady tended her bunions even more than she did her goldfish, and buddy, those were some spoiled goldfish."

Tyler didn't laugh anymore. His sweet locks had been torched, and those richy-boy good looks were now covered with knobs from the stingers of so many wasps. I didn't think he'd scar, but then maybe I was an optimist. He looked like a bad dream. That's what a fire and a pack of marauding wasps could do for a guy. I'd been right there with him, of course, but it wasn't the same for me. I had some singes and stings, but I wasn't the chicken. That had become Tyler's burden, so I liked him better now.

"Will you be all right?" I asked.

"No," he replied in a hoarse voice. "I have to explain this to my parents."

"That's all right. I heard your folks are cool."

He shot me a glance like what I'd said was ridiculous.

"Okay…" he began. "My folks are cool. Do you know what my father will say? I'll tell you what he'll say. He'll laugh at me.

Truly, he will. He'll say that I look stupid. My mother will get ticked off only because I ruined my clothes, but they'll both accept anything I tell them as long as it's halfway believable. They don't want to deal with it. They just want to watch their shows." Then in a low voice he said, "Say...did I ever tell you that we own the biggest TV in town? I'm serious. My dad literally called every store from here to Shreveport to get the most colossal one he could find. It's silver with a remote and we even got a Betamax to go with it. You should see it, man. It's television paradise."

After another mile, the rain abated to a sprinkle and then stopped. From the star hidden behind the clouds, rays burst outward in long golden arms. Tyler and I eventually had to cross Summerhill Road, so we waited until there were no cars in sight and then went over. Once there, we took a secluded road that would eventually snake its way to the park.

"Soon, we'll be home free," I said. "We didn't get caught."

"You don't think they'll figure it out?"

"That old man with the fishing pole doesn't know who we are. Nobody over there does."

"There'll still be descriptions. There was a deputy at the lake for crying out loud."

"They don't know where we're from or where we went. It's been raining and everybody else was inside anyway."

"Which makes us stick out even more."

"You sure sound paranoid."

"Have you seen my head!?" he exclaimed and broke into tears. "I'm hideous!"

UNDER THE LIGHT OF FIREFLIES

I needed Tyler to get it together. He was more of a pansy than I would've ever thought, but he still could help me with my cause. I'd literally gone through the fire with him, and I wanted him to stick up for me at their club's meeting. I had to get my dad's medal back. That's all I cared about now, even more than getting busted.

"I'm so tired of running," he groaned. "We're always being chased. You never have any choice but to go along."

"Why don't you just quit?"

"I can't quit. You should understand that by now."

"I won't be voted in."

"That'd be your good fortune."

"How do you mean?" I asked.

"Don't ever tell anybody what happened today."

"Are you nuts? I don't want people knowing."

"You don't understand. If you tell anybody, and the others find out, they'll get you. Watch out for Fenton's big brother, Sloan. He's not who you think." He paused to look at me before he continued, "And don't talk about how I got trapped under that bed. I'll say you're a liar. I'll say it was me who saved you."

"I won't tell anybody about that," I assured him.

"How can I believe you?"

"Because maybe I got scared and did the same kind of thing once, but I just can't remember it."

That seemed to satisfy him, or at least placate him. We took the road under the interstate and soon after arrived in the park. This was where we parted ways, and I'd become anxious. I desperately needed his help.

"We had good luck today, if you think about it," I said as we came to a stop. "It could've been a lot worse."

"I bet you didn't know that was our first trip to the bridge, did you?"

"What? But that's where you took your test, isn't it?"

"No. We didn't take any test. It was Connor who told us about the place. We never went there before today."

"You've gotta be kidding me," I said, thinking of Billy screaming at me while Fenton smirked. Despicable.

"Connor crossed that bridge, though," Tyler added. "At least that's what he said."

"What happened between him and all of you?"

"We ran together for a while. He became unpredictable."

"Like when he pulled that knife at the store?"

"Not like that. Connor was honest. With all the stuff we've done, he couldn't be trusted."

"He never ratted you out," I said.

"He wasn't a saint either."

"There was a lot of trash talked about him. Now he's dead, people sound sorry."

"People won't shut up."

"What about those teachers' editions?"

"There's nothing to talk about. Even if there was, the club must come before everything."

"I need to get my dad's medal back."

He wouldn't look at me.

"Could you help me? *Please?*"

"There's only one way to get that back, Noah. The test."

"It's not my fault that old man caught us at the bridge."

"Sure. Like you weren't happy he stopped us."

UNDER THE LIGHT OF FIREFLIES

"I only want my dad's Purple Heart," I said, pulling the patch from my pocket and holding it out in despair. "Here. Take the patch. And Fenton's backpack too. You can say you saved our skin. You can say whatever you want. Just get the medal back for me. Please. You've got to help me."

"You're stupid for offering me your token. If I took it and showed it to them, the backpack wouldn't mean a thing. There's no telling what they'd do to you."

My breath turned choppy, and I began to panic. The guilt and shame were swelling. Tyler gripped the handlebars and adjusted his gears.

"Are you leaving now?" I asked.

"Yes."

"You don't have to go yet. Can't you stay longer?"

"I have someplace to be."

"Where's that?"

"I'll know when I get there."

He forced a weak smile, leaned on his handlebars, then biked away. I couldn't stop him. He went to the cut-through at the railroad tracks where he wavered. I thought he might turn back, and I felt a ray of hope. After another moment, though, he took his bike across the tracks and disappeared without another word. Summer would end, and many seasons would pass before I ever saw Tyler again.

Against Billy's earlier threat, I biked across the park and over the avenue towards Fenton's house. Up above, the clouds had separated into wispy pewter filaments with an azure canvas of sky showing behind. As I drew closer to the entrance, my

314

anxiety increased. I asked myself whether I should go onto the property against their explicit command. I felt a terrible urgency, though, to personally hand Fenton the backpack right then and there. Surely, he and Billy could appreciate that I'd rescued evidence from the doorstep of a burning building started by their own hands.

Then we could straighten things out. I would offer them the patch, and they'd return the Purple Heart. I knew they didn't want me in their club. I didn't have to join. I only wanted to make a deal. What kept eating at me now was the thought of my dad in a military hospital with that medal pinned onto his pillow. The symbol of the sacrifice he'd made, and I, his son, had simply given it away. I felt worse than ashamed. I didn't know myself anymore, but I had to get it back. My father's memory was the only thing that mattered, and the weight of it was killing me.

With that pushing me, I decided to continue on. When I made it to the end of that back street, I ducked through the brush onto the Felchers' property. From the rain, puddles had pooled in the gravel drive while drops fell off the leaves above. The air itself seemed painted green from the backdrop of grass, moss, and ferns. Marshall's truck sat in the carport, but otherwise there was no sign of life.

On the chance Fenton had parked his bike out of sight, I looked beside the shop. There was nothing. Through the front window, I saw Marshall busy at his workbench. Deciding that I might risk bothering him for some information, I stepped to the shop's door and bravely knocked three times.

"Who's there?" Marshall shouted.

UNDER THE LIGHT OF FIREFLIES

"Noah Ellis."

He squinted his eyes and looked at me through the smudged glass. I gave a friendly wave before respectfully taking a step back. Put off, he dropped his work and strode over. Cracking the door against his shoulder, he laid his other hand on the jamb and looked down at me.

"What do ya need?" he asked.

"Hi, Mr....I mean, hi, Marshall. I was wondering if you saw Fenton lately?"

"Is his bike here?"

"I didn't see it. But I thought maybe he came by and said where he was going."

He slowly shook his head no and then asked, "What's that behind your back?"

The backpack was gripped tightly in my hands behind me. I didn't want to show it to him, but I couldn't say no. With some trepidation, I pulled it around. His eyes sharpened as he looked at it.

"Where'd you get this?" he asked.

"Fenton left it at...at...the creek."

"At the creek?"

"There was a run-in with some wasps, so we had to bolt," I said and displayed the line of stings on my arm. "I went back later and found this."

Marshall listened to my words suspiciously before he reached down and took the backpack from me. Just like that, my bargaining chip was gone. As he glanced at Fenton's name written on the outside, he stepped back from the door.

"I think you better come inside, son," he said.

316

My heart sank into my stomach and my blood curdled. Somehow, I'd miscalculated this move too. The backpack was now out of my hands, but even worse, I had no choice but to go into Marshall's lair under heavy suspicion. I knew my story was incredibly thin. Matching wits with this brute filled me with dread because I didn't know what would happen if he caught me in a lie. Not to mention what the other guys would do to me after he asked them about it. The whole thing was on the verge of unraveling. I took a hard gulp and plodded inside.

Marshall pointed at a chair for me to sit in. He tossed the backpack into a wheelbarrow and grabbed the oval ring with a key on it. Crossing the room, he rolled the tool cabinet away from his security closet. Next, he spun a combination, turned the key, then opened the door and disappeared inside. I wondered what kind of torture device he was going for. I considered making a break right then, but it would only make me a coward. Inside the chamber, I could see shelves stacked with books and junk. On the ground sat a strange mound covered by a blanket, but that was it. Then Marshall reemerged carrying a huge rifle.

"You ever seen one of these?" he asked as he shut the door then walked back to his workbench.

"No, sir. We mostly had shotguns."

"I doubt that's all you had," he said with a short laugh.

He displayed it to me. The gun was clean and black with rails fitted along its sides. It had a sleek, sturdy frame and contoured stock. A blunt cylinder was fixed over the barrel which I recognized to be a silencer. All of it appeared state of the art and outclassed anything I ever saw.

"What kind is it?" I asked.

UNDER THE LIGHT OF FIREFLIES

"It's a German model. Very rare. I modified it myself."

"I never saw one like that. It's nice."

He pulled the bolt back, checked the chamber, then released it with a snap. A click sounded as he pulled the trigger, showing it wasn't loaded. He regarded it in his arms like it had come from his own loins, then he held it out to me.

"Go ahead," he said. "See how she feels."

I looked at him, questioning, but he nodded yes. So, I accepted the gun and let it sink into my arms. Marshall's eyes shone as I pulled it close against my chest. The rifle was heavy and long, though it felt perfectly balanced, even to a novice like me. I gripped the stock then peeked through a large mounted scope.

"You've handled guns before," he said without asking.

"Yes, sir. My dad taught me."

He went back to his chair, relaxed, and watched me. His hands were calloused and scarred. A black tee-shirt clung to his sinewy body, half exposing the tattoos on his arms. He saw me looking and pulled up a sleeve.

"I got these in my younger days," he said. "That one right there says USMC. You know what that means?"

"You're a Marine."

Marshall nodded with an approving eye. He liked seeing me with a gun on my lap. Brawny and muscular, the gun seemed like a reflection of Marshall himself. It felt dangerous, yes, but that was part of the allure.

"I've shot that gun with your dad," he said out of nowhere.

"With my father?"

"You've heard that me and your dad have a history. Right?"

318

"I heard a little."

"He knew guns. I bet he never told ya that, did he?"

"No, sir. He didn't."

"No, sir," he whispered back. "Walter wouldn't mention that."

He bounced his knee as thoughts bounced in his head.

"Dad was a Marine too," I said.

"I know he was. I know it well."

A long pause came like he was waiting for me to say something else, but I didn't.

"We was Marines together," he told me at last. "Didn't you know that?"

"You two? Like, at the same time?"

"We served side by side."

"Wow. I never heard that. Did you go to college with him too?"

"Ha ha!!" He laughed and threw back his head. "No, I ain't been to no college. Everything I learned is with these hands and my instincts."

"Dad didn't talk about that stuff. About the war, I mean."

"I guess he never had the time to tell ya about it," he said. "Walt was a fine soldier."

I bowed my head in silence. When I looked up, his eyes were still on me. I wanted to delve into it more, but there was some hermetic force around the subject that I was afraid to broach. I examined the gun again to avoid his stare.

"That's a hand-crafted silencer on the end," he told me. "I made it myself. I make 'em better than anything on the market. That's a fact."

319

UNDER THE LIGHT OF FIREFLIES

My finger rested on the trigger. If it was loaded, I could squeeze off a round and no one would hear it. It was a wild thought.

"That's about enough," he said and stood with his hands out.

I gave the rifle back as an oily film stuck to my fingers. After laying it on his work bench, Marshall paused with his back to me, doing nothing. A moment later, he turned and walked to the door where he opened it and waited. Dutifully, I got up and went outside.

On the step, I looked at him again with the question on the tip of my tongue, battling whether I should ask it. Could you please help me get my father's Purple Heart back? *Could you please save me from my shame?* His granite face and stare, though, intimidated me. To ask for it would lead to more questions. I shrank from that possibility.

"Goodbye, Noah," he said.

"So long, Marshall."

The door shut, and my hopes vanished. I felt like a child. I looked up at the empty treehouse. Their church. Those guys hated me. I didn't even have their backpack anymore. All my credit was spent. To add to the misery, I'd included them in a lie that they knew nothing about. Marshall would certainly ask for an explanation to which they'd have no answer. I was in deeper than ever. And what would I say to my family when the phone rang and a policeman said that I was wanted for burning down a house? Without a doubt, the others would blame the whole fiasco on me. I wasn't a Star. The life I saved, the bravest act I ever committed, would go forever unknown. It had become a

320

bad day for me too. A very bad day indeed.

Wrought with guilt, I left their property and randomly rode the wet streets of Texarkana and headed south, passing through neighborhoods, over bridges, and beyond the places I normally went. I kept riding farther and farther away until I arrived in a poor part of town and rode amongst its tired and huddled houses. At last, I came upon a road lined with dogwoods and crepe myrtles. I went down to where it narrowed into a single track and followed it through a gate into a broad orchard. The earth there was good, and the pecan trees rose to magnificent heights, some over a hundred feet high. Squirrels skittered about the grounds picking nuts while a dove called from a tree.

A creek of spring water ran through the heart of the property where halfway down an ancient bridge stretched across to a noble cemetery. On that side, cars sat parked with visitors mingling about. I rode over the bridge and got off my bicycle. At the stream, I stopped and splashed my face and took a long drink. After that, I walked to a kneeling stone angel with his wings draped around his body. I left my bicycle there and continued past an obelisk and later a statue of Mary.

A few rows down, I found my father's grave. It was clean and washed from the rain. Upon the gravestone was a stone pot filled with flowers, white with yellow buttons in the center. Someone had visited that day, and I wondered who it could've been. I did not have any flowers to give. I stood at the foot, careful not to tread, then sat down. I read the inscription on his gravestone over and over again:

Theodore Walter Ellis

June 1st, 1944—November 7th, 1979

UNDER THE LIGHT OF FIREFLIES

"I have fought the good fight, I have finished the race,
I have kept the faith." 2 Tim 4:7

A breeze touched my face while the flowers swayed. The dove lighted and passed over to the orchard. Dropping my head, I wept bitterly.

"I'm so sorry, Dad," I lamented. "I really messed up this time. I don't know what to do anymore. I wish you were here to help me."

Everything I'd been putting off now rushed upon me. I was not a man, but I was guilty of a terrible sin. Wrapping my arms around myself, I held in the pain as tears pattered the grass below. While I shook and trembled, the breeze turned into a wind and swept through the trees. Then a hand came upon my shoulder, gentle and warm. It squeezed and rubbed my back. I breathed deeply and slowly as this stranger consoled me unseen. I turned at last, and there stood a Black lady with bouffant hair and horn-rimmed glasses, giving a gracious smile. It was Mrs. Johnson, the mother of my old teammate, Donovan.

"Oh, Noah Ellis," she said and kneeled next to me. "You got such a big heart. I'm so sorry, son. I'm so sorry."

She laid her long arm across my back and pulled me close. She had on a starched yellow dress, and I was afraid she'd muss it, but she didn't mind and held me while I cried. We didn't say anything for a long time. With her there was no shame. After a while, I caught my breath and felt strong enough to stand.

"Is that your bicycle parked by that angel?" she asked.

I nodded and tried to speak, but my throat was too tight.

"You're a long way from home, son. You came here on a

mission." She looked at the flowers and asked, "Did you ride all that way with these little daisies in your hand?"

I shook my head no.

"Those ain't your flowers?"

"No ma'am," I said.

"Well, there you go. People loved your daddy."

Those simple white flowers wouldn't last forever, but for one day it was enough. I would've loved to have had one more day with my father. I remembered our last night together and thought, *If only I'd known. I never had the chance to say goodbye.* Mrs. Johnson stood respectfully before his grave with me until the wind stilled.

"Thanks, Mrs. Johnson," I said.

"God bless you, Noah. You had to grow up so fast, but that's just gonna make you that much stronger. Everybody sees what you've been through, and what a good heart you have."

"I wish I was good. I wish everything was easier. Life is hard."

"I know it is," she said and raised my chin with her hand. "Life is a furnace sometimes. But you can either burn up in it, or you can come out shining like gold."

"I'm tired of going around and around. Everything changes, but nothing gets any better."

Her eyes were deep, soulful, understanding, the eyes of a dancer who'd danced the dance, who'd performed with grace, and who'd done it for no applause. She understood the splinter.

"Listen to me, son," she said. "It's not about whether you go into the dark house. It's about whether or not you make it out. God made you decent, Noah Ellis. Just be yourself, and never give up hope."

CHAPTER EIGHTEEN

"In Dramatic Twist, Case Dropped
Against Russian Zookeeper"
The Texarkana Gazette, July 11, 1981

As if the grisly deaths of a man and teenager from a tiger attack wasn't drama enough, the ensuing case against the communist immigrant charged with their manslaughter took another wild turn yesterday when Justice Whitaker Caraway dismissed the case. Just as the trial looked to be turning towards a conviction, defendant Hendrik Magi—a maintenance worker at the local zoo who previously escaped the Soviet Union—was acquitted when seemingly out of thin air missing evidence appeared.

Early this week defense attorney Clive Longbranch, the maverick from Tyler who famously defended the fugitive Jeb Strahan, made a motion for a second sweep at TPD in hopes of locating two critical pieces of evidence. The first piece was a service request for a new lock to the tiger cage; the second, a hand-

LEE SANDERS

written note left at the zoo which warned against moving the tiger. Both were claimed to have been penned by the defendant.

The prosecution argued against the motion, stating that an inspection had already been performed and another would only be a waste of the court's time. Justice Caraway, however, sided with the defense. Shortly thereafter, the startling evidence was discovered sitting in a drawer at a vacant desk.

The find indeed contained the documented request for a new lock which was signed by Magi, verified to be his handwriting by the judge himself. The same file also held the handwritten note in question. On the day of the attack, Magi had posted a notice upon the outer security-door which warned that the lock was unreliable, and it would be a danger to move the tiger back into its original pen.

When court reconvened, Longbranch immediately made a motion to dismiss the case which Justice Caraway agreed to hear. The counselor argued that the new evidence showed Magi had acted with duty and conscience and should not be held accountable for the victims' deaths. He referred to the documented request as well as the handwritten letter found on the dead park director's person. Then in a dramatic scene Longbranch held up the blood-stained note.

In the prosecution's rebuttal, lead attorney Jeffrey Palmer admitted that it appeared Magi had indeed made the request for a new lock. Regardless of the warning, however, Magi was negligent in leaving his post when such a possibility even existed. He then reminded the judge that because of that negligence, a teenage boy along with a father of two were dead, and another boy was scarred for life.

325

UNDER THE LIGHT OF FIREFLIES

In his counter, Longbranch argued that Magi had waited for his superiors well beyond any reasonable length of time. He contended that the zookeeper and his assistant were both inebriated and most likely disregarded the note. The defense then presented paid receipts which showed that during the time in question, the zookeeper and his assistant were carousing at a drinking establishment named Mother's until 8:00 p.m. The combined bill accounted for nineteen cocktails. The argument against Magi for any kind of negligence, Longbranch insisted, was totally unsustainable and hypocritical.

With the gallery astir, Justice Caraway declared a recess for deliberation. After a two-hour wait, the court was reconvened. When he returned, the judge opined that negligence and dereliction comprised the central argument of the prosecution's case. The newly discovered evidence undermined that argument. The judge agreed with the defense that Magi was in no way responsible for the accused deaths, and that the case no longer held merit. With a strike of the gavel, the charges were summarily dismissed and the defendant released.

As he stood on the steps of the courthouse in his custom-made boots and silk suit, the fiery Longbranch lauded Justice Caraway for administering swift justice.

"Judge Caraway is a man of honor," he said. "Few men who wear the robe have the guts to do what he just did. Everyone should understand that Mr. Magi is an innocent man with a right to due process, the same as any American. I saw to it that he got his due. He's now free to go as he pleases. It's a victory for justice."

The prosecution had a less than glowing appraisal of the

result.

"Justice went unserved today," prosecutor Palmer dourly remarked. "Two innocent people are dead, and a young boy will never be the same. Somebody should have paid for it. It's hard to explain away what happened in there."

When asked if another indictment would be forthcoming, Palmer offered no comment. A second arrest for the same crime is rare. With the case against the Russian zookeeper officially over, this tragic tiger tale could be nearing its conclusion. To date, however, the actual tiger remains uncaptured.

CHAPTER NINETEEN

After visiting my father's grave, I went home and stayed in my room with my head on my desk, watching the fish swim. Fish didn't have any responsibilities. They didn't understand they weren't free. I sat there wishing I could be like them. I'd turned my back on my father, on my friends too, and along the way, a house got burned down. There was no doubt that the police would have a report and a description of us. That old man got a very good look, after all. There had been other vandalism right around the corner from me. Would they link them together? And if they found out who did it, which they always did, who would take the rap? I knew what Tyler had said was correct. The club came first. I'd have it pinned on me. And to add insult to injury, they still had my father's Purple Heart. A pit formed in my stomach and my head throbbed as I languished in despair. I tried to watch the fish swim, but it didn't help.

Downstairs, Sally sat at the kitchen table doing crafts with Grand'Mere who was most impressed by Sally's artistic prowess. At the counter, Mother cleaned shallots on a chopping board. She gave me a soft look when I walked up. I never considered all the effort it took to raise us, but she looked amazing to me right then. I came next to her, and she breathed deeply. She liked me coming around.

"So, the swimming trip got cancelled today?" I asked.

"Yes. It started raining right when we got out of the car."

"Was Sally upset?"

"A little, but she has her Grand'Mere to keep her entertained," she said and dropped the shallots into the pan with some oil. "I saw that you got wet today, though."

"I got drenched."

"Where were you?"

"I was at the creek hunting for crawdads."

Next, she cut the squash.

"How was your movie last night?" I asked.

"A bore. Lots of explosions. That seems to be the theme for summer movies nowadays, but it's hardly entertaining if you ask me."

"So, who was that man that brought you home?"

Her face flushed and she pulled her hair behind her ear.

"Why, Noah Ellis," she said. "Were you spying on me?"

"I was riding up when you arrived."

"You were supposed to be home already."

"I promised that it wouldn't happen again."

"You'll be held to that promise."

We sat there with my question still lingering as she continued to cut.

"Lloyd Graham is his name," she told me at last. "He's a

UNDER THE LIGHT OF FIREFLIES

friend of a friend."

"He walked you to the door."

"Men are supposed to do that."

"Was it a date?"

She tossed the squash into a pot, grabbed some carrots, but stopped.

"Yes," she said. "It was a date. I thought it would be nice to have some company. I'm allowed to have a life, you know."

"I know. It's okay."

She turned to see if I was really okay, then laid down the knife and put her hands on my shoulders.

"You look just like your father. Do people ever tell you that?"

"All the time."

She squeezed my shoulders and watched me quietly. As we stood there, I thought about everything I'd done and all I'd lost, yet I still had her. I didn't want to let her down.

"Those stings look terrible," she said to change the subject.

"They don't hurt anymore. But they itch a lot."

"Keep putting calamine on them."

"I'm pink all over."

"Did you hear that Nancy Thomas's house got vandalized while they're out of town?" she asked, turning back to the stove.

"*Again?*"

"Yes. It happened last night. They threw furniture, firewood, and everything else they could find into the pool. They even smashed pots and vases. Maniacs. The authorities are on the lookout."

I didn't respond because I had a good idea who was responsible. It started with Billy and ended with Fenton. This was the

330

second time that Nancy's house had now been hit. The cops would definitely be snooping.

"You're not running around with hoodlums like that, I hope," she said.

"Of course not."

"Where's Dusty been?"

I didn't answer, which was an answer in itself.

"Is it about a girl?" she asked.

"It's not like you think."

"It is or it isn't, son."

I shrugged.

"It's a bad choice to let a girl come between friends."

"I'm just doing my own thing for now."

"Do as you please, but Dusty, Sam, and you have always been a team. Whatever your issue is, I think you should settle it and move on."

"Sam hasn't been around anyway," I said.

"He got back two days ago."

"Is that right? I haven't seen him."

"Maybe you haven't been looking."

Mother lighted candles and served us dinner in the dining room. Sally got to wear her nicest dress. Jack slicked down his hair and put on a tie which made the ladies laugh. All the fixings were there including dessert. Under other circumstances, I would've enjoyed it. I put on my best face, though, complimenting the meal, trying to smile at jokes, thinking of how blissful it would be to have a simple dinner in innocence. Then the phone rang. I choked and halted, terrified the cops were calling to report I was wanted. This beautiful family dinner

UNDER THE LIGHT OF FIREFLIES

would be shattered with the knowledge that I'd done the impossible; burned a house down.

Sally loved telephones, so she ran down the hall to answer it. After she picked it up, she called my name. I clinched in jittery anticipation. *Please be Sam*, I thought. Tell me his parents had figured out the tiger wasn't stalking them in particular.

"Hello?"

"Noah," I heard a teenager's voice say.

"Who is this?"

"You know who."

"Sloan?"

"Am I interrupting something?"

"No, no. I can talk."

"What have you been doing all day?"

"Nothing much," I replied, unsure if this was a test.

"I was wondering," he said in an intimate tone. "Did you hear about that fire down Shillings Road?"

"Yeah. I actually saw the firetrucks. Lightning must have hit something."

"Must have. So, did the firetrucks see you?"

"No."

"Interesting. Let me ask you something else. Were there any ambulances?"

"Not that I saw."

"Then everyone is okay. Everyone made it out."

"Yeah. It was a close call, but everybody came out okay."

Muffled tones seeped through the earpiece as Sloan spoke with someone.

"What are you doing tonight?" he asked as he got back on.

332

"Staying in."

"You need to come over here."

"I'm not allowed to ride my bike this late."

"I'll come and get you."

"What's going on?"

"You passed your test."

My heart jumped. I looked in the other room where my family was enjoying dinner, oblivious to the situation.

"I'll be waiting at the dead end of your street," he said. "Thirty minutes."

"I really can't come out at this hour. I got in trouble the other night for doing it. My mother put her foot down."

"Then that's too bad for you, tiger man."

"Wait a minute. Can't we just do it tomorrow?"

"This is your only shot."

"But why?"

"Because I said so," he replied sharply.

I sat there gripping the phone, my mind racing.

"See you later, Noah."

"Okay, okay," I said. "I can meet you at the end of my street like you said."

"That should've been your first answer. Be there at eight o'clock or else. And another thing, keep your mouth shut."

The line went dead. I stood there blankly and held the phone. This was it. This was my chance. If I could make it over there, I'd be saved. Somehow, I had to pull this off with my mother, but it would be a hugely difficult task. My only option was to lie. I hated to do that to Mother, especially after everything we'd discussed, but this was where the path had led me.

"I'd love to!!" I then exclaimed as if still on the call. "But I'll have to ask my mother. Talk to you later!"

After I hung up, I went to the doorway of the dining room and motioned Mother to come over. She squinted at me curiously then slowly left the table and came into the hall.

"What is it?" she asked.

"That was Dusty on the phone. He called to talk things over. He asked if I could come by to watch a movie."

She held up her hand and stopped me.

"No," she answered. "We talked about this just last night. You can't go out."

"But it's only Dusty's house. He lives behind us."

"You kept breaking the rules without any reservations, and this is where you've ended up."

"Please, Mom. I know what we said, but I haven't hung out with him this summer since...since the whole thing happened. You said that him and me were a team."

She shook her head a few times and looked away. She couldn't believe I was doing this, but I had to press.

"Please, Mom? Please?"

"You're bent on making things difficult."

"I want to see my friend."

"Did you do your chores today like we agreed?"

"I scrubbed the bathroom earlier, but I couldn't mow the lawn because it was wet. I'll mow it tomorrow, I swear."

"I don't know if this is a good idea."

"I'll be back by bedtime. You can call Dusty's house if you need to."

It was a gamble saying that, but I had to do it. Mother bit

334

her lip. "You be back here by nine o'clock," she said.

"But the movie will run longer. Can't it be a little later?"

She laughed and gave me an odd look.

"9:15. How's that?"

I gulped. Hopefully my business at the Felchers would be done by then. Mother was one step from telling me no, so I accepted.

"Eat the rest of your supper," she said.

I finished eating and quickly cleaned off the table, watching the clock the whole time. With five minutes to go, I said goodbye under Mother's disapproving eyes then rushed to the garage and grabbed my bike. As I walked it outside, Sam unexpectedly appeared on the driveway. It felt like ages since I'd last seen him. More than that, I couldn't believe he was outdoors. He sat on his bicycle like he wondered if I remembered him.

"Sam," I said. "Where've you been? I thought you were staying away all summer."

"I've only been gone a month."

"More like a month and a half."

"Well, we took a vacation too."

"You never had anything to worry about, dude."

He was delicate, disappointed by my greeting so far. I got on my bicycle and started to go. I didn't want him to follow me, but I couldn't bring myself to say that.

"I know why your parents shoved you off to your cousins," I said as we started down the lane.

"I go to my cousins all the time."

"That tiger is gone. They'll never catch it."

"I heard it got some chickens in New Boston three days ago."

335

UNDER THE LIGHT OF FIREFLIES

"And a pig in Queen City. Plus, another one in Ida. That three states in three days. That tiger can really move."

Sam looked in the distance as he pondered this super tiger.

"Tigers don't go around people unless there's nothing to eat," I told him. "I'm pretty sure there's plenty of deer and possums in the woods."

"The tiger ate Connor, though," he said then gasped at what he'd said.

"I know it did."

"I'm sorry."

"Don't worry about it."

"You can't remember anything yet?"

"I remember earlier in the day when I was with you and..."

I stopped. I couldn't say Dusty's name. Sam timidly waited but didn't ask anything more. We rode together to the dead end where I got off my bike and stood at the trailhead. I knew he wouldn't go beyond that.

"Where are you leaving to?" he asked.

"I've got something I have to do."

"What is it?"

"I can't tell you right now. I need to leave."

He looked around anxiously then started to squeeze his hands together like he did whenever something was eating at him.

"Listen," he said. "I've got something you should know about."

"What is that?"

"If I tell you, please promise not to get mad."

"Humph. You don't want me to get mad. I know what this

336

is about."

"I don't think you do."

"Oh yeah, I do. I heard it straight from the horse's mouth. Dusty hooked up with Jill. Everybody knows, right? Well, they can laugh all they want. I don't care about anything anymore."

"That's not what I was gonna say."

"Then what is it?"

He took a few more breaths and shifted his weight uneasily. I didn't have time for Sam, and I truly didn't care. Sloan would be coming any minute. I decided to leave.

"It's about your dad," he said.

I stopped in my tracks and whipped around. He stood there like a statue as I read his face. There was no lying in that face. My pulse quickened.

"What about him?"

"Please don't get upset. I've been wanting to tell you, but my folks said not to. Your mother said it isn't..."

"Shut up, Sam. I don't have the time. Tell me what you're talking about."

"Okay then," he said with a big swallow. "It's about the river. It's about the day your dad died."

I felt butterflies swirl in my stomach as my body flinched.

"There's nothing more to know about the river," I said in a gravelly voice.

"There's one thing. It's about Fenton's dad. Mr. Felcher. He was there that day too."

"No. That can't be true. My brother would've told me. It's impossible."

"I also heard that Mr. Felcher was alone with your father

UNDER THE LIGHT OF FIREFLIES

right when...when it happened."

That hit me like a pile of bricks. It was too incredible.

"I don't believe it," I said. "Gary Donald was the only one with my father."

"Mr. Donald had gone to his truck. He heard a gunshot. When he went back, he says that Mr. Felcher was pacing up and down the bank's edge, looking into the water."

My heart pounded in my chest. Sam had just described the moment my father died. It was as heavy as anything I could've dreamed of. Adrenaline flooded my bloodstream while my thoughts darted in my head. My reality was coming unhinged.

Then far away I heard the tinkering of hard-rock music and the low rumble of an engine. I peered through the gate, and on the opposite end of the park road, I saw Sloan's car curving around the pond.

"I've gotta go."

"Can't you stay for a little longer?"

"You should be home by now. It's past your curfew."

"I have a few minutes."

"I can't."

"Please?"

"Not this time!" I said with a grimace. Then I started to walk away.

"Noah, wait."

I held still for one last second. His big lucid eyes shined in the early evening.

"I'm sorry for what happened to your dad," he said. "I'm sorry for what happened to you and to Connor too. I only wish that you and Dusty...I wish you could be friends again."

338

"I can't talk about it. I've gotta go."

"Okay. But wherever you're going, please be safe."

Without a goodbye, I walked to the trailhead and disappeared. Down the path, I found a patch of saplings and hid my bike underneath. I stood on a crop of rocks and watched Sloan's car speed past. Across the road, the park rested from the brunt of the day. The storm had cleared, but a few clouds still hung in the ebbing light. Everything was quiet and at peace.

I walked back to the trailhead, peeked out, and found that Sam had thankfully left. Then Sloan arrived with his loud music blasting out the windows as he rode with the T-top off. When he wheeled up, he had a cigarette hanging from his mouth and a beer in his lap. I slid into the car where he barely acknowledged me. Putting it in reverse, he peeled backwards through a plume of tire smoke, then slammed it into drive.

We rode back the way he came and turned down the cross street. As we did, I saw a boy standing beyond the curb near a tree, and our eyes met. It was Sam. His face drooped and his hands dropped by his side. I had to look away.

For me, joining the Stars would no doubt be a betrayal. I felt more compelled than ever, though, to do so. Along with retrieving my father's Purple Heart, questions about his death now crowded my mind. Was Marshall really at the river that day? Why wasn't I told? And though it initially seemed like a foul and inconceivable notion, as the seconds ticked away, I couldn't help but ask myself—did something criminal occur? That question alone constrained me. For if there existed even the small chance something happened, I could not abandon my father's memory into the hands of his possible killer. Sloan pulled onto

UNDER THE LIGHT OF FIREFLIES

the park road and mercifully turned down the racket.

"Tell me something," he said. "Have you heard anything since you last saw Tyler?"

"Not since we made it back."

"Made it back to where?"

"Here in the park."

"What'd Tyler do after that?"

"He just took off," I said.

"Tell me where."

"He wouldn't say. He was pretty upset."

"Tell me why."

"Like I said before. We had a close call."

"And what does that mean?"

"His hair got burned, and he had wasp stings all over his face. It's really bad. At least he's alive."

Sloan took a swig of his beer and stared straight ahead.

"Is there something wrong?" I asked.

"Don't ask questions," he answered and put the music back on blast.

His inquiry was strange. Why hadn't they asked Tyler himself about what happened? What was with all the intrigue? I glanced at Sloan who acted like he was doing duty on an unwanted mission. I realized what was happening. It was simple. Tyler had gone AWOL.

They'd abandoned him in a blazing building and now couldn't find him. The boys had done a lot of bad things in their time, but burning down a house had to be at the top, and they needed to keep this under wraps at all costs. So, unwilling to have two wildcards out on the scene, they had no choice but

LEE SANDERS

to initiate me into their club. It wasn't about me passing any test or them wanting me in. It was about shutting me up.

We arrived at the Felchers' property. The earlier green atmosphere had now turned brown in the deepening shadows. The loamy smell of wet earth saturated the air, and everything was still. Along the edge of the culvert, a school of fireflies danced about, spawning arcs of golden light. Sloan parked his car and took us straight inside the shop.

Florescent lighting illuminated the place while that slight aroma of gasoline still lingered. The boat had been finished and now rested on a small trailer. Beside the refrigerator in the back, the door stood cracked open. There at the workbench, facing me, sat the man himself. Marshall. He had on clean jeans, boots, and a white tank top while he casually rolled a silver dollar across his knuckles. His mere presence sent a pang of dread that began to choke me.

"Not a minute too soon," he said gruffly.

"Not a minute too late," Sloan replied.

A heavy thought seemed to pass between them. Marshall looked at me, stopped rolling the silver dollar, then flicked it my way. I instinctively reached up and caught it. Sloan giggled as he walked towards the back.

"Don't take all my beer," Marshall said.

"I put more in there earlier."

As Marshall rose, I noticed that he was free of his keys, knife, and dog tags. He walked past without a word, and I could smell the musky scent of cologne and felt ill.

"Get that thing going," he told Sloan. "And don't go in the den. A movie's on."

341

UNDER THE LIGHT OF FIREFLIES

"I'm heading out afterward."

Marshall pushed back the screen and left. I pocketed the coin. Sloan strolled to the refrigerator, grabbed a beer, then took Marshall's place at the workbench and cracked open the can.

"Right about now is when I ask for that patch," he said, taking a sip.

"I got it right here," I replied and reached into my pocket.

"First things first. What've you said to your brother?"

"Nothing. He doesn't care what I do."

"Ain't that sweet. How were you planning on getting your daddy's Purple Heart back?"

"I don't know."

He put down the beer and came and stood before me. I handed him the patch. He pocketed it then removed a buck knife from his belt and held it in front of me. It reminded me of Connor that day at the store.

"You came here on your own choice, yes or no?" he asked.

"Yes."

"In order to get something, you gotta give something, and I ain't talking about no purple hearts."

He twisted the knife so that it glinted in the light.

"You ever heard of blood brothers?" he asked.

"Yes."

"That's the ultimate oath. Once you mingle blood, you can't ever turn your back. You better be ready for that."

He then took my hand and held up my palm.

"After tonight, you'll be a Wandering Star," he said. "Or you'll be dead to us."

I stood without movement as the blade drifted above my

342

skin. Naked light flashed off its sharpened edge. I thought about my own brother, and I felt anguish for what was about to happen.

"It is what it is," I said quietly.

Sloan gave a sardonic smile and wrenched my fingers, pulling me closer. He breathed into my face, but I refused to wince. After a painful few seconds, he tossed my hand aside and re-sheathed his knife.

He went back to the workbench with his eyes on me and pulled their oval key ring from a box. Striding to the steel door, he shoved aside the tool chest and inserted the key into the lock and turned it. After spinning the combination a few times, he pulled down the lever and the closet opened. He stepped into the darkness before reappearing a moment later. In his hand, he held the lavender and gold-lined box. Kicking the door shut, he strode back across the room with a surly look and flipped open the box so I could see the Purple Heart.

"Look familiar?" he asked as he held it within reach, daring me to take it.

"Yes, it does."

He taunted me with the medal a bit longer then snapped the box shut. He pointed me to a chair and I sat down. With my father's medal in hand, he grabbed his beer and walked to the front.

"We'll be back down when we're good and ready," he said. "Stay there and don't move."

He exited and slammed the door shut. As soon as he was gone, I exhaled and collapsed over my knees. Nausea started to grow. The smell of gas seemed thicker than before, the room more cloying. I rose from the chair and paced the floor, returned to the chair, then stood up several more times, trying to find relief in the exercise, but to no avail.

As I toiled, I saw the back door open and thought I'd try for some fresh air. I noticed that the tool chest was still pulled away from the closet. As I lumbered towards the exit, I stopped to have a look. The closet door was built with a solid steel frame like a bank's safe, which seemed like overkill. *Why all the security?* I asked myself. Were stacks of money or dead bodies stuffed in there?

I noticed that Sloan had forgotten about the key in the lock. Staring at it, I wondered if this was the bait. Were they watching to see if I'd break in? I looked about and listened, but nobody was around. I thought about trying the door, but I'd never been the snooping kind. I was too afraid of getting caught. However, I wasn't myself at that moment, standing in a cold sweat, reflecting on how much I didn't belong there. If I committed the soulless act of joining their club, I knew I'd be treated lower than low. After all, they'd abandoned one of their own brothers right in front of me. What more would I receive?

So, for the hell of it, I turned the key. Without the slightest resistance, I felt the chamber click and a bolt roll under. I didn't know the combination, so I didn't even try, instead grabbing the lever and jerking it down. Then to my surprise, the door magically opened.

Shocked at what I'd done, I held onto the frame, afraid to turn around, listening for any hint of a sound. Nothing came except the whir of fluorescent lights and my heart pounding in my ears. I stood indecisively at the threshold, grappling with whether to risk it and go inside, or shut the door and stay safe. Then again, what was safe? I'd done this much, so maybe I could take one tiny peek.

Inside the closet was pitch black, and I blindly fumbled along the wall for a light switch which didn't exist. As I ventured further, my feet kicked some cans and a loud clang rattled out. That jangled my already battered nerves, so I decided to reverse course before I got nailed. While I stumbled towards the door, though, I felt a string drag across my face. I knew what that was, so I pulled it down whereafter a burst of light filled the closet.

The chamber had been built long and wide. On one side, crates were piled chest high with markings from a language I didn't recognize. In the back, rusted steel lockers stood with shelves full of junk hanging above. Looking to the opposite side, I saw a long set of double-racks stacked from top to bottom with machine guns, assault rifles, and handguns. Dozens upon dozens of every kind, each one clean and bristling. Underneath the racks sat more cartons with other unknown markings. In trash cans, a myriad of long rods poked up with fat metal bulbs on the ends. From the movies, I recognized them as being rocket grenades. Even I knew those were illegal. Then I understood what all this meant and almost had a heart attack. Marshall was a gun runner. I'd just wandered into the middle of his stash.

As I frantically turned to leave, I noticed the covered mound near the entrance that I'd observed the one time before. It looked awkward, bulky, as if it didn't belong. I put my hand on the blanket and felt a steel molded figure with a short,

UNDER THE LIGHT OF FIREFLIES

ridged back. When I moved my hand up the body, I touched something like a head with pointy ears. That made no sense at all. Confused, I yanked back the cover where I was suddenly met by the fanged visage of a wild animal. Unlike that day in the park, though, this animal would never attack. It was the hog from the marquee in front of Arkansas High School.

Then something else caught my eye. Hidden against the wall behind the hog laid a stack of dusty books that looked familiar. Upon closer inspection, I spied the top book's cover which read, *English-Literature Teacher's Edition*. A jolt went through me. These were the books that had gone missing from the junior high last spring. I dropped the blanket and stumbled to the door while my stomach churned and my mind brimmed with foul thoughts.

I stumbled out half dizzy, shut the closet, and pulled the lever. Inside the shop, I found that I was still alone. Leaning back against the door, I rubbed my temples and tried to reason everything out. But the truth was plain. Connor took the rap for those books. He'd been set up. And here I was about to mix blood with the culprits, including Fenton and Sloan, which also meant the blood of their father. The room spun. My nausea grew worse. I needed air fast.

The back door sat halfway cracked, and in a haze I staggered through. Outside, I saw the school of fireflies still bobbing and swirling along the edge of the yard. They were magnificent. As I watched them blink in the final light of dusk, my body started to tingle, and goosebumps covered my flesh.

I remembered back to Grand'Mere's cabin where thousands of the bugs had appeared hovering over her deck. Sally

LEE SANDERS

had been so excited. I caught one and put it in a jar, but she wanted to let it go, so we did. Then I remembered the other time in the park after Connor and I had crossed the bridge to the playground. Along the banks of the creek, fireflies blinked and flickered like strings of Christmas lights. Connor said they were beautiful. It surprised me that he would say such a thing, but he had. Then he looked in the distance and got quiet. I asked him what it was, but he didn't answer. He kept staring, and an uneasiness came over me. Something was out there. Something was watching us. What was that? What could it be? What in the world could that... *Oh no. Connor!*

CHAPTER TWENTY

"What is that?" I asked, pulling Connor's shirt.

He didn't answer, but I could tell he was greatly disturbed.

"Tell me, Connor."

"Something ain't right."

"What is it?"

"I don't know. But something's stalking us."

"Something? Stop kidding around."

"It's watching us. Whatever you do, don't move."

Then that something itself moved, lurking low beyond the playground before hiding behind the spinner. Whatever it was, it blended in perfectly with the rusty browns of the landscape. As I stood up, my nervous hands unintentionally rattled the chain.

"*Stay still*," Connor said.

"What is that thing?"

"I can't tell."

"We should run for the water. It can't get us in the water."

"You'll never make it, Noah."

"We've got to try."

"It wants us to do that. Just wait. A car might pull up."

I stayed frozen next to the swing, rapt by this unknown creature watching us. Then after a few anxious moments, ever so softly, it slipped quietly from the shadows into the open. At first, I couldn't believe my eyes. I soon found out, though, that it was real enough. For what I saw coming right at us was nothing less than a tiger.

The thing was enormous. Just looking at it, I thought this truly had to be the king of the jungle. Its body was sleek, its eyes lustrous, and it carried a strange foreign presence. As it crept over the pine straw, its stare remained locked on us, intently watching every twitch we made. After crossing the grounds, it slunk behind the top of a rise where it laid flat to gaze at us with those magnetic eyes.

"We can't just stand around," I told Connor, terror swelling in my voice. "We've got to run."

Connor wouldn't say anything. He just watched the tiger as the tiger watched us.

"Come on, Connor. We've got to go now."

"It's only watching. So we stay put and wait."

"Wait for what?"

"It's not doing anything."

"Yes, it is. Let's run for it."

"Don't make it chase you, man."

With its paws the tiger scraped some dirt and adjusted itself. It wasn't there to sit all night long, I knew, and at last my fear got the best of me. Grabbing Connor's shirt, I begged him

UNDER THE LIGHT OF FIREFLIES

one last time to run, but he didn't move. So, I decided to go it alone. With a whimper, I took off and the chase was on.

It was no match. The amazing thing was I never heard it coming. I made around fifteen steps towards the water when out of the silence, the tiger's claws slammed into my back and shredded my flesh into ribbons. It knocked me to the ground with such force that the tiger went tumbling over my head while my mouth and nostrils filled with dirt. Being the cat it was, it hopped instantly to its feet and crouched, its eyes blazing like amber pearls.

As I sat paralyzed in fear, the warm flow of blood trickled down my back. Next, the tiger roared so loudly that I thought my eardrums would burst. Death was imminent. Being fully aware that this was the end of my life, I involuntarily convulsed and ejected a stream of vomit that caught the tiger just as it got ready to lunge, smacking it squarely across its snout and eyes. Recoiling violently, it fell several steps backward where it wildly pawed and drug its face in the dust with snorts and growls.

Next came a noise came from the other direction. The tiger heard it and perched, its snout filthy, its watery eyes searching the playground. The sight of my attack had evidently made a strong impression on Connor because he'd now broken into his own mad dash for survival. His mistake was that he'd emitted a small cry, the same as I'd done.

The tiger shot forward like a loaded javelin, its claws digging and spraying up dirt as it sprinted. I so very dreaded what was coming to Connor for I'd just experienced it firsthand. What was in store for him, though, would be much much worse.

Connor made it inside the little stone tower where he

350

quickly hustled up the ladder. Unfortunately for him, the tiger arrived only seconds later. Through the door, I saw its hindquarters hunch low before suddenly the animal sprang upward and disappeared from sight—though not from sound.

Growls and hisses reverberated through the windows alongside frantic cries for life. *"Nooo!!! Nooo!!! Please stop! Please please please go away,"* Connor begged, followed by squeals and shrieks of terror so horrific that it would shudder even the steeliest soul. Next, his body fell to the bottom in a pile. A second later, the animal dropped beside him and rolled Connor around while the boy groaned in a voice that wasn't human anymore.

After tormenting him a while, the tiger pulled Connor outside by the leg and left him there as it ducked around the corner to hide. Disfigured and dazed, Connor managed to get to his feet where he walked mechanically across the park entrance. He staggered along without expression, detached and deformed like a puppet hanging from half-broken strings. From the fall, he'd gotten a badly broken arm that now hung weirdly at his side. His face was streaked in blood. His empty eyes peered into the distance.

After he got several steps onto the drive, the tiger bounded from behind the tower, batting at the boy like it was a game. But it wasn't a game. When its victim wouldn't play, the tiger sunk its teeth into Connor's broken arm whereafter a sickening caterwaul of pain rang out. As Connor fell backward, he grabbed the tiger's ear and jerked back and forth, trying to steer the beast away. Twenty yards over, Jill's home sat as peaceful and quiet as a sun cloud.

351

Watching Connor's struggle, a deathly pall came upon me. This tiger was bloodthirsty. I surely would be next. I had to get out of there. Woozy and bleeding, I forced myself to my feet and bumbled towards the water which waited thirty feet away. The nausea and blood loss had weakened me to semi-consciousness, and after several steps, I vomited again and collapsed only yards from the water's edge, terrified the whole time the tiger would hear me and switch victims yet again. I refused to look back.

With my good arm, I clawed towards the pond until I discovered that it was no longer a mirage. Once there, I reached out and let the wetness cover my hand. The simplicity of feeling water became beautiful to me. I yearned to be in its darkness. I pulled and strained with all my strength until at last, I gently rolled over the bank. The water was warm and accepted me without judgment. I clutched the soft mud at the shallow bottom while around me a cloud of crimson grew. Above the surface, I could see the dying light of day and small blinking orbs of fireflies. I didn't want to come up for breath. I wanted to remain in that liquid state, safe from the sounds in the park.

As if from an unseen power, I thrusted upward from the water and gasped for air. The taste of it was sweet and filled my famished lungs. Fireflies flickered all around me. On the park's drive, Connor's cries had lowered into tough grunts, as if the eating of his flesh took great endurance. I watched and listened as a succession of struggling sounds devolved into a final groan of agony, and then there was no more. Connor was dead.

In the water, the pond's deepest point reached only chest high, and onward I churned towards the tiny island where

LEE SANDERS

ducks listlessly waited. My heart pumped and pumped inside my blood-drained body while my mind slid further away. My fear of death never waned. At any moment, I expected to hear a splash as the beast sought me out for its next plaything. But I made it to shore.

Ducks waddled away and turtles plopped into the water at the loss of their tranquility. On the bank's edge, the water was shallow enough for me to crawl up, which I struggled to do. I ultimately made it onto the grass where I collapsed onto my back with my feet hanging off. I laid there and sucked in breath after breath. When I'd slowed down enough, I sat up on an elbow and looked out, hoping the tiger wasn't coming.

Twilight had fallen, so I couldn't make out the scene, but then headlights appeared on the park road as a truck drove around the pond to the park's entrance. Once inside, it suddenly jerked to a stop from a shocking discovery. For there in its headlights was the sight of a living tiger. A tiger that sat hunched over the corpse of a dead boy.

In the glare, the tiger squatted and greedily guarded its prize, hissing at the mechanical beast. The truck quickly reversed and slammed to a stop. Then it revved its engine several times and lurched forward, blaring its horn. That confused and spooked the animal, and after another honk, it begrudgingly moved off its prey towards the shadows. The horn kept going, and after checking its kill one last time, the tiger darted into the night where it was never heard from again.

With the animal gone, a man appeared from the truck to check Connor's remains. That man was Derek Mayfly who later rescued me from the water. My sight was blocked as

353

UNDER THE LIGHT OF FIREFLIES

he knelt over, but as soon as he went back to his truck, I saw Connor's body in the light, lifeless as a doll. Blood was everywhere. His shirt had been torn off his maimed body, and his blank eyes stared across the pond directly into my own. With that sight, my mind cracked wide open, and my consciousness flew upward like sparks from a campfire.

I laid back again on the soft grass, my heart straining to beat, my head spinning through space and time. Above me I saw a distant star, silent and unmoving, blinking its faint light across the cosmos. I felt surely that's where I was going, and that my father would be waiting. My last thought was about my little sister, Sally. What would she hear except that a tiger had killed her brother? Monsters would become a real thing, haunting her sleep as she dreamed of me dying upon the park's island. *Poor sweet Sally*, I thought. I wished there was something I could do, but I couldn't hold on any longer. I prayed a last prayer in silence, for my sorrow was unspeakable. The night was very still. I went to sleep.

That was the end, and I remembered it all.

Outside the backdoor of Marshall's shack, I smelled the syrupy odor of gasoline mixed with the thick scent of wet earth, and I dropped to my knees and puked violently. My soul rocked with the memory, sharp and pale and gruesome. For a moment I felt like I'd been sent back to that tiny island where the stitches of my psyche were stretched to their breaking point. If it split again, would my mind heal a second time? The tidal force splashed and roiled, rising higher and higher until at last it broke, retreated, and washed back into its beginning.

LEE SANDERS

After it was over, I asked myself if this was it. Was this what I'd been yearning for, the liberation of this repulsive memory? Was this the truth, nauseating and horrific, that I'd so desperately sought to know? Well, now I knew. My town would be ecstatic to hear about it, that was for sure. And these other vermin—Sloan, Fenton, and Billy—they'd lick it up like cream. They were a menace, a disease, but they had my father's Purple Heart.

As the fireflies blinked, a notion occurred to me. What about the Purple Heart? If my father were alive, what would he say, that the medal had meant so much to him? Or would he say that the Purple Heart was only a memento, an image that could not speak or hope or love? He mounted fish on the walls and put a baseball on display, but the one item commemorating his wound, he kept in a drawer. He didn't need a reminder. The bullet went with him to the grave. All that remained was to learn the truth of his death.

From the treehouse, I heard a clatter and then the opening of the trap door. Fenton's conspicuous torso squirmed out first, followed by Billy and Sloan. They hit the ground like gunfighters and strutted to the front of the shop where I heard the screen door swing open and clang shut. Inside, they chatted briefly before a lull ensued as they realized I wasn't there. After a look around, accusations of backsliding ensued while they argued whose fault it was. Finally, Sloan noticed the back door open and saw me outside on my knees.

"There he goes," Sloan said. "Playing with the lightning bugs." The others laughed. "Whatchya doing out there, tiger boy? Did you bring your little jar?"

355

I didn't respond. After waiting a few seconds, Sloan called again, this time more severely.

"Say, boy! This ain't no time for picking daisies. Get your fool ass over here before I come and drag you over here."

I refused again to move which further stoked his anger. As he issued his final decree, I curiously heard a car's tires rolling onto the gravel drive. Then a second set pulled behind and both came to a stop. Doors opened and shut, followed by the low murmur of men's voices. I couldn't see them, but a moment later, I heard the unmistakable chatter of a CB Radio. Then the treehouse's trap door flew open again. To my surprise, it was Marshall who came flying down the trunk this time, shouting threats the whole way. All of a sudden, a barrage of spinning red and blue lights lit up the property. With that, the boys grew very quiet, and the shop light went dark.

Inside the commotion, Connor appeared in my head. It wasn't about how he'd died, but how he could never vindicate himself. I was his only witness. These other guys were the ones who cut in line, stole, and vandalized houses until, in the end, they burned one down. They'd even abandoned their own blood brother because blood oaths didn't apply to them. Weakness didn't have to be real, it only had to be perceived. That's when they turned on you. To them, the most important aspect of their club wasn't fraternity. It was impunity.

In that moment, I loathed them more than anything I ever knew. Then I asked myself, was I only joining them to follow in my father's footsteps? Or to earn some notoriety this time instead of having it thrust upon me? If my dad could've been there, would he have wanted me to stick around just to learn how he died? No. He'd want me to do the exact same thing he did. Leave. Yeah, they might've had my father's medal, but they didn't have me yet. And if they wanted me, they'd have to come and get me. But they'd have to go out the front door to do it.

I rose to my feet and slammed the back door shut, leaving them inside without any lights. Along the outside wall laid a pile of scrap iron beside a stack of rusted metal chairs. I found a crowbar and wedged it into the door jamb. Then I rammed a chair under the knob and barred it fast. I didn't know if the barricade would hold, but to hell with it. I was getting out either way.

In the middle of the backyard grew a large tree. As quiet as a church mouse, I ducked and scurried across the lawn. At the tree, I crept behind the trunk and waited for the chance to make another dash. Yet another police car pulled up. As the cops gathered for a discussion, the door started to bang from the boys trying to get out. They called out my name with vicious threats, but what they didn't know was that their threats didn't mean a damn thing to me anymore.

While they continued to work on the door, I hurried for another tree. I slipped around and listened for any hint of detection. Marshall had calmed momentarily, but soon enough he broke into more slander and curses after which a colossal feud erupted. While he and the cops shouted accusations at each other, the shack's backdoor finally burst open and the three excited boys fell out.

I knew that I shouldn't wait. I had to take my chances right then. In the growth along the culvert, I spied a recess that

UNDER THE LIGHT OF FIREFLIES

I thought would be a good place to try. After surveying the scene one last time, I took a breath and went for it. As I bolted full steam ahead, Sloan spotted me and yelled, "*There goes that dirty rat.*"

I sprinted as fast as I could, my feet splashing through mud as I went, yet the cops never heard a thing. At the recess, I skidded to the culvert's edge, stepped off, then plopped neatly onto the creek's concrete floor inside a band of fireflies. As I knocked the mud off, I heard the boys coming behind me, jabbering foolishly. A spotlight swung and hit them, followed by a command to halt. When they didn't obey, a full chorus chimed in with more orders. Even Marshall sounded off.

"Have you lost your damn mind?!" he cried. "Stop your butts right there!"

Their feet slid through the mud and stopped just a foot in front of me. As they stood there on the edge looking down, I'll never forget their faces.

"You can't run this time, boys," I said with a long grin.

"You wanna talk smart?" Sloan said. "Don't think you're getting off this easy."

"What are you going to do, turn me in? How would your pop feel about you becoming a rat?"

His eyes burned with venom, but there was nothing he could do or say. Fenton and Billy had to choke it down too. All of them stood there with their teeth bared, hating me, wanting to be standing right where I was standing, but this time I was the one who got away. Staying for one last delicious moment, I wagged my finger at them, then turned and booked it out of sight.

358

Going up the channel wasn't an issue. The creek had ebbed into a small stream while the floor was clear on both sides. Streetlamps and yard lights lit my way enough for me to trot at a brisk pace, and I didn't stop.

After a good while, I could hear the growl of traffic coming closer and I figured that must be State Line. Further down, I found iron rungs stapled onto the culvert wall. I climbed up and left the creek.

I didn't know how late it was, but I knew the minutes were ticking away. I was easily a mile or two from home, so I decided to go to the boulevard on the wild chance my brother might be around. Other than that, I didn't know what to do.

I found the boulevard and wandered down it for blocks until I saw a glowing sign that read "Diggs Burgers." I turned in, harboring that frenetic hope that I'd find Jack. In the parking lot I desperately searched for him, or anybody else I might know, but found no one. Through the kitchen window, a clock read ten minutes past nine o'clock. I only had five minutes left.

By the bathrooms, I located a payphone, but I didn't have a cent to my name. I rushed back to the lot in a frenzy, wandering in front of cars like a lost child, but there was nobody. I pulled my hair, acting half mad, when I heard the quick honk of a horn. Turning, I saw a red sports car chugging near the front. As it got closer, a girl's voice called my name.

"Noah Ellis!" she cried. "Noah! Come over here!"

Cutting past curious onlookers, I raced up the pavement to the red car where a teenager leaned out of a back window and waved. It was Lisa, my brother's old girlfriend. She was with Rip and Desaray.

UNDER THE LIGHT OF FIREFLIES

"What are you doing out here?" she asked.

"Lisa!" I said as I ran up, out of breath. "Could you help me please? I've got to go home. Could you please please help me?"

"What's going on, Noah? What's wrong?"

"I was just at somebody's house, and...and I had to leave," I said and pointed in the distance. "I really need to get home, though. Like right now. Will you help me?"

Rip listened in perplexity to my panicked pleas, but seeing me in that wild state of mind, he opened his door and let me in.

"Jump in the back, bro," he said. "I'll take you home."

"Thank you," I said. "Thank you so much."

I crawled in and Lisa moved over to make room, then Rip drove around the lot and pulled onto State Line. Desaray sat sideways so she could see me as Lisa put her hand on my shoulder and rubbed it.

"You look awful, Noah," she said. "You're dirty. Tell me exactly what happened."

"I was just at a house with some fellas and they...they were gonna....Well, I can't say. I just had to leave."

"Were they being mean to you?"

I didn't want to sound like a child, so I simply shook my head no. I saw Rip watching me through his rearview mirror and I thought about his school's mascot hidden in Marshall's closet. Telling him where he could find it, though, was out of the question. My brother had explained that I could never give up my own countrymen, no matter who they were, and that was still the rule.

"Do you want to tell us about it?" Desaray asked and rested her exquisite face on the seat to look at me.

360

"I'd rather not," I replied. "I do appreciate the ride, though."

"Anytime, hoss," Rip said. "So talk to me. What's your brother been up to lately?"

"Nothing really. He finished with baseball and has been lifeguarding a little more."

"I don't see him much anymore."

"Join the club."

Lisa took a deep breath and gazed out her window. Though not a stunning beauty like Desaray, I still thought she was great. If I'd been old enough, I would've snapped her up in a heartbeat. *That's how the world works*, I thought. *The good ones always get passed over.*

"I'll tell Jack that you helped me," I said to Lisa. "That all of you helped me."

We came down the park road and turned onto the street towards home. Lisa's wristwatch read that I had less than a minute. I'd have to leave my bike on that trail, but I figured it was a small sacrifice. When we got to my house, the garage door was raised and Jack and his buddy Keith were sitting in lawn chairs, doing exactly nothing. Rip pulled in front where I got out and told them all thanks. As I did, Jack walked over to see what this was all about.

"Rip here gave me a ride home from Diggs," I told Jack in the yard.

"What were you doing there?"

"I had to get away from some folks."

Jack leaned down and saw Lisa sitting in the back seat. She gave a strained smile and a small wave. He waved back.

"Who'd you have to get away from?" he then asked me.

"You remember that talk we had about the Felchers the other day?"

"Yeah."

"I don't have anything to do with them anymore."

He nodded slowly as if he understood. Rip's car idled as he and the girls sat there waiting. Jack told me that he'd talk to me later, then he went to the car. Keith came out as well, so Rip cut the engine. As I got to the front porch, I looked back and saw Lisa in the window with Jack on his knee speaking with her.

Inside, the house was empty and quiet. The clock on the shelf read 9:15. I blew out a long breath and took a moment to gather myself. As I walked to the stairs, I heard Mother and Grand'Mere in Sally's room. It was well past her bedtime. I guessed she'd had a bad dream. As I climbed up, they began to sing her favorite song together.

Daddy finger, daddy finger, where are you?

Here I am, here I am, how do you do?

I peeked inside and they were all resting on the bed with Sally in the middle. I gave them a smile. I told Mother that I'd be in Dad's office and asked her to come down when she was done. That's where I would tell her.

In the office, I clicked on the desk lamp and the light to the cabinet. There was no need to get the key from the clock because there was nothing for me to return. After a while, Mother appeared in the doorway and looked at me with her intuition, her power to sense that something wasn't right. I knew that she loved me. Tears welled in my eyes and my lip trembled.

"*Noah*," she said. "What is it, son?"

"It's all my fault."

"What are you talking about?"

"I shouldn't have run," I told her. "But I did."

"Whatever do you mean?"

"I shouldn't have run. That's why it happened. That's why Connor's dead. I ran and it's all my fault."

Her eyes never left me as she strode across the room. Putting my face into her hands, she looked at me as I told her with unspoken words of what I'd become, and how heavy my burden was. She saw it all.

"Do you remember?" she asked. "Do you know?"

"Yes," I replied, fighting the tears. "I ran away, but I shouldn't have. That's why the tiger got me and got him too."

"You didn't know, son. You didn't. Do you understand? It is not your fault."

"But that's not everything," I said, choking. "I gave away Dad's Purple Heart too."

"You gave it away? I don't understand."

"To join a club. I thought I was doing the right thing, I swear, but I was wrong. I was so wrong. I didn't mean to let you down."

"You haven't let me down. Whatever happened, son, it doesn't matter. Do you understand? It doesn't matter."

"I don't want to feel this way anymore," I said as I broke into sobs. "I don't want it. I hate myself so much. Please make it go away."

Then I collapsed into her arms and poured it all out as Mother rocked me back and forth. She stroked my hair and told me that everything would be all right. My cries rang through the house, and soon my family heard and came into

363

UNDER THE LIGHT OF FIREFLIES

the office. They put their arms around me, and together we wept. For me and for Dad, but as much as anything, for the pain we all shared.

My memories and scars would remain forever; this was the hand I'd been dealt. But I learned the cards were incidental. Life goes on either way.

My heart still beat and my eyes saw clearly.

That was enough.

CHAPTER TWENTY-ONE

Justice Caraway's office shone clean and bright, the same as the first time I'd visited. Glass paper weights rested on neatly stacked papers, photos hung on the walls, and flags stood behind his desk. This was a Saturday morning, though, and instead of donning his usual starched shirt and tie, the judge wore a navy blue jogging suit and tennis shoes. His commanding presence remained unchanged, though, even if he gave off a more casual tone.

I told him everything I remembered about Connor, and how he'd died. It needed to go in the official file, so rather than visiting the cold police station, Mother took the judge up on his offer that she could contact him about anything. The judge listened thoughtfully and didn't ask me any further questions once I'd finished. After that came the moment I was dreading. Mother and I had agreed that I should confess my involvement with the fire. Except I didn't have to.

The night before, something curious happened. After Tyler

UNDER THE LIGHT OF FIREFLIES

left me at the park, he slipped into a stupor whereafter he aimlessly wandered the city streets. Perhaps he couldn't face the fact that his courage had failed him, or that his head looked like a car pileup, but the pain he felt was real. After his heart was laid bare for him alone to look at, he couldn't deal anymore with what had previously been concealed by fancy shirts, fat allowances, and shiny toys.

Eventually, Tyler made it downtown and stopped on the steps of the bi-state justice building under the looming eyes of the Hotel Grim. As frightful as he looked, a couple of cops took notice and sat down to ask him a few questions. Tyler was unresponsive, almost catatonic, so the policemen decided to escort him inside.

There, they requested his name and phone number, trying to reason that his parents would be worried about him. Hearing that, Tyler went into hysterics and even fell off his chair. That was rather unusual, so the cops decided to call a doctor who drove over to assess the situation. After an evaluation, the doctor reported that Tyler wasn't crazy, and he wasn't physically abused. He was neglected.

The cops resumed their questioning, asking him where his stings and burns had come from. Tyler answered remotely at first, even abstractly, but as he got going, the hotter he became. After a few increasing minutes, he broke onto a roll that gave up everything about the fire including all the participants—but he didn't stop there. He talked about breaking into schools, vandalizing the Thomas's house, plus a myriad of other niceties the boys had indulged themselves in over the years. He played like a free juke box before the cops finally figured out who he was.

366

Tyler's father was a notorious sleaze attorney who happily gamed the system for anybody and everybody who could pay his fees, and people paid plenty. Over the years, his reputation had grown beyond the city into the four-states sphere at large. His clientele revolved around contractors, accountants, doctors, and of course the occasional drug dealer who always paid in cash. Naturally, his closest friends and their kids received special service. This sirloin-faced lawyer was about to get a big surprise, though, because this time it was his own son who sat downtown, and his son was spewing like the mad hatter.

The whole thing eventually leaked, of course, and soon afterward the gossip groupies with phones grown to their ears had their new scoop. Tyler didn't realize that his mother was a gold star member who was about to be devoured by her own brood. He just kept rattling off stories like it was open mic night. Those carnivorous scandalmongers had never eaten so well.

Tyler did me right. Perhaps it was because of what I'd done for him, or maybe it's the person he wanted to be, but when he told the authorities I was with them at the burning house, he also said I didn't have any hand in it. He even generously offered that I helped him escape alive. Tyler added that the boys were supposed to initiate me into their club that very night. He talked about the blood ceremony and how they would slice open my palm to make me a brother. He was breaking their cardinal rule of secrecy, but the others had abandoned him in the blaze, and for Tyler, the oath stopped there.

After he got done, a buzz started around the water cooler concerning me—the tiger victim without a father who'd saved this punk from a fire. Now those other punks were about to

UNDER THE LIGHT OF FIREFLIES

cut that boy's hand open and mix their sorry blood with his. It was disgusting. After several minutes of grumbling, the lieutenant himself finally had heard enough and decided to drive over to the Felchers' place for a chat. Marshall was a dubious character with a reputation, so they found it best to take a few squad cars and flash the red and blues just in case they got confused for interlopers. The rest is history.

I didn't learn most of this until much later, though. On that specific morning, the judge merely said he knew where I'd been, and that a meeting of minds had occurred. In other words, the others took the rap. I'd be left alone.

"I hope this has been a lesson for you," Judge Caraway said to me. "You might've gotten hung up in some other foolishness, and I don't have to mention how serious this otherwise could've turned out."

"Yes sir."

"Judge," Mother said. "We'll pay our portion of the damages."

"That's none of your concern. Reparations have been arranged," he replied. Then to me he said, "I think you'll agree that you've had enough drama for one summer."

"Yes sir."

"I'll make a bold prediction right now: no more visits to my chambers, and no more wild adventures. Your family will enjoy a nice peaceful finish to the summer before school begins. What says you?"

I had a lot that I wanted to say, but I figured he'd already heard every excuse in the book, so I saved him the platitudes.

"Is it true that Bonnie and Clyde once stopped by the Hotel

Grim?" I asked.

"That's what they say."

"And they got away?"

"Afraid so. But why are you asking; are you thinking of robbing a bank?"

"Maybe. I mean, I'm already pretty good at running from the cops."

The judge looked at me puzzled before he raised his eyebrows and let out a hearty chuckle, slapping his desk. Mother blushed and shook her head.

"Boy, that's your one get out of jail free card," he said. "But here's an interesting nugget. Do you know about the hog that disappeared earlier this summer from Arkansas High?"

"Yes."

"Why, in the wee hours of this very morning, right out of thin air, it suddenly reappeared on the steps of that school. Now isn't that a peculiar thing?"

At home, I told Mother there was one more favor I had to ask. There was one thing left that needed to be done. After hearing my request, she rose and paced the kitchen several times. She didn't like it. The favor I was asking for was better suited for a man. I explained that it was something I needed to do because I didn't want someone else, particularly her, to bail this one out for me. After much bargaining, she grudgingly agreed to this final favor.

I left and walked to the dead end of my lane into the field. Under the saplings hidden in the brush, I found my bicycle safely waiting for me. I pulled it out, hopped on, then embarked upon one more ride over the avenue. I crossed into the other neighborhood until I coasted down that empty street to the entrance covered by vines and branches.

Inside the Felchers' property, Sloan's car sat in the drive and Fenton's bike rested underneath the treehouse, but I wasn't there to see them. I rode to the shop and got off. At the door, I knocked hard a few times then waited respectfully.

"Yeah, who is it?" a voice shouted.

"Noah Ellis," I replied.

A portending silence ensued before footsteps stomped across the floor followed by the door jerking open. Marshall stood fiercely on the other side of the screen, wearing his usual bicep-friendly apparel while staring at me with burning eyes.

"I'll say one thing," he said. "You've got some brass coming over here, boy."

"I just came to talk."

"Then start talking."

"Can I come inside first?"

He continued to stare at me, slapping the door frame.

"You wearing a wire, boy?" he asked.

"Are you serious?"

He grunted then said, "Half of me wants to throw you down a drain, and another half wants to give you a right education."

"I didn't come here to bother you. I only want to talk."

He slapped the frame some more, looking at me suspiciously, then at last he turned the knob and opened with menacing gentility. Inside, he yanked out a chair and pointed me to it. Then he pulled his own chair forward, sat down, and eyed me closely.

"Don't come here with that sharp tongue today, boy," he

370

started. "You're on my property. Now you're gonna tell me everything I wanna know."

"Yes sir."

"Why ain't you in the Juvie with my boy and Billy," he asked, his mouth barely moving. "They're sitting in a cell while you're all comfy here in my shop."

"I went and saw Judge Caraway this morning."

His eyes opened wide and his intensity seemed to build, if that was possible.

"A squirming rat," he seethed. "What'd you talk about, pray tell?"

"I had to tell the judge what happened to Connor Strait."

He tilted his head and leaned back, mulling it over.

"You remembered how that boy died?" he asked.

"Yes sir. The police needed it for their report."

"Ain't that something. What else did you tell him?"

"Nothing."

"I can smell a lie. You're here and Fenton's not. Explain that."

"Judge didn't ask one word about any of them. I promise."

"You ain't innocent either. Nobody is."

"Connor was," I said. "He never stole those books. It wasn't fair what happened to him."

"What are you talking about?" he asked with a squint in his eyes.

"You know. The books. The ones that were..."

Then I stopped. He looked genuinely puzzled. I asked myself if it was possible he'd never known about those teachers' editions. Maybe he never saw them, or maybe he didn't want

UNDER THE LIGHT OF FIREFLIES

to know. One thing became clear, though. Connor was no rat. He'd never given up a single name. Neither would I.

"Never mind," I said. "I was thinking of something else."

He looked at me dubiously as a thought pricked his mind.

"Somebody got into my storage room," he said. "That light was on."

I nodded yes.

"You want to talk about that?"

"I went in there."

"You little punk! You ever heard that curiosity killed the cat?"

I gulped and nodded yes again.

"What'd you see in there?"

"Everything."

"You think you're clever?!" he shouted and jumped up. "You go swimming in dangerous waters and you're gonna get eaten. Even that judge won't be able to save you."

"I swear I never told anybody a thing."

"You expect me to buy that? Snoops and informers go hand and hand."

"Not one soul. I promise."

He kept a rigid scowl, and a bad feeling came over me. He'd been in dark places. He'd seen things I'd never see, and he'd done things never do. I could smell smoke and gun oil on him. He stayed there many seconds with his eyes trained on me before he slowly calmed down and retook his seat.

"I suggest you stick with that policy," he said. "Or you'll be sorry."

"Yes sir."

372

"Well, then. Have you said all you needed to say?"

"I came here to find out the truth. That's all I want."

"The truth? You tell me, what is truth?"

"Why'd my father and you quit being friends?"

He looked at me incredulously then showed that blaze of silver teeth.

"Boy, you are something else," he said. "I never thought I'd meet another person like your daddy, and then here you come walking right through that door." He sat back in his chair with his thick arms pulled over his chest. Then his eyes darkened, and his face grew somber. "You wanna know about me and your daddy?"

"Yes sir. I do."

"Here it is. Your daddy didn't want nothing to do with me anymore."

"But why?"

"It ain't for you to ask."

"Did he walk out over money?"

"Money?? We went deeper than money, boy. We got history. Hell, the day he got shot, it was me who carried him out of that godforsaken jungle and got him onto the chopper. I never said he had to be beholden, but some things don't fade. Even if he did stop being my partner. I will say this for your sake, though, and it's the last word I'll ever speak on it. Whatever business I got, it's legit. I know people like to say I'm outside the law, but that don't make it true. When you get grown, you'll understand."

You'll understand when you get grown. What a great non-statement. That's how adults always talked to kids, especially

UNDER THE LIGHT OF FIREFLIES

when they didn't want to tell the real story. Sometime later, though, I did learn about it. When Dad healed from his gunshot wound, he returned to Texas while Marshall stayed overseas and enrolled in special forces. At home, my father went back to college and graduated in engineering. One day, Marshall showed up having completed his final tour. He wanted to start a business, but he couldn't do it alone. They were young yet tested, and Marshall eventually convinced dad to co-sign for a shipping truck and a storage lot. Dad felt like he owed him.

Quickly enough, that little company expanded. While my father designed bridges, Marshall wasn't exactly hauling refrigerators around. There were a few customers, but the bulk of Marshall's business was supplying some very vague clients with some very specific merchandise. It was through contacts that he'd made in the war. The lines got blurred. Dad received assurances, but it felt like the fringe, and even if it technically might've been legal, being legal didn't make it right. My father could not abide. So, he sold back his share and afterward the friendship crumbled.

In the shop, my presence was becoming non-grata. Marshall's demeanor had grown edgy.

"I know why you're here," he said. "They've done told you. Ain't they? All the lies and innuendo. Every word they say is filthy."

"What'd they say?"

"Don't pretend to me."

"All I want is to know what happened to my father."

He reached for his cigarettes and lit one up. He sat there thinking. I could tell that whatever happened at the river had never left him, which was an affront to the image he'd built of himself.

"Tell me what you do know," he said at last.

"I know you were at the river when Dad died. I heard you were alone with him."

"Did you hear about a gunshot?"

"Yes."

"What'd you think about that?"

"I know Dad wasn't hit. Otherwise, I can't say."

"Well, other people sure as hell can. Humph. 'They didn't have a duck.' Like that mattered."

I looked at him blankly.

"When did you hear about it?" he asked.

"Yesterday."

He blew out a stream of smoke and stroked his chin.

"Your momma kept it away from ya," he next said. "I can see that. You didn't need to know about them other things anyway."

"What other things?"

"The lies."

"What lies?" I asked.

"Criminal intent."

He was now visibly upset and started to bounce his heel.

"I was never officially charged, mind you," he started. "Our buddy Gary was there. He stated on record that I could've never done harm to Walter. But the rats in this town just can't help themselves. People say, 'They hadn't seen each other for eight years, but they were alone when Walter died?' I can't go anywhere without whispers. 'There's Marshall Felcher. The

UNDER THE LIGHT OF FIREFLIES

scoundrel.' Them with all their gossip and lies, and they call me a scoundrel?!"

He flung his arms up and glared at me as if he were the most innocent man on earth. Realizing I happened to be the dead man's son, he eased up.

"The police checked my hands for residue," he said. "Gunpowder. They know I didn't take the shot. Check the records."

His shoulders drew down and he exhaled a quiet breath. I could now see the miles on him, from the scars across his hands to the lines on his face, yet somewhere inside there was a splinter. I knew then that this man didn't murder my father.

"Can you explain what happened?" I asked.

"I'm sure you've heard enough."

"No, I haven't."

"I can't do it."

"I deserve to know."

"Everybody deserves something, but we don't always get it, do we?"

I must've been the picture of perfect distress because he couldn't look at me.

"All I've heard," I said, "is that my dad went hunting and drowned. But my dad was a top swimmer. Surely, you know that. And he wasn't dumb. He was an engineer. He could figure anything out. He built my treehouse. He built airplanes that could fly, and then he'd just give them away. He helped people stranded on the road even when he had important places to be. He was the greatest man ever. I just can't believe..."

Then to my own contempt, I let out a small sob and put

my fist to my mouth. I squeezed as tight as I could because I'd told myself not to cry. Marshall flicked ashes on the floor with a strained look.

"Why won't you tell me?" I finally asked.

"It ain't my place. How come you don't you ask Lauren, your momma?"

"Because it's too hard for her. I'm here now. Please tell me."

He sat there ruminating, not moving a muscle. What if it had been him who'd drowned in that river instead? Would he want his own sons to know how it happened? He took several more drags, struggling with the decision, then put out his cigarette and sat with his elbows on his knees.

"I don't want your momma mad," he said. "So you keep this in here 'til you get older."

"I will."

He let out an ironic laugh as if he couldn't believe this, then sank into the bleak memory and stared at the floor.

"Gary Donald was a mutual friend of your daddy's and mine from way back. He hated seeing us at odds. After many years, he decided it was time that we patched things up. So, he suggested a hunting trip. After some debate, we both said fine. We stayed cordial on the ride out but didn't talk much. We were gonna do that later, I guess.

"At the river, we put on our leg-waders and set up the blind on a sand bar. It was cloudy that morning and bitter cold. There wasn't a lot of birds flying, then Gary went to his truck for coffee. While he was gone, a few ducks showed up. As they came along, I told Walt to take the shot. A duck cut upstream, and your dad popped him. One shot. The bird hit the water

UNDER THE LIGHT OF FIREFLIES

and started floating our way. Walt took the dog and went to fetch it.

"The riverbank was tall and dropped straight down. When they made it there, the dog wouldn't jump in. She just tucked her tail and whimpered. The duck was floating by, so Walt found a limb and stretched over to fish it out. He was holding onto a shrub, but the ground was too soft there. The roots tore out and he went over. I heard a splash and that was all. I couldn't help but chuckle because it reminded me of a time when we were kids.

"I walked up thinking how we'd have a laugh, but when I peered over the edge, all I saw was current. The river at that turn was deep and full of sand and eddies. His waders must've filled up. While I searched back and forth, Gary came over and I told him what happened. We patrolled those banks for an hour, but Walter was gone. He was just...gone."

He drew in a breath and cleared his throat. My own breath came out in a long rasp. That was the last time anybody saw my dad. My poor wonderful dad. Marshall's fists unclenched and his body slumped over. It's a moment I'll never forget. The first moment I ever saw a man broken.

"There was nothing I could do," he said under his breath. "I couldn't find him. I couldn't help."

My father had encountered a lonely place where all people are destined to go. His time came where the dark forces had gathered at a crook in a river, and that's where he died. There was no cause, no purpose, no fault. I realized that at last. I knew my dad, so I also knew what his intentions were that day. He was there to do the right thing and to make amends. I decided that I should do the same, and so I followed. I rose and went and stood next to Marshall. He turned to me with his face ashen and his eyes bloodshot.

"Accidents happen," I said to him and laid my hand on his shoulder. "Even to strong men."

Then from my hip pocket, I produced the silver dollar that he'd tossed to me the night before. I put it in his hand.

"That token is not mine to keep," I said to him. "But I do promise that I will always hold onto this."

I then pulled out the Two of Hearts that he'd given me after his card trick all those days before. His eyes searched over it and he drew in a long breath. Next, he slapped his knee and rose to his feet.

"I guess it's settled then," he said. "Since you're a man now, you can show yourself the door."

I looked at him, and without a word, I walked to the door and went through. Outside the sun was shining. From my bicycle's handlebars, I plucked off my Franklin Cardinals baseball cap and pulled it on. I mounted and raised the kickstand, ready to leave, when I heard the shop door swing open. Footsteps crunched across the drive. Marshall stood beside me.

"I'll tell you one thing, Noah Ellis," he said. "You are your father's son."

In his hand, I saw that he was carrying a lavender box with gold trim. He held it out to me. "I don't want nobody calling me despicable," he said.

I took the box and ran my fingers over its smooth top and gold stripe lining.

"Thanks," I said.

379

UNDER THE LIGHT OF FIREFLIES

"Open it up. You'll see. That medal's in there."

"I don't need to see it. Thank you."

His face was worn and his trails were hard. He stood still a moment and looked at me as if he were looking at a long time past. I held out my hand, and he obliged and shook it. With nothing else said, he turned back to his shop and disappeared inside. Taking one last look, I gazed around at the place knowing it would be my last: the covered gate, the steel workshop, the lawn, the bank, and the red oak with its treehouse resting in the heights where words were scrawled in faded luster, "To thine oaths be true." I put my feet on the pedals, my face forward, and rode away. with my father's Purple Heart in hand.

CHAPTER TWENTY-TWO

The rest of summer came and went quietly, though Mother had to ground me. I'd blatantly lied about going to watch a movie at Dusty's, and that came after a collection of other misgivings like sluffing off chores, staying up past bedtime, then that little incident where a house got burned to the ground. She didn't beat me down with guilt, though. My contrition sufficed.

In the meantime, I got used to reading books, writing in my journal, or taking the occasional ride to the farmlands with my brother, though we didn't return to the river. Sally and I played mini-golf a time or two, and we all attended some get-togethers with friends. Once, I noticed Mother sitting next to a man. She introduced him as Lloyd. He was the same man she'd gone on a date with. He worked as an accountant. I was naturally suspicious of any person who chose to do math all day, but he appeared decent enough and pursued Mother at a proper distance, so I reserved my right to disapprove of him later.

We decided on another trip to the cabin under the shadow

UNDER THE LIGHT OF FIREFLIES

of the glorious dogwood tree. Grand'Mere cooked every kind of delicacy, and we rode the canoe all the way across the lake. The camp itself was absent of Elliot and most everyone else except for a few permanent residents, including the blue hair herself who avoided us by mutual consent. Summer's buzz had faded, the fruit harvest ended, and the fox was gone.

Back home, the dog days trickled away until the end finally came into view. As always, the taste was bittersweet. Every child anticipates a new school year, to be a grade older and a notch higher, but it only comes with the final kiss of summer. That restless season, and the death and misery contained therein, would soon be no more. Then one warm September morning, it began.

My seventh-grade year arrived and with it the first day of junior high. I took a shower, combed my hair, then put on my new school clothes and back-pack. After breakfast, Mother loaded me and an exuberant Sally into the car and drove us to school. We arrived at Pine Street Junior High where kids mingled out front with fresh faces and bright eyes. I sat in the car and took a deep breath.

"Here goes," I told Mother.

"Be brave," she said.

"Summer is finally over."

"Yes. You now have a whole year to do what you're told."

We smiled at each other, and in the morning light, the wrinkles around her eyes seemed to vanish.

"Sally," I said over the seat. "Enjoy your first day of kindergarten."

"I can't wait to count to a hundred."

382

"I'll help you with it."

I opened the door and got out. Mother gave one last wave as she drove away, and then I was alone. Our junior high was a magnet school fed by three different elementaries. Many of the kids I didn't recognize, although they certainly recognized me. The first person I scanned for was a blonde-headed girl, but she wasn't around. Without further hesitation, I walked to the mob as they waited to see what I would do. When I got there, I stopped and gave a friendly nod.

"How'd everybody's summer go?" I asked.

A throng of chatter ensued while I stood and listened patiently. They crowded in tightly, eager to speak, but I didn't let it bother me. This would all pass eventually, and I'd become just a regular guy again. Out of excitement, a girl clumsily asked me how my own summer had gone. With a light gasp, the crowd halted to listen. I took it in stride.

"I spent most of my summer chasing fireflies," I replied.

The first bell mercifully rang and broke up the party as kids scrambled to search for their new homeroom. I followed the hall and checked the doors too. Halfway down, I found the roll with my name, *Roosevelt N. Ellis*.

After locating my desk in the rear, I pulled off my backpack and sat with my chin held high just like I'd practiced in my mind. In the room, boiler heaters stood along the walls while a rickety air conditioner blew from a window. A fresh coat of paint had been applied, but no concealment was great enough to disguise that school's age, which went back generations. The tardy bell rang, the last student scuttled in, but no teacher. As we waited, kids surreptitiously turned their heads to peek at me,

UNDER THE LIGHT OF FIREFLIES

then quickly popped forward after catching a glimpse. I stayed quiet.

Through a frosted window, an outline of a woman appeared as she spoke to someone across the hall. After a moment, the door opened and an elegant Black lady waltzed inside with an armload of books that she plopped onto her desk. Without a word, she turned and wrote her name on the board, "Mrs. Turner." Dropping the chalk in the tray, she sat down, opened a binder, and called roll.

When she came to me, she addressed me as Roosevelt while everyone stole another glance to make sure I hadn't disappeared. In a clear voice, I responded that I went by my middle name Noah, which the teacher noted and continued without pause. After finishing, she rose and formally stepped before the class with her hands pressed together.

"Students," she said with a grand smile. "I am Mrs. Turner, your new homeroom teacher. Welcome to Pine Street. I know that you all are brimming with excitement about your first day of junior high, but first let's get a few things straight: you are here to learn; I am here to teach; and that's just what we shall do. Open your books to chapter one."

I'd never been more relieved to hear a lesson in my life. As Mrs. Turner taught us the essentials of subject-verb agreement, I sat in my stiff desk and actually listened. Before I knew it, the first class was over, and not far behind it, half the day had ended too.

During lunch, I found a seat with a couple of kids from my old elementary, one of them being Alex who owed Sam the dollar from paper football. They were nice to me, if not a little

384

amazed I was at their table. Little by little, though, their intrigue melted away. I asked Alex about his bet with Sam from the prior school year. He grimaced and said he'd finally paid it off just to get Sam out of his life.

Across the cafeteria, Sam himself was seated with Dusty and Donovan. I wanted to join them, but feelings were still unsettled, and I was unsure of what to say. I left them alone.

Between classes, I saw Fenton stalking the hallway as superior as he ever had. As we got close, he caught sight of me but gave no reaction and kept moving. I guessed that his dad, or the judge, or somebody else had established the rule to lay off. It would remain that way for good, and that was fine by me.

As for his buddy Billy, he got moved to a different school. That was part of the deal after he'd been fingered for starting the blaze—not to mention about a dozen other indiscretions that Tyler had so generously revealed. He and the gang were forced to split up.

For Tyler, leaving town was his best option. I don't think he could've survived after everything he'd exposed. He got shipped off to a boarding school where, from what I heard, he did fine. There were plenty of other neglected kids he could relate to.

As the hours wore on, my first day simply became a school day, and I began to feel normal again. When the final bell rang, I shoved some books into my backpack and made for the bus. Arriving, I climbed aboard and strolled down the aisle while the other kids stared at me. In the back, I saw Sam with his head against the window as he sat with Dusty. I walked up and stood beside them.

"Has anybody taken this seat?" I pointed across the aisle.

385

UNDER THE LIGHT OF FIREFLIES

"Nope," Dusty replied without looking.

Sam sat up and shook his head no. I took my seat and watched out the window while the bus clanged into gear and got going. Occasionally, I'd sneak a peek at them, but Dusty never moved. Sam, though, had turned all the way sideways and never took his eyes off me. Words danced on my lips, but I remained uncertain and kept to myself. While the bus went through its drops and kids exited one by one, I decided that I should talk to Dusty after we got off. We had the same stop, and nobody else would be around except Sam. When we arrived at the park, though, Dusty stood up to leave before our usual drop off.

"Why are you getting off here?" I asked, alarmed at how quickly that came out.

"I've got a meeting at the bridge," he said and motioned over his shoulder.

"A girl?"

He nodded yes.

"Sandra?"

"Yep," he replied then turned down the aisle.

I clutched my backpack, wondering whether I should follow or just forget about it.

"I'll stay with you, Noah," Sam said and scooted closer to the aisle.

Dusty went to the front of the bus where he hopped down the steps and walked into the park alone. Afterward, the driver jerked the handle and shut the doors. The bus cranked into gear and slowly moved forward. As we pulled away, I suddenly cried out.

"Wait!" I hollered and jumped to my feet. "Please. I need

386

LEE SANDERS

to get off here too."

Everyone turned around and stared. In the rearview mirror, the bus driver gave a tired headshake. She stopped the bus, pulled the handle again, and opened the doors.

"Come on, Sam," I said and grabbed his arm.

"But my dad will be looking for me."

"Your old man's a gun freak now. He'll be fine."

We scooted past the remaining kids with their wondering faces and dashed down the steps outside. Far under the pines, Dusty marched onward, and Sam and I had to run to catch him. When we got alongside him, though, Dusty kept his eyes forward and didn't say anything. Sam drooped his head. It was all too obvious what the deal was, so I came out with it.

"Look, guys," I said. "I know I haven't been too cool lately and that I blew you off without explanation. It's been kind of a hard summer, you know? I just want to say I'm sorry."

Dusty sighed and kept going. Sam didn't talk.

"Come on," I said. "Can't we just forget about it?"

Dusty's pace grew faster. His legs were longer than mine and I had to really stretch my stride to keep pace. Sam decided that skipping was his best option. We must have looked ridiculous, three boys fast-walking and skipping through the trees like we'd been forbidden from running. As it neared total absurdity, Dusty decided to give it a rest and we all stopped for air.

"Listen, man," he said at last. "I know you wanted to be Jill's first kiss, okay? And I know I messed that up. But honestly, I didn't mean for it to happen. Honestly."

"I know," I responded. "It doesn't matter now anyway. I ended up kissing Jamie Jimmer this summer at the lookout."

387

UNDER THE LIGHT OF FIREFLIES

"Say what?" he cried in horror. "You kissed Jamie Jimmer?"

"Sure did."

"What were you *thinking*, man?"

"Like you haven't thought about it before."

"I've thought about a lot of stuff."

"Thinking's a normal thing to do."

"But I didn't actually go through with it."

"I couldn't help it. She ambushed me."

Dusty listened unimpressed while Sam stood with his jaw agape.

"Okay," I said. "So maybe things got a little weird."

"A little weird?" Dusty said.

"I was lonely, vulnerable, and I'd been tanking vodka all day."

"Uh huh. So, how was it?"

"The kiss? It wasn't that bad actually. Jamie's a little ahead of her time."

"Now *that's* weird."

"Hold on a second," Sam interrupted, still shocked. "Noah. You're saying that you're in love with Jamie?"

"What? No! I'm in love with Jill. Wait a second. No, I'm not."

"Well, that's good because Jamie Jimmer is going with Joey now."

That's a lot of Js, I thought. Thinking it over, though, it made a lot of sense. They were both quirky. She probably played Princess Leia while Joey ordered her to give up the rebel base. He was certainly a better option than Fenton, though. At least the fellas and I were talking again, but Dusty and Sam stood

388

there brooding.

"What's wrong?" I asked. "What's with you two?"

At first they didn't say anything. It was Sam who finally spoke.

"Tell us one thing," he said. "Did you join up with those other guys or not?"

Inevitably, the word had gotten out. There was no sense in fretting, though. The truth needed to be told.

"No, I didn't," I answered. "They did invite me to join their club, but I don't live over there. I'm from the park. The same as you."

They both looked at each other with unsure faces.

"Once a Loafer, always a Loafer," I said and stuck my hand in the middle.

They checked each other once more before the lines melted from their faces. Then they reached in their hands too. Together, we nodded at each other and counted off to three.

"Loafers ride!!!"

After a short silence, Dusty reached over and squeezed my neck.

"Old Rosie!!" he said and shook me. "What took you so long, baby?"

Breaking away in laughter, we scampered across the park and talked about our summers. They wanted to hear what happened with me, naturally, but they were respectful about it. I couldn't help but think back to Connor and how I was the only kid who ever knew him. I decided from that point forward to tell his story right. So, I gave them the account, without the gory details, beginning with how Connor had saved me from

UNDER THE LIGHT OF FIREFLIES

the bridge at Waterworks.

We passed the pavilion and went towards the pond. As we approached the creek, I noticed some girls hanging out on the bridge. One of them was a blonde with her hair pulled into a ponytail. All day long I'd looked for this one. Now, here she was.

As my heart jumped, I began to wonder what Jill thought about me now. Surely, she'd have heard most everything. Had she also heard about Jamie? Whatever she might or might not have known, I only hoped she didn't think less of me. Of all the people I knew at school, she was the most decent. My crush on her hadn't faded a single shade.

"Ladiez, ladiez, ladiez," Dusty said as he strutted onto the bridge. "All the women to the dance floor. All the ladies prepare to groove. It's time for a big booty shake-down."

Sandra and the other girls giggled into their hands.

"I can't believe you're my boyfriend," Sandra said. "You're so cheesy."

"Check this out. I can moonwalk."

Then he scuffed backwards with his arms flailing up and down in a way that was nothing short of hilarious. We couldn't help but laugh, but Jill kept her eyes on me. I glanced away, then slowly looked back. This time when our gazes met, she pointed at me and dropped her jaw.

"Roosevelt Noah Ellis," she said. "Where in the world have you been?"

"Me?" I asked with my hand to my chest. "Umm... I've been around. Well, for the most part. I actually spent some time in the hospital. Then I went on a trip. Some other stuff happened

390

that I won't get into. You see, sometimes a person gets mixed up and..."

"Well, duh," she said. "I was gone too, but when I got back, I thought we were supposed to do something?"

She dropped her hands on her hips with her head tilted in that coy manner. I didn't know what the hell was going on.

"You don't remember, do you?" she asked.

She stumped me again. I was such a stump.

"You're a ditz," she said. "Just stay right there."

She ran across the playground towards her house as I stood there awkwardly. I tried some small talk with the others, but I couldn't keep from watching her door. After a minute, she came out with something behind her back. When she made it on the drive near the park's entrance, she summoned me over with her finger.

"What's up?" I asked when I got there.

"Look and see," she replied and pulled around a booklet.

On the outside cover in block letters, a title read: *Kennedy Elementary, '80-'81.*

I opened it, and on the inside sleeve I found my name written. It was my yearbook. Now I understood. I'd left it on Jill's desk that last day of school.

"You sly dog," I said. "You've had this all summer?"

"I figured I'd just give it to you when school started. Check out what I wrote."

Dear Noah, Here's to our last day in elementary school. I hope you have a wonderful summer full of starry nights and grand adventures. I'd love to toss the horseshoes

UNDER THE LIGHT OF FIREFLIES

with you. Here's a little hint: I'll kick your butt. See you then. Your friend, Jill

Relief washed over me like water. What I'd written in her yearbook all those months ago wasn't a tragedy after all. I'd have to tell my brother the sage about it. Then I noticed we were standing shoulder to shoulder, and she wasn't moving. I'd never been this close. I could feel her warmth. I caught her eye and her cheeks flushed which made me wonder—could it be that she felt the same? I'd always been shy, but that inner voice found me and told me that the door was cracked, to take a chance, that this was the time. So, I tentatively reached out my hand. To my delight, she reached out hers too. We touched then held them together and squeezed.

"I've got to leave," she whispered in my ear.

"Where are you going?"

"I have to practice clarinet and then get started on my homework. I have a reputation to keep, you know."

She scrunched her nose and grinned, and I grinned back.

"So I'll see you soon?" I asked.

"I'm just across the bridge," she replied with a wink.

We squeezed hands again and she left. At her house, she gave me one last glance over her shoulder then went inside. I'd never been to cloud nine before, but I was pretty sure this was it because I felt like I was floating right into the sky. Hope had finally found me, and no other memory remained.

I went back to my friends, and Sam was naturally scared that his parents might show up any second with a search party. I said I'd walk home with him. After a goodbye to the girls,

392

Dusty and I slapped five and promised to talk later. No need for any hugs with that guy.

Sam and I hurried to his house with him fretting the whole way, but when we arrived, by the grace of the gods, his parents' cars were still there. He was so relieved that I thought he'd kiss the ground they were parked on. Unlike Dusty, though, he did give me a hug. An emphatic one. He was a good kid.

Coming to my own house, I saw a green car leaving the driveway and found the garage door open with my brother at the work bench, tinkering with the plane.

"Was that Lisa leaving just now?" I asked.

"Maybe."

"What's the deal?"

"You ask a lot of questions, don't you?"

"I'm your brother."

"Yeah, you are," he replied and gave me a wink. "We're all good."

"So, how much longer until the plane is finished?"

"It's done."

"Which part?"

"The whole thing."

We stared at it incredulously, wondering if that could be possible.

"So, now what?" I asked.

"We fly the darn thing."

We both laughed. We never believed that it would actually get finished. It was like a mountain that men swear they'll climb but never do. There the plane was, though, gleaming bright yellow and baby blue. Under a curved glass sat a tiny pilot wear-

UNDER THE LIGHT OF FIREFLIES

ing goggles as he waited at the wheel. A brand-new steel engine sparkled. It was raring to go.

"Fire it up," I said.

Jack laid it on the floor and pressed a button on the remote. A click sounded and the plane suddenly roared to life. Jack worked the throttle and it lurched forward as if it were alive. Holding the breaks, he revved the motor loudly while the body trembled.

"What are you doing?" a little voice called from behind us.

Turning, we saw Sally standing on the step with her Teddy in hand.

"Jack finished the airplane," I told her.

"You did?" she said and bounced over. "Are you going to fly it like Dad used to?"

"You remember Dad flying planes?" Jack asked.

"Of course I do, silly. Who could forget that?"

Jack hit the kill switch and the engine stopped.

"Aww," Sally said.

"It's not over. We'll take it to the park."

"Yay!" she exclaimed then ran inside for her shoes.

Jack tossed the plane into the car's trunk. Next, the front door opened where Sally reappeared with Mother.

"Is there room in your car for two ladies?" Mother asked as Sally pulled her along.

"It's a perfect fit," Jack replied.

Everyone got in, and Jack drove us to the back of the park where the meadows were. There, he turned down an asphalt drive and parked in some grass. After we climbed out, he pulled the plane from the trunk and lined it up on the drive. He

394

repressed the button, and at once the plane sparked back to life.

"Can you fly it?" I asked.

"Dad taught me how," he replied with a nod. "I'll remember."

We all sucked in a collective breath as Jack held down the brakes and pressed the gas, revving the engine louder and louder into a high-pitched squeal. Right when we thought it might break, Jack let go whereafter the plane bolted forward and went bouncing down the strip. Like a baby bird on its first flight, the craft fledged and flagged along, trying its best to get airborne, but it couldn't quite make it. Jack wasn't giving up. While the end of the line approached, the plane's tail straightened, its body settled, then at last it lifted skyward.

We cheered gleefully as the plane took flight and zoomed over the fields, free at last to soar. With its wings arched sideways, it made a hard bank then turned proudly into the western sun. Blazing across the road, Jack swung it for a long loop around the pool, past the old fighter plane,, then back towards us. Over the fields again, the plane hung just above the ground where a dove lighted and a breeze swept through the grass. As it rushed our way, Sally squeezed Mother's legs and giggled, her eyes sparkling with excitement. Right when it reached us, Jack pulled back the control and the plane gracefully surged upward, its wings spread wide, rising higher and ever higher into the immortal sky of summer.

—The End—